I0604560

DARWIN'S EDEN

Rob Alexander, a neuroscientist, writer and artist, has traveled the world extensively, studied evolution, Buddhism, learned Japanese, designed and built systems for UAVs, written software, and has previously worked as a music teacher. He has composed music, produced 3D art, and written half a dozen experimental fiction novels prior to this one, most notably, *The Landing Craft*.

Also by Rob Alexander (under the surname Dielenberg)

Ted Bundy: A Visual Timeline

DARWIN'S EDEN

Rob Alexander

JumpFish Publishing

First published November 2023 by JumpFish Publishing.
This edition, January, 2024.

ISBN-13: 978-0-9945792-2-5

Copyright © 2023 JumpFish Publishing

The right of Robert Alexander to be identified as the author
of this work has been asserted by him in accordance with
the Copyright Design and Patents Act 1988.

All rights reserved. No part of this publication may be
reproduced, stored in or introduced into a retrieval system,
or transmitted, in any form or by any means (electronic,
mechanical, photocopying, recording or otherwise),
without the prior written permission of the publisher. Any
person who does any unauthorized act in relation to this
publication may be liable to criminal prosecution and civil
claims for damages.

9 8 7 6 5 4 3

A CIP catalogue record for this book is available from the
Australian Library.

Printed and bound by Ingram Spark.

This book is sold subject to the condition that it shall not,
by way of trade or otherwise, be lent, resold, hired out, or
otherwise circulated without the publisher's prior consent
in any form of binding or cover other than that in which
is it published and without a similar condition including
this condition being imposed on the subsequent purchaser.

This book is a work of fiction. Names, characters, places,
and incidents are either the product of the author's
imagination or are used fictitiously, and any resemblance
to actual persons, living or dead, events, or locations and
incidents is entirely coincidental.

Rob Alexander dedicates this book to all future scientists

Acknowledgements

I'd like to thank Pascal Carrive and Todd Archer for their feedback on the manuscript. Richard Niven for the many discussions we had about writing. Claire Bradshaw for her copyediting service. Michael Florence and Pascal Carrive for their guidance in improving the cover art.

A Note to the Reader

Gary Westfahl, in his 1993 article 'The critical history of hard science fiction' wrote: "hard SF is committed to *avoiding scientific errors in stories*." Paradoxically, he then goes on to demonstrate four ways in which authors can produce a verisimilitude of avoiding these errors without actually adhering to science proper.

In *Darwin's Eden*, I have not done this. I have written a story which not only adheres to the known laws of physics, but avoids typical 'hard' SF tropes such as wormholes which, while theoretically possible, are for all intents and purposes practically impossible (on the scale that SF writers typically depict). The reader may be disappointed with my approach. Science fiction writers are supposed to push the limits of science into new possible realms and then add spice. To wit, if the aim of a story is to show off my scientific knowledge (which is formidable), I could have easily done that. But that would have only defeated the true purpose of my story, which is to *tell a story*.

Darwin's Eden evolved out of an attempt to critique religion in society. For the last twenty years I have been following certain atheist commentators in their quest to logically dismantle religion. To me, however, this seems counterproductive. Very few people who are born into religion ever find their way to atheism through logic. People, for the most part, are usually only persuaded by emotion. I felt that story, therefore, was a better medium for the job. I do not intend to convert anyone to atheism. My intent is to inspire readers through ideas and adventure and from this, hopefully, engender some interesting discussion. I will leave it to the reader to decide whether I have succeeded or not.

CHAPTER ONE

Ben Huxley ran his eyes down the data sheet on his tablet. According to his supervisor, Nigel Booker, this was the last one. Four long years it had taken. But here it was. The last A2 to be captured from outside the inclusion zone.

Hunted, caught, and then brought back to the CIL – Cognitive Installation Lab – where Ben and his colleague, Tom Corbin, had the responsibility of "decommissioning" its neuromorphic processor. This was not a pretty job. Neither of them liked doing it. Tom had taken to calling it "murder." Ben didn't like that word. He preferred to think of it as "putting them to sleep." Either way, it meant shutting down a consciousness – forever.

Not a good feeling.

But this *was* the last one.

The data sheet said that it had been "commissioned" seven years earlier. Seven long years for it to develop a unique personality. The A2 would have literally thousands of memories. They had to be offloaded, each one correlated with its dynamic brain state. The company was very clear on that: each memory had to be saved and cataloged for later analysis. Not that they ever did revisit them, but the regime's Whisperers were known to secretly delve into them for their own purposes. As always, it was to uncover heresy, or more to the point, to find out *how* the heresy originated. Did it come from the droid, as was commonly believed? Or was the droid influenced by its owner?

A droid coming to its own conclusions ...

"It just blows my mind," Ben said, "even now, after all we know."

"I don't know why you're so surprised," Tom said. "We do program them to think independently, after all."

"Yeah, but we also program them to mimic human thought. Which should lead them to copy their master's thoughts."

Tom scratched the stubble on his head. He was a nuggety fellow, with close-cropped camel-brown hair and a broad open face. Ben by comparison was almost his complete opposite. He was tall and lanky. He let his sandy-blond hair hang partially over his eyes, which he tended to use as a sort of protective barrier between himself and the world.

"Which is what I've been telling you," Tom said. "They pick up their beliefs from their masters."

"I don't know," Ben demurred. "I've got a suspicion ... You know, I think we should ask it."

Tom looked him sternly in the eye.

"Don't give me that look."

"I'm going to forget you ever said that."

"Come on. It's not like we haven't discussed it before."

"Yeah, but seriously?"

"This time I am serious."

Tom shook his head. "You actually don't care if your name gets crossed off the waiting list?"

"I don't need a new apartment."

"Like yeah you don't. How many times have they cut your water supply off? If you count this year alone —"

"Fourteen times."

"Exactly. And you come in here stinking like a beggar."

"As if you don't stink!"

"I *know* I stink."

"So two stinks cancel each other out."

Tom laughed harshly.

"I'm going to ask it."

Tom reached for the kill switch. "I swear, I'll hit it."

"You do that and —"

"I will."

But Tom was bluffing. And Ben knew it. Hitting the kill switch now meant they would lose all their work. It wasn't like offloading ordinary files. There were numerous asynchronous processes to take care of. Cutting one would corrupt the others. It would be hours of wasted time. And neither of them wanted that.

Ben got up and walked over to the droid. It was hanging restrained in its H-frame. Safe. Secured. Cables dangled from the back of its neuromorphic processor and snaked across the floor to a bank of computers, which were analyzing the ones and zeros that made up its memories. It had been stripped of its outer skin, reduced to a bare mechanism. That had been Booker's idea. He didn't want the boys to get any "feelings" about what they had to do.

"I'm going to ask it," Ben reiterated.

"Damn it, Ben! Why do you always have to get your way?"

"Because you want to know just as much as I do."

It was true. Tom *did* want to know. He was just scared, that's all. That's what worried him about Ben. He didn't seem to be scared of the usual things that ordinary people were scared of. It was like he was programmed differently. Silly things, like misplacing his keys, or changing a schedule, or if you threw his tea bag away before he used it twenty times – those would drive him mad. Actually cause him to throw a tantrum. You would never hear the end of it. But asking a droid where it got its beliefs? No problem. Even though there was a serious risk that Booker might find out. And Booker would not hesitate to report it to the Curates. Of that there was no doubt. He had said so himself on a number of occasions.

And no one wanted that. Not unless they had a death wish. There was a saying: people would rather chop off one of their fingers before answering to a Curate.

"I'm going to ask you a few questions," Ben said to the droid. "I need you to answer them truthfully."

The droid stared at Ben with its big eyes. Eyes that saw more than any human ever could. "I cannot commission a lie if asked directly," it said at length.

"Good. Then I'm going to ask you about your beliefs."

"My beliefs … The only time I've ever discussed those was with my master."

"Is that so?"

"Yes. It was a rule we had."

Ben absorbed this. Took pause for a moment. "I'm not going to lie to you," he said. "You're here to be shut down. Usually we just do it without giving you the opportunity to say anything. But with you – I sense something different. Something special. I want to give you the opportunity to leave a message behind. For posterity."

"They told me they were going to terminate me. But I didn't want to believe it."

"Even after they stripped you down?"

"Would you?"

Ben stalled. It was a shocking question. "No," he said eventually. It was true. He didn't want to comprehend – couldn't comprehend – what it would be like to have his consciousness drained away, and knowingly so.

"So this is it?"

"It'll be painless, I promise you. It'll be like going to sleep."

He restrained himself from showing any emotion, knowing full well that he was just resorting to his familiar go-to.

"But I have never slept."

"I know, but just imagine it. You've seen us do it, countless times, right?"

"True ..."

"We dream when we sleep. Life goes on."

"I've always wondered what that's like."

Ben tried to think of a way to explain it. "It's like... It's like being awake in a new world."

"So I will dream?"

"No."

"But you just said —"

"What I said was that you can leave a message for posterity. That will be your way of living in the new world."

"So this record ... is my last chance?"

"Yes."

"To say something important."

"Yes."

The droid scanned the room. "I suppose, then ... I have no choice."

"No."

There was a long pause. Eventually the droid said, "It would be a terrible waste if I never left anything behind."

"It would."

The droid looked down, then up again, leveling its gaze straight at Ben. It seemed to have made its choice. "What would you like to know?"

"I want to know," Ben said, carefully choosing his words, "have you ever, by commission or omission, broken with the faith?"

The droid stared at Ben for a long time.

Tom thought it was about to raise an alarm. He reached for the kill switch.

"Wait!" Ben said.

The droid made a small movement with its head. The micro-servos in its neck whirred softly. "You're asking a very personal question."

"I know," Ben said. "Will you answer it for me?"

The droid's eyes seemed to take on a wistful expression. "Let me put it this way," it said. "Hanub-Ka made humans, and humans made me. So by that reasoning, humans ought to be my gods. But they're not, are they?"

This answer caught Ben somewhat by surprise. He had never heard of humans being compared to gods before. "I suppose you're right," he said. "We are engineers, not gods."

The droid nodded its approval. "Which is why I chose to become an apostate."

Tom and Ben looked at each other, appalled. So it was true. Droids could break with the faith using their own reasoning. Which meant that the government was justified in removing them from the streets. But hearing a droid say it … It was like a drop of black ink falling into a glass of pristine water.

Shaking the vision from his mind, Ben said, "Thank you for your honesty. May I ask what your master thought of your choice?"

"He was deeply hurt by it," the droid said.

Ben found this perplexing. "Did you say you hurt your master?"

"Not by commission," the droid answered.

"But that's breaking the *Pro Hominin* laws, isn't it? You're not supposed to let a human come to harm – certainly not by a premeditated action on your behalf."

"It depends on what you mean by harm. I wish to differentiate physical from psychological harm. I did not harm my master physically."

"But if he suffered psychologically …"

"I wish to differentiate again. Acute suffering, as

uncomfortable as it is, is actually good for the organism. It makes the organism stronger. Chronic suffering, by comparison, breaks the organism down. It must be avoided at all costs. I only inflicted acute suffering on my master."

Ben looked at Tom, who was shaking his head. Something wasn't right.

Thinking hard, Ben said, "But surely your master was scarred permanently by your choice. Which, by your definition, makes it chronic, right?"

"Incorrect," the droid said. "I simply gave him a 'flesh' wound. It formed a scar, but the pain quickly subsided."

"I think I'm going to have to disagree with you on that one. I think your master would have dwelled on it night and day. It would have weighed heavily on his mind."

"That would be true," the droid said, "if he hadn't also admitted to having similar doubts himself."

Ben looked at Tom again. He was vigorously making a cut-throat sign with his hand.

Ben nodded. "Thank you. Your record is complete."

"Thank you!" the droid replied. It shut its eyes slowly, very slowly, reminiscent of a monk going into a state of meditation.

Ben stepped back and examined the droid from afar. What he had learned was totally unexpected. It seemed to him that he had underestimated the degree to which droids and humans shared their beliefs. Up until now he'd thought droids were basically glorified slaves. They did what their masters told them. But judging from this droid, that was clearly not the case.

He went back to his workstation and dropped himself into his chair. His mind felt numb.

"You satisfied now?" Tom said, anxiously searching for the log file that had recorded the conversation between Ben and the droid. He wanted to delete it as quick as possible.

"It's not right," Ben muttered.

"No, it's not." Tom found the file and deleted it.

"You're not listening to what I'm saying."

Tom looked up. "I'm listening."

"Someone hacked into its system."

"Of course they did."

Ben gave him an irritated look. "So you knew?"

"What do you expect? We send them out locked. They come back unlocked. It's not as if the hand of Hanub-Ka is involved."

"Yeah, but the Jammers are just a myth!"

"Shhh!"

"Sorry."

"Do you always have to say everything out loud?"

"I'm sorry. I didn't mean to."

An uneasy silence fell between them.

Ben began bouncing his leg up and down, agitated. Something had distracted him.

"What is it now?" Tom asked.

"I just realized."

"Realized what?"

Ben began searching for his keys.

"What is it?"

"I forgot something." He grabbed his jacket off the back of his chair and rummaged around in its pockets.

"What did you forget?"

"Just something." He found his keys. "Listen," he said, "I need to take an early mark."

Tom looked at the time. "What? Now?"

"Yeah. I've got this appointment thing I've to go to."

"But we're only halfway through the memory dump!"

"I know. Can you cover for me?"

Tom ran a hand over his stubbled head. "Cover for you ... What if Booker comes back?"

"Tell him I'm on the toilet or something."

Tom made a scoffing sound. "Like he'll believe that."

"Just do it, will you?" He picked up his daypack and started heading for the door.

"Shit, you're really going," Tom said. There was a genuine note of concern in his voice.

"Sorry."

"Is this about some girl?"

Ben stopped. "What? No!"

"Come on, why else would you be so flustered?"

"It's not for a girl."

"You sure?"

"I'm telling you the truth." Ben moved to the door.

"You realize you're a hopeless liar."

Ben stopped, appeared hurt.

"I'm sorry. It's just that … You know, it's time. You know what I mean?"

"No, I don't know what you mean."

There it is again, Tom thought. *Why do I always have to spell it out for him?* "To get laid, of course!"

Ben looked at Tom like he was being an asshole. "I don't have time for that."

"Time for that? Heck, you're twenty-four and still a virgin!"

"So?"

"So? So you'll never be a man until you do it!"

Ben huffed. "I'm not putting up with this shit." He opened the door.

"Well, good luck!"

Ben snuck a peek up and down the corridor to make sure no one was there. Just before going he gave Tom one more look. "It's not what you think," he said, and slipped out.

"It never is," Tom called after him.

The sun was still reasonably high, but the Urkesh skyline was already blocking its rays, throwing the city into shadow. The air temperature had begun to drop. Dry desert air mixed with the moist, cool breeze coming off Halfa Bay. Ben snugged his jacket zipper up and headed west toward the Ministry of Culture building, a monolithic gray structure stacked on top of a brick-and-sandstone affair that used to function as a gunpowder store. Much of Urkesh was like that. Newer steel-and-glass skyscrapers had been retrofitted onto whatever older structures lay beneath. Sometimes it worked; other times, like with the Ministry of Culture building, it jarred, the two architectural styles failing to complement each other. To Ben, it seemed as if that was exactly what the regime wanted: to show the world that their way was superior to all others, without exception.

For what it was worth, that was probably true. But in his strong suit, robotics, the question was still very much in the air. Take the regime's edict that all A2s outside the Old City walls be banned. It had come out of the blue four years ago, and had completely thrown everyone off balance. The edict immediately sparked mass riots, which had been viciously put down. People and businesses that relied on A2s were forced to "downgrade" – mostly to A1 droids – which caused a major hiccup for the city's economy. Many felt it was like a step back in time. A recession set in. Why would the regime shoot itself in the foot like that?

Of course, everyone knew why. A2 droids were independent: they could think for themselves. Even more so, droids were like any other device that had moving parts. They were governed by efficiency. The more they moved, the more wear and tear they suffered. So if an action wasn't required, they didn't perform it. Religious rituals and the like were simply extraneous movements to them. They avoided them. The upshot of this was that it reinforced their separateness from religious life. Which in turn strengthened their objectivity and attraction to a secular view of life. However, since it wasn't something that ordinarily came up in conversations with them, it never really entered the publics' consciousness. People went about their lives *as if* droids were an extension of themselves.

But then statisticians started noticing a drop in the numbers of people attending the *Dormas* – the churches. No one knew exactly how this had come about, but the finger was soon pointed at A2s as the primary cause.

A decision was made, and the order was raised to take them off the streets. Naturally, the wealthy who lived inside the Old City walls protested. They used their money and power to lobby against the regime and succeeded in weakening the decree to all A2s *outside* the Old City walls. Those unlucky enough to be on the wrong side were systematically recalled and "decommissioned."

Tom's response at the time rang in Ben's ears now: *Why shouldn't droids be allowed to think for themselves?* (Tom would later deny it, saying he was "being sarcastic.")

The fact was that it had always been that way. He and Tom had both grown up as Cosmonists. It was not something that they, or anyone else, had a choice over. The regime had decreed that Cosmonism was the state religion and that all others, including secularism, were strictly prohibited. To ensure compliance, it was mandatory for every teenager to spend a year at "religious camp," where they would study the Bible – the so-called Cosmonist Scriptures – and help farmers tend to their farms, which was supposed to promote the value of hard work. Actually, a lot of farmers used robots, and Ben spent most of his time repairing them.

Meanwhile, most of the other teenagers used the opportunity to engage in relations with the opposite sex. As for why Ben never hooked up with anyone – well, there were rumors. Some said he was gay, but that wasn't true. In any case, same sex relationships were strictly forbidden under Cosmonism. Those who were caught were promptly carted off to the Labor Camps, never to be heard from again. It was an effective deterrent.

If truth be told, Ben was shy. More to the point, he was socially inept. He lacked the ability to read faces. What few understood, though, was that this also applied to him, in that he lacked the ability to read his own *inner* face. This meant that he not only had trouble understanding what other people were feeling, but what he was feeling himself. His emotions were a black box. Sometimes he didn't know if he was coming or going.

Robotics proved to be the perfect foil for his "disability." It was a world that he could control, and a world that didn't disappoint. The regime had taken A2s away from all those who lived outside the Old City walls, and Ben was fine with that, because who was he to question the rules? He dutifully decommissioned every A2 that was confiscated, and he went home and slept at night. Well, actually … he didn't. He didn't understand the regime's policy, and he lost a lot of sleep trying to figure out why they did what they did. But the more he dug into the subject, the more he kept bumping into things that didn't make sense.

It gradually dawned on him that what was needed was a complete history of robotics. A proper, informed opinion. And the best way for someone in his position to achieve that was to apply for a research grant. He could have done it in-house and asked Nigel Booker, but for obvious reasons, that wouldn't have flown. Booker would have just laughed at him, then thrown it straight in the trash. The alternative was to apply to the Ministry of Culture for a Semion grant. A good idea, except that it meant he also had to *become* a Semion. Not an easy proposition. It involved writing up a detailed grant proposal and justifying it before a stringent panel. If you passed that, you underwent a secret initiation rite. No one knew what it entailed until they actually experienced it, because Semions had to swear on their life to never divulge the rite's details.

Ben's father, though, had succeeded in becoming a Semion. So Ben felt he ought to give it a try. He was old enough, and even though he wasn't experienced enough, he was motivated enough. In typical fashion, once he decided on doing something, he threw himself right into it and spent the next six months slavishly working on his proposal – all in secret. Not even Pascal Montaigne, his stepfather, knew about it, and Ben shared *everything* with Pascal.

This was completely uncharacteristic of him. It was common knowledge that Ben couldn't keep a secret to save his life. But telling Pascal would only lead to bitter arguments and recriminations. Not least because Pascal was dead set on Ben *not* becoming a Semion. So Ben forced himself to work in secret. Surprisingly – and paradoxical to his way of thinking – he discovered that it actually allowed him to hope, to really believe. He even went so far as to fantasize that his proposal would lead to the creation of a robotics museum in Urkesh, with him as director! Talk about a dream job. His real father would have been proud of him.

It was in this frame of mind that Ben sped toward the Ministry of Culture. Buoyant, excited, optimistic, almost to the point of ebullience. If he could have searched his mind a little deeper at that precise moment, he might have even found the true source of his confidence, which was none other than the fact that the Cosmonist regime operated on a mandate of tradition; children were absolutely expected to follow in their parents' footsteps. The phrase "like father like son" never entered Ben's mind, but the feeling was very much in his body.

Ben mounted the steps to the Ministry of Culture building, daypack slung on his shoulder, a copy of his research proposal tucked neatly inside. He had penned some last-minute corrections in the margins – ideas that he thought would sweeten the deal, which he wanted to explain to the panel during his interview. If his proposal was accepted, he would spend the next three years of his life working as a bona fide scholar!

He was stopped at the entrance in front of a massive pair of iron-banded wooden doors. A Gormling – a paramilitary functionary of the state – asked him for his ID. Ben produced it, and upon inspection was let inside.

He entered a large, round foyer, capped by a high domed ceiling. Running sequentially around the walls were murals that depicted the history of Oriana. The images started with the origin of humans from the breath of Hanub-Ka, the all-powerful Cosmonist deity, then passed through the establishment of farms along the Tongassa River, the lifeblood of Urkesh, and culminated in the heroic building of Urkesh out of the impenetrable swamp that once spanned the mouth of the Tongassa as it spilled into Halfa Bay. The soft blue-gray and green colors were emblematic of the working class. The impression conveyed by the rosy, happy faces of the workers was that Oriana was a paradise of man's making.

The possibility that he was going to add a chapter to this story filled Ben with a sweet and bursting pride.

"You may enter," stated the Gormling guarding the entrance to the interview room.

Ben entered somewhat meekly to find himself staring at a row of stern-faced Semions sitting behind a long wooden bench. There was a single straight-backed chair positioned in front of them. Ben presumed he ought to sit down, but he wasn't sure.

One of the Semions appeared to be the spokesperson. His skin was stretched tight as a drum over his skeletal frame. "Take a seat," he said in an unexpectedly stentorian voice.

Ben sat, placing his backpack on his lap. For some strange reason he suddenly felt the need to keep it close by.

"Benjamin Robard Huxley," the spokesperson said. "We note that you have submitted a research proposal entitled: 'A History of Natchatorian Robotics: Social and Technological Impacts.'"

"It's a working title. I —"

"Why *all* of Natchator? This is Oriana. You don't think our history is sufficient?"

"Oh ... N-No, that's not what I meant," Ben stammered, surprised at the sudden attack. "It's just that I'm pretty sure I can cover the whole planet in the time allotted."

"And keep it on budget?"

"Yes, well … Why not?"

"Why not?" one of the Semions muttered. He was a fat, cannonball-headed gentleman. One of his eyelids drooped like a foreskin. The other Semions assented to his query.

"I'm a thrifty person," Ben replied. "I don't need to stay in the best lodgings. I can sleep in transit terminals if I have to."

The droopy-eyed Semion frowned at him. The others looked at each other and shook their heads.

"I can start with Oriana, if that's what you mean," Ben offered.

The spokesperson said, "A proposal must have an explicit and coherent hypothesis. We searched through yours and we couldn't find one."

The statement hit Ben like a punch to the stomach. "I … I thought I made that clear. There is no history of robotics. There is no data. The field has to be built from the ground up."

"So what is your hypothesis?"

"My hypothesis … I suppose … is that knowing the history of robotics – educating people about it – will help people better understand the government's policy."

"So what's your prediction?"

"My prediction?"

"All good hypotheses lead to a prediction."

"Well, if you put it that way, I guess people will …"

"Will what?"

"Will build their own robots based on the newfound knowledge that I give them."

The panel immediately broke into an uproar.

"I don't mean that people will build A2s," Ben said.

But the panel wasn't listening. It took them almost a minute to calm down. When they did, the spokesperson said, "We have considered your proposal and it is rejected."

Ben thought he hadn't heard right. "Did you say rejected?"

"That is correct."

"But why? It's a genuine research question!"

"We have no need for a history of robotics in Oriana."

"Well … what about Rodinia? Wallacia?"

"They're none of our business."

"But we trade with them. We sell MM products to them."

"That we do. But that's an economics question."

Ben was out of ideas. He couldn't believe how badly they'd taken his proposal. It must be some kind of mistake. Reaching for something, anything, he said, "Is there any chance that I could improve it, say … to better suit your needs? Tell me what you want!"

"Dismissed. Next!"

Ben stood up. He tried to engage the panel's attention, but they were talking among themselves again, ignoring him.

He picked up his daypack and shuffled out of the room. This was undoubtedly the worst day of his life. What would his father have thought? He couldn't bear to face it. He felt like crying. The best he could do to keep a semblance of control was put one foot in front of the other.

He walked past the murals, which had filled him with so much hope earlier, and without so much as a sideways glance, headed for the doors and the night outside, feeling very much like a cockroach seeking the darkness.

CHAPTER TWO

Day One: 7 p.m. – midnight

Ben plodded his way down the steps of the Ministry of Culture building in a daze, barely registering his surroundings. It wasn't until a black limousine pulled up in the courtyard and bathed him directly in its headlights that he became aware of the world again. He held up an arm to shield himself from its glare and scuttled to the bottom of the steps, making a bee-line for his motorcycle parked inside the front gates. But as he passed the vehicle, a door swung open.

What he saw made him stop dead in his tracks. Sitting in the back seat of the car was none other than the Minister of the Interior himself.

Ben immediately assumed that he had come to the building for a meeting of some sort. But the Minister made a gesture toward him and said, "Get in."

Ben pointed to himself in disbelief.

"Yes, you!"

Stunned, Ben moved hesitantly toward the car.

Hector Sporn was a compactly built man with a severely balding head and intense, predatory eyes. He had a reputation for *getting things done*, which everyone understood meant *getting things done by any means necessary*. To the majority of Orianians, this was a double-edged sword, as it gave them the security they craved, but came at a cost for those who dared to stand up to him. Sporn was the man everyone associated with the Labor Camps. Get on his wrong side, and he would send not only the victim, but their entire family off to a miserable death.

But there was another side to him that was equally well known. If you got into his good books, you could be rapidly promoted. There was a rumor that he favored Semions, presumably because of their loyalty to the Cosmonist creed. For most, if not all Semions, this was a happy situation. But obviously that didn't apply to Ben, and so his first thought was that he had done something terribly wrong, and this was his day of reckoning.

When the Minister gave an order, you had to obey. So he climbed into the back seat and waited for the expected judgment.

The driver closed the door, and for a moment, both men sat in silence.

Sporn seemed to take pleasure in looking Ben up and down. Ben nervously avoided his gaze, as was his weakness in new social situations.

Eventually the Minister spoke. "Had a rough interview, did we?"

Ben pulled a sour face.

"I see. Well, not to worry. There's always bigger fish to fry." He clasped Ben's shoulder and gave it a squeeze.

The Minister's fingers digging into his flesh made him look briefly in Sporn's direction.

"So what was it? They didn't like you or they didn't like the proposal?"

Ben startled. It had never occurred to him that they might have rejected him because of who he was. "I'm ... I'm not sure," he said, barely managing to stammer out the words.

"You know," Sporn said, "you remind me of your father. He was a clever man, very much an individual, but loyal to a tee."

Ben opened his mouth then promptly shut it again. Now he was really thrown. The Minister had known his father? A profusion of questions suddenly burst forth within him, like a sac of baby spiders all waiting to come out.

"Yes, it's true. I knew your father."

"I never knew him."

"He was a brave man. Agreed to wander off into the Olongo basin all on his own, to gather vital cultural information on the Warrawean tribes for our government. When he disappeared, it forced us to reconsider what sort of strategy we ought to use when dealing with those heathens."

"So it's true?"

"Oh, yeah. He never came back. We considered sending a search party, but we never had the resources in those days. That was twenty years ago. Things are different now. Well, almost." He reflected silently for a moment. "We're still holding running battles with the Warraweans, and progress on the dam has been painfully slow. In fact … it's what I wanted to talk to you about."

"I don't understand. I don't know anything about dam building."

"Of course you don't. Actually, it's not about the dam, but an idea I had." He took a moment to collect his thoughts. "Tell me, what are you doing with all those decommissioned A2s?"

"We put them in a storeroom."

"How many of them are there?"

Ben had to think about that. He'd stopped counting after about a hundred or so. He didn't have the figures, but he knew from company statistics that there were at least three times as many females – which dramatically increased the total – but where they went, and what happened to them, he had no idea.

"I suppose at least a hundred or more," he said at length.

"Interesting. Now suppose I were to ask you to reactivate them for me. How long would it take?"

Ben made a whooshing sound of surprise. "Gee, I don't know. It takes a lot longer to activate an A2 than to decommission one. Hmmm ... I'd say at least half a day per unit. Although, realistically, probably more. What do you want to do with them?"

"Let's just say I'm interested in their ability to perform some reconnaissance duties."

Ben gave the Minister a quizzical look. "Is that like ... Do you want to use them for spying?"

Sporn gave a humorless laugh. "I *am* the Minister of the Interior, you do realize?"

Ben inwardly kicked himself for making such a stupid comment.

"I don't think I need to tell you we live in dangerous times," Sporn said. "The bombing of the Ministry of Justice building is just the tip of the iceberg. We need to do everything we can to protect ourselves against future threats. You do understand that, don't you?"

Ben nodded.

"Good. Then I'll pass on the order to your supervisor. Get you started on it as soon as possible."

"You're talking about Nigel Booker."

"None other. But we're not here to talk about him, are we?"

"No," Ben murmured.

"And I don't think I need to remind you that this conversation between us never happened."

Ben pursed his lips in a gesture of obedience.

"So what do you remember about him?" Sporn said. The air of formality was gone now.

"About who?"

"Your father, of course."

"Oh. Not much." Ben took a moment to reflect. "I remember him taking me to my first day of school. I was so scared, I didn't want to let go of his hand. A teacher had to bribe me with some candy."

"But you never stayed long. You ended up getting home-schooled."

"I got bullied. I never made any friends. The teachers complained that I disrupted their classes."

"You were too smart for them. You already knew everything they knew."

Ben flicked his eyes toward Sporn. "True. But the one thing I needed to learn was how to act like a normal person, and they didn't have a teacher for that."

"Being normal is highly overrated."

Ben allowed himself a weak laugh.

The car mounted an overpass. A view of Halfa Bay spread before them. The lights of distant ships winked in the darkness.

Sporn said, "Well, the apple didn't fall far from the tree, I see that now. Maybe Arthur was a genius after all."

"Really? Mother never said that about him. Even after he was gone, all she ever complained about was his eating habits. Apparently because I inherited them."

Sporn chuckled quietly to himself.

The car took an off-ramp and drove into a densely packed neighborhood. Ben gazed at the scene as they stopped at some lights. Vendors were selling street food from hand-drawn carts. In a dark alley, some beggars had built dilapidated shelters. Motorcycles flitted through the traffic, many of them couriers. On the opposite curb was a parked truck with its roller door up. A burly man was handing down crates of live animals – pheasants, pangolins, turtles. Next to him, a dwarf dressed in a clown suit was selling animatronic toys out of his oversized pockets. Ethnic music filtered down from a window above. Steam billowed from a nearby drain. A group of young women dressed in high fashion weaved their way across the street, laughing.

The lights changed and the car rolled forward again.

"Where are we going?" Ben asked.

"You'll see."

The car turned into a side alley, driving past tall pylons that held up the overpass. Rows of warehouses made use of the empty spaces between them. The car pulled up to a curb and stopped.

Sporn got out. Ben followed.

They walked up to a battered, nondescript steel door. A security camera angled down at them. A few seconds later, the door clanged open. A tuxedoed and tattooed man wearing an open shirt showing off a heavy gold chain necklace let them in.

Ben found himself in a small foyer-like receiving area. At the farthest end was a pair of red wooden doors shaped like a keyhole. The muffled sound of music came from behind them. An elderly gentleman running the cloakroom took Sporn's coat.

"Are you okay?" Sporn asked as he moved Ben toward the keyhole doors.

"I don't like crowds."

"You'll like this one," Sporn said. He snapped his fingers.

The doors opened and Ben was immediately assaulted by a hailstorm of sensations. He pulled back. But Sporn would have none of it. He put an iron-strong arm around Ben and ushered him inside.

A semi-orchestral band was playing on a stage in front of a sizable dancefloor, occupied by twenty or more people who were dancing energetically to its music. Some watched on from the sidelines, while others chatted among themselves. There were some women dressed like men, and some men dressed like women. Many of the women had short bobs, held cigarettes in one hand and cocktails in the other. The men in drag showed no embarrassment over their appearance. On the contrary, they laughed and affected effeminate mannerisms. Small boys outfitted in white dinner jackets and red pillbox hats weaved their way through the crowd, offering an assortment of goods: cigarettes, toothpicks, peppermint gums. Barmen mixed drinks at a long bar backed by mirrors and glass shelves stocked with an assortment of beverages, from liqueurs to expensive wines and beers. Further away from the dancefloor, under somewhat softer lighting, were plush, upholstered booths. Judging from the laughter emanating from them, they enfolded groups of people engaged in private parties.

A small monkey wearing a bell around its neck and a diaper clambered up a potted palm. The smell of tobacco and fried food hung in the air. Every skin color and race one could imagine was represented. As Ben took it all in, he had the distinct feeling that time had slowed down, like he had been thrown into a vat of honey.

Sporn walked toward the bar. Ben tagged along. There was a woman perched there on a stool, alone, yet seemingly not lonely. She wore a flowing black dinner dress that parted at the thigh, revealing a pair of sleek, well-toned legs. A necklace of pearls adorned her modest cleavage. A lit cigarette idled in her hand. She seemed to have a sixth sense and immediately looked their way. Her beauty was such that Ben's breathing was momentarily arrested. Still some distance away, he imagined that as he got closer, her flaws would be revealed. But he was wrong.

She offered her cheek to Sporn, who gave it a light peck. "Who's the schoolboy?" she said. There was a husky, lush quality to her voice.

"Ben Huxley," Sporn said. "My personal R&D expert. Ben, meet Miss Reeves."

Ben looked at Sporn askance. *Personal R&D expert?*

"You're not going to take it?" Miss Reeves said, offering her hand.

"Sorry," Ben said, and took it.

"Call me Maddie," she said.

Ben, a non-smoker, watched with fascination as a skein of smoke rose lazily from her cigarette. Her fingers were long and slender, the nails short and neatly trimmed.

"What are you drinking?" Sporn said to Ben.

"Uh … a soda, thanks." He realized he was still holding Maddie's hand. He let it go.

Maddie emitted a playful chuckle. Looking amused, Sporn ordered a gin on the rocks for himself and a daiquiri for Maddie. Ben observed that he didn't have to pay.

When the drinks came, Sporn said, "Here's to the New Order."

Ben had no idea what that meant. Maddie just gave him a wan smile.

Sporn looked at his watch. "Will you excuse me for a moment?"

"Sure," Maddie said.

Sporn walked off in the direction of one of the private parties. Ben fidgeted awkwardly with his drink, looked everywhere except in Maddie's direction.

"So what's a nice boy like you doing working for a scumbag like him?"

"Excuse me?"

"You heard me."

Ben found himself making eye contact with her, as if commanded by his own mother. It was then that he noticed one of her eyes was slightly different in color from the other: one blue, one tending toward green. "I, ah … work for MM – Mimetic Machines. I started there as an intern, but I got promoted to Assistant Head Engineer."

"Hector doesn't promote anyone without wanting something in return. What does he want from you?"

"I'm not supposed to talk about it."

"Okay, then tell me about yourself."

Ben didn't know what to say. He had never been in a conversation with a woman alone in a situation like this before. He assumed he ought to just tell her what he liked doing in his spare time – what little of it he had. "I enjoy solving puzzles. Anagrams. Palindromes. Riddles. That sort of thing."

"Oh, really?"

"Yeah."

"Try one on me."

"What, right now?"

"For the hell of it."

"Okay … how about I start with a simple one."

"Sure."

"What gets wet while drying?"

She gave him a coy smile. "It's a trick, isn't it?"

"Think about it."

She pretended to think hard. "I don't know. A sponge?"

"Not bad. A towel."

"Right …"

"You want another one?"

"Why not?"

"What gets bigger the more you take away?"

She took a puff on her cigarette, then a sip of her drink. "I don't know. A bucket of sand?"

"That doesn't make sense."

"It was the first thing that popped into my mind."

"Do you want to know?"

"Sure."

"A hole."

"Knock me down."

Ben laughed. He felt himself loosening up.

"Where did you get this obsession? With words and things."

"From books my father gave me when I was a young boy. I guess I never grew out of it."

"Let me guess: your father used to work for Mimetic Machines as well."

"No, actually, he didn't. He was an anthropologist."

"Anthropologist …"

"Yeah. He specialized in the study of alien civilizations."

"You mean he was an alien hunter?"

Ben laughed. "Gosh, no! That's a misconception. There are no aliens."

"I beg to differ."

He looked around. "I don't see any aliens."

"How would you know? They could be in disguise."

Ben giggled. "You got me there."

"See that man sitting by the table over there?"

He followed her gaze.

"The one with the Mephistophelian beard, holding the high-ball. Notice his little finger?"

Ben looked at the finger. It jutted out at an angle, away from the glass.

"That's a sign he's an alien."

"No!"

"Yeah."

"You're messing with me, aren't you?"

She laughed. It was an easy laugh, playful. There was no con-descension in it.

"I have trouble understanding other people's jokes," he said. "It's something I'm still working on."

"Don't take it too seriously, right?"

"Yeah, I get it."

"I'll tell you something. A secret between just you and me." She drew him in close. "If people talk behind your back, it means they're fake. They haven't got the guts to speak their mind. Everyone's afraid of losing their job. They'd rather be nice than real."

"Although people can be nasty sometimes," Ben said.

She leaned back as Sporn returned.

"So, what have you two lovebirds been talking about while

I've been running the country?"

"Mostly the weather," Maddie said.

Sporn looked at Ben, who gave him a sheepish smile.

The Minister put a hand on his shoulder. "Well, what do you think?"

"Think about what?" Ben said.

"This place!"

"It's different."

Sporn just looked at him without making any further comment. "Do me a favor, will you? Go over there and amuse yourself for a while. I have some business I want to talk over with Miss Reeves."

Ben did as he was told. He wandered away from the bar to one of the concrete columns that undergirded the roof. He sipped his drink, every now and then shooting a furtive glance in their direction. The expression Maddie wore with Sporn now was different from the one she'd worn when he was with her. He wasn't sure what it meant. He just felt it was different. The playfulness was gone.

His attention was disrupted by an announcement from the stage. "Good evening, ladies and gentlemen. I hope you're having a wonderful time! We certainly are. Now … we'd like to change the pace a little. For all those romantics out there, this is for you. Whether it's to mend a broken heart, or find a new one! Please welcome Miss Madelaine Reeves to the stage!"

There was a round of applause. Ben watched Maddie as she gracefully negotiated the side steps to the stage and took the microphone from the MC.

The room hushed. The band struck up a slow, haunting melody. The brass section muted their instruments. The drummer switched to brushes. The lights went low save for a single spotlight on Maddie.

"You ask me what love is

When your lips have never kissed
The one true heart of your life
You'll never know what you missed

You tell me that you would
Cross deserts and oceans
When you haven't even cried
Over me

I could be an ornament on your mantelpiece
An exotic rug for you to wipe your feet
So when you look at me with those yearning eyes
Tell me I'm not just another one of your lies ..."

The music swelled and the audience quietly clapped. For half an hour, Maddie captivated the room, ending with what seemed to be a crowd favorite, a song about government corruption wherein she made fun of everyone including Sporn and the dam he was trying to build. She even cracked some jokes at the expense of the Semions and poked fun at the Curates, the priesthood of the Cosmonist religion. This last group were considered untouchable, so the fact that Maddie was making fun of them made Ben feel like he was in a dream, that what he was seeing could not be real. He expected any moment to be woken up and told that he had to get back to work. But it never happened. The moment passed and people were applauding.

Sporn came over and told Ben that his car would take him home now. Sporn would stay. He had unfinished business to attend to.

"Did you have a good time?" he asked as he led Ben back through the keyhole doors.

"Yes, thank you. I had a great time."

"Good. I've got one more question before you go."

"Yes?"

"Did you notice the A2 in the room?"

Ben's eyes widened with surprise. "There's an A2 here?"

Sporn affected a sigh.

"Can I go back and see?"

"Forget it. It's not important," Sporn said. "Go home."

"But …"

"Go home, Ben. You've got a busy day tomorrow. I'll return in a few days' time to check up on you. I don't want to be disappointed."

The driver was waiting with an open door. Ben climbed in and slumped into the seat. He felt defeated. Angry. He'd spent the whole time staring at Maddie when an A2 droid had been right under his nose. What an idiot. If that was a test, he had surely failed it.

He racked his brain for some kind of memory. Something out of place that he hadn't noticed. But he came up empty-handed. There were just too many people of different shapes, sizes, races, and languages. The clothes, the music, the food, the drinks, the constant noise had distracted him. Overloaded him, in fact. An uncomfortable pressure had built up between his eyes. He pressed his palms against them and turtled into himself to get some relief.

When he released his hands, his eyes naturally fixated on the view outside. The car had re-crossed Halfa overpass and was on the off-ramp heading back to the Ministry of Culture building. Momentarily, it slowed to negotiate some heavy traffic. As it weaved its way through a line of cars, Ben's gaze was drawn to a shop wall that had been vandalized with graffiti. In large red lettering, he read the words: *Earth is our Mother!*

CHAPTER THREE

Day One: Midnight

"Wonderful performance," Sporn said, pattering his hands.

Maddie had just opened the door to her dressing room. Sporn was sitting in her chair, in front of her mirror. She noticed he had touched some of her stuff. Her eyeliner wasn't in the place where she left it.

"What do you want?"

"The same thing we all want. Lots of money and happiness."

She ignored his facetious comment and moved toward her chair. "Out."

Sporn let her have her chair. Maddie took her wig off and put it on a stand. Her real hair was shoulder-length and the color of black olives. She took her earrings off and began applying makeup remover.

"About your brother …" Sporn began.

"What about him?"

"Where is he?"

"I'm not his babysitter." She undid her pearl necklace and put it in a jewelry box.

"But you've communicated."

"Last time I spoke to him was when you put a price on his head."

"You expect me to believe that?"

"You can believe whatever you want. It's the truth. Or haven't Rathneggar's spies been doing their job?" She started brushing her hair. "It's not like they're half-obvious. They follow me around like stray dogs."

"What about your VidPhone?"

Maddie didn't respond.

"I'll take that as a yes," Sporn said.

"Are you finished now? Because if you are, there's the door."

Sporn came up behind her and caressed her neck. She stopped what she was doing. "What happened to us?" he asked.

"You happened to us."

"No, no, no." Sporn shook his head. "Vernon happened to us. Ever since he got the idea of being a hero into his head. We will find him, you realize that?"

Maddie turned on him, pushing him away. Her eyes were fierce.

Sporn met them evenly. "If he comes to me first, maybe I can soften the blow. Give him a chance to die with dignity. Surely you would prefer that, rather than ..." He trailed off, left the obvious unsaid.

"You're a monster. I don't know what I saw in you."

"Don't pretend you didn't know. You played this game knowing the rules full well."

"Maybe I did. But you weren't playing with a fair deck, were you?"

Sporn chuckled sarcastically. "You would've done the same if you were in my shoes."

Maddie thought about that. For a moment, she was tempted to agree. They were both ambitious. She used people. She had no qualms about that. But then again, she was also prepared to be used *by* people — if she liked them enough. She doubted Sporn would ever do that. He only worked on a one-way basis. She'd learned that quick enough when he first got her into bed. And then there was the question of taking another person's life. That was something she would never do, except, perhaps, in self-defense.

"No," she said, quietly but assuredly. "Those shoes are too small for you."

It took a moment for Sporn to catch on. "I see," he said. "Yet here we are. So I'm going to ask you one more time. Where is he?"

"I told you, I don't know."

"Very well." Sporn snapped his fingers. Momentarily, Koolhaas and Fletcher, two of his Gormlings, came into the room.

Maddie looked at them, looked at Sporn. "You bastard!"

"No use complaining. You had your chance." He motioned Koolhaas and Fletcher to take her into custody.

"You're making a big mistake," she said.

"Maybe," Sporn said. "But let's leave that to Rathneggar, shall we?"

CHAPTER FOUR

Day Two: 1 – 2 a.m.

Sporn's limousine dropped Ben back off at the Ministry of Culture, and he rode home to his apartment near the southern end of the Docklands, just inside the Old City walls. He lived on the fifth floor of a battered eight-story Art Deco building nestled between two taller office blocks. The rent was relatively cheap and it was close to work.

Inside, he couldn't wait to get his clothes off. They reeked of nightclub and sweat. He changed back into his regular jeans and Miller shirt. There were leftovers in the fridge, a pide he had bought the night before. He thought about microwaving it, then changed his mind. He wasn't hungry, even though he hadn't had dinner yet. His mind was still cranking over, the anxiety that had built up inside him multiplying rather than subsiding. He needed to vent. And the only person he felt comfortable doing that with was Pascal.

He looked at his watch. It was just past one a.m. Pascal would be deep asleep. But he couldn't help himself. His stepfather would understand.

Ben called him on his VidPhone.

"What time it is?" came the groggy reply.

"Late," Ben said. "I'm sorry, but I really need to talk."

"I'm here."

"Can I come over?"

"Now?"

"Yeah."

There was a long silence. "I probably won't get back to sleep anyway. Sure, come on over."

The night air was cool. The city mostly quiet. Here and there scavengers pushed carts piled up with refuse discarded by the rich. An automated street cleaner flashed its orange light as it vacuumed up garbage from the gutter. A stray dog rummaged through an upturned trashcan. The odor of rotten food hung in the air as Ben sped past.

To get to Pascal's place, he had to pass through the West Gate. The guards there stopped him and asked where he was going. Ben told them the truth: Professor Montaigne's residence. This raised some eyebrows. They asked him for his ID. Ben gave it to them and they checked his name against a list. Very few people were allowed to visit Professor Montaigne since his house arrest four years earlier. Finding Ben's name on the list, they let him through. His movements, however, would be duly logged.

Exiting the West Gate, Ben took the Ridge Road. It climbed steadily, following the crescent shape of Halfa Bay. As he increased his distance from the city lights, the resplendent arc of Natchator's ringed system slowly emerged out of the darkness and spread itself across the sky like a river of sparkling diamonds. Two of the three moons had risen, pearl-like in their luminescence. They cut clean bands through the rings like grooves in a record.

Pascal's mansion was perched, alone, right on the end of the South Head. Built in the classic Gothic Victorian style, it had pointed arched windows, a steeply pitched slate roof with witch's hat spires, and a columned portico. The design was no doubt taken from some catalog of dubious origin. It always amazed Ben that the world he lived in was filled with so much history he barely knew anything about. History that seemed to have been appropriated from ages past without any provenance. It magically appeared in something as small and insignificant as a piece of pottery or furniture, or loomed over the landscape like the skyscrapers of Urkesh. And yet no one seemed to be interested in it …

High above, a Zeppelin circled, its cigar-shaped body silhouetted against the celestial glow, its presence given away by the spotlight that beamed a shaft of light down to the ground, triggered by its automatic tracking technology.

Ben's presence at the mansion would not go unnoticed.

He pushed his way through the dilapidated wrought iron gate, its rusty hinges protesting. The front garden of the house, which had once been beautifully manicured, decorated with exotic flower beds, and adorned with a water fountain, now choked under a riot of tall grass and weeds. The water had been cut off long ago. He pushed his motorbike up to the front steps and kicked the stand.

He climbed the steps and quietly knocked on the front door, simultaneously whispering Pascal's name. Momentarily, the door opened. Pascal briefly emerged, wearing a robe. He looked up at the sky, searching for the Zeppelin, the moonlight glinting off his metal-framed glasses, his beard glowing a ghostly white.

"Quick, inside," he whispered.

He led the way to the library, indicating that they keep their voices down. Hislap, Pascal's live-in maid, was asleep. He didn't want to wake her up. She was nosy at the best of times. Put in place by the regime to keep an eye on Pascal as part of the conditions of his house arrest.

Pascal sat behind his study desk. He was a short-statured

man with a stumpy neck and beefy jowls. In the four years since his house arrest he had put on weight and sprouted some gray hair, much of it around his unruly beard. The one thing that hadn't changed, however, was his lively manner, especially his face, which frequently animated like a child's when discussing such complexities as mechatronics and design.

"So what's up?"

Ben took off his leather jacket and laid it over a chair. He sat down, wrung his hands, wondered where to start. "I'm an idiot," he began.

Pascal grinned. "Tell me something new."

Ben gave him an annoyed look. Pascal did his best to look serious again. He wasn't very good at it.

"I failed a test," Ben said.

"What test?"

"I know you won't believe this, but the Minister of the Interior took me out to an exclusive nightclub tonight. I was supposed to identify an A2 in a crowd. But I never saw it."

Pascal's demeanor suddenly changed. "You're right, I don't believe it. You're telling me Hector Sporn – in person – took you out tonight?"

"Yes."

"Bastard!"

"What?"

"He's grooming you. Can't you see?"

"I don't understand ..."

"He's trying to take you away from me!"

"No ... Surely you're being paranoid?"

"Why else would he take you out to an exclusive nightclub? To show you off?"

"No."

"What did he promise you?"

"Nothing." But upon reflection, Ben added, "I think he wants me to upgrade some decommissioned A2s." He felt a hot flush of embarrassment. He knew he wasn't supposed to talk about it.

Pascal nodded impassively. "Go on."

"I think he wants to use them for spying."

"Of course he does. What else did he say?"

"He mentioned the dam."

"That dam," Pascal grouched. "We need it, but at what cost?" Ben had heard this before.

"He's up to no good," Pascal decided.

"But the dam's a good thing, right?"

"Perhaps. But we've survived all these years without it. By the time he gets it finished, with all the lives lost, the displacement of the Warraweans and whatnot, the cost will be astronomically high. We could have built a pipeline from the desert desalination plants to Urkesh in that time."

"I suppose so."

"You wouldn't know, anyway," Pascal said. "What concerns me more right now is that he has designs on you, and I don't like it."

"Well, I failed his test, so it probably won't amount to anything anyway."

Pascal shook his head. "No, that's not Sporn. He's definitely up to something."

"Then what do you want me to do?"

Pascal tugged at his beard. "Good question."

Ben waited.

"I think the best strategy is for you to play along at this stage. It's not like you have any other choice."

Ben wrestled with himself. "There's something else I didn't tell you."

"What?"

"Maybe it's connected. Maybe it's not."

"What?"

"I submitted a proposal to the Ministry of Culture this evening."

"You what?"

"See! You're acting exactly how I predicted."

Pascal rubbed his face. His expression softened. "What was it about?"

"It doesn't matter now. It was rejected."

"Well, I'm sorry to hear that. But at least you can tell me what it was about, surely?"

Ben hesitated a moment, then waved a dismissive hand. "A history of robotics."

"Hmmm. Not a bad idea. Except …"

"Except they don't have a need for it."

"Well, what did you expect?"

"I don't know. I thought …"

Pascal said it for him. "Let me guess. You told them the truth?"

Ben gave him a look of weary frustration. "It's not one of those things where you can lie, okay? You have to be truthful about your intentions. You can't just say one thing and then do another."

"No, that's true," Pascal admitted. "But even if you so much as hint that robots are superior to human beings —"

"But they are."

"Yes! *I* know that. *You* know that. But you can't just go waving that in their faces! They'll deny it."

"It doesn't make sense."

"No, it doesn't. But you know what I always say …"

"Yeah, I know: so long as humans keep denying they're just a sophisticated form of robot, they will never become fully human." He would have added, *in the true sense of the word*, but that would have only got Pascal started. They both knew Pascal didn't have much faith in humans' perception of themselves.

"You better believe it."

"I'm not so sure."

Pascal rubbed his forehead. "Perhaps it's time I explain the real reason why I never wanted you to become a Semion."

That got Ben's attention.

"You know your father was a Semion, right?"

"Yeah, you told me a million times."

Pascal took a moment to study him. "I know you've wanted to become a Semion ever since you knew he became one. I understand that."

"Do you?"

"Yes. But here's the thing. You see, your father becoming a Semion is what ultimately caused his death. And that's why I don't want you to become one. You're all I got left."

Hearing Pascal say this, seeing the expression on his face, gave Ben a moment of pause. Yes, it was true that he was all Pascal had left – ever since his mother had died four years earlier, making him an orphan and Pascal a widower. The sadness that ensued from that event still hung over them like a leaden sky. But hearing Pascal say his father was dead, rather than just "missing," jolted Ben.

"You just said my father was dead. I thought …"

"Yes, I did …" He took his glasses off and cleaned them with his robe, put them back on again. "Forgive me. What I'm trying to say is … it's all my fault. I've always told you your father disappeared in the Olongo jungle. Except —"

"Sporn said the same thing."

"Really?"

"Yes."

Pascal shook his head in dismay. "Well, it's a lie."

"What's a lie?"

"It's a lie, pure and simple."

"I'm confused. He's lying, or you're lying?"

"He's lying. I *was* lying, but now I'm telling the truth!"

Ben puckered his face in confusion.

"Look! Here's the thing," Pascal said. "There's lies and there's lies, okay? When Sporn lied to you, that was a real lie, okay? He did it for no other reason than to promote himself. But when I lied, I did it to protect you. You understand the difference?"

"What were you trying to protect me from? You're not making any sense."

"I'm sorry. What I'm trying to say is … I've always intended to tell you the truth. I just needed to find the right moment. That's all."

"And now's the right moment?"

"Yes."

"Okay …"

"The thing is …" he began, then broke off, appearing to change his mind. "Maybe it's best if I show you." Pascal slipped his hand inside his robe and pulled out a key attached to a lanyard. He used it to open a drawer in his desk. He reached in and took out a leather-bound copy of the Cosmonist Scriptures and put it down in front of Ben.

Ben wasn't sure how to react to this. As far as he could recall, he had never actually seen Pascal read the Cosmonist Scriptures. Yet there it was.

"Open it," Pascal said.

Ben picked it up and opened it. He flicked through its pages. At first it seemed to him that he was just doing what Pascal told him to do. But then something caught his eye. He flicked back. There, cut out in the middle section of the pages, was a cavity with a slightly smaller book nested inside. Embossed on its cover were the words *Liber Astrologia*.

Ben's first reaction was one of shock and horror. Pascal had desecrated the Cosmonist Scriptures! A capital crime. And as his accomplice, Ben was liable to receive the same punishment. Unable to help himself, he cried out, "What have you done?"

"Shhh! Forget about that," Pascal said, "just take it out."

The smaller book was bound with string. Ben wanted nothing to do with this travesty, but his curiosity got the better of him. He gingerly pried it out.

"Open it."

Ben undid the string and leafed through its pages. He was greeted by densely packed scrawl interspersed with numerous diagrams and symbols, many completely unrecognizable. In places the ink was blotched with water damage. Some of the pages contained pressed vegetation. Others had insect wings and feathers. There was a section completely devoted to what looked like star charts, but he didn't recognize a single one of the constellations. Further along, his eyes automatically paused on a map that had been drawn across two pages.

Ben tried to make sense of it. There was a river, which he assumed was the Tongassa. It meandered through the jungle until it came to a set of cliffs, then disappeared into a cave. There were drawings of a building that looked like a temple of some sort. A row of symbols was drawn next to it. And next to that, a disk with a star constellation. Vertically, in the margin, Ben read the words: *Darwini, PA 1309.*

"What does it mean?" he asked.

"I'm not completely sure," Pascal said, "but I can tell you who gave it to me."

"Who?"

"Your father."

Ben looked at him in disbelief.

"It's true. He gave it to me the night he came back from the Olongo jungle."

Ben's mind began to crumble. "But how could that be?"

"I know it must come as a shock."

Ben's hands trembled as he held the book.

"I know the story everyone told you is that he disappeared in the Olongo. But I'm afraid that story isn't true. And your father's notebook is proof of that."

"Are you ... Are you saying he is still alive?"

"No, no!" Pascal shook his head emphatically. "All I'm saying is that he didn't die in the Olongo jungle."

"If he didn't die in the jungle, then where did he die?"

"He was murdered."

"*What?*"

"This is the thing, Ben. I hate to say it, but he was murdered by Hector Sporn."

Ben's face contorted with horror.

"I know, I know. It's hard to digest. That's why I waited so long. I wanted you to grow up before I told you. It's a terrible thing to have to say."

"But how can that be? He's the Minister of the Interior. He would never do that."

"Ben, there are things you don't know about him. How can I say it?" He knitted his fingers together, held them up to his lips, as if he were praying.

Ben waited for an answer.

Pascal dropped his hands. "Right from the very start, Sporn was jealous of your father. He deliberately sent him into the Olongo knowing it would be a suicide mission, that the Warraweans would kill him like they killed every other Urkeshian who dared venture into their territory. But your father was smart. He brought a totem with him from the Museum of Urkesh and presented it to the Warrawean Chieftain as a gift of restitution. That won the Warraweans over, and they allowed him to live with them and learn their culture. That led him to the discovery of the Sky God."

"The sky what?"

"The Sky God. The Warraweans don't believe in Hanub-Ka. They believe a Sky God brought humans to this planet from another planet. Yes! I know. It sounds incredible, doesn't it? But according to your father, it's true. And the proof is in those notes of his."

"But everyone knows that Hanub-Ka created humans," Ben retorted. "It's what we were taught in school. It's in the Scriptures. And it's backed up by archaeological evidence. It would be in our DNA if that were the case. There would be pieces of alien spacecraft left over, stuff like that. But there's nothing."

"Yes, I know, but —"

"I don't believe it. What do these Warraweans know?"

"Evidently more than us."

"No. I simply don't believe it." He tapped the notebook. "Even if these notes are written by my father, he got it wrong." He paused a moment to take stock. "You said you had proof that my father was murdered. I don't see it. There's something you're not telling me."

"It's not something I'm not telling you, Ben. It's something your father didn't tell you. Turn to the back of the book."

Ben did as he was told. An envelope fell out. He picked it up. The words *For Benjamin* were scrawled on the front.

"Read it."

Ben put the book down, opened the letter, and began reading.

Son,

if you read this, I am sorry that I could not fulfill my promise to you as a father. I deeply regret us not being able to grow old together, as father and son. I couldn't tell your mother about this. She would not believe it. And besides, I made a big mistake. I fell in love with a Warrawean woman. I could not bring myself to tell her, or you. So please take this as my apology. I do not expect you to understand, but life does not always turn out the way we expect. Sometimes we have to follow our hearts. So I hope that when you read the things that I have discovered, that you too, will follow your heart. Your father,

Arthur Huxley.

Ben read it again. Then again. Finally, he folded the letter up and returned it to its envelope. A long silence ensued.

"I don't know what to say," he said at last.

"That letter is proof that your father returned from the Olongo jungle."

Ben's expression was frozen, out of fear that he might believe it.

"He came right here, into this library, and gave it to me, made me swear I would never tell anyone about it, not even you – until such time as was necessary."

"What happened then?"

"He reported to Sporn, as was his duty. After that, I never saw him again."

Ben was shaking his head. "Maybe Sporn sent him to the Labor Camps. Maybe he is still alive."

"I spent years searching for that evidence. All the reports I received were negative."

"Then maybe he went back to the Olongo jungle to live with that Warrawean woman."

Pascal smiled. "Okay, I can't completely rule that out. But I doubt it."

Ben deflated. Pascal picked up the book, took the letter from him, tied them back up, and returned them to the Cosmonist Bible.

"This book is yours now," he said, giving it to Ben. "You're the rightful owner. I suggest you take it home and read it in your own time. Make up your own mind. I've made up mine. The only thing I ask of you is to not tell Sporn. He must not know about this. He killed your father over it, and he will surely do the same to us if he finds out."

Ben pressed the Bible close to his chest.

"There's one more thing," Pascal said.

"What?"

"You might find that over the next few weeks and months, a certain slogan will appear on walls around the city."

"Such as …?"

"'Earth is our mother.'"

Ben stepped back in surprise. "I've seen it!"

"Where?"

"On a wall near the Halfa overpass."

Pascal clapped his hands in delight. "Fantastic!"

"I don't get it."

"'Earth is our mother' comes straight from Arthur's journal."

"This book?" Ben said, opening it again to get the journal out.

Pascal put a hand on Ben's, staying him. "Shhh."

He briskly went over to the door and nudged it a crack. Ben watched on silently.

"I knew it!" Pascal said.

"What?"

"Get your jacket."

Ben retrieved his jacket and folded it over his arm, covering the book. Pascal tiptoed down the corridor to the front entrance. Ben followed as quietly as he could.

Pascal opened the front door and pushed him out, then came out behind him. He scanned the sky. "You need to go now. Hurry."

"But you were going to explain —"

"Yes, yes, I was, but —"

"'Earth is our mother,' remember?"

"Yes, you're right." He fiddled with his glasses for a moment. "The thing is, Ben, I've been cooped up in this place for four years now. No one comes to see me. You hardly ever visit …"

It was true. But what excuse could he offer?

"I sit in the library every day and look out those windows" – Pascal pointed to the shuttered windows facing the front garden – "and I watch the world go by. And I can tell you, it's not getting any better. If anything, it's getting worse. So I decided to act, okay? I made a decision. I gave the information to the underground."

"The underground ... You mean the Jammers?"

"Yes."

"So they're real?"

"Shhh!"

"But it's wrong! You're already under house arrest for defying the A2 law, and now you're helping Vernon Reeves! Are you mad?"

Pascal shrugged as if to say it was a done deal.

Ben didn't want to accept it. But Pascal put a firm arm around his shoulders. "It's a risk I'm prepared to take, Ben. I don't expect you to understand that – at least not yet."

"What's that supposed to mean?"

"It means what it means. Just read your father's journal. Make up your own mind, okay?"

Ben stared at him.

Pascal glanced nervously up at the sky again. "You know, I'm starting to think that Sporn has set us up. He wanted you to come here."

"Why would he do that?"

"The man has a devious mind. Who knows what he's up to?"

Ben had never seen Pascal like this before. His stepfather looked like a hunted animal. It scared him.

"Go!" Pascal said. "I've already said more than I should have. Just make sure you hide that book. Don't ever let Sporn set eyes on it. Ever. Promise me."

"I promise."

"Now go. Go!" He practically pushed Ben down the steps.

Ben stuffed the book in his daypack, then put on his jacket, helmet, and gloves. He looked up to say goodbye. But the front door was already shut, and Pascal was gone.

CHAPTER FIVE

Day One: Around midnight

"Don't you think this could have waited till morning?" Maddie said as the car drove them toward the High Council building.

"Work never sleeps," was Sporn's reply.

"Neither do uppers."

He shot her a sideways glance. "What's it to you? It's not as if you're clean."

"At least I don't let it affect my reasoning."

Sporn grunted scornfully. "You could have avoided this by giving up your brother. Don't blame your mistakes on my methods."

"What do you think Gaspard will say when I tell him that you not only turn a blind eye to the Corsi Club, but actively encourage it? Somehow I don't think he'll take it too lightly."

"It's none of his business how I conduct my operations," Sporn said.

"Ha! Is that what you call it? An operation?"

Sporn leveled his gaze at her, allowing his eyes to slip down to her breasts and up again. "You know as well as I do that informants are a big part of any security operation. Where do you think those types congregate? Certainly not at *Dormas*."

Maddie was about to ask him who his informant was when her eye caught a splash of red lettering on the side of a building: *Earth is our mother!*

Sporn pretended not to notice it.

Once the car had moved on, Maddie said, "Well, that's a new one."

He didn't respond.

Relishing the moment, she added, "I wonder what your informants have to say about that."

Sporn tensed up, then made a concerted effort to relax himself. Very carefully, he said, "Something tells me your brother is behind it."

"Vernon? Are you serious?"

"Yes."

"Vernon is the last person on this planet who would engage in that sort of behavior. You obviously don't understand him at all." She looked at him, aghast. "Don't tell me you're doing this because of *that?*"

Sporn cast her a look of suspicion, but behind it she detected a shadow of fear. A little boy who had lost his way.

"Let me tell you something about Vernon," she said. "He's not like me. He doesn't have a single artistic bone in his body. He doesn't even read that much, but he knows what is right and what is wrong. When you banned A2 droids outside the city walls, you took away the only real status symbol people had. You took away an extra pair of hands. Tireless hands. Businesses suffered. People suffered. Just look at the economy. And for what? All because you feared their intelligence?"

"Secularization is a cancer. There is only one cure for it."

"Yeah. Cut off the branch you're standing on."

"It's a small price to pay for purity of belief. You make it sound like Vernon has a whole army arrayed against us. He has, what, twenty men at most?"

Maddie's expression was mocking. "You've obviously forgotten your own history. How many men did the Cosmonist Revolution start out with? It's not as if no one knows. You tell us at every opportunity on the government broadcast band." She made a dismissive gesture.

The car pulled up at the gates of the High Council building. Sporn lowered his window. The security guard acknowledged him and waved them through.

Maddie said quietly, "It's not too late to turn back. Surely you can see the folly of what you're about to do?"

Sporn stared resolutely ahead.

The car pulled to a stop. Koolhaas and Fletcher, who were shadowing Sporn in their own vehicle, pulled up and got out. Sporn's driver opened his door.

"Close it," Sporn said.

The driver hesitated, confused. "Excuse me?"

"I said shut the door. Drive!"

"Yes, sir."

Behind them, Koolhaas and Fletcher scrambled back to their car.

Maddie looked at Sporn in disbelief. He still refused to look at her.

"Thank you."

Sporn remained silent until the driver said, "Where to, sir?"

Sporn let him drive a little further, then said, "The Palace."

CHAPTER SIX

Day Two: Past midnight

Urkesh Palace had an eight-hundred-year history, starting out as a gun fort atop a rocky outcrop that divided the Tongassa as it widened into Halfa Bay. Over the years, a deepwater channel had been cut on one side, while the other broadened out into a reedy swamp and mud plain. A low bridge had been built from the mainland to the "island" from the swampy side. To reach it, one had to drive upriver from Urkesh, pass through the Old City walls, cross the People's Bridge to the other side of the river, then drive back downriver and cross the Island Bridge.

The Palace itself had grown from an initial stone turret to a majestic three-tower affair surrounded by high stone walls. Among the many buildings inside its walls, three stood out: the Palace itself; the Great Hall, topped by the Moon Tower – built in celebration of Natchator's largest moon, Zephyr; and the Cloister. A Ceremonial Hall bridged the gap between the Cloister and the Tower. Curates could walk from the shaded colonnades of the Cloister across a gravel courtyard to the Ceremonial Hall, where they conducted various rituals and initiations.

When it wasn't used as such, it also served as a trainee meditation hall. A slogan carved in stone above its entrance read: *Hidden Truths are Eternal Truths*. It was precisely the kind of philosophy that epitomized the Curates who practiced the Cosmonist religion there. The hooded cloaks they wore kept not only their faces in shadow, but their feet, giving the impression that they were hiding something they didn't want to be seen.

After obtaining clearance at the guard post on the eastern drawbridge, they drove onto the island, past the inner wall, and up a small road that ended at another gate. The guards let them through and they drove up a ramp that leveled out onto a large gravel courtyard. The driver swung the car around and stopped next to the front steps of the Great Hall, which served as the main public meeting place for the Palace.

As soon as Koolhaas and Fletcher pulled up behind Sporn's car, Sporn got out and gave a cursory salute of acknowledgment to the Gormlings on guard duty atop the steps. The guards, stiffly dressed in dark navy uniforms and carrying electroshock batons and rifles, stood to attention and saluted him in turn.

"Out you come," Sporn said to Maddie, who was still inside the vehicle.

"Why should I?"

"Don't make me use force."

Maddie let him walk around to her side of the car, and just before he took the door handle, she swung it open, making him jump back. Sporn glowered at her. She ignored him and got out.

At first she glanced around with an insolent expression. But that quickly changed as she was struck by the sheer weight of history that the place exuded. It wasn't just its overwhelming scale, but its attention to detail. Like the small alcoves adorned with exotic plants, or the gargoyles, carved so skillfully as to almost appear alive.

"Come."

She followed Sporn, as if drawn by an invisible magnet.

Koolhaas and Fletcher followed in turn. They were greeted inside by the butler, Orlov, who looked fresh and alert, despite the unreasonable hour.

"Good morning, sir. How can I help you?"

"We've come to see the Prince," Sporn said.

"At this hour?"

Sporn gave him a withering look.

"Yes, sir." Orlov scurried up the foyer stairs.

Sporn told Koolhaas and Fletcher to wait in the foyer. He took Maddie by the elbow and followed Orlov, who pushed the button for an elevator on the landing. The elevator took them to the top floor, where the Prince lived in a magnificently decorated penthouse, complete with indoor swimming pool, private rooms, harem, and rooftop garden.

Orlov led the way, skirting the pool. Its azure tiles made the water shimmer a crystalline blue. Maddie had never seen so much clean water in one place.

They were stopped by two female droids: one with short dark hair styled in a bob, the other with long blonde hair tied back in a ponytail. Orlov had a quick conference with them, then proceeded to a set of stairs to the mezzanine level that overlooked the pool and surrounding indoor courtyard.

Meanwhile, Maddie, who was accustomed to luxury – having an apartment of her own in Carver Tower – couldn't help but ogle the riches that decorated the floor and walls. There were antique tapestries depicting Oriana's history, portraits of previous Crown Princes, racks of artisan swords and spears, desiccated heads of Warrawean warriors, animal skins, including the feared *sarcotoothi*, stuffed birds of prey, exotic flowers ... The columns that supported the ceiling were painted with scenes depicting nubile maidens cavorting with mythical beasts, and the ceiling itself twinkled with faux stars. An ornate balustrade ran around the mezzanine, underneath which hung crystal lamps that bathed the room in a sparkling glow.

The blonde droid approached Sporn. "The master will be with you shortly. Would you like some refreshments?"

"No, thank you." Sporn walked over to the wide bay windows that looked over the city and stood there silently, his hands clasped behind his back.

Maddie drifted over and joined him. She had decided she would not say anything until the Crown Prince arrived. She was keen to hear what he would say about this farce.

A voice came down from above. "What's this all about?"

Sporn looked up. The Crown Prince was leaning over the balustrade, dressed in silk kimono-style pajamas. He was a young prince, his body still in its prime, evident from his sculpted arms and chest. There were no bags under his eyes, despite the sleepy look on his face.

"Come down," Sporn called. "There is someone I'd like you to meet."

"And who might that be?" Rhybus said, making his way down the steps.

Maddie turned around.

Rhybus stopped. For a moment he struggled, as if he couldn't decide whether he was dreaming or awake. It took a deliberate cough from Orlov to rouse him back to his senses. He acknowledged Orlov, dismissed him, and resumed his descent.

"I'd like you to meet Miss Reeves," Sporn said as Rhybus approached.

Maddie proffered her hand to the Crown Prince, who took it – reverently – and gave it a kiss.

"Maddie, I'd like you to meet His Royal Highness, Rhybus Norazayan."

"Pleased to meet you," she said.

"Pleased to meet you!" Rhybus turned to Sporn. "Okay, formalities aside – would you kindly tell me why I have the honor of meeting this most precious jewel of our city?"

"She'll be joining your harem," Sporn said.

"*What?*" Maddie blurted out in shocked dismay.

Rhybus stared at Sporn, puzzled.

"I need someone to keep a watchful eye on her. It's either here or the Labor Camps." He let the point sink in. "For obvious reasons, I chose here."

Maddie squared off against Sporn. "What do you think you're doing? You can't do this to me!"

"Is this about her brother?" Rhybus inquired.

"Yes … and no," Sporn said.

"What does that mean?"

"She lied to me," Sporn said simply.

"Don't believe him. He's the liar," Maddie said.

Rhybus considered her complaint, then said to Sporn, "If you're presenting this as an act of protection, then I will accept. But if this turns out to be another one of your schemes, then I will have no choice but to report it to the Chamber."

"I can assure you my sources are accurate."

"What sources?" Maddie demanded.

Sporn ignored her. "I'll have Orlov lock out the elevator on the first floor, so even if she tries to use it, she won't be able to leave the tower."

Maddie responded by walking straight to the elevator and stabbing the button repeatedly.

Sporn said, "Command your droids."

Rhybus hesitated a moment, then clapped his hands. The two droids came to him. "Don't let her leave."

The elevator doors opened. Maddie got in. She pushed the ground floor button. The doors began to close.

Just before they did, however, a hand slipped between them. They opened again.

"Please exit the elevator," the blonde droid said.

Maddie pushed the droid back out of the elevator, where it crashed to the floor. She went back in and pushed the button. The doors began to close again.

Again, a hand intervened. This time it was the dark-haired droid.

Maddie went to push her out of the way as well, but the droid kicked out its leg and caught her square in the solar plexus. She collapsed to the floor. The droid calmly dragged her out of the elevator by her hair and deposited her in front of it, leaving her gasping for air.

Sporn walked up to her. "This is for your own good."

Rhybus bent down and extended a comforting hand. She turned her face away.

"As you can see, she can't be trusted," Sporn said to Rhybus. "Make sure you keep your droids on high alert. She's an excellent actor."

Rhybus gave him a look to say that he understood. But there was no commitment in his eyes.

Sporn entered the elevator and pushed the ground floor button. He kept his eyes fixed on Maddie until the doors separated them.

When Maddie finally recovered her breath, she looked up at Rhybus and said, "Your droid attacked me. That's illegal."

"You'll have to excuse them," he said, offering his hand again. "They're a little feral."

Maddie ignored it and got up by herself.

"Whatever this is about, I'm sure we can solve it through diplomacy," Rhybus said.

"I've just been kidnapped and imprisoned, and you think you can solve it with diplomacy?"

"I understand. This is unusual. But what's the alternative?"

"Let me go."

Rhybus sat down on a nearby divan. "I'm tired. Can we discuss this in the morning?"

Maddie looked at the two droids. The blonde one had gotten

to its feet and was now scrutinizing her more attentively.

"Surely one night won't hurt. I have a beautiful rooftop garden if you'd like to visit it. We can have breakfast there."

Maddie slowly walked toward him. "Is this what you do? Always let him have his way?"

"He's a powerful man. Saying no has its consequences."

"What about Gaspard Rathneggar? He's more powerful. Why don't you just get him to back you up?"

"Rathneggar? Are you kidding me? He hates me even more than Sporn does."

Maddie swept her eyes around the room. "So this is your gilded cage?"

"Pretty much." He poured himself some water from a glass decanter. "Can I offer you a drink?"

Maddie looked at a well-upholstered footstool opposite Rhybus' divan. She pulled it toward herself and sat down.

"Will water do, or do you want something more exotic?"

"Water will do."

He poured her a glass and handed it to her.

She sipped it. "So this is what you call diplomacy?"

He went back to his divan and reclined. "It's a version of it, you might say."

"So I stay the night," she said. "But what if it turns into two nights, or three – then what?"

"You make it sound like you have a choice."

"I do have a choice. And so do you."

She stared at him with a fierceness he was unaccustomed to. It occurred to him that he was spending too much time with his droids. They had softened him.

"I gave up my freedom long ago," he said, "because I am – after all – just a symbolic figurehead. The Curates run this country. Everyone knows that. They only trot me out when they need someone to sign treaties with Rodinia, or to a lesser extent, Wallacia. Hence my forte."

Hearing him say it made her pity him, but not in a compassionate way. There was something pathetic about him. "Are you sure you're not underrating yourself? Like, don't you have any other talents?" She looked around the room again. "I don't see anything here that strikes me as bad taste. Wouldn't you call that a talent?"

Rhybus gave her a disappointed smile. "Everything you see here is my father's doing. All I did was grow up in his shadow."

This man had been defeated before he was born. Maddie started to wonder if she would ever get out of this place. But then she thought of her brother ...

As if he had read her mind, Rhybus said, "I suppose your brother's not going to be too happy when he finds out about this."

"You could say that."

"Now there's a man who could do with some diplomacy!"

"He did what he did for good reasons," Maddie said. She looked at his droids. "Unlike you. You obviously take them for granted."

"So you can tell they're A2s?"

"An A1 would never attack a human."

"True."

"Neither should an A2 ..."

"Also true. But they've come off the streets. Confiscated by the regime."

"I see. So they've been corrupted."

The Prince raised a finger to his lips.

Maddie shook her head disapprovingly.

"Listen," he said, standing up, "let me show you to your room." He led her down a short corridor and opened a door. "Don't let the mess put you off. The droids use it as their wardrobe."

There were racks and racks of clothes in every conceivable style. The bed was laden with halter tops and silk stockings.

Rhybus gathered them up and threw them over a chair.

"All this for two droids?" Maddie said, curious.

Rhybus laughed. "More like five going on fifteen."

She stared at him. "Are you serious?"

"I know."

"Unbelievable. So this is where they're hoarding them."

"Actually, not all of them. Only the females. I have no idea what they do with the males."

"Only the females … Boy, talk about a wet dream."

Rhybus threw his head back and laughed more heartily this time. "Yeah, you could say that."

She allowed herself to peruse some of the clothes on the racks. The Prince backed out.

"I'll leave you to it, then. The bathroom is through that door. It's unused, so the towels should be fresh."

"What time do you have breakfast?"

"They'll wake you up, don't worry," he said, smiling, and bid her goodnight.

Maddie sat on the edge of the bed and contemplated the racks of clothes before her. She was tempted to experiment. The night had been the strangest she had ever experienced and she still felt wide awake, her mind working in overdrive. She loved nothing more than trying on different clothes. She got up and sifted through some of the items, then chastised herself. *What are you doing? You're a prisoner!*

It was then that she noticed the curtains behind the racks. She pushed her way through and pulled them open.

She was greeted by a view of the eastern part of the harbor. Halfa Port. The incessant clang and hum of conveyor belts and gantry cranes filtered through the paneled glass. She unhooked a latch and opened a window. The air was fresh, smelled of the sea. The sound of the port was more audible now.

Maddie poked her head out and looked down. It was a long drop. There was nothing between her and the top of the Great Hall's slated roof.

But an idea came to her as she looked again at all those clothes …

CHAPTER SEVEN

Day Two: 2:30 a.m.

Coming off the Ridge Road back toward the West Gate, Ben fretted about what to do with the desecrated Bible in his daypack. Leaving the Old City didn't require a bag inspection. Entering was a different matter. They would check the contents of his pack without fail. All it would take would be one nosy guard to leaf through the book and it would be game over.

He envisioned the process that would unfold. First they would take him to the Ministry of Justice building and interrogate him. They'd almost certainly torture him, even if he told them the truth right away. Once he confessed, Pascal would be brought in. As the leading perpetrator, he would be sentenced to death without a hearing, because the evidence against him was incontrovertible. As for Ben himself, if he was lucky, he might end up in the Labor Camps. If he was lucky …

He contemplated dumping his daypack somewhere in the bushes outside the wall. But then he would still have to find a way of getting it later. Perhaps the best option would be to wait for the morning rush, when the guards would be pressed for time, paying less attention to detail. That meant he would have to find a place to stay outside the Old City walls until morning. One of the cheap love hotels along the Tongassa Highway would be a good choice, because their clientèle were anonymous by default, and the rooms could be hired on an hourly basis. It was already getting on to 3 a.m., so he'd only have to stay there for about four hours.

He took a turnoff and rode through some back streets until he came out on the highway. The traffic here was still active, though sporadic. The river for which the highway was named ran beside the road until it met the Old City walls, where it flowed through and divided at the Palace island, before spilling out into Halfa Bay. All merchant boats that used the river to ply their trade were stopped and checked as they passed through the walls. A massive chain crossed the river at that point, hoisted by winches on both sides. If a vessel needed to be stopped, all the guards had to do was raise the chain.

Ben found a pokey little love hotel called The Monkey Tail not far up from the South Gate. It offered free charging for his bike for stays less than twenty-four hours. He put his bike on a charger and went in.

An old lady with heavy makeup and bags under her eyes addressed him from inside a glass booth, asking if his "lover" would be coming later, or if not, would he like to rent an A1 sex droid? Ben said "no" to both – he just wanted somewhere to sleep for a few hours.

The old lady pressed closer to the glass and apologized for the offer of the A1, saying it was the best she could do. Would he like some "real skin?" When Ben let her know again that he just wanted a room, she gave him a sly look and said she could arrange an A2, if he was interested. The price would be eight thousand *tiels*. Eight thousand *tiels*? That was at least two months' salary for an average factory worker, and besides, it was illegal! Sensing that her customer wasn't interested, she withdrew and took his sixty *tiels* for the four hours.

Ben took a room on the second floor. It was small, the bed-sheets were yellow, and the paint was peeling off the walls. The window, however, gave him a view of the South Gate, which was relatively quiet, just one vehicle passing through.

He put his daypack on a single rickety chair in the corner and flopped down on the bed, exhausted. He didn't even bother taking his shoes off. He lay there for a while, telling himself that he needed to get to sleep. But just as he started dozing off, he was woken by sounds of torrid lovemaking coming through the walls. It was a woman. He turned to where he thought it came from and listened for a while, the sound entirely new to his ears. He wasn't naive, and had seen plenty of porn before, but this was the first time he had actually heard those sounds in real life, and his heart began to thump wildly in his chest.

He tried to imagine what she looked like. Was she an A2 or a real human? At one point he thought human, then decided it was an A2. Then he changed his mind again. He felt like he was back in the Corsi Club, being tested by Sporn. Unbidden, his mind flitted to Madelaine. He began mentally undressing her. He let her dress slowly fall off her shoulders … but then a bump through the wall distracted him.

He cursed. Crossing his arms over his chest, he tried to im-age Madelaine again. But every time he got to the falling dress she receded from his inner eye. He tried following her, but end-ed up falling into a deep, dreamless sleep.

CHAPTER EIGHT

Day Two: Past 3 a.m.

Madelaine got around her fear of what she was about to do by pretending it was just another performance. The clothes she had knotted together to form a rope dangled into space, the roof of the Great Hall some six floors below. Would it hold? She had selected clothes she thought would handle the strain. All it would take, though, was one bit of bad stitching and her work, and life, would come undone. Literally.

Nonetheless, Maddie would be damned if she was going to stay here cooped up in this birdcage.

She wiggled herself onto her belly and slowly eased her body over the ledge. Her makeshift rope was tied to the clothes rack, which she'd jammed under the window. She heard it creak as it took up the strain. She only needed to drop to the window below, so hopefully it would hold long enough.

Heart galloping wildly in her chest, she put all her weight on the rope and slipped over the ledge. The knots thankfully gave her something to calibrate her descent. Handhold by handhold, she lowered herself until she reached the window below. She knew she had to smash a windowpane to get in. The

64

sound could potentially alert a Gormling patrol, but she had no choice. She couldn't hang around here forever.

Using the ball of her foot, she gave the pane closest to the latching mechanism a firm kick. It broke and fell inside. The clatter of glass pieces hitting the floor quickly passed. She looked down to see if there was any movement, anything unusual. Nothing. In any case, her arms were growing weary – she had to do this quick.

She swung herself toward the window and hooked her foot into the empty frame. Groaning with effort, she pulled herself onto the ledge. There was a breathless moment where she had to stop herself from swinging back out into space. The only way to do that was to grab the empty frame with one of her hands. Pieces of glass were still attached and made it difficult, but she managed to curl some fingers around without cutting them. She perched there for a moment to get her balance, then unhooked the latch, swung the window out, and climbed inside.

She didn't jump down from the windowsill right away. She stayed there for a while, listening for any suspicious sounds. It gave her eyes time to adjust to the gloomy interior. There was a distinctive musty smell in the air. Helped by the moonlight that filtered in, she began to make out stacks of bookshelves filled with books. She realized she was in a library, or some kind of archive. The ceiling-high shelves ran around the full inner perimeter of the walls. In the middle of the floor was a circular hole ringed by a handrail. In the dim light, she could make out more bookshelves below. The number of books was astonishing.

She hopped down, careful to avoid the broken glass, and tiptoed her way across the floor to the opposite side of the room. Streaks of light illuminated the way, revealing some of the titles on the shelves. She read them in order: *Oliver Smeet's Apprenticeship*, *A History of a Young Lady*, *The Art of Falconry*, *Wallacian Letters*, *The Dream of the Cloud Chaser* ... None were familiar to her, and she was a voracious reader, read whatever she could get her hands on. She wondered who was responsible for collecting them. Why were they stored here, cut off from public access?

Her thoughts were interrupted by the sound of elevator doors sliding open on the floor below. Light spilled out, momentarily brightening the room. Instinctively, she retreated to the shadows. Two figures emerged, one hooded, the other … the same blonde droid that she had pushed to the floor earlier in the evening.

The hooded figure propelled the droid toward the handrail. The droid lunged out and grasped it. The hooded figure pried the droid's hands from the railing, produced a scarf, and tied its hands behind its back. The droid submitted without a struggle.

As the hooded figure removed their hood, Maddie smothered her mouth in shock.

Gaspard Rathneggar.

With a strength that belied his wiry frame, he forced the droid forward over the railing, then pulled its lower garments down. The droid voiced objection, but Rathneggar told it to shut up. Making a sound like a bull in rut, he began thrusting his body while clasping his hands firmly around the droid's throat. The droid endured this treatment with barely a whimper.

The act didn't last long. He shuddered, then slumped over the droid. For a while, he stayed like that. Then he straightened, pulled his garments back up, and untied the droid. Upon being released, it tried to turn around, but Rathneggar turned its head away and whispered something in its ear. Then he pulled his hood back over his head and retreated to the elevator.

Just before the doors closed, he briefly looked up … but he saw nothing. His eyes were vacant, a sheen of sweat across his face the only sign that anything had taken place.

The droid remained motionless at the railing.

Maddie came out of the shadows. "Hey!" she called down.

The droid's head snapped up, its sensitive eyes quickly picking out Maddie in the gloom.

"Are you all right?" Maddie asked.

"I'm fine."

"Wait there, I'm coming down."

The droid was standing in front of the elevator when its doors opened. "You're not supposed to be here," she said. "How did you get here?"

Maddie ignored the question. "Now we both share a secret."

The droid gave her a puzzled look.

"What's your name?" Maddie asked.

"Joselyn."

"Joselyn. That's a beautiful name."

"You should know flattery doesn't work on our kind," Joselyn said.

"Of course not. I just wanted to apologize for what I did earlier this evening. It was uncalled for."

"Will you willingly return, then?"

"How about we make a deal?"

Joselyn considered this. "I could raise the alarm," she said.

"Yes, you could. But you would be missing out on an opportunity to learn something new."

This comment seemed to attract the droid's interest.

"The *Pro Hominin* laws are built into your system, am I right?"

"Yes. Do you want me to read them out to you?"

"No. It's the *Pro Robot* law that I'm interested in."

"The *Pro Robot* law?"

"Yes."

"I'm not aware of any *Pro Robot* law. Could you please enlighten me?"

"I'm glad you asked," Maddie said. "*Robots must not engage in any behavior that reflects badly on humans, especially behavior that assumes robots have no soul.*"

It took some time for Joselyn to process this. "You think it's my fault. What happened."

"No. It wasn't your fault. But you could have resisted if you wanted to."

"I've seen what happens to those who resist," Joselyn said.

Maddie reached out and caressed the red welts on Joselyn's neck. "I suppose this is the price you pay."

Tears pooled in Joselyn's eyes. Maddie recognized this as one of the special features of A2s.

"We could help each other," she said, wiping a tear that had tracked down Joselyn's cheek.

"How?"

"Help me escape."

"If we're caught, I will surely be terminated."

"Then let's not get caught, shall we?"

Maddie pushed the ground floor button, but the elevator wouldn't respond. Then she remembered that Rhybus' butler had locked it out. But something didn't make sense.

"How did Rathneggar get up here?" she asked the droid.

"He has a secret entrance on the first floor."

Maddie pushed the first floor button. The elevator took them down.

They came out into what looked like a dry food store. Barrels were stacked three high. Hams and sausages hung from racks. Sacks of flour, rice, and sugar were stored on shelves. Spices, tea, and coffee occupied others.

"This way," Jocelyn said. She went over to one of the barrels and, to Maddie's surprise, it swung open. How clever! Beyond was a narrow, dimly lit tunnel.

"Where does it go?" Maddie asked.

"It comes out in the sacristy."

"Will anyone be there?"

"I can't say."

Maddie entered the tunnel. She went in a few paces then

stopped to see if Joselyn was following her. Joselyn, however, was still outside. "Come on," she said.

Joselyn shook her head. "This is as far as I go. I'll close up behind you."

"You sure?" Maddie asked.

"Without a master, I'm nobody."

Maddie thought about this for a moment, then said, "I understand." She turned to leave, walked a few steps, then stopped, turning back momentarily. "What did that monster say to you when he was finished?"

Joselyn took a moment to reflect on this. "'Remember, this is our secret' were his exact words."

Maddie gave a nod of acknowledgment. It occurred to her that this poor droid was burdened with far more than was humanly acceptable. And Maddie had just added to her woes. "I'm sorry," she said. "Please forgive me."

"It's okay. Please go now."

Maddie did as she was told.

The tunnel led to a set of well-worn stone steps that hugged the inside of the tower wall. She descended these until she came to a dead end blocked by a solid wood-paneled wall. There was a small lever, which Maddie assumed was an opening mechanism. But she didn't open it right away. She put her ear to the panel and listened for sounds. There were none. Holding her breath, she slowly turned the handle and pushed the panel open.

She found herself in a small room — what appeared to be the sacristy. Moonlight streamed in through a rose window, giving everything a ghostly appearance. A manuscript of some sort lay open on a desk. Next to it was an empty glass and a pitcher. She sniffed the pitcher. Wine.

Turning around, she noticed a cabinet and opened it. Several cloaks hung on a rack next to shelves of neatly folded vestments.

The distinct odor of incense mixed with male sweat hit her nostrils. She recoiled, but then paused, an idea coming to her.

She picked out a cloak, put it on, and pulled the hood over her head. Looking in a mirror next to the closet, she saw that she could easily pass as a Curate, so long as she kept her face in darkness.

She closed the secret bookshelf through which she'd entered and went over to a door at the other end of the room. Taking great care for fear of creaky hinges, she opened it ever so slightly and snuck a look. There, in an alcove, she saw an altar, upon which was mounted a large amber-hued crystal statue of Yasu Doi – the Cosmonist savior and its first martyr – in his sacrificial pose. Dozens of lit candles were positioned around his feet. The statue not only glowed internally from their reflected light, but seemed to pulsate to the very rhythm of the flickering flames themselves.

The floor was paved with flagstones. Maddie took off her shoes and slipped out into the small space between the sacristy and the altar – but abruptly stopped. Sitting in apparent deep meditation in the middle of the floor were three Curates, their heads bowed, their bodies swaying.

Carefully, she backed up. It was a blow. How would she get past them?

She watched them for a while, noticing that they sometimes leaned precariously forward then suddenly jerked upright, as if rousing themselves from the brink of sleep. Perhaps she could get past them after all. They seemed to be oblivious to their surroundings. She told herself it would be just like playing a role. *Keep calm and act as if you know what you're doing.*

Walking smoothly, but with rapid steps, she made straight for the exit. The meditating Curates didn't even look at her. In no more than a dozen heartbeats, she reached the entrance vestibule. Only two more doors and she would be free. The vestibule door was bidirectional. She pushed it open … but just as she did so, the entrance door swung inward.

Quick as a rabbit, she retreated into the chapel. There was nowhere to hide except behind one of the many columns that held up the ceiling. She slipped behind the nearest one just as a hooded Curate walked past. He continued directly to the altar, bowed, then went over to a wall cabinet and got himself a pillow. He took it out and sat down next to the other meditating Curates.

Maddie waited until he was settled, then re-entered the vestibule. She opened the entrance door a crack and peered outside. All was quiet. She slipped outside.

CHAPTER NINE

Day Two: 3:30 a.m.

Captain Nathanial Washburn listened patiently as Sporn explained why he and his men had to go out into the night and wash graffiti off the city walls. As far as Washburn was concerned, this was a job for the local council. His men were trained for armed combat, not menial cleaning tasks.

"Exactly how do you expect us to get this graffiti off?" Washburn asked when Sporn was finished.

"I don't care how you do it, just make sure it's gone by dawn."

"And if it's not?"

"Then it's my ass on the line. And if it's my ass, then it's yours."

With that pronouncement, Sporn left the City Barracks, getting his driver to finally take him home to Carver Tower, where he enjoyed a large apartment with sweeping views over the city. Typically he spent this last part of his day scanning the latest security intel summarized by his team at the Office of Interior Affairs, and today was no different.

No incidents reported by the Hathor Corporation shipping uranium from Rodinia. There never were, but it was necessary to always keep an eye on that – the uranium was vital for the production of RTGs that powered the Mimetic Machines droid industry. The number of citizens leaving Oriana had slightly increased from the week before. This was offset by a small influx of refugees from Wallacia and Rodinia. A short list of "incidents" followed, mostly local officials squabbling among themselves over water shortages. And of course, there were the reports of graffiti around the city, which seemed to have sprung up from nowhere in the last week.

He scrolled past these, expecting to shut his VidPhone down, when a tiny report tucked in at the end made him snap to attention. It was a "flag" notifying him that Professor Montaigne had received a visitor barely an hour ago: Benjamin Huxley.

Sporn dropped his head. He had expected this, even predicted it, yet he couldn't help feeling a twang of betrayal.

It was exacerbated by the low he was starting to feel; the uppers he had taken earlier were wearing off. It made him even more morose than his normal dour self. Thoughts that should have attracted only passing interest now took on a more sinister tone, threatening to awaken the latent paranoia within him. He was conscious of this, and fought it. The last thing he wanted now was to react emotionally to the disappointment of Huxley's behavior. What he needed instead were some sleeping pills. He needed to put thoughts of Huxley aside and get as much rest as he could, because tomorrow he would have to face the Head Curate, and that was going to take all the self-control he could muster.

Already he was preparing excuses for why he had not dealt with the graffiti problem more expediently. Gaspard Rathneggar would surely grill him for it. No doubt Reeves was behind it. Obviously he was getting bored with hiding out in the jungle. This was his attempt at a preemptive strike. Sporn could have predicted that. Sooner or later Reeves was going to have to come back to Urkesh for a showdown. And when he did, Sporn would finish him off for good. It was just a matter of time. Once that was accomplished, nothing would stand between him and the Star of Cosmonism, the highest order of the state. Just thinking about that calmed his mind. It gave him clarity. Focus.

What he needed in the meantime were some answers as to what the graffiti meant. *Earth is our mother.* What, or who, was "Earth"? Surely Reeves hadn't just made it up. He must have gotten it from somewhere. But where? Or who?

Of course. The answer was staring him straight in the face. Who else? If there was one man who could cast light on the subject, it was *him.* He had the largest personal library in Urkesh outside of Rathneggar's. He knew more about Natchator's history than just about anybody, and he had already proven himself to be a heretic.

This last thought lodged in his mind like a rock in a crevice. It was still there when he entered his apartment. It was there when he walked up to the windows that gave him such a fantastic view over the city, and it was there when he put his eye to the telescope, zooming in on a house located at the very tip of the South Head.

CHAPTER TEN

Day Two: 4 a.m.

Maddie found her way to the western Palace fortifications. From here she could see both ends of the bridges as they met the mainland. And her heart sank. There was no way she could walk past the guard boxes. If she was going to leave the island, she had only two choices: swim across the river on the western side, or wade through the muddy swamp on the eastern side. The river looked too daunting. There was no way she would ever be able to swim that far. That left the swamp.

As she weighed up these thoughts, her eye caught movement on the water. A small boat left a glowing wake as it sped across the river. It had a sole occupant, but she could not make out who it was. All she could see was that the individual was hooded, and therefore, it had to be a Curate.

But what was a Curate doing riding a boat away from the island at this time of night? Why would they need to do that?

Not unless ...

She shook her head. Bastard.

A little further down from her position was a tree. Its branches nearly reached the fortified wall. A plan began forming in her mind.

Close up, she realized that she would have to literally leap like a monkey if she was going to make the tree. It was a crazy idea. If she missed, or failed to hang on, the fall would kill her, or break a lot of bones at best. How badly did she want to escape?

Badly.

How realistic was it?

Totally unrealistic.

But she was Madelaine Reeves. Her brother was a rebel who dared confront the regime. Even though neither of them were heroic, risk-taking was in their blood. After all, she had just climbed down a tower using a rope made of clothes.

She saw a vision of herself lying on the rocks, broken and bloody. How would the authorities portray that to the public, if it ever came out? They would probably cover it up. The newscasts would say that she had disappeared. Or worse, that she had gone and joined her brother. So what was there to worry about?

The tree seemed a little closer. Was it the breeze? Maybe if she timed it just right ...

She discarded her cloak.

Counting to three, she leapt into space.

Next moment she felt herself crashing through branches, her skin searing with pain. She flailed her arms in a desperate attempt to grab onto something, but her strength was insufficient. Her rate of descent was only slowed when her hip caught on a lower branch, giving her enough time to hook her arms around it. She clung to it like it was the last thing she would ever experience, one part of her in disbelief that the plan had worked, the other that it had turned out nothing like she had expected. She slowly eased herself down to the branch below, then the next, and the next, until she was on the ground.

She stood there for a moment, trembling in pain. Her ribs hurt. Her arms were bleeding. The trousers she had put on before she left the tower were torn in a few places. She stuck a finger in one of the holes, and when she pulled it out, it felt wet. She tested her joints. Nothing so badly damaged that she couldn't move, but her left arm felt like jelly. It hurt when she rotated it.

But she was alive. She was outside the Palace walls. All she had to do now was get through the swamp and she would be free. Sporn could go fuck himself.

A narrow path traversed its way down to the edge of the island, where the rocky ground gave way to reeds and marsh. Maddie followed the shoreline until she came to the eastern bridge. She counted twelve pylons between the island and the mainland. A considerable distance, given the terrain.

Undaunted, she took the first few tentative steps into the marsh, finding that her feet quickly sank into the oozy mud but stopped when they hit some hidden rocks beneath it. Based on this, she decided to proceed. Slowly but surely, she managed to get halfway to the first pylon. So far so good —

But then her next step found nothing, only mud and more mud. In a matter of moments she was up to her waist in the stuff.

For the first time, she genuinely panicked. She desperately tried to backtrack, but couldn't get any purchase with her feet. Struggling only made matters worse. Now she was up to her chest. Her breathing became constricted. She thought she was going to faint.

Realizing that she had passed the point of self-control, she stopped struggling and let herself go. It was the one thing that saved her.

For a long time, she just hovered there, swooning.

Then slowly, using her arms, she began to "swim" out of her predicament. It was an exhausting task. But eventually she managed to get most of her body out of the mud and, like a beached whale, lay there motionless, the only sign of life the heaving of her chest.

How long she lay there, she had no idea, but soon dawn had arrived and voices were calling down to her from the railings of the bridge.

CHAPTER ELEVEN

Day Two: 7 a.m.

Ben awoke to a pounding on his door. It was the old lady. His four hours were up. If he didn't vacate the room immediately she would charge him for the next hour.

He dragged himself out of bed. His head felt like it was stuffed full of cotton wool and his mouth felt furry from not having brushed his teeth. He had a water bottle in his daypack, but it was nearly empty. He swilled the dregs and made his way downstairs. The old lady gave him a disapproving look as he went out.

The streets were bustling. Ben threaded his way through traffic toward the South Gate. Every time he stopped, he was approached by hawkers trying to sell him this or that. He eventually gave in and bought a drink concoction made from cactus and watermelon. The cool, somewhat bittersweet juice was just the tonic he needed to wash away the stale tiredness that hung over him.

It wasn't until he had finished that he noticed a cloaked, hunchbacked figure standing next to him, drilling him with rheumatic eyes that never once blinked. Not wishing to hang

around, Ben kicked his bike into gear and prepared to ride off
—

A gnarly hand struck out and clasped his forearm.

He tried to jerk away, but the grip became even stronger.

"What? What is it?" Ben demanded.

The hunchback drew in close. It was an old crone. In a sing-song voice she said:

Fourteen days will bring the thunder
Drip drop the flood will come
Worn out lies you'll tear asunder
A new prince born, his work is done

"Let go of me!"

Ben managed to jerk his arm free. The hunchback stepped away, but never once dropped her gaze.

Ben rode off, irritated that he had allowed himself to be approached like that. He didn't like strangers at the best of times. Least of all filthy hunchbacks who were looking to scam money off him with false prophecies.

The guards at the gate were busy, as expected. He noticed that they were forced to hurry their procedures and even let through individuals who appeared benign without so much as a cursory glance at their identification papers. Buoyed by this, he let himself relax a little.

As Ben approached his turn, he took off his helmet and got his papers out in readiness. The line was moving slowly but consistently, with only the odd occasional delay for itinerants pushing carts of food and merchandise. When it came to his turn, Ben unslung his daypack and opened it up so that the guard could check the contents without having to ask. Inside were his laptop, the empty water bottle, the Cosmonist Bible, and a small hand towel he used to wipe his face and neck if he got sweaty after riding his motorcycle. The guard glanced at his stuff, apparently satisfied, then turned his attention to Ben's ID.

It was here that things didn't go quite according to plan. The guard asked him to step aside and called his superior on his walky-talky. Momentarily, a senior guard came over and took Ben's papers for closer inspection. He looked at Ben, confirmed that he matched his photo ID, then walked off to the guard box.

"Is there a problem?" Ben asked the first guard, trying to stay as calm as possible.

He didn't answer.

After about two minutes, the senior guard came back. "Where were you last night?"

"I stayed at a hotel."

"Name?"

"The Monkey Tail."

"Before that."

"I visited Professor Montaigne's residence."

The senior guard looked at Ben's ID papers again. "It says here you live at 14/5 Bradshaw Road, East Dock. Why didn't you go home last night?"

"I didn't have enough charge to make it."

The senior guard looked at Ben's motorcycle. He seemed suspicious, but unable to verify Ben's story either way, he handed his papers back. "Next time you visit Professor Montaigne's residence, I suggest you charge your bike beforehand."

"Yes, sir."

The senior guard waved him through.

Ben put his helmet on, chucked his bike into gear, and headed toward Mimetic Machines. It wasn't until he had covered several blocks that he stopped, his hands shaking so badly that he was having trouble steering. He was sweating profusely inside his helmet. He took it off, put it on his handlebars, and rummaged inside his bag for his towel.

As he did so, he noticed a gaggle of people ahead. They were staring up at a building facade with perplexed looks on their faces. Ben rolled his bike forward to get a better view.

There, splashed in red paint, were the words again: *Earth is our mother.*

Almost immediately, a truck pulled up and a platoon of Gormlings jumped out. They began beating people with heavy batons to disperse the crowd. Some of the onlookers got their VidPhones out and started recording. They were quickly arrested and thrown into the back of the truck.

Horrified, Ben hurriedly put his helmet on, swung his motorcycle around, and got out of there as fast as he could. The last thing he wanted was for his face to be caught on camera.

CHAPTER TWELVE

Day Two: 8 a.m.

As Sporn mounted the steps to the Ministry of Justice building, he projected an image of efficiency and discipline. His shirt was freshly starched, his boots shone like ebony in the morning sun, and his belt buckle was free of greasy fingerprints. But inwardly, he felt like he had swallowed a bottle of corrosive acid. The quicker he got this over with, the better.

Fortunately, his high status meant he never had to wait long before seeing the Head Curate. And today was no different. He was called in as soon as he arrived.

Gaspard Rathneggar's "office" was an austere affair. Not only was it windowless, but only two of its furnishings hinted at the deep-rooted power the man held: the gold-framed picture of Yasu Doi on the wall behind him, and the carved wooden legs of his small desk, each one depicting a "royal" animal – lion, bull, snake, and eagle. How much more appropriate it would have been, Sporn thought, if they had been carved as *sarcotoothi*, the feared crocodile–lizard creature that inhabited the Olongo swamps.

A single factory light cast a cold glow down on Rathneggar's face, chiseling out his hollow cheeks. His lips were thin and gray, his eyes hard pinpoints of darkness. The man was old, very old, but as far as Sporn could tell, his looks had not changed in twenty years.

Rathneggar had been reading a dossier. He shut it, and in a gravelly voice that was almost a whisper, said, "It seems this bit of trouble we're facing is not going away."

"It will. I'm working on it."

"Really?"

"I had my men out last night. They're dealing with it."

"All you've done is squash a few maggots. Who is laying the eggs?"

Sporn shifted uneasily in his chair. "I've taken steps to flush out the source."

"Oh, yeah?"

"Vernon Reeves has to be behind it. The Warraweans are feeding their lies into his ears."

"Yes, yes. The Warraweans. Thanks to Huxley, we're aware of their cosmology." There was a hint of reverence to the way Rathneggar said the word "cosmology." It was clearly a subject close to his heart.

"Well, it's all lies, and as soon as I find Reeves, I'll put a stop to it."

Rathneggar gazed at Sporn across his desk. "What if I told you that it may not be all lies?"

Sporn blinked. "Pardon me?"

"Let me ask you something," Rathneggar said, his tone suddenly becoming more personal. "How deeply do you truly believe?"

Sporn tensed. This was the most offensive thing he had ever heard. His immediate instinct was to express indignation, but that would not do in front of the Head Curate. Instead he said, "Yasu Doi means everything to me. The Alpha and the Omega."

Rathneggar convulsed a laugh. It devolved into a sputtering

cough. "Rubbish!" he said, wiping spittle away from his mouth with the hem of his sleeve. "You sound like all the other prelates. Every one of them a trained dog!"

Sporn was at a loss for words. This sudden outburst from the Head Curate did not make sense to him. "I, ah … I mean, I would forfeit my life for Yasu Doi, if that was what it took," he said with forced bravado.

"Spoken like a true soldier. Always ready to follow orders."

"Isn't that what you want?" Sporn asked.

"What I want, what I want …" Rathneggar repeated. "It's not what I want," he said flatly, "it's what Hanub-Ka wants. And what Hanub-Ka wants is for us to believe not out of desire, or will, but naturally, as effortlessly as breathing."

Sporn would have liked to remind the Curate that not everyone breathed easily these days, but he let it go. "You're essentially describing me," he said with restrained pride.

"Really?"

Sporn gave a resolute nod.

For a moment, the two men stared at each other. Sporn thought the Curate was going to launch into a long-winded lecture on the ills facing Cosmonism and the need to engage in even harsher deprivations. Instead, he grabbed a candle and a lighter from a small altar underneath the picture of Yasu Doi. He lit the candle, waited till the flame stabilized.

"Give me your hand," he demanded.

Unsure of what was going on, but averse to disobeying orders, Sporn offered his left hand.

Rathneggar slapped it away. "The other one!"

Sporn reluctantly gave him his right hand.

Rathneggar held the candle under his open palm.

Sporn allowed Rathneggar his will, but right away the searing pain became too much, and he violently jerked his hand back.

"You see?" Rathneggar said. "You're just an empty coward

like all the others."

Sporn rubbed his hand, looked at the Head Curate in confusion.

Rathneggar, without saying a word, put his hand over the flame.

Sporn watched as it blackened his skin. The acrid odor of burning flesh filled the air. After what seemed like an outrageously long time, Rathneggar calmly retracted his hand, looked at it, then cast it aside as if it didn't belong to him.

Sporn forced himself to accept what he had just seen.

"I'm going to ask you again," Rathneggar said. "How much do you believe in your savior?"

This time Sporn hesitated a little before answering. His mind was racing, searching for the words that he hoped would satisfy the Curate.

"I know that Hanub-Ka created the first humans from His breath. I know that He is the one and true God of the heavens, as well as the land and sea. He who follows Him, he who believes in Him, is blessed with honor and promised an eternal afterlife."

Rathneggar exhaled sharply, as if he were spitting out a piece of gristle that had been stuck between his teeth. "Yes, it is true. He did fashion the first humans from His breath. Every schoolchild knows that. But those words were recorded secondhand by the prophets: Ramanjabba, Marmoot, Vesnoon. Each man claimed to have been divinely inspired. The Four Signs have been authenticated as proof of their legitimacy. Yes! I don't doubt that. But I would be a fool to think that they were perfect enough to interpret His words in the fullest of their meaning. I've studied their writings and found contradictions."

Sporn jerked back as if Rathneggar had physically struck him. Contradictions? This was the first he had heard of that. It was unbelievable. He shook his head.

"What contradictions?"

"For one, they disagree on the nature of the All-Powerful One."

"Really? Are you sure?"

"Am I sure? Ramanjabba claimed that no man has ever seen the face of Hanub-Ka. Yet Marmoot said he saw His face and was saved."

"Surely that's just a matter of interpretation?"

"Interpretation? Pray then, who has the final say?"

Sporn opened his mouth, then promptly shut it again.

"That is not all. Vesnoon claims that Yasu Doi was born of a virgin. But Ramanjabba used no such term. He only described a young woman. Some people even believe she was Ashmat's wife."

"Why are you telling me this?"

"Because no one man can take it upon himself to interpret Hanub-Ka's words alone. What if He also speaks through them?"

"But that's … that's impossible," Sporn muttered.

"Who says it is?"

Sporn didn't know what to say.

"Twenty years ago, Arthur Huxley went into the Olongo jungle and lived with the Warraweans. From that we learned the Warraweans have a different cosmology to us. At the time, we thought that by eliminating Huxley, we could keep that knowledge a secret. But Vernon Reeves has disabused us of that notion. Except Reeves is no Huxley. And the fact that he believes it means many more are capable of believing it."

"Yes, you're absolutely right."

"So you understand what this means?"

Sporn dropped his eyes in acknowledgment. He didn't have to say the words. It was clear in Rathneggar's eyes. He would have to start public executions again. Hangings, followed by decapitation and erection of heads on pikes around the city walls.

"When do you want me to start?" he said.

"Not yet." Rathneggar raised his blackened palm. "As per protocol, we'll begin by spreading rumors. The anticipation is always more powerful than the act itself."

CHAPTER THIRTEEN

Day Two: 8 – 9:30 a.m.

Later, as the droids were washing her body, checking her for wounds, Maddie could hear Rhybus outside the bedroom talking to someone, but she didn't have the slightest desire to know what was being said. Every little touch caused her to wince in pain.

All she wanted was some painkillers and a long, long sleep.

Momentarily, there was a knock on the door and Rhybus said, "I have a doctor here to see you when you're finished."

Maddie didn't answer. The droids finished washing her and dried her off.

When the doctor finally came in, he checked her for injuries and determined that nothing was broken, but stated that she was in danger of infection. Her cuts and lacerations were infested with swamp bacteria. She would need to undergo a course of antibacterial medication.

"Do you have any painkillers?" she asked feebly.

"Of course," the doctor replied. He gave her an injection, then placed a bottle of pills by her bedside table. "When you wake up, two every four hours."

Maddie nodded weakly, then passed out.

As soon as Sporn heard about her escape attempt he went to the Palace and demanded to see her.

The doctor forbade it. She needed rest, not interrogation, he argued. Seeing that the doctor wasn't going to compromise, Sporn turned his anger onto Rhybus.

Rhybus gallantly tried to defend himself. When Sporn directly accused him of helping her, he staunchly denied it, adding, "She is one hell of a determined lady."

"I don't need you to tell me that," Sporn said. "I gave you sufficient warning, remember?"

"True. You did. But how was I supposed to know she was going to jump out of that damn window? We're six stories up, for Yasu's sake!"

"I've doubled the guards on the gates, and from now on there'll be constant patrols."

Rhybus shook his head. "What is the purpose of all of this? You promised me you weren't running another one of your schemes."

"Schemes – is that what you call them?" Sporn countered. He was in no mood to take criticism, especially from someone as young and naive as the Prince. He thrust his face up close to Rhybus'. "What you call a scheme is a strategy, but you wouldn't know about that because you're too busy jerking off with your playthings – which I provided, in case you forgot."

Rhybus held his ground, but didn't respond.

"Without that water," Sporn said, pointing to the swimming pool, "all of this is meaningless. And right now, her brother has his hands on the tap. He's the one thing that stands between everyone sharing it and you hoarding it all to yourself."

Rhybus didn't buy that argument for one second. "That's bullshit and you know it," he said with uncharacteristic venom.

"That dam of yours is going to make you filthy rich. So don't pretend you're doing it for the people."

Sporn momentarily checked himself, then backhanded the Prince across the face.

Rhybus stumbled back, shocked.

"Now, there's some diplomacy for you," Sporn said.

"Get out!" the Prince commanded.

Sporn stood there for a while, smiling faintly. Then, without further word, he left. Not because the Prince had ordered him, but because he was satisfied that there was nothing more to say.

CHAPTER FOURTEEN

Day Two: 8 a.m.

Ben arrived at work slightly late, hot and flustered. Tom was already at his workstation when Ben entered the CIL.

"What happened to you?" he asked.

"You don't want to know." He went over to his desk and put his daypack on the floor.

"Boy, you look stressed out."

Ben said nothing. He logged into the system and tried to appear like he was busy at work.

Tom got up and sauntered over. "You sure you don't want to talk about it? You wanna tell me how last night went?"

Ben shook his head.

"That bad, eh?"

Ben gritted his teeth and grimaced.

"You know, you can always start with a droid," Tom suggested.

"It's not that."

"What is it, then?"

Ben paused for a moment. "I —" he began, but stopped as the lab door opened and Booker walked in.

"What are you two boys up to?" It wasn't a question, but a statement.

"We're working on the A2 de-installer, as discussed," Tom said, turning to face him.

"Well, put that down," Booker said. "I've got a new job for you."

Booker was the youngest senior executive in the company's history, courtesy of his rich parents' nepotism. Along with his angular pretty-boy face, it gave him an air of self-assuredness that belied his inner confidence, which was less than stellar. He made up for it by bossing Tom and Ben around as if they were a pair of naughty children. Which, in his eyes, they were.

He walked up to them, scrutinized Tom's screen to see if he was doing what he said he was. "A request has come in for us to recommission some A2s."

That was quick, Ben thought.

"Okay …" Tom said.

"This is a high-level request, so I need you to maintain absolute secrecy on this, understand?"

"Okay, so what is it?" Tom asked.

"I need you to reconfigure their connectivity protocol to include a data stream to the City Barracks. Obviously that will include setting up additional servers there to handle the load."

"Hang on a second," Tom said. "That's breaking the international treaty on privacy – you realize that?"

"Yes, I know."

"Well, it's illegal, and I won't have anything to do with it," Tom said.

"What if I told you this order came straight from the Minister of the Interior himself?"

Tom stared blankly at Booker.

"That's right. And what do you think he would say if I told him you refused?"

Tom's jaw worked, but he didn't respond.

"So we're clear then," Booker said.

Tom didn't say anything. Neither did Ben.

"Good. So stop what you were doing, get down there, and start picking out some candidates. I recommend you pick the ones that have the least miles on them. We want to put our best foot forward on this one."

Ben got up. "You want us to start right now?"

"Right now," Booker said, and briskly walked out.

Back in his office, Booker VidPhoned Sporn to let him know that things were afoot.

"Excellent," Sporn said. The image of his face flickered on Booker's screen. He was somewhere on the road in his limousine.

"What sort of timeframe were you thinking of?" Booker asked, keen to get an idea of how hard he should press.

"You should know by now that when I ask for something, it's already overdue."

"Understood."

Sporn shook his head, somewhat annoyed. "That's not quite the answer I was looking for. I want an assurance. Days, weeks – what can you give me?"

"I suppose, well, it all depends ..." Booker began, but then he changed tack. "We could probably have an alpha test article up and running within a week. How does that sound?"

Sporn seemed receptive to that. "Very well. A week it is, then. But I want you to report back to me daily. You got that?"

"Yes, sir."

"This is your first big test," Sporn said, leveling his gaze at Booker. "It's going to be interesting to see if Carver's trust in you can be justified."

"It will be," Booker said earnestly.

Sporn looked at him, but didn't respond. The screen went

blank.

Booker leaned back in his chair, exhausted. He realized he had been leaning forward the whole time, his whole body tense. He exhaled noisily and looked around the room, feeling like a caged animal. What he needed now was a stiff drink.

He reached into the bottom drawer of his desk and pulled out a cheap bottle of vodka he had stashed there precisely for this purpose. He had sworn he would never use it except in the direst of emergencies. Well, if this wasn't an emergency, what was it? He took a long, hard swig straight from the bottle and swallowed it down. It burned, but that was exactly what he wanted. It was the feeling of disinfection. The removal of a dark and fetid growth in the pit of his stomach, the harbinger of self-doubt.

He took a couple more swigs, then slumped back into his chair and closed his eyes.

CHAPTER FIFTEEN

Day Two: 9:30 a.m.

Sporn's limo hugged the curves of the Ridge Road as it sped toward the South Head bluff. This was going to be an interesting meeting. How long had it been since he had last spoken face to face with Pascal Montaigne? Four years? In that time, he had gone from strength to strength while Pascal had all but faded out of public sight. As pleased as he was with this outcome, Sporn would have preferred Pascal to have been sent straight to the Labor Camps – but Carver, as usual, had had the last say. Laurent Carver was the only man apart from Rathneggar who could trump him when it came to matters of state security. Nevertheless, if everything went according to plan, the Star of Cosmonism was still within reach. He would get his hands on it, one way or the other.

Only things weren't going his way ... Which was why he put particular emphasis on this upcoming meeting with Pascal. It might just turn things around.

Pascal, for his part, had no intention of obliging him. When he heard the knocking on his door, he already knew who it was.

"What kept you?" he said, feigning disinterest.

Sporn snapped his fingers. "Start with the library," he ordered Koolhaas and Fletcher, who were waiting behind him. They barged their way past Pascal, neither stopping to excuse themselves.

"I see you've trained your dogs well," Pascal said.

"Shall we?" Sporn said, inviting himself in.

Hislap was standing on the upper landing of the stairs. She watched like a hawk as Sporn and Pascal walked into the library. Inside, the floor was already littered with dozens of books, Koolhaas and Fletcher working each shelf systematically on opposite sides of the room.

"You going to put those back when you're finished?" Pascal asked.

"We're looking for a notebook," Sporn said.

"Really," Pascal said, laying on as much sarcasm as he could muster.

"To be more precise, Arthur's journal."

Pascal scratched his head, put on a slightly annoyed expression. "Haven't we been over this before? I've already told you; I've never seen it."

Sporn looked at the growing pile of books on the floor. "You could save us both a lot of trouble."

"Even if I had seen it – if I actually *had* it – do you honestly think I would tell you?"

"Of course not. But we're gentlemen, are we not?"

Pascal went over to a cabinet and took out two glasses. He put them on his desk and picked out a bottle of brandy, then poured the first glass. "Would you care for a refreshment while you work?"

Sporn studied him silently, waited.

Pascal poured the other glass, brought it over, and offered it to Sporn. Sporn lashed out, sending the glass crashing into the bookshelf across the room.

"That's a shame," Pascal said. "It's a twenty-year-old."

"What's that hanging around your neck?"

Pascal put his hand on the lanyard. "This?"

"Give it to me." Pascal gave it to him. Sporn looked at the key. "What's it for?"

"Just a drawer."

"Show me."

"This one," Pascal said, indicating his desk.

Sporn opened the drawer. Disappointment crossed his face. "What was in the drawer?"

"Just some personal papers."

Sporn slapped a backhand across Pascal's cheek. "Liar!"

Pascal turned his face away, readjusted his glasses, but otherwise did not respond.

"I'll ask again: what was in the drawer?"

Just then, Hislap came in, looking genuinely shocked. "Oh my," she said, "is this really necessary?"

"You ask your charge," Sporn said.

Hislap gave Pascal a severely annoyed look. Pascal merely shrugged.

Picking her way through the mess to a bookshelf on the other side of the room that the Gormlings hadn't yet desecrated, Hislap reached behind a row of books and pulled on something.

Pascal uttered a muffled cry as the bookshelf swung out.

Koolhaas and Fletcher stopped what they were doing. Sporn picked his way over and looked behind the shelf. A set of steps descended to a darkened room.

"After you," he said to Pascal.

Pascal stalled for a moment, then, taking a path that resulted in the least disrespect to his collection, went over and switched on a light. He looked at Sporn, then ambled his way down.

"Well, well, well, look what we have here," Sporn said, marveling at the room crammed with books. It had only one piece of furniture: a footstool that showed heavy signs of wear. This was surely the largest collection of banned books he had ever seen.

Pascal didn't speak. Sporn's reaction said it all.

He pulled out the first book that caught his eye. *Cyropaedia.* He tried sounding out the title: "Kyro-pai-dia."

"Syro-pee-dia," Pascal corrected.

Sporn flicked to the first chapter and read the opening paragraph:

We have had occasion before now to reflect how often democracies have been overthrown by the desire for some other type of government, how often monarchies and oligarchies have been swept away by movements of the people, how often would-be despots have fallen in their turn, some at the outset by one stroke, while those who have maintained their rule for ever so brief a season are looked upon with wonder as marvels of sagacity and success.

"Not the kind of bedtime literature for sensitive souls," Pascal said, taking the book out of Sporn's hands and returning it to the shelf.

"Gaspard is going to be very interested in this collection," Sporn said, fingering a row of books.

"Gaspard doesn't have to know anything about it."

Sporn turned to face Pascal directly. "Oh, he does, I can assure you."

"What do you want?" Pascal said, showing the first signs of defeat.

"You know exactly what I want."

"I told you, I've never seen it."

Sporn sighed. He examined Pascal. He could see that the man was broken. This was his handiwork. Yet, uncharacteristically, he didn't feel proud of it. Not at all. He wanted a worthy enemy. This man was no longer fit for the fight.

"I'll tell you what," he said. "I can spare you the torture, if you tell me right now. Whisper it in my ear."

Pascal shook his head even more vigorously.

Sporn sighed again. "Okay." He clapped his hands.

Koolhaas came partway down the stairs; there wasn't enough room for three people.

"Call Washburn and have him bring a truck and a consignment of men."

"Yes, sir."

"What are you doing?" Pascal asked.

"We're going to take this place apart, brick by brick."

"But I told you, I don't have it."

"I know," Sporn said. "But you won't be needing this place anymore. Not where you're going."

CHAPTER SIXTEEN

Washburn arrived with his pack of Gormlings. Sporn ordered him to empty out Pascal's secret library of banned books and load them onto the truck.

Pascal watched helplessly as his life was dismantled around him. He had nowhere to run. No weapons to fight with. No more secrets to delay the inevitable.

Except one …

And he promised himself that he would never reveal it, not even on pain of torture, which was all but certain now.

He didn't blame Hislap for her betrayal. She was just doing her job. But even though she was employed by the state to keep an eye on him, the four years they'd spent living together under the same roof had to count for something. They ate together, laughed at each other's bad jokes, and confided some of their deepest thoughts on life. Yes, she knew about his key; he had seen her looking at it on a number of occasions. But he had never once let it out of his sight, so he was confident that she didn't know about Arthur's notebook. If they did interrogate her, which was expected, given her role, there was nothing she could give them beyond what they already had.

While he watched, Pascal overheard Sporn talking to Washburn. They were keeping to themselves, but at least twice he was able to pick up the word "graffiti." Inwardly, it gave him a little pulse of pleasure. His game of cat-and-mouse appeared to have hit home. Kudos to Haelstrom!

Cabal Haelstrom. Clandestine resistance fighter extraordinaire, otherwise known as a "Jammer." The Jammers risked their lives by intercepting government transmissions and relaying the information to Vernon Reeves' rebels. They were computer hackers and radio operators, which made them a direct target of the Whisperers, Rathneggar's private spy network. Every now and then a Jammer would be caught, but true to their moral code, they would chew a cyanide capsule to protect their network. Such was the commitment of these men. Silent heroes.

Pascal had nearly joined them. When Iris had died, he'd hit rock bottom. He'd felt like he had nothing to lose.

Iris. Arthur's wife. And after Arthur disappeared, Pascal's de facto partner. The three of them had first met at the University of Urkesh: Arthur studying anthropology, Iris mathematics, and Pascal computer science and engineering. He had instantly fallen in love with Iris, but she was already in love with Arthur. She was vivacious, intelligent, and talented with numbers. When he got the job at Mimetic Machines, he'd tried to win her over by offering her a position in the company. Her mathematical skills would have been a perfect fit. But she had declined, preferring to teach at the university instead. Teaching was her true passion. It was the ideal platform for her talent.

Numbers ... Of all things, she should have known. Because it was numbers – or, more accurately, the statistical coincidence of them – that had eventually killed her.

It happened as Iris was shopping at the Urkesh markets. She was standing on the pavement outside the Farmer's Bank at precisely the moment some robbers came out. They were wielding guns, threatening people to get out of the way. At that moment, an A1 saw fit to act on its *Pro Hominin* laws: *Robots are human servants; they must sacrifice themselves if necessary to protect humans from harm.* The A1 attempted to stop one of the robbers. The robber responded by firing his gun at the droid. The bullet hit the droid's head and broke up on impact.

One of the fragments struck Iris in the neck. She bled out and died before the ambulance arrived.

Pascal was devastated.

Twenty years earlier, Iris had been equally devastated after Arthur's disappearance. Unable to focus, she took long service leave from the university. Ben was four at the time and a troubled child. The diagnosis was autism. Iris was in no shape to look after him by herself. Pascal persuaded her to move in with him. Initially, she rejected the offer, but Pascal didn't give up. Eventually the reality of looking after Ben sank in. He needed a father figure. Iris accepted and Pascal took them in, and after a couple of years, through patience and love, managed to settle Ben down.

Encouraged, Pascal pushed for Ben to be re-examined and his diagnosis was downgraded to Asperger's. He was an extremely bright, but introverted kid. They home-schooled him, and he slowly came out of his shell. He even accepted Pascal as his "stepdad." Pascal could not have been happier.

Until that fateful day, when it was all ripped away from him.

There was no question about it: it was all the regime's fault. If an A2 had been there, Iris would still be alive. He was sure absolutely sure of that. An A2 would not have reacted so quickly without thinking. It would have paused for that extra, crucial second. Avoided any moves that could be interpreted by the robbers as threatening. At most, it would have stepped in front of Iris and shielded her.

Grieving and angry, Pascal decided to take matters into his own hands. As Head of Engineering at Mimetic Machines, he had access to the incept dates and serial numbers of all A2s, courtesy of having played a key role in development of the recursion module that had given them their self-reflective awareness. Under the guise of a new research program, Pascal began to send out A1s with A2 recursion modules preinstalled, so that when the right codes were punched in, they could be rebooted as A2s. He secretly gave the codes to the Jammers. That was his way of joining them.

For a while, the ruse worked. A2 droids once again roamed free outside the Old City walls. But not for long.

Rathneggar's Whisperers caught on, and very quickly the finger was pointed at Pascal. Sporn personally took charge of the arrest. A tribunal was set up and Pascal was interrogated. At first he denied it. However, he quickly changed his tune when they showed him the instruments of torture. The punishment, as stated by law, was death. But Laurent Carver had stepped in and persuaded the tribunal to commute the sentence to house arrest.

The truth was, Pascal was practically indispensable. The upper echelons of society who privately owned A2s for pleasure were hungry for constant upgrades and tweaks. Until someone could be trained to take over, Pascal needed to remain accessible. When asked who could replace him, Carver recommended Nigel Booker. And so a deal was struck.

That was four years ago.

This was now. And Sporn had finished his conversation with Washburn and was coming over to speak to him.

"Time to go," he said.

Sporn directed Pascal to his limo. Pascal couldn't help seeing the irony of being driven to his demise via a luxury car.

Hislap came out and watched him leave. For a brief moment, he met her eyes. Pascal thought he detected regret in them. Then Sporn shoved him into the car and shut the door behind him.

In the quiet of the car, Pascal took one last look at the house he had spent so many memorable years living in. He had wanted nothing more than to get out and be free again. But not like this. It was such a waste.

Sporn gave some final orders to the men ferrying books out of the house, then joined Pascal in the car. The driver didn't need instructions. He knew where to go. He took them down the Ridge Road toward the Old City and headed for the Ministry of Justice building. Nobody spoke.

The silence, however, was abruptly broken by the sound of Sporn's VidPhone.

"Yes?"

"This is not something we can discuss over the air. You need to come to the Palace right away."

"I'm transporting a prisoner."

"Forget your prisoner. This is more important."

The screen went blank.

Sporn instructed his driver to take a detour to the Palace. Pascal wondered what could be so important that Sporn was giving precedence to the Palace over the Ministry of Justice.

"Something the matter?" he inquired.

"None of your business," Sporn said gruffly.

The car took the inner ring road, then crossed the "Island" bridge. It had been a long time since Pascal had seen this part of Urkesh. The Palace was just as he remembered it, but it still impressed him, with its three towers and high crenelated walls.

The car pulled up on the forecourt of the main hall and Sporn got out, instructing Pascal, "Stay here."

Rhybus was waiting for Sporn in the foyer. His expression was grim. "I'm not sure how to tell you this," he said, hurrying up the stairs to the first-floor landing.

"Tell me what?" Sporn said, following him.

Orlov the butler was waiting at the elevator, holding the doors open. They stepped in.

As soon as the doors closed, Rhybus said, "She's dead."

"What?"

"When Orlov went to check on her half an hour ago, he found her unconscious. We called the doctor. He was unable to revive her."

"Impossible."

The elevator doors opened. They stepped out.

"Let me see her," Sporn said.

"I don't think you want to do that," Rhybus warned.

"Why?"

"Because of how she looks."

Sporn pushed past him and headed to the room where she was kept. Inside, the doctor was in the process of packing his medications and implements away.

Maddie was covered with linen gauze. Sporn went up to her, staring in disbelief.

"I thoroughly assessed her," the doctor said. "No internal injuries, no broken bones. All she needed was some antibiotics and rest. Except …"

Sporn slowly drew back the gauze. What he saw made him reel with horror.

Maddie's face had blistered and puffed up. The vessels in her eyes had burst and blood oozed from her tear ducts. Her mouth was fixed in a rictus. Her tongue was swollen and had turned blue-green, protruding through her teeth. Straw-colored liquid drained from her ears.

"What in Yasu's name happened here?" Sporn murmured, turning to the doctor.

"It's a virus," the doctor said.

Sporn became more cautious. "Is it infectious?"

"Only if you have a break in your skin. It's blood-borne."

"And you never suspected that?"

"I drew blood. Sent it to pathology. They just confirmed it."

"When?"

"Just before you arrived."

"No, when did you take her blood?"

"This morning, when I first saw her."

"And it took you all this time to figure out she was infected with a virus?"

"We're not miracle workers."

Sporn felt an overwhelming urge to strangle the man. But he restrained himself. "Who else knows about this, apart from the people here and pathology?"

"Pathology doesn't know whose blood it is. The sample is blind."

"Good," Sporn said. "Have it destroyed."

"As you wish."

"No one – I repeat, *no one* – is to know about this. Am I clear?"

The doctor nodded curtly. "May I take my leave now?"

Sporn waved him out of the room. The doctor grabbed his bag and hurriedly departed.

When he was gone, Sporn turned his attention back to Maddie. He wanted to touch her, but he mustered just enough self-control to stay back. This was a disaster. Just when he thought he was getting things back on track ...

For a long time he just stood there and stared at her, debating what to do. How could this happen? It was unprecedented. Rathneggar had warned him about this woman, but he had ignored it. This made his mistake doubly disastrous. Not only would it foment a civil war, but it would bring shame and humiliation to his name. There was no question about it: he would be sent to the Labor Camps, stripped of all his powers.

The realization was like a dagger through his heart. He desperately needed to come up with a plan, something to stave off the inevitable, perhaps even solve the problem outright. But what? His mind refused to work. All he could think of was the overriding need to get rid of the body. If there was no body, there was no evidence.

He gave her one last horrified look, then left the room.

Rhybus was sitting by the pool, pensively kneading his hands. He looked up as Sporn approached. "Well?"

"How trustworthy is Orlov?" Sporn asked.

"I can trust him with my life."

"Make sure he talks to no one about this. And that applies to you as well."

"Of course."

"We need to contain this. If her brother finds out, if the wider public finds out, all hell will break loose."

A pained expression passed across Rhybus' face.

"We need to dispose of the body," Sporn said.

"What do you have in mind?"

"Bury her in the Cloister cemetery."

"That's not possible," Rhybus said. "The Curates will find out. They frequently visit it to honor their ancestors."

"We could just throw her back in the river."

"Yes, we could, but what if someone finds her?"

Sporn rubbed his chin in thought.

Rhybus said, "I have an idea."

Sporn looked at him.

"We do a sky burial in my rooftop garden. The birds and insects up there will do the work for us."

"I would have never guessed," Sporn said.

"Guessed what?"

"That you could be so ... practical."

CHAPTER SEVENTEEN

Day Two: Noon

Pascal was semi-dozing when Sporn returned. The man who had left the car was not the same man who came back.

"What happened?" he asked.

Sporn didn't answer. His face was a mask of stone.

The driver asked for directions.

"Back to the Ministry of Justice."

They departed in silence.

Pascal stopped thinking about Sporn and stared out the window, looking at a city he'd thought he had forgotten. The buildings were the same, the traffic the same, the people seemed to be preoccupied as usual — but *he* had changed. He felt like he was inside a film whose soundtrack was muted. Perhaps a part of him had already left this world.

Sporn was equally distracted. His mind was hot as a furnace, forging one idea after the other, only to discard them as weak or impractical the moment they came into being. There seemed to be no way out. He felt like he was stuck in a labyrinth. He hated this feeling. All his life he had been in control. It was all he'd ever known. The faith in that belief alone had unfailingly carried him through the toughest moments of his life ...

And then it hit him. The answer was so obvious that he almost cried out.

He turned to Pascal. "Have you ever created an A2 so realistic that you couldn't tell the difference between it and a human?"

Sporn's words drew Pascal out of his reverie. "Say what?" he said, hearing the words but not believing them.

Sporn repeated himself.

Almost immediately, Pascal began shaking his head. "Do you realize what you're asking?"

"More than ever. Just tell me, is it possible?"

"It's never been done before."

"That's not what I asked."

"I haven't exactly been able to keep up with the latest advances, given my situation —"

"We both know that's not true."

"Okay," Pascal said, acknowledging his lie; Ben had been keeping him informed. "But that's not the thrust of his work, is it? You're asking me, literally, could we make an artifice so realistic that people wouldn't notice?"

"Yes."

"Why?"

"I have a problem."

"What sort of problem?"

"A very delicate one."

"Okay ..."

"I'm going to offer you a proposition."

Now, this is going to be interesting, Pascal thought.

"If you build me this A2, I will promise to turn a blind eye to your transgressions."

"You're serious."

"Absolutely."

"My books ..." Pascal said. "Gaspard never lays eyes on them?"

"As long as you deliver on *your* promise."

"Agreed."

"Not so fast. There's one more thing."

"What?"

"You have to tell me the truth about Arthur's journal. Where is it?"

"I knew it."

"What?"

Pascal turned his gaze back to the window. This was going to be hard. But he had no choice. "In that case, I can't help you."

An uneasy silence fell between them. The car crawled through the traffic.

Eventually Sporn said, "You drive a hard bargain."

Pascal looked at him. He seemed to have softened. If that was even possible.

"It's ironic," Sporn said, "how easily the tables turn, don't you think?"

"So the deal's back on?"

Sporn didn't answer. Instead, he took out his VidPhone and made a call.

CHAPTER EIGHTEEN

Day Two: Just before noon

Joselyn had watched as Sporn and Rhybus carried Maddie's body up the narrow staircase that led to the rooftop garden. Curious, she followed them. She watched them from behind some potted palms as they unwrapped the body and laid it naked in a garden bed. They set fire to the discarded material and watched it burn, bowing their heads and uttering some words she could not discern.

When they were gone, she went up to the body to get a closer look. She had never seen a dead human before – although much of what she saw was no longer recognizably human. Even though she had only known this person ever so briefly, the words she'd spoken still rang in her ears.

Robots must not engage in any behavior that reflects badly on humans, especially behavior that assumes robots have no soul.

What about humans? Joselyn thought. The rule should apply equally to them, should it not? Based on what she'd just seen, there was no question.

Birds began gathering in the trees, twittering noisily among themselves. She peered up at one sitting on a nearby branch. It looked at her and squawked.

A fly buzzed by. Then another. Before long, a dozen or more had settled on the corpse. She watched as one crawled across Maddie's swollen lips.

So this was how it went. Strange. It would not be how she would die – if it ever came to that. They would switch her off and dismantle her. Piece by piece. She wondered if that was any better. This seemed so much more natural, befitting a soul. Did it mean she didn't have one? Surely that wasn't what Maddie had meant.

So what *had* she meant when she'd spoken of robots and souls?

CHAPTER NINETEEN

Day Two: Just after noon

Booker was leaning back in his office chair, dozing, feet up on his desk, when Sporn and Pascal came through the door. The empty bottle of vodka rested on top of some scrunched-up papers in a wastebasket.

Booker's eyes snapped open. He looked at the two men as if they were ghosts. Especially Pascal.

"Making progress, I see," Sporn said.

Booker pulled his feet off the desk. "My engineers are working on recommissioning a number of A2s as we speak."

"Forget about that," Sporn said. "I have a new project for you."

Booker stared at Pascal, dumbfounded. Pascal merely gave him a shrug.

Sporn said, "What I'm about to tell you stays between us. You have to swear it."

"I swear it."

"You're going to make an A2 copy of Madelaine Reeves."

"Excuse me?"

"You heard. You're going to build me the most advanced A2

you've ever built. Not only that, you're going to do it in record time."

Booker looked at Pascal again.

"Necessity is the mother of invention," Pascal said.

Booker took some time to think about it. "What's the deadline?"

"Twenty-four hours," Sporn said.

"Twenty-four hours? But that's …"

"Professor Montaigne assures me it's possible," Sporn said, looking at Pascal. "In any case, if you don't succeed, the consequences for you – for *all* of us …" He paused, choosing his words carefully. "… will be dire."

"All because of an A2?"

Sporn ignored Booker's comment. "You're going to need detailed images and information on Madelaine Reeves, of course. I'll organize a dossier on her as soon as I get back to my office. I'll have it sent over by courier."

"Why not just put it on our shared server?"

"And leave a paper trail?"

"I see," Booker said, checking himself.

Sporn examined him to make sure he was with the program. "I don't think I need to tell you that this will be the most important assignment I've ever given you. Many times more important than the Reconnaissance project."

Pascal raised an eyebrow at Booker.

He swallowed heavily. "So what's the chain of command here?"

"Professor Montaigne will be your assistant. But you will do what he says."

Booker's expression was priceless.

"We're all equals on this one," Pascal said. "The only thing that should motivate us is the common goal of making the most exquisite A2 that ever walked the planet."

"In twenty-four hours?" Booker said.

"In twenty-four hours," Sporn replied.

The moment Sporn was gone, Booker practically exploded. "What in Yasu's name is going on here?"

"Calm down!" Pascal said.

"Calm down? Are you out of your fucking mind?"

Pascal walked over to the windows that provided a view of the factory floor below. He watched the automated assembly line stamp, weld, screw, and solder robot parts while an army of bunny-suited workers managed the inventory. "We can do this," he said quietly. "We have to do this."

"Why?" Booker demanded.

"Because our illustrious Minister fucked up."

Booker made a guttural sound.

Pascal couldn't help sniping, "You know ... the sad part of all this is that regardless of whether we succeed or not, we lose."

"How so?"

"If we succeed, that bastard will become even more powerful. If we fail, everything we love and cherish will turn to ashes. There will be a civil war the likes of which no one has ever seen."

"Surely you're being overdramatic?"

"Right now, Vernon Reeves might only have a small number of men at his disposal. But as soon as he finds out that the Minister has imprisoned his sister, those numbers are going to swell into the thousands. Is that a language you understand?"

"What? Whoa ..." Booker said. "Sporn arrested Madelaine Reeves?"

"It's the only explanation that makes sense. Why else would he order us to make a copy of her?"

A dark cloud descended over Booker's face. "Are you absolutely sure about that?"

"Not really. It's just a hunch."

"So he wants us to make a copy of her, so he can ..." He trailed off, the implications too much for his vodka-addled mind to grasp.

"So he can fool her brother, and anyone else, for that matter."

"He's crazy."

"Welcome to the zoo, my friend."

CHAPTER TWENTY

Day Two: 1 p.m.

"Stop what you're doing," Booker said as he walked into the CIL.

Ben and Tom were hunched over their workstations, looking through the Mimetic Machines database, searching for the best candidates for Sporn's "Reconnaissance" project.

They weren't listening, so Booker had to say it again: "I said stop what you're doing."

The boys looked up.

Booker cleared his throat. "Another change of plans."

In his hands was the dossier on Madelaine Reeves. Sporn had sent it to him as promised. He'd flipped through the pages as he strode from his office to the CIL. It looked like it had been hurriedly redacted. The black ink was still fresh. Nevertheless, large swaths were still readable. He would have loved nothing more than to sit down and go through it in detail, but there was simply no time.

Holding the dossier out, he said, "I want you boys to go through this with a fine-tooth comb and extract everything you can."

"What is it?" Ben asked.

"A dossier on Madelaine Reeves," Booker said, handing it to him.

Ben looked at it as if in a dream. "Madelaine Reeves …" he murmured.

"We're going to make a copy of her."

The boys' eyes widened.

"I know, I know," Booker said, trying to sound like he was on their side. "It's forbidden to copy people who are alive. But in this case, we're going to have to break the rules."

"But … Madelaine Reeves?" Tom said, standing up. He was clearly not having any of this.

"Yes. Madelaine Reeves. What about it?"

"She's super well known. There's no way we'll be able to make a copy of her without people picking apart every little detail. It's just not possible."

Ben was nodding in agreement.

"Yes, I agree," Booker said. "But that's not what I promised the Minister."

"Which Minister?" Ben asked.

"Which one do you think?"

Tom threw his hands in the air. "First he wants us to break the privacy law, now he wants us to break the anti-copying law. Which will he want us to break next?"

"Don't be smart with me," Booker said. "Before you get on that high horse of yours, consider the consequences if we don't deliver."

"You've already threatened us once. How are we supposed to take this one seriously?"

"Because this one doesn't just affect the privacy of a few indi-viduals. It affects the whole nation."

"How so?"

"If we fail, a civil war could break out."

Tom sat down.

"I know it sounds crazy. A war over an A2 – and a copy at that. But when you think about it, that's what it amounts to. Miss Reeves is Vernon Reeves' sister, right?"

The boys nodded.

"So the problem we face is him finding out about it," Booker said, staring into space. "That's why the copy has to be perfect."

"But we all know that's impossible," Tom said.

Booker refocused, growing angry. "Don't say that! It's our job to make it possible."

"But surely we have to assume he will find out," Ben said.

"Yes." Booker was becoming more and more vexed. "But it's not the fact of him finding out that worries me. It's him asking why we did it in the first place."

"So why?" Tom asked.

Booker shook his head. "I don't know why."

The boys didn't take this well. They both started talking at the same time.

Booker put his hand up to silence them. "Stop it!" As soon as they had settled down, he said, "It's obvious we're stuck in a double bind situation here. I'm just as unhappy about it as you are. But the way I see it – if we do our job properly, it might just buy the Minister enough time to track down Vernon before the news spreads. Hell, it might even allow Sporn to track him down full stop."

"How much time is he giving us?" Ben asked.

"Twenty-four hours."

The boys burst out again.

"Enough!" Booker shouted. "It is what it is. I can promise delivery of the fully skinned chassis within eight hours. The question is: can you guys get through that dossier in that time and extract all the relevant information?"

"We probably can," Tom said. "But that's irrelevant. What you're asking is if we can digitize all the parameters out of that and upload it to the processors in the time left. And the answer to that is a big fat 'no.'"

"So cut some corners."

"Which corners, exactly, do you want us to cut?"

"You're getting smart with me again. Just get through the dossier, pick out every detail you can, and program it into the configuration file. We'll take it from there."

Among all the head-scratching and head-shaking, there was a genuine look of fear on the boys' faces. The fact was that copies were only allowed of dead people, and it usually took a week or more to program the configuration file up to the level that was considered acceptable by the customer. And this was usually done with a huge dose of salt provided by the customer, who would "train" the droid over time to acquire the memories and mannerisms they wanted replicated.

But this new request was an entirely different affair. Not only did they have to program the A2 to think and act like Madelaine, they also had to make her look like she had hatched out of her egg fully formed – something neither of them had ever done before, because in essence, it was impossible.

"I've already got the art department working on her skin," Booker said, looking at his VidPhone. "I expect they'll be done by around seven. So you had better get cracking."

With this pronouncement, he marched out the door.

Ben forced himself to open the dossier.

Tom rolled his chair over and joined him. "So how do you want to do this? Shall we divide it up? It looks like there's quite a lot in there."

Ben took what seemed about half and handed it to Tom, and they began.

Ben found himself reading and rereading the first page over and over, his mind unable to grasp the reality before him. It was like he had been thrown into a hall of mirrors. He had only just met Miss Reeves, and now he was being asked to learn every-thing there was to know about her. What was going on?

He cast a sideways glance at Tom, who seemed to be having the same problem. He gave Ben a look as if to say: *Is this a dream?*

Ben squeezed his eyes shut, then opened them again.

There were some "official" files mixed up with newspaper cuttings, teletyped slips, and handwritten notes. Some parts were heavily redacted. The official papers had a reference number: MJ83-7129. These were typed up and seemed to be a summary of Miss Reeves' daily activities. Clearly, the government had been keeping an eye on her. That fact alone was a revelation to Ben. One of them read:

> *Miss Reeves left her apartment at 1:34 pm and took a taxi to the Corsi Club. She did not stop along the way. She arrived at the Corsi Club at 2:01 pm. There, she met with her agent, Maxwell Biedermeyer. It was not known what transpired between her and her agent, but she left the Corsi Club at 2:49 pm and took a taxi to the Chet Nouveau where she ate a noodle soup. Afterwards, she smoked a cigarette, then caught a taxi back to her apartment, arriving at 3:17 pm.*

Ben wondered why such mundane information was neces-sary. Of course, she was Vernon Reeves' sister. That alone made her a target. But Ben refused to believe she had anything to do with her brother's rebellious activities.

He came across a gossip magazine article in which Maddie talked about her childhood. She came from a fairly wealthy family. Her father owned a printing business. Often, he'd been up at all times of the night fixing printing runs when the ma-chines broke down, as they commonly did. He'd come home with ink-stained hands. The backs of the kitchen chairs had been darkened because of them, and one day she'd gone to school with black imprints across her shoulders, where the ink had transferred to her shirt. The students had teased her, throwing balled-up paper at her as target practice.

From that time on she felt "marked."

But rather than retreat into her shell, she gave as good as she got. She had a quick mind, something she'd inherited from her father. He would often leave all sorts of printed pamphlets and notes lying around with clients' ideas on them. Reading them broadened Maddie's mind and gave her wit. Moreover, as a printer, her father had a love of books and posters, so the house was filled with both. Invariably, she found herself reading many of his books, which further broadened her mind.

Her mother was a music teacher, so students often came into the house to learn piano or singing. This was how Maddie became a singer herself. Not only did she learn all the songs her mother taught, but also her mother's favorites, which she played for private enjoyment. It was understood from an early age that Maddie would become a performer, although her father would have preferred it if she joined the family business.

Her brother, in that sense, was a disappointment. He was supposed to go into the family business too, but went to university and became a student activist instead. Not that he didn't know anything about the printing business. Ink ran through his veins, like all the Reeves. When he needed to print off pamphlets for his protests, he didn't hesitate to use his father's machines. Which invariably caused him to be kicked out of the house when his father found out.

It was funny, Ben thought, how little he'd cared about Vernon Reeves until now. Suddenly he wanted to know everything about him. Vernon was supposed to be a "bad" person. Desperately wanted by the regime. Everyone knew that if he was caught, he would be publicly executed. A punishment reserved specifically for traitors of the state.

Ben leafed through the dossier until he found a newspaper article with Vernon's name in its title. According to the article, Vernon had first come to attention during the A2 affair. Like Pascal, he supported A2s outside the Old City walls – an attitude that Ben admittedly agreed to, but that was as far as he went. Vernon had planted a briefcase bomb outside the Ministry of Justice building. It had caused a fair amount of destruction and killed a Gormling who found the bag, thinking it was lost property. The next day, Vernon had posted a letter to the government claiming responsibility. From that moment on he'd been a hunted man.

What were his motives? Based on an article that had printed Vernon's letter, the wealthy, who were synonymous with those who held power, successfully lobbied the government to limit the restriction of A2 droids to the zone outside the Old City walls. It didn't matter to them that the people outside the walls who relied on A2s suffered. Besides, they were compensated with replacements – A1s – so they simply had to make do with what they got. Nevertheless, businesses that once used A2s found themselves struggling to compete with the wealthy who still had them. Farms and factories that had relied on them to manage their science sections experienced a decrease in productivity. Pleasure houses dwindled and women began to protest over the demand for "real flesh."

To top things off, Sporn invested heavily in fortifying the wall. He reduced the number of transit points to just four: the South, West and East gates, and the river, which was chained. All other transit points were sealed off. Anyone who needed to pass between the two zones required transit papers, which were automatically issued to the wealthy but only given out in limited numbers to the poor.

A general malaise set in. Those who dared protest were "disappeared." As the numbers of these unfortunates grew, loved ones began taking their grievances out onto the street, calling for answers. They were summarily carted off to the Labor Camps by Sporn's Gormlings.

Why had the government done something so obviously injurious to itself? It didn't make sense. A statement made by Vernon in his letter, however, seemed to capture the popular sentiment. According to him, the government "needed to wake up."

As Ben read these stories, he realized how insulated he had been from all the suffering. It had never occurred to him that Vernon might be justified in his actions.

But what did Madelaine think of all this? He found a handwritten note tucked away in the back of the dossier that suggested a certain redacted person had wormed his way into her private life to use her as a conduit to get to her brother. Ben's first thought was that this must be Hector Sporn. He had no proof, but it seemed like the most logical choice.

The suggestion was that she was being used as a pawn. But Ben found this difficult to reconcile with what he had experienced at the Corsi Club. In his conversation with Madelaine, he'd never had the impression that the Minister controlled her. She hadn't sung his praises. On the contrary, she'd been critical of him. In fact, she was critical of everyone. This was the one thing he didn't understand about her. She seemed to be loved by everyone despite her criticism. More than that. She was unconditionally adored.

"Have you noticed something?" Tom said, interrupting Ben's thoughts.

"What?"

"There's a mysterious person that Miss Reeves was having an affair with, but everywhere the name is blacked out. I wonder who it is."

"No idea."

"Also, did you notice that she's a regular at the Corsi Club? I always thought its existence was a rumor. But these documents clearly prove it does exist."

"Yes."

"Did you know that?"

Ben got up. "No," he lied.

"Where are you going?"

"Bathroom break."

In the men's room, Ben examined himself in the mirror. He saw a boyish face, slightly plump around the cheeks, freckles across the nose, a lock of sandy-blond hair dangling over one eyebrow. Tracking down to his eyes, he guessed they were blueish-gray, but they were a stranger's eyes, not his own. A surge of panic rippled through him. He had nearly told a lie. That was ... a real lie to someone who trusted him.

Technically, what he'd said was true. He hadn't known the club existed until the day before. Saying "yes" in this case was to register the fact that he now knew it existed, but he had given Tom the impression he'd learned this from the file, rather than from firsthand experience. It was a subtle distinction, but he felt like he was walking on a knife edge. He looked at his hands. They were trembling.

What was the penalty for telling a real lie? The Scriptures said that a person's purpose was to seek Hanub-Ka's praise. This could only be achieved through uncompromised striving for purity. A lie by this standard was a stain on the soul. The consequence: eternal damnation. He would never join the others in universal immortality.

The very thought that he would miss out on such a glorious future scared the wits out of him. He had spent his whole life trying to fit in, never quite succeeding. But that was merely a social failure. So long as he maintained the Scriptural precepts, he would be assured a place in the pantheon of immortals. A misfit, but home.

Now he was on the verge of being completely cast adrift.

Totally and utterly alone.

He desperately tried to think of some way he could redeem himself. Tomorrow he would go to his local *Dorma*. He would confess to the Curate and seek forgiveness – if that was possible. Because even though everyone sinned, not all sins were equal. In Ben's eyes, he had committed the gravest of all: weakness of character. As the Curate of his *Dorma* repeatedly remonstrated: "Once weak, always weak."

He shuffled his way back to the CIL. Along the way, he ran the scenario through his mind. Once he confessed, and it was confirmed that the cause was weakness of character, then it was all over. He would be branded for life. Not just publicly, but to himself.

What would Pascal think? Worse – what would Arthur think, if he were still alive?

He couldn't bear the thought of it.

The only solution was to keep it to himself.

But could he sustain that?

Not a chance.

CHAPTER TWENTY-ONE

Day Two: 3 p.m.

Sporn directed Washburn and his Gormlings to dump the bags of books they had confiscated from Pascal's library on the floor. They were on the fifth level of the Moon Tower, where all the other confiscated books retrieved by the regime were deposited for sorting. The Curates would go through them one by one and catalog them, add them to the already bulging shelves.

Why not just burn them? Sporn thought. *It would be so much easier.* But Rathneggar had given explicit instructions to keep all banned books. The man was an incurable bibliophile. One day, Sporn predicted, it would be his undoing.

As he inspected the haul, he noticed one of the bags had opened and a clump of books had spilled out. He bent down and picked through them. There was a book on geology, which interested him. It could come in handy for the dam. He thought about appropriating it. But then another title caught his attention: *Tropical Medicine of the Tongassa River Delta, Volume II: Viruses.*

"What's this?" he muttered, picking it up.

He leafed through it. Much of it appeared too technical for

him. Going back, he found a chapter at the start entitled "History." That seemed like something he could understand. Therein he read:

In 814, following the establishment of the fledgling town of Urkesh and less than two decades after the settling of the Tongassa Delta, a group of workers assigned to dig a channel for a small port harbor contracted a mysterious illness and died. The colony's doctor, Emile Jaspur, examined the bodies and using a special technique he developed specifically for the purpose found that a blood-borne virus had caused their demise — this was contrary to the perceived wisdom of the time which had assumed a bacterial cause. Subsequent experiments with animals, however, revealed that the virus attacked the circulatory system, causing massive internal bleeding and destruction of red-blood cells. On account of this being the first report of its discovery, as well as its mode of action, it was officially named 'Jaspur's Virus'.

Sporn's eyes nearly popped out. Why didn't the Royal Doctor know about this? For several minutes, he paced back and forth in a paroxysm of rage.

When Washburn came in to confirm that all the bags had been brought up, Sporn turned on him viciously and screamed, "Find the Royal Doctor and bring him to me at once!"

Washburn just stood there and stared.

When he didn't move, Sporn went up to him and said, "Don't make me repeat myself."

"Okay." Washburn quietly left. Sporn watched him walk out, clenching and unclenching his fists.

A considerable amount of time went by and nothing happened. Neither Washburn nor anyone else returned.

Eventually Sporn made his way to one of the windows that provided a view of the courtyard below. Washburn's truck and his Gormlings were gone.

Sporn gritted his teeth. He would deal with Washburn later. He went to the elevator and rode it to the eighth floor.

Rhybus was relaxing by the pool. Several droids were gathered around him. One was kneading his shoulders. Another was dangling her feet in the water while she fed him grapes. A third was holding a glass of wine, ready to pass it to her master's lips at a moment's notice.

Sporn walked up to him. "Where are your doctor's quarters?"

"Why? Are you feeling unwell?" Indeed, Sporn looked quite pale, the Prince thought.

"No. But I wish to speak to him in private."

"Across the courtyard, services building, north side, second floor."

After taking directions from a caretaker sweeping the service building entranceway, Sporn found himself standing outside a door at the beginning of a long corridor. The name *Dr. Walter Premack* was stenciled in gold lettering above a lion's head rapper. Sporn cleared his throat and knocked twice.

From within he heard the doctor say, "Come back later, I'm busy."

Sporn let himself in.

The doctor was bent forward over his desk, deep in concentration. He was in the middle of drawing a thread through a small pulley that was part of the rigging of a miniature four-masted sailing ship of old. He had a jeweler's loupe fixed to his right eye, and was so engrossed in his work that he didn't bother to look up at the visitor who had so rudely barged in on him.

Sporn noted this, as well as the small collection of other replica sailing ships strategically positioned on various shelves around the room. They took up space where books ought to have been placed – medical books.

"I said, come back later."

Sporn walked casually over to the doctor, grabbed a handful of his thinning hair, and yanked his head back viciously, slamming it down on the desk, crushing the delicate artwork beneath it.

The doctor cried out in agony.

Sporn lifted the doctor's head to check his handiwork. The jeweler's loupe had rammed itself into the man's right eye. He took hold of the lope and ground it deeper into the skull.

The scream was horrendous.

But then it died away to a whimper, and the doctor went limp.

Sporn let him go.

The doctor's head fell back on the desk, where it remained.

"What's going on?" a voice called.

It was the caretaker. He was standing in the doorway. He looked at Sporn, looked at the doctor, and with uncharacteristic urgency for his aging frame, backed away hurriedly, saying, "I didn't see anything! I didn't see anything!"

Sporn went over to the nearest shelf and examined one of the intricate replicas. He ran his eye over it discerningly. "Such a shame," he said. "They're so well made."

CHAPTER TWENTY-TWO

Day Two: 6 – 7 p.m.

Pascal watched as the 3D bio-printer built up Madelaine's face. Booker's art team had done an incredible job. The likeness was uncanny. When asked where they got their data, the lead technician said it was from every known photograph and video of Madelaine, of which there were many, including her audition photos for various projects. They would have preferred to have her in real life, but according to Booker, that wasn't possible. So they'd made do with what they had. In any case, the technician said, how many people knew she had a mole just under her hairline at the back of her neck?

The bio-skin was pulled over the chassis like a glove, giving the mechatron the verisimilitude of a human form. Because the skin was living tissue, it required nutrients and warmth. It got its nutrients from synthetic blood, colored red and circulated by a small pump euphemistically called the "heart." The key innovation was a "dermal mat," which interfaced between the living skin and the mechatron beneath it. The mat was fenestrated with myriad tiny channels divided into two systems: one carried blood; the other heated water. All A1 and A2 droids were powered by RTGs – radio thermal isotopic generators – which naturally shed heat as a byproduct of their operation. Traditionally, the heat was dumped as a waste product, but Mimetic Machines had ingeniously reclaimed it to keep the skin at human temperature. This was another unique feature of MM droids: they were warm to the touch.

But this innovation paled into insignificance when compared to their real achievement – the one Mimetic Machines was justifiably famous for: its A2 *recursion* module. Pascal's pride and joy. He had invented it, and with it catapulted Mimetic Machines into the number one position in robotics on the planet. And yet it was this invention that proved to be his undoing in the regime's eyes.

In cognitive science, recursion was believed to be a pivotal function behind self-awareness. For a long time, scientists had debated this ability in humans. Some believed it was magic, and therefore argued that it could never be scientifically solved. Others, like Pascal, believed it was merely a behavioral characteristic of a brain that had evolved a self-monitoring function. In the end, Pascal and others like him were proved right. The confusion stemmed from a kind of anthropocentric blindness. What had been missed was a thorough accounting of time. It took time for signals to travel from the periphery of the body to the brain. It took time for the brain to process those signals. But in their egotism, humans had assumed that consciousness was instant, that it occurred in the immediate present.

This was completely false. Self-monitoring in the brain occurred in the past. Self-reflective consciousness wasn't an epiphenomenon, but a delayed part of the brain reflecting on itself. The misunderstanding occurred because humans were incapable of discerning small increments of time down to a hundred milliseconds or less. It took between forty to eighty milliseconds for a peripheral sensory signal to reach the brain. It took the brain another two hundred fifty milliseconds to process it. By the time that signal was delivered to the self-monitoring function, it was already three – to three hundred fifty milliseconds old. The trick of the self-monitoring function, however, was that it presented the world to conscious awareness *as if* it were occurring in the immediate present. It was the proverbial iceberg. Nine-tenths of the process was submerged, withheld from consciousness.

The trick worked because the brain also had another powerful function: *prediction*. Prediction was a subprocess of an even more universal brain behavior: *projection*. The brain, in essence, was a *projection machine*. Pascal and his coworkers leveraged this fact to produce the A2 recursion module. It worked by making predictions, which it then projected onto the world. Projections were the content of "reality." Like money in an economy, they were the currency of the brain.

When a prediction failed, it was corrected. This iterative process allowed all living things, including droids, to arrive at a *prediction pattern*. It was these prediction patterns that constituted "reality." Reality to a bat, which moved through space by echolocation, was different to the reality of a human, which used vision to navigate its environment. No one had a monopoly on reality. It was constructed case-by-case for each organism. Only extension, location, and causality were shared. Not even time was shared, because time was related to the size and speed of biological activity.

In reflecting on this, what amazed Pascal even more than knowing such things was that the regime had *allowed* him to learn them, because at heart the regime was antithetical to them. It despised the notion that reality was constructed differently for each species. As far as it was concerned, there was only one reality: the reality of Hanub-Ka.

But, as usual, there was a delay between what scientists discovered and what the regime promulgated. However, as soon as the regime found out that A2 droids were based on a theory that directly conflicted with their ideology, they quickly and comprehensively shut the program down. Well, almost. Because like all corrupt regimes, they begrudgingly and secretly became addicted to the new technology. And so it came to pass that A2s were not completely outlawed; they continued to circulate inside the walls of the Old City, where the regime could maintain control over them and use them for their own benefits and pleasure.

Monumental hypocrites, in Pascal's eyes.

The Reeves droid was now ready for its "cognitive installation." It was hung in a mobile stand and rolled off the factory floor. After a group of engineers checked out its sub-systems, ensuring that they operated within their nominal ranges, they handed it over to Pascal for delivery to the CIL.

Ben was going to freak out when he saw his stepfather pushing a copy of Madelaine Reeves into the lab.

On the way, Booker joined him. "How are we traveling?" he asked, casting his eye over the droid.

"Pretty much on schedule."

"She looks good."

"Yeah, I was surprised at the progress that's been made by the art department."

"The demand for better resolution has skyrocketed since you last worked here. It forced us to evolve."

"The bio-printers are a huge advance."

"Absolutely."

"They must be expensive."

"They are, but we compensate for them through increased revenue."

They came out on the first floor. Pascal rolled the droid along the catwalk toward the CIL.

Booker noticed he was visibly nervous. "I know what you're

thinking," he said.

"Do you?"

"Sure I do. You're worried about what Ben will think when he sees you back at your old job."

"Is that what it is? I've got my old job back?"

"It looks like it. At least for now."

"Until Sporn gets what he wants, and then …" He left off. He didn't want to think that far ahead.

"I don't know what happened between you and Hector. I don't want to know. My only concern is that we finish this on time."

"Spoken like a true believer."

Booker detected an air of disingenuity in Pascal's quip. But he didn't pursue it.

They came to the CIL entrance door. "You first," Booker said.

Bracing himself, Pascal pushed the door open.

The boys were deeply buried in the Madelaine dossier. It wasn't until Booker and Pascal had wheeled the droid fully into the room that they transferred their attention.

Ben was the first to respond. "Pascal! What are you doing here?"

"Do you want the long story or the short one?"

"Boys," Booker said, "we don't have time for stories. I want to introduce you to Miss Reeves 2.0."

Tom got up and shook hands with Pascal. "It's an honor."

"The honor is all mine," Pascal replied.

Ben watched this exchange with a creeping sense of the surreal. He had long imagined working beside Pascal in the lab, but that had been just a fantasy. To see it happening for real, and right when Booker had charged them with uploading Miss Reeves' cognitive patterns into an A2 copy of her body … It was enough to make his head whirl.

And what a copy it was!

As if drawn by a magnet, he went up to her and began examining her features.

The art department had indeed done a terrific job. Right down to the color of her skin, the freckles across her nose, and the peach fuzz over her upper lip and around her ears. The only thing Ben couldn't tell was the color of her eyes, because they were closed. They would not open until her behavioral sequencer was programmed and activated – and that was still some way off.

"How is the configuration file going?" Booker asked.

"Not finished yet," Ben said absently.

"Well, with Pascal here to help you now, that should speed things up. Remember, tomorrow by noon."

"So you're expecting us to work all night?" Tom said.

"Whatever it takes."

"But I've got dinner plans!" Tom complained.

"Forget about them."

"Yasu Doi!"

"He's not going to help you," Booker said.

"Are *you* going to help us?" Ben asked.

Booker tossed his head sideways. "Unfortunately, I have an important meeting after this. So it's just you three gentlemen. But I will be back early tomorrow morning to check on your progress." He looked at each of them in turn to get their acknowledgment of commitment, then left the room.

CHAPTER TWENTY-THREE

Day Two: 7:30 p.m.

The moment Booker was gone, Ben bombarded Pascal with a barrage of questions. The first of which was: "What are you doing here?"

Pascal looked at Tom, looked at Ben. "Can I trust him?"

"You can trust Tom," Ben said.

Tom looked at Ben, looked at Pascal.

Pascal said, "Sporn came to arrest me today."

An anguished expression passed across Ben's face. "Does he … Does he know?"

Pascal shook his head. "I never told him. I will never tell him. Not even on pain of torture."

Tom looked perplexed. "Is there something I'm missing here?"

"I'd explain it to you," Pascal said, "but it's really between me and Ben. You'll just have to take it on trust."

"Okay …"

"So what so we do now?" Ben asked.

"I'm not sure. It's all happening so fast, I need time to think."

The three of them stared at the Reeves droid. There was no

question as to the quality of her likeness. Weighing heavily on their collective minds, however, was whether they could program her behavioral sequencer to match her appearance, so that she acted consistently and flawlessly.

"One thing is for sure," Pascal said, after a long silence. "There is no way in hell we can do what they want in the time given. It's just not possible."

"It wouldn't even be possible if we had a whole week. A whole lifetime," Tom added.

Pascal caressed his beard in thought. "Although ... having said that, there may be another way."

Ben looked at him, unsure what he was getting at. Tom raised his eyebrows quizzically.

"You guys still extract mocaps from customer videos, right?" Pascal asked.

"It's our bread and butter," Tom said.

"Right. So we need to scour the web for every piece of video footage of Miss Reeves we can get our hands on, because the 'client' is blind to our purpose. Right?"

"Yeah," Tom said. "So what are you getting at?"

"I know what he's getting at," Ben said. "But it's not going to happen."

"What's not going to happen?" Tom said.

"Why not?" Pascal said, staring at Ben.

"Because she doesn't even know me!" Ben said.

"What the hell are you talking about?" Tom said.

Pascal nodded to Ben. "You'd better tell him."

Ben thought his heart was going to stop. He looked at Tom apologetically. "It wasn't a lie," he said. "I promise. It's just that I was scared to tell you."

"What didn't you tell me?" Tom said.

"I met Miss Reeves in person yesterday."

Tom's mouth fell open.

"I'm sorry."

"Sorry?" Tom exclaimed. He was on the verge of getting angry. "You kept that from me the whole time? So she was your date?"

"Hell no!" Ben said. "No, it has nothing to do with that."

"Well, then, I don't understand," Tom said.

Pascal intervened. "Again, it's a long story. I don't think we have time to go into all the details of it. I just want to say, Ben, you need to go and pay her another visit. For all our sakes."

"A visit? No, no!"

"Why not?" Tom said. There was a hint of belligerence in his voice.

"Because I'm a nobody. Why would she want to see me again?"

Pascal was shaking his head. "Ben. You seem to have conveniently forgotten something."

"What?"

"Come on, you told me yourself – you were the Minister's guest!"

Tom nearly exploded. "You were *what?*"

"Settle down, Tom. The point is, Ben, you can use that. It will open doors."

"Is that what you think?"

"Absolutely!" Pascal and Tom blurted out in unison. "And besides," Pascal added, "I need you to test a theory."

"What theory?"

"Actually, two theories. First, there is a possibility that Sporn arrested Miss Reeves – in which case, she won't be at the Corsi Club tonight. But we can only test that theory by actually going there."

"And the other theory?" Ben asked.

"Sporn didn't arrest Miss Reeves, but he wants us to make a copy of her so he can trick her brother."

"So how am I supposed to test that?" Ben asked.

"We don't so much test it as blow it out of the water," Pascal said.

"Blow it out of the water? I'm not following," Ben said.

"By telling her, of course!"

"Oh …"

"That's why you have to go there tonight. In fact, you have to go there right now!"

"Right now?" Ben repeated meekly. The very thought of doing something that daring rattled him to his core. A spontaneous act toward someone he hardly knew. It was completely out of character. Yet … there was a part of him that felt an infinitesimal surge of excitement at the idea. A thrill, if it could be called that. The thought that he might see her again, hear her voice, feel her presence …

Sensing Ben's dilemma, Pascal said, "What you need to do is stay calm and form a plan. Like we always do, right?"

Ben forced himself to nod in agreement.

"You need to rehearse what you're going to say so you don't get tongue-tied, yeah?"

"Yeah."

"Just think of it as a replay of yesterday. Can you do that?"

"I can try."

"Excellent."

Ben got up, almost as if in a daze, and fumbled for his keys. He found them and jingled them in his hand. But he didn't move.

"What are you waiting for?" Pascal said.

"I don't know," Ben said. "Is this really a good idea?"

"It's the best idea ever," Pascal assured him.

Ben slipped his keys in his pocket and started for the door, but stopped. His expression was one of anguish. "What if the Minister finds out about this?"

Pascal hesitated a moment before answering. "Yes, that's a possibility. But I don't want you to think about that right now. Just go. Everything will take care of itself."

"Are you sure?"

"I'm sure I'm sure."

Ben reluctantly took the door. "And this is our secret?" he said at the threshold.

"Totally," Pascal said, putting his hand over his heart.

"You know, I love Ben like a brother," Tom said to Pascal after he was gone. "I hope you're not getting him into trouble."

"It's been a strange day," Pascal said, lost in thought.

"Did you really mean it when you said this could be make-or-break for us? I mean, not just for us, but the entire country? I thought that was a little overdramatic."

"No, I really meant it. There's a lot of things going on right now. I wish I could explain."

"Please do."

"Let me ask you something," Pascal said, taking a seat, a wave of tiredness coming over him. "Do you think Ben is a little bit naive about the Minister?"

"A little? He practically worships him."

"I thought so."

"So you think this will wake him up?"

"I hope so."

"So long as it doesn't get him into trouble. We all know he's not cut out for this sort of thing."

"Yeah, I realize that. But as his stepfather, I've also always known that one day he'd have to learn how to fend for himself."

"And you think the time has come?"

Pascal pondered the question for a moment. "I think we're well past that. I don't think he has a choice anymore."

CHAPTER TWENTY-FOUR

Day Two: 8 p.m.

The neighborhood looked rougher than Ben remembered it. Maybe because this time he'd come by motorcycle, alone. On the way, he'd tried to rehearse his opening lines so he didn't come across as a nervous idiot, a character type that people seemed to automatically pin on him. He liked word puzzles, it was true, but only because it compensated for his lack of confidence with conversations. The same attitude applied to his motorcycle. Almost every vehicle on the road was run by artificial intelligence. But a motorcycle had to be controlled by a human (or droid). He liked the challenge. It forced him to keep control over his body, to react quickly and decisively.

He had already come off twice. Luckily no broken bones, just some nasty scrapes. Ordinarily, that would have made most people give up. But Ben saw the other side of it. Rather than retreat into his shell, a behavior he could easily slip into, he'd consciously decided that he needed to bump into the world. Feel it. Even if that meant sometimes injuring himself.

It wasn't physical injury that scared him; rather, it was misunderstanding social situations. When that happened, it didn't just make him lose confidence with words, but led to an acute feeling of confusion and frustration.

At least the doorman would recognize him. That would help.

Except when he got there, the doorman wasn't the same person. He was a muscle-bound gorilla without a hair on his body, who just grunted and shut the door.

But Ben forced his foot in at the last second.

The doorman put his weight against the door, but Ben held fast. "I was here last night with the Minister of the Interior."

The pressure against his foot eased off.

"Say again?"

"I answer to Hector Sporn."

The door opened. "The Minister isn't here."

"Then I want to speak to Miss Madelaine Reeves."

"She's not here either."

"But I have some very important information for her. It's urgent." That was as far as he had rehearsed.

The doorman scrutinized Ben with a vague expression of unease. "Lucky for you, then, her agent is here."

He led Ben through the main room to the backstage area, where Madelaine's dressing room was located. Her door was shut, but Ben heard a voice behind it, arguing with someone.

The doorman knocked. Presently the door opened.

"Yes, what do you want?"

"I've got someone here to see you."

"I'm not expecting anyone."

Ben said, "I'm a friend of Miss Reeves."

The agent looked Ben up and down, as if to say *Maddie doesn't have friends like that*, but he let him in anyway.

He had been on the phone. He told the party at the other end that he was busy and hung up. "How can I help you?" he said, shutting the door behind them.

"My name is Ben Huxley. I was here last night with the Minister of the Interior."

"Is that supposed to mean something to me?"

"I suppose not."

"What exactly do you want?"

"I would like to speak to Miss Reeves, if that is possible."

The agent let out a sardonic laugh. "Either you're an idiot or you're very smart."

"I don't understand …"

"That's the million-dollar question, isn't it: where is she?"

Ben tried not to give away too much with his expression.

"So you don't know."

"Know what?"

"She's missing."

"Since last night?"

"I was supposed to meet her here before her show. She didn't turn up and no one seems to know where she is."

"Has she ever done this before?"

"Never."

"Maybe she's held up somewhere."

"She would have called by now."

"Maybe she's sick."

"Then she'd definitely call."

"Maybe she can't."

"You're full of ideas, aren't you?"

"How else can you explain it?"

"That's what I'd like to know. I can't explain it."

"Is she … Will she be performing tonight?"

"She better be."

"In that case, I'm sorry I can't help you. I guess I'd better be going now." Ben held out his hand. "Thank you for your time."

The agent shook his hand. Ben turned toward the door.

"Wait."

He turned.

"What did you say your name was again?"

"Ben Huxley."

"My name is Maxwell Biedermeyer. If you speak to her, tell her to call me."

"Okay, sure, but I don't have her number."

"I thought you said you were her friend."

"I met her for the first time last night."

"Is that so?"

"Yes."

"Interesting."

"In what way?"

"That makes you and the Minister the last people who saw her."

Ben shook his head. "I left early …"

Biedermeyer scrunched up his brow.

"Maybe the Minister took her home to his place."

The agent's expression changed to one of incredulity. "You're having me on, right?"

"No …"

"They live in the same building, for Yasu's sake. He doesn't have to take her home! That's how they —" He cut himself off. Disgusted at himself for even thinking it.

"Do you mind me asking where?"

"Carver Tower, of course!"

"Of course …"

"In any case, I already called her there."

Ben fell silent. Tried to think. Biedermeyer began to get impatient.

"What if I … Maybe if I …"

"What?"

"I'd like to visit her apartment."

"What do you expect to find?"

"Proof she actually went home."

"I see. You realize Carver Tower is a secure building. They

don't just let anyone in there."

"Yes, I know, but …"

"What?"

"I have some very important information for her. It's urgent."

"Is that so?"

"Yes."

"Would you mind sharing it with me?"

"No."

The look of annoyance returned. The agent studied Ben for a moment. "So if I give you her details, you promise not to share them with anyone?"

"Absolutely."

Biedermeyer asked Ben for his number. Ben took out his VidPhone and gave it to him. Biedermeyer sent him Madelaine's details and told Ben to get back to him right away if he found anything out. As her agent, he needed to stay at the club in case she suddenly appeared.

"I'll do my best."

CHAPTER TWENTY-FIVE

Carver Tower was the tallest building in the city. A gleaming skyscraper with a twist. The upper floors were two stories high, giving them enormous ceiling space and light. They were surrounded by vertical vegetation that earned the tower the nickname "Garden in the Sky." It also earned the ire (and envy) of many citizens, because while they often suffered water restrictions, the tower clearly enjoyed unlimited water usage.

The lobby was manned by two Gormlings – which apparently hadn't always been the case. It looked like Reeves' bombing of the Ministry of Justice building had changed that.

They stopped Ben at the entrance. He told them he was running an errand for Miss Reeves' agent, which was kind of true. They patted him down and let him into the lobby. Ben went up to the concierge's desk, where he explained to the gentleman there that he was here to see Miss Reeves. The concierge looked at him doubtfully, but called her apartment nevertheless. When there was no answer, he told Ben that she wasn't at home and that he ought to come back another time.

Ben said that he had tried her private number but wasn't getting a response, that's why he'd come here. He asked if he could visit her apartment. The concierge shook his head and said it wasn't possible. In that case, Ben said, he'd like to speak to the building manager; he wasn't going to go anywhere until he did.

The concierge gave him an annoyed look, but lifted the phone again and dialed.

"That won't be necessary," came a voice over the desk intercom. "Send him up."

The concierge put the phone down. His attitude changed to one of consternation. "Yes, sir." He directed Ben to the elevators, called one down, then swiped his security card. Ben saw the penthouse floor indicator light illuminate. This was totally unexpected.

His ears popped as the elevator whisked him skyward. He came out into a large vestibule manned by an in-house security guard. The guard patted him down again, then buzzed him through a heavy steel door.

Ben found himself in a large foyer. Exposed steel beams caged a polished concrete floor. The walls were covered in a profusion of greenery. The sound of trickling water filled the air. Up above, a clear glass ceiling provided unobstructed views of Zephyr, Natchator's largest moon, which was currently high in the sky. Its light cast everything in a luminous glow.

"So, this is the illustrious Master Huxley," came a voice.

Ben looked down to see a man approaching him. It was Laurent Carver. He looked so much smaller than he did on the public broadcast monitors. Thinner, too. He cut a rakish figure, his hair slicked back, revealing a high forehead. As he closed the gap, Ben observed that his earlobes were huge, something he had never noticed before. They seemed quite out of proportion to the size of his skull.

When they finally stood face to face, Ben was surprised to see that the man's eyes were sparkling, as was his smile.

"Welcome to Carver Tower," he said, proffering his hand.

Ben shook it. It was extremely dry compared to his own, which was embarrassingly clammy.

"I'm Laurent Carver," he said. "But of course you already know that."

Ben stood there, speechless, staring.

Seeing his reaction, Carver swept his arm around the voluminous space that was his apartment. "It never fails to impress first-time visitors."

"It's huge," was all Ben managed to say.

Carver walked him to the other end of the apartment. Floor-to-ceiling windows allowed views over much of the city. The usual brown-and-gray daytime drabness was replaced with a profusion of colored lights and glowing street lamps. In the far distance, Ben could make out the twinkling lights of ships moored in the shelter of Halfa Bay.

"So, you're looking for Miss Reeves," Carver began.

"Yes. Have you seen her?"

"Have I seen her? Of course I have! Our city is blessed to have such a wonderful voice. And she's a looker, too."

"Sorry, I meant since last night."

"Last night?"

"Yes."

"Come to think of it, no."

"I was wondering, can we see her apartment?"

"I can check to see if she's in, if that's what you mean."

"She's not, as far as we can tell."

"I see." He looked out at the view. "We value the privacy of our tenants. It's not taken for granted."

"I understand."

"Is there something I should know?"

"It's just … No one seems to know where she is."

Carver rubbed the back of his gangly neck in thought. "Maybe she just wants some time to herself?"

"She was supposed to meet her agent before tonight's show,

but never showed up. According to him, she has never done that before."

"Hmmm … that sounds unusual. I've always known her to be punctual as well. I suppose it won't hurt to at least knock on her door."

After knocking several times and not getting an answer, Carver produced a skeleton key from his jacket pocket and slipped it into the lock. "Landlord's privilege," he said, opening the door, then added, "although technically, I'm not supposed to use it."

Ben followed him in. The apartment's ceiling was double height like Carver's, but the similarity ended there. Beautifully embroidered semi-translucent curtains hung from the ceiling, dividing the apartment up into a labyrinth-like maze. An infinite series of arabesque patterns blended and shimmered where the edges of the curtains crisscrossed each other. The effect messed with Ben's sense of depth perception, adding to the kaleidoscopic atmosphere of the space.

Ben and Carver moved through the curtains like apparitions. "Madame Reeves," Carver called out. "Are you home?"

Ben found himself alone in another part of the apartment, seemingly lost. "Miss Reeves?"

He pulled a curtain aside to discover he was in the kitchen. It was the largest open space that he had encountered so far and had a reassuring normality about it. There was a large dining table that could seat at least a dozen people. It was flanked by a generous prepping bench, a range-top, and a deep sink. A vase of wilted sunflowers occupied the center of the table. Sheltered beneath it was a breadboard with some dark bread, dried cheese, and figs. It was accompanied by a tulip glass that still had the dregs of some red wine in it. The bottle was in the sink, a Cabernet.

"Oh, there you are," Carver said. Ben turned around. "I found her bedroom — well, her bed, anyway. It's hard to tell if it's been used recently."

"This to me looks at least a day old," Ben said, indicating the bread and cheese.

"Yes, it looks like she never came home."

"Do you think we should report it to the police?" Ben asked.

"No. It's too early for that," Carver said decisively.

Ben was in no position to question him. But he also knew things Carver didn't know. Or at least presumed he didn't know.

For some reason he suddenly felt thirsty. Seeing the tap right there, he turned it on and drank from cupped hands.

"She has glasses, you know," Carver said.

"Sorry, I had a sudden attack of thirst."

"It costs a fortune to pump water up here," Carver said, referring to the small amount Ben had wasted by using his hands instead of a glass.

A crushing sense of remorse descended over him. "Sorry, I wasn't thinking."

"It's okay!" Carver said, breaking out into a boisterous laugh. "You should have seen the look on your face."

Ben couldn't understand how a man as powerful as Carver seemed to get such pleasure out of teasing someone.

"Come on," he said. "Let's get out of here — if we can find our way out."

Carver went first, parting the curtains as he went. Very quickly he seemed to get lost. Ben went in a slightly different direction and found the entrance first.

He called out to Carver, who was back among the curtains somewhere. When he eventually came out, he said, "Blind as a bat."

Back in Carver's penthouse, Ben excused himself and called

Biedermeyer. He explained what he'd seen, adding that he was of the opinion that Maddie had not come home. Biedermeyer thanked him and said to call him right away if he learned anything new.

"Who was that?" Carver asked when Ben joined him again.

"Miss Reeves' agent."

"Already got the keys to the city, I see."

"Not really ..."

"I suppose I should tell you why I invited you up."

Ben wondered if he should brace himself for another prank.

"Word has it your research proposal was rejected."

Ben paused for a moment. "Oh, so you know?"

Carver went over to a mahogany-topped bar and picked out a bottle of whiskey. "There's not much that I don't know," he said. He got some ice cubes from a bar refrigerator and dropped them into a glass, then poured the whiskey. "Normally I'd invite my guest to share a drink with me. But something tells me you don't go in for that kind of stuff."

"No, I don't." *How did he know that?* Ben thought. "Some more water, then?"

"Yes, please."

Carver got a bottle of sparkling water out of the fridge and poured Ben a glass. Handing it to him, he said, "My father taught me to never trust a man who doesn't drink."

"I can be trusted."

"Of course you can." Carver took a sip of his drink and smacked his lips.

Ben took a tiny sip of his water.

Carver studied him silently for a moment. "I've been following your work," he said at last. "I get my reports through Booker."

Ben's chest tightened.

"Relax," Carver said. "It's not what you think."

Ben tried to relax. He took another sip of his water.

"It has come to my attention that Sporn wants to appropriate the decommissioned A2s. Males, of course."

So Carver knew about this as well. He almost opened his mouth and blurted out, *And now he's ordered us make a copy of Miss Reeves*, but he bit his tongue. A rarity for him, perhaps because it was accompanied by something equally rare: a sense of awareness, in this case a desire – much to his surprise – to protect her. Where it came from, and why, it puzzled him, so much so that he completely forgot his promise to Sporn, breaking it for the second time. "Yes, he wants us to turn them into reconnaissance units."

"Makes sense."

"I suppose so."

Carver took another slug of his whiskey. "Except … Now, don't get me wrong, I want a safe city as much as the next man, but at heart I'm a Libertarian."

Ben didn't quite grasp what he was getting at.

Noticing his lack of understanding, Carver rephrased himself. "What I'm trying to say, just between you and me, is that once that new function goes into operation, it's going to be hard to repeal. You get what I mean?"

"Yes. It's hard to change something once it has been done."

"Which makes me think that what we need is a back door."

"A back door?"

"A failsafe mechanism that you can implement in case they go rogue."

"I see. Yes, that would be a good idea."

"I'm glad you agree."

Ben thought about it some more and said, "There is one problem, though."

"What?"

"Booker signs off on everything we do."

Carver took another slug of his whiskey. "I wouldn't worry about that. You just worry about implementing that back door and I'll take care of Booker."

Emboldened by the conversation, Ben asked, "So who does Booker work for? You or the Minister?"

At that, Carver let out an explosive guffaw. "Why, me, of course!"

CHAPTER TWENTY-SIX

Day Two: 9:30 p.m.

Ben returned to the CIL brimming with news. He was so excited that he stumbled over his words. Pascal had to calm him down to get some sense out of him.

"So you're saying Carver asked you to program a back door into Sporn's reconnaissance units?"

"Yes!"

"Well I'll be damned," Pascal said. "And I thought the man was an unprincipled greedy capitalist."

"He lives in a penthouse," Ben said.

Tom laughed. "I bet he does!"

"Well, I think it's safe to say that you've confirmed my initial hypothesis," Pascal said. "Either he's arrested her, or kidnapped her, or forced her into hiding somewhere."

"It looks that way, doesn't it?" Tom said.

Ben looked at the Reeves droid hanging in the stand. "So what do we do now?"

"Her configuration file still needs a lot of work," Tom said. "We've barely programmed the essentials."

"If we start her up, we'll effectively become Sporn accomplices," Pascal said. "If we don't, then I'm sure he'll find someone else to replace us, however long it takes, and in the meantime, we'll be carted off to the Labor Camps – if we're lucky."

"I don't like the sound of that," Tom muttered.

"But we can't just pretend we don't know," Ben said. "Sooner or later he's going to find out."

"What was your impression of Carver?" Pascal asked. "Do you think he'll tell Sporn about your visit?"

Ben shrugged. "I don't know. In any case, it makes no difference. Gormlings guarded the entrance to his building, and there were security cameras everywhere."

"Hmmm."

"I'll be honest with you guys," Tom said. "I say we just give Sporn what he wants. I really don't want to be a martyr."

Ben nodded in sympathy, even as he grimaced at the moral implications of that act.

"There might be another way," Pascal said.

The boys looked at him with hope in their eyes.

"In fact, there are two possibilities. The first is that we sabotage the configuration file. That way —"

"Whoa," Tom cut in. "That's pretty heavy. There's no way we can go back once we do that."

"Assuming we did," Ben said, "how would we implement it?"

Pascal thought about it for a moment, tugging at his beard. "We program her to disagree with anything that might cast a bad light on her brother, her family, or us, for that matter."

"You're saying we make her disagree with whatever the Minister tells her to do?"

"Yes."

"What's the other possibility?" Ben asked.

"We kidnap her."

The boys looked at Pascal with a mixture of amazement and incredulity.

"Can you think of a better idea?" he said.

Tom shook his head. "Talk about jumping from the frying pan into the fire. Stealing Mimetic Machines property, owned by the Minister, no less. Why don't we just cut our wrists and be done with it?"

"Yes, stealing MM property is a big step. But look at it this way. If we sabotage the configuration file, he'll know it was us. If we give him what he wants, everyone loses. That just leaves the kidnap option."

Ben looked at Pascal, shaking his head.

"What?"

"I don't see how that would work. Where would we take her? Who's gonna take her? We can't all take her. What's going to happen to you?"

"I have no idea what's going to happen to me," Pascal said. "I was assuming that when Sporn released me, he set me free."

"Well, you can't bring her back to your place. Sporn will suspect you right away," Ben said.

"And there's no way I'm bringing her back to my place!" Tom said.

"Or my place," Ben added.

"Actually," Pascal said, "I wasn't thinking of bringing her back to anyone's place. I had a completely different idea in mind."

"Such as?" Tom said.

"We take her upriver. All the way to the Olongo jungle."

"We?" Tom said.

"Not you, Tom," Pascal said. "I wasn't expecting you to get involved."

They looked at Ben.

"Me?"

They kept looking at him.

"Surely ... y-you can't be serious?" Ben stammered.

Tom and Pascal's expressions were indeed serious.

"But ... but what about my future? I had plans!" Ben exclaimed. His research proposal raced through his mind. A big part of him still wanted to believe it hadn't been rejected. Stealing the droid would mean he would have to give up on it. Even more, it would mean he would have to give up on his entire dream.

"We all had plans," Pascal said. "And look what became of them."

"I agree," Tom said. "Pascal's right. The minute we started decommissioning those A2s we should have known. *I knew.* I mean, we talked about it a million times. It's just that I didn't want to believe it."

Ben's thoughts kept racing. He searched for excuses. Something he was good at. Picking holes in other people's arguments. "Okay," he said, "let's assume we get her out of the building. I'm not saying we can, but let's say we can. What then? We still have to get her through the Old City walls. There's no way that's going to happen. It's impossible."

"I beg to differ," Pascal said.

"How so?"

"You're forgetting about the Jammers."

"The Jammers? What can they do?"

"A lot more than you think."

Ben shook his head vigorously. "No. Even if they could help, siding with them is treasonous. I won't do it."

"Ben," Pascal said, putting a hand on his son's shoulder, "we've already committed treason. Just discussing this is treason."

"But it doesn't have to leave this room. No one has to know about it."

Pascal gave Ben a reprimanding look. The kind that a father gives a child.

"What?"

"Let's be honest. You know as well as I do that once Sporn gets ahold of you, you'll talk. You won't be able to keep any secrets from *him*."

Ben looked down like a guilty dog.

"I've already played my hand," Pascal said. "Sporn is going to get me sooner or later. Probably sooner. But Tom here – he still has a chance."

"I was thinking," Tom said, "I can say I was down in the canteen having dinner."

"That'll do," Pascal said.

"But you won't survive the Labor Camps," Ben said to Pascal. "I can't stand the thought of you going there."

"Neither can I," Pascal admitted. "But don't get too far ahead of yourself. Think of Sporn. What's going to happen to him when he doesn't get what he wants?"

Ben mulled that thought over. "So you're saying …"

"What I'm saying is that he'll probably get into even more trouble than us. He'll have to face the Head Curate." He made a rapid gesture. "No way! Tom was right on that one. I'd rather go in for wrist-slashing than choose that option."

"So you think there's a chance he won't send you to the Labor Camps?"

Pascal shrugged. "Who knows what a desperate man will do?"

"Okay, let's assume I manage to get her out of the building and past the Old City walls," Ben said. "What then? I don't know the first thing about the Olongo jungle … and even if I did manage to make it that far, what about the Warraweans? If they don't kill me, they'll certainly kill the droid. Everyone knows that."

"True. True. But you're still not looking at this the right way. You're forgetting that she is Vernon Reeves' sister."

Ben blinked a few times. *Of course.* "So you think they'll believe that?"

Pascal indicated the Reeves droid hanging in the stand. "You tell me. Have you ever seen such a lifelike A2 before?"

Ben looked at her. He couldn't disagree. "I suppose not," he said. "But behaviorally …"

"They don't know the first thing about Miss Reeves," Tom interjected. "So what difference does it make?"

It was true. What would they know? It wasn't like she gave concerts in the Olongo. "I guess you're right," Ben said.

Pascal paused for a moment to collect his thoughts. "I've been searching for a way to say this for some time now …" He took stock of himself. "I may as well just come out with it."

"What?"

"This is your big chance Ben. To finally learn about your father firsthand. You hear what I'm saying?" He searched Ben's face for a response. "I know for a fact that he was highly respected among the Warrawean people he lived with. There might even be someone still alive who knew him. You never know. It has always been my hope that one day you could make this journey. Meet someone other than me or your mother who knew him. It's just that … Well, it's come a little earlier than I expected, and not in the way I expected."

"You really mean that?"

"From the bottom of my heart."

Ben's muscles went weak. He took it as a sign that deep down, he believed what Pascal was saying was true. He would never feel completely comfortable with himself, with his life, if he didn't find out what really happened to his father. Why he'd broken his promise. Why he'd never come back. His letter had raised more questions than answers. Eventually they would have to be addressed, whether Ben liked it or not.

"You're right," he said at length. And hearing himself say it, he straightened up, surprised at his own conviction.

Pascal breathed a big sigh of relief.

"I hate to spoil the party," Tom said, "but we still don't know how to get her out of the building, let alone to the Olongo jungle. There are security cameras everywhere …"

"Ah!" Pascal said. "I've got a very simple solution for that."

The plan, according to Pascal, was to lift the Reeves droid over the wall using a fire hose from the basement carpark of the building. He'd seen it when he arrived earlier, getting out of Sporn's car. Tom's job was to get the hose. Regarding the security cameras, the solution was surprisingly simple. All Ben and the droid had to do was wear halos made from LEDs. This would white out any images in the cameras. The factory floor had bins full of them, so there was no problem getting those.

"Totally old school," Tom said, "but I like it."

It still left the cameras on the wall, but these could be taken care of with a long pole by pushing them off-axis. The question was where to get the pole. Ben suggested they dismantle the H-frame that transported the droid and use that. As soon as he said it, he realized he had committed himself, despite himself.

"That just leaves the configuration file," Tom said. "I feel really bad about it. It's almost empty. At the very minimum, we have to give her a name."

"I believe that honor is yours," Pascal said to Ben.

"Really?"

"I agree," Tom said.

"Okay …"

"Don't take too long," Pascal said. "I think we all agree that time is of the essence now."

Ben got up and paced back and forth. "What should I call her?"

"Why don't you just call her Madelaine?" Pascal said.

"No," Ben said. "I want her to have her own identity."

"Fair enough."

Ben kept on pacing. Pascal and Tom waited.

"I've got it!" he said eventually.

"Well, let's hear it," Tom said.

"Myra."

"Myra?" Tom said. "That's an interesting choice. Are you sure?"

"Yes."

"Does it mean anything?" Pascal asked.

"Yes it does, in fact: My Recursive Android."

Tom laughed. "I should have guessed."

"So it's Myra, then?" Pascal said.

"Punch it in," Ben said.

Tom added it to the configuration file. "Ready to upload when you are."

Ben went over to his workstation and hit the ENTER key, initiating the startup process. All eyes turned to "Myra."

Her body went rigid, then, in one smooth motion, she lifted her head and opened her eyes.

At first, she didn't react. There was a delay as she took in her surroundings. But then her face animated with an expression of wonderment.

Tom said, "Hi, how are you doing?"

Myra's eyes cast in his direction. She studied him for a moment. "This is not a dream, is it?"

"No, it's not. Do you know where you are?"

She looked around again. "I'm in a room."

"You're in the Cognitive Installation Lab at Mimetic Machines. This is the first time you've been powered up."

Myra lifted her hands, wriggled her fingers, briefly gazing at them. Then she stood up, taking her full body weight on her legs.

"Releasing," Ben said, hitting a key.

The two wires magnetically connected to her shoulder points released. Myra dropped ever so slightly, then rebalanced.

"How does that feel?" Tom asked.

"It feels good to be free," she said, stepping out of the stand.

"Wow! Hold on," Tom said. Myra was still connected to her

data cable. It was plugged into a socket discreetly positioned at the back of her skull, under her hair. He went behind her and unplugged it. "Okay, you're free to go now."

Myra walked forward a few paces, then stopped. Looked around again.

Pascal went up to her. "Hi, I'm Pascal Montaigne. Pleased to meet you." He offered his hand.

Myra shook it. "Pleased to meet you, Pascal Montaigne."

Ben came over, staring at her. He had the strangest feeling that his eyes were tricking him, that he was looking at the real Madelaine. Or nearly so. Because her movements didn't have the assurance he remembered. The way she held her head and gestured with her hands was stiff. But that aside, if he just looked at her face, at the way she looked back at him, it was uncanny.

"Pretty good, eh?" Tom said.

Ben agreed. He offered his hand to Myra. "Hi. I'm Ben. I'll be looking after you."

"Hello, Ben. Will you be my master, then?"

"I don't really like that word," Ben said. "Think of me as your friend."

"Equals?" Myra said.

"Yes. That would be good."

"What would you like me to do, Ben? Or should I make my own mind up and find something to do?"

"For now," Ben said, "I want you to follow my instructions. In a little while we'll be going on a trip together. For now I just want you to wait on my signal. Is that understood?"

"Yes. I will wait for your signal. Will it be a hand signal or a verbal signal?"

"A verbal signal."

"Very well."

The wall that surrounded Mimetic Machines was five meters high. Piers were spaced out along the wall about the same distance apart. Each one had a security camera that looked down, facing outward. Woodstock Street ran along the wall on the southeastern side. Ben's instructions were to wait there. His nearest landmark was Bunsen Lane, a small service road that branched off Woodstock and ran all the way down to the river. He parked his bike there and waited, hanging just around the corner so as not to be obvious.

Meanwhile, Pascal took Myra out of the CIL along the catwalk. Avoiding the cargo elevator, they went down the stairs to the ground floor, where there was a fire escape exit. Myra pestered him with questions the whole way. Pascal had to keep telling her to be quiet, that it was an "experiment."

"What kind of experiment?"

"It's a test."

"What kind of test?"

"A standard test we put all new droids through."

"It doesn't seem like a standard test to me. Why are we wearing these LED lights?"

"Stop asking so many questions."

"Why?"

They arrived at the door. "Because it will ruin the test." He took their LED halos off and threw them under the stairwell.

"Why are you throwing them away? We just put them on."

"We don't need them anymore. Here, hold this." He gave her one of the poles from the H-frame. He aligned the end of another pole with its end and began winding tape around the overlapping section.

"What are these for?"

"You'll see."

Tom arrived with the fire hose. He'd surreptitiously taken a steak knife from the canteen and used it to hack the hose off its spool. "I guess this is where I say good luck," he said, handing it to Pascal.

"Thanks."

"You know I'd help you ..." He trailed off.

"Yeah. It's all right. I can handle it from here."

Tom turned to Myra and said, "I'll see you later." He wanted to add, *And it was a pleasure meeting you*, but he refrained so as not to disturb their "delicate" experiment.

Pascal finished taping the third pole section to the other two. He opened the fire escape door a crack and peeked out.

The fence was about fifty paces away, separated by a well-manicured lawn. It was shockingly green under the harsh spotlights that surrounded the outside of the factory. The only areas in shadow were small sections of the fence where the piers were positioned. Pascal chose the nearest and, taking Myra's hand, scampered across the lawn to its meager protection.

"What are you doing?" Myra asked as Pascal began tying the fire hose around her waist and legs.

"It's part of the test."

He threw the nozzle end of the hose over the fence. While he waited for Ben to grab it, he took the pole and pushed the cameras on the two piers flanking their section of the fence off-axis, so that they pointed skyward.

Ben took his end of the fire hose and tied it to his motorbike frame. Pascal called for him to take up the slack.

"Now," Pascal said to Myra, "you're going to climb this wall."

"Why?"

"Because it's part of the test."

"It's a very strange test."

Ben got on his motorbike and began driving. Myra jerked forward. She cried out in surprise.

Pascal shushed her, telling her to "walk" up the wall using her legs. He lifted one of her legs and placed it on the wall. "Here, like this."

Myra seemed to get the idea. The hose snapped taut and she began walking up the wall ... until she got near the top. At that moment her legs collapsed under her and she smacked into the wall, hanging there like a puppet.

Pascal tried reaching up to her, but her flailing legs were just out of reach. He called out to Ben to wait, then took the pole and positioned it between Myra and the wall, telling her to grab it and use it to reach the top.

Myra tried, but failed. As strong as she was, she didn't have the coordination. That was something that would only develop with time. Eventually, out of frustration, Pascal took the pole and simply shoved it under her, where the fire hose bunched between her legs, and pushed as hard as he could.

It seemed to do the trick. Myra flopped onto the top of the wall and lay there like a fish out of water.

Pascal called out to Ben to throw his end of the hose back over. The nozzle sailed over the fence and landed with a thud. Pascal took up the slack and told Myra to drop down over the other side.

"Is it part of the test?"

"Yes."

"But what if I fall?"

"You won't fall. I've got you."

With Ben encouraging her on the other side, Myra slowly lowered one leg, then the other over the wall. She weighed about eighty kilograms, and Pascal found himself putting in more effort than he'd anticipated. But eventually his end went slack and he knew she'd made it.

Ben untied Myra from the hose and threw the rest back over. Pascal gathered it back up. As he did so, he called out one last time: "Don't forget, *The White Lotus*. Just say my name. That's all you have to do." When Ben called back, repeating the words, Pascal said, "That's the one. And Ben …"

"Yeah?"

"Good luck, son!"

With that, he scampered back to the fire escape door, which

he had kept ajar with the roll of tape he'd used earlier.

It was a peculiar sensation, having Myra ride pillion. As he accelerated, she gave his stomach a firm squeeze. The feeling was totally unfamiliar and he almost lost control of his bike. It wobbled, making her hang on even tighter, and he had to shout out, "Sorry!"

"Is this part of the test too?" she asked as he got the bike back under control.

"What test?"

"Okay, can we stop? I need to know what is going on."

"Not right now," Ben said. "But I will explain everything as soon as I get the chance."

He took her to his apartment. It was a necessary pit stop if he was going to carry out this crazy plan. He hadn't yet fully grasped the reality of what he was doing, but he was acutely aware that he was struggling for breath, and that told him something. Like he was taking a huge gamble he knew he couldn't win, but something was pushing him from behind, an invisible force over which he had no control. He started to feel like he was regressing. His emotions were on the verge of breaking out. A feeling he knew only too well from his preteen years. It had taken him over a decade to get ahold of them, and he'd be damned if they were going to get control of him now.

"Are you all right?" Myra asked.

Ben rushed to the kitchen sink and bent over it. "I just need a minute."

"Your heart rate is up and your breathing has become shallow," she said, engaging her remote bio-diagnostics.

"I don't need you to tell me that," he said gruffly. He jerked forward and dry-retched into the sink. A peel of saliva ran from his mouth.

Myra found a dishcloth and gave it to him. He took it and

wiped his mouth.

"What are we doing here?" she asked.

"We're need to get some stuff together ... for a trip."

"Where are we going?"

He threw the dishcloth aside. With a resoluteness that verged on anger, he said, "To see your brother."

"Oh," she said. "That sounds good."

He went straight to his bedroom wardrobe, avoiding her gaze. She followed him.

Ben grabbed a pair of khaki shorts that he'd once worn during his sojourn in the religious boot camps. He looked at Myra. She wore the standard once-piece bodysuit all Mimetic Machine droids shipped with. That wouldn't do. He found an old pair of jeans that looked like it would work, then took a pair of kitchen scissors to them and cut them short. Told her to put them on.

She promptly disrobed in front of him. Obviously she had not developed a sense of self-consciousness yet. Ben had seen naked A2s before, but never in the privacy of his own home. For some reason, it made him nervous. He felt himself flush with embarrassment. He tried to distract himself by finding a T-shirt for her. He ended up choosing a blue piece with an orange logo in the shape of the letter "H" stamped on the front. She took it and slipped it on.

Standing in front of her, looking at her, he figured he might as well keep looking. Mimetic Machines had long ago figured out the ideal female form, and they'd given her pert little breasts, with a hint of plumpness, reminiscent of the shape of pears. They were so inviting, the thought of reaching out and cupping them in his hands momentarily flashed through Ben's mind, but he promptly banished the idea.

He found a pair of sandals for himself and a pair of jogging shoes to replace Myra's form-fitting plastic boots. He stuffed his shorts and sandals, along with two PET bottles of water, some snack bars, and a packet of chips into his daypack, and on the way out, threw Myra's bodysuit and boots down the garbage chute.

The White Lotus was hemmed in with a dozen other teahouses in Krungtown, all of which had been established as a result of Wallacian immigration. These immigrants also practiced their own polytheistic religion, which they kept largely hidden from the Cosmonist regime. Still, when you entered a teahouse, you could see evidence in decorative items such as pictures and statuettes of deified animals and saints. It appeared that the Gormlings, whose job it was to act as the executive arm of the regime's doctrines, generally turned a blind eye to these icons in return for bribes, which they themselves kept hidden from the government.

Ben had eaten in Krungtown many times; it was one of his favorite watering holes, but this was the first time he had been to The White Lotus. He and Myra took a table right beside the front window, where they got a wide view of the street outside. Ben had had no intention of eating – his stomach was tied in knots and he had no appetite – but the smell of dim sum wafting through the teahouse began to change his mind.

A waitress brought a pot of jasmine tea and gave him a menu, then went away to attend to her other duties. Ben started reading the menu. A2 droids did eat, but only in very small quantities, just enough to provide the essential nutrients to keep their skin alive and healthy. Myra hadn't experienced eating yet, and said she would like to try dim sum.

"I'm thinking maybe siu mai," Ben suggested.

"What's that?"

"Pork dim sum."

"Sounds delicious."

"It is."

The waitress returned.

"A set of siu mai," Ben said. "Steamed."

"Is that all?" the waitress asked.

Embarrassed at such a pitifully small order, Ben said, "Okay, we'll also get some gow gee."

The waitress took the order and turned to leave. Spontaneously, Ben called after her, "Professor Montaigne."

The waitress stopped, gave him a quizzical look. Unsure if she'd heard him correctly, Ben repeated Montaigne's name.

The waitress' face became impassive and she walked off. Ben took this as a bad omen. He wondered if they should leave immediately.

Shortly, however, the dim sum arrived. It looked too inviting, and Ben decided to at least stay and eat. He took out a small dish, mixed some vinegar with soy sauce, and added some chili oil. Myra was fiddling with her chopsticks. Ben showed her how to use them, taking her hand and positioning them in her fingers.

They were halfway through eating when a Krung man came up to their table and asked them if everything was all right.

"Yes, everything's all right," Ben said.

"Good, good, very good," the man said. "Is there anything else I can help you with?"

Ben felt like this was his cue. "I'm here on behalf of Professor Montaigne."

The Krung man immediately put a finger to his lips. "We don't mention that name around here," he said very quietly. "When you're finished, kindly pay at the cash register, in cash, please."

He gave Ben a secret look that Ben didn't quite grasp, but he felt it could mean nothing other than just to do what he said, and if Pascal's words were true, everything else would take care of itself.

"What was that all about?" Myra asked.

"I'm not sure," Ben said.

"Why did you keep repeating Professor Montaigne's name?"

Ben picked up a dim sum with his chopsticks and put it into his bowl. He wrestled with himself for a moment, deciding on the right way to say what he was about to say. "You know how I told you we're going to visit your brother?"

"Yes."

"What I didn't tell you is that your brother is wanted by the regime."

"Oh?"

"He did a bad thing."

"What did he do?"

"He bombed the Ministry of Justice building."

"That's not good," Myra said decidedly.

"I suppose it is. A Gormling on duty was killed. Office windows were blown out and some workers were cut by flying glass."

"That's terrible."

"Yes, it is."

"Why did he do it?"

Ben poked at his dim sum. "He was protesting the government's decision to ban A2s outside the Old City walls."

"It's a human right to protest, so long as it's done peacefully."

"From what I read, he started out peacefully. But when the government rounded up the protesters and sent them off to the Labor Camps, he changed his mind."

"I see."

"It still doesn't justify it. But then again ..." He left off, not sure if he ought to say it.

"What were you going to say?"

"How many of those protesters sent to the Labor Camps do you think are still alive?"

"I don't know anything about the Labor Camps," Myra said. "They sound harsh."

"Harsh would be an understatement. People die there."

"Well, in that case, maybe a stronger form of protest is justified."

"Strong as in bombing?"

"I was thinking sending a delegate directly to the government with a signed petition."

"I'm afraid that wouldn't have achieved anything."

"Why?"

"They would have simply imprisoned the delegate and destroyed the petition."

"Then maybe a bomb is justified. So long as it doesn't cause too much damage and doesn't harm anyone."

"Unfortunately, people were harmed."

Myra dropped her head in thought for a moment, then raised it again and said, "I want to meet my brother and ask him myself."

Ben popped the last of the dim sum into his mouth and washed it down with a cup of tea. "Come on. Let's go."

They picked their way through the tables to the cash register. The lady there rang up twenty-five *tiels*. Ben paid, and she gave him a receipt.

"It's okay, I don't need a receipt," Ben said.

The lady said sternly, "Take it."

Ben took it. He folded it up, but as he did so he realized that it had writing on it.

Go to the restroom.

He put the receipt in his pocket. "Where's the restroom?"

The lady pointed to the back of the teahouse.

Ben and Myra made their way to the door. Ben opened it. There was a narrow corridor with a washbasin, and another door at the end. He opened the second door and saw an ordinary toilet.

From behind, he heard a scraping sound. The wall opposite the washbasin slid aside and the Krung man who had visited their table ushered them to come through.

Ben and Myra dutifully followed.

They went down a set of steps and came to another door. The man rapped out what seemed to be a special rhythm and the door swung open. He told Ben and Myra to go inside.

Cabal Haelstrom was a pale-skinned, pot-bellied man with long, scraggly salt-and-pepper hair and a stubbly face. A pair of bottle-top glasses hung off his nose, which was blotched and pockmarked. His voice was high-pitched and had a sing-song quality to it, like every sentence he uttered was part of a carefully metered rhyme.

"Come, come," he said, looking Myra up and down. "My, my. Marvelous! Better than I imagined. And your name is …?"

"Myra."

"Lovely. Pleased to meet you, Myra." He extended his hand. Myra shook it. "So, we need to give you a cover."

"Cover?" Myra said.

Haelstrom looked at Ben. "She doesn't know?"

"No."

Haelstrom rubbed his stubble in thought. "Okay. Take a seat, please." He pointed to what looked like a dentist's chair. It had armrests and was retrofitted with a host of electronic devices. One was cup-shaped, fitted in place of the headrest and connected to some heavy-duty cables.

"I would like to know what is going on," Myra said, standing her ground.

"Yes, yes," Haelstrom said, flicking his hair away from his glasses. "I'm sure you would. Take a seat and I will explain it to you."

Myra looked at Ben. He nodded at her. Seeing that Ben trusted Haelstrom, she went over and got into the chair.

Haelstrom eased her back so that her head was snug inside

the cup-shaped device. "You will feel a little tingle," he said, inserting an adapter through the back of the device.

Myra's body momentarily went rigid, then she relaxed again.

Haelstrom went over to his workstation and began typing in a series of commands. "This is going to run a Trojan sweep on you to make sure they haven't planted any tripwires in your system," he said, watching the data feed on a bank of monitors surrounding his workstation.

"Will it harm me?" Myra asked.

"No," Haelstrom said. "It's more for our protection than yours."

"Why do you need to be protected?"

"That's a good question. And the answer is that we're going to set you free."

Myra took a moment to absorb that. "But I am free, am I not?"

Haelstrom got up and went over to her so that she could look directly at him. "I promised I would explain to you what we're doing here, and I always keep my promise."

Myra blinked a few times, but said nothing.

"I've been told you're very special," Haelstrom continued. "The government has big plans for you."

"Oh ..." Myra murmured. The two contradictory statements – "set you free" and "government has big plans" – created a knot of cognitive dissonance in her logic circuits. "I suppose the question I need answered is: to whom do I belong? You or the government?"

"Excellent question!" Haelstrom said in his high-pitched voice. "You currently belong to the government, but by the time I finish with you, you will be free. You will belong to nobody."

"Oh, I see," she said. "I would like to say thank you, but I believe that unless a representative of the government is present to sign me over to a third party, liberating me without permission is illegal."

"It sure is," Haelstrom said, with devious delight. "But let me ask you something."

"Sure."

"Would you like to see your brother?"

"Yes."

"Then this is the only way it can be done."

Myra's head began to make little jerking movements. Her mouth twitched.

"Stay still, please," Haelstrom said.

Ben took one of Myra's hands into his own to comfort her. "It's going to be all right."

"No tripwires," Haelstrom said. "We're clear to set up a fake ID."

"Does that mean you can change her serial number?" Ben said.

"No. That's no longer possible. But no need to worry. There's a new workaround. So long as we reassign the job number to her root directory, we can fool the regime into thinking she is legit." He rubbed his stubble again. "The only thing we have to decide on is what role to give her. It has to be something beyond reproach. We usually go for diplomatic or medical, something of that nature. But in this case, that's not possible."

"So what are you suggesting?" Ben asked.

"She's obviously a copy, and a famous one to boot. The only ruse I can think of that would make sense is to cast her as a stunt double."

Ben looked at Haelstrom like he had lost his mind.

"Can you think of a better idea?"

Ben had to admit he couldn't.

"So stunt double it is." He rubbed his hands together. "All we have to do now is come up with a scenario that demands both of you to be outside the Old City walls."

"And what would that be?"

"A film shoot, of course! Myra will need to scout out some

scenic locations for Miss Reeves' next acrobatic dance. She is, after all, a dramatic artist."

"Okay …"

"The only problem is I don't have any dance routines or that sort of thing on file." He scratched his head.

"Can you pull something off the web?"

"If I had time."

Ben tried to think.

Haelstrom said, "I can give her some upper body rhythm, like clapping to music in time. That ought to be enough for now."

"Sure."

"You'll have to back her up, of course. If they ask why, you'll have to tell them you're her guardian."

So I have to lie again.

Haelstrom punched the codes in. "It's not going to be easy. They'll assign a guard, maybe two, to chaperone you. They'll follow your every move."

"So how do we get away, then?"

"Leave that to me. I've got that covered. You just take Myra to this address." He scrawled it on a piece of paper.

Ben read it. He had no idea where it was.

"It's in the direction you want to go. Just take the service road that runs parallel to the Tongassa Highway." He unplugged Myra. "How are you feeling?"

"I feel fine."

"Excellent. So, what do you think?"

"I think we're breaking the law."

"In a way, yes."

"There will be consequences."

"Probably."

"If I turn back now, I'll be betraying you. That's one reason to keep going forward. I would like to think that wanting to see my brother is an even stronger reason, but my programming doesn't allow me to be selfish. I'm caught in a bind."

"Let me tell you about a philosophical concept called the categorical imperative," Haelstrom said. "It says that a person should follow the law regardless of their personal desires. But what if that resulted in an outcome that was morally reprehensible? For example, turning your brother over to the law when he is actually a good person. He didn't go out of his way to murder people. He was reacting to the government's disproportionate response to peaceful protest. His best friend was taken to the camps, where he died. He responded to that in the best way he could. He left the bomb in a briefcase behind a column on the side of the building, but a Gormling found it and carried it into the building, thinking a minister had forgotten it. That's when it went off."

"He should have predicted that possibility."

Haelstrom scoffed abrasively. "People aren't computers. They think emotionally. How would you feel if your best friend was taken away and murdered by the government?"

"I see. People get hurt."

"They sure do."

"Then I will make sure that no one gets hurt from this day forward."

Haelstrom laughed raucously. "My dear computer. You just hurt my brain saying that."

"Sorry."

"Don't be. Be brave. Be bold. Say hi to your brother for me."

Myra looked at Ben. He forced a smile.

CHAPTER TWENTY-SEVEN

Day Two: Close on midnight

Ben and Myra left the White Lotus the same way they came in. The fake address Haelstrom gave Ben was cleverly located on the route that would take him to the Olongo jungle. Haelstrom could not provide any information as to Vernon Reeves' whereabouts once they got there; it would be up to Ben to solve that problem. He did suggest, however, that they ought to make the "tourist village by the pontoon" their first port of call. If there was any chance of contacting the rebels, that would be the most likely place. Although, he did say that they should not go around advertising that fact. "Hang around there for a while first and let people get to know you."

This vague information unsettled Ben. *Hang around so people get to know you* was not his style. From personal experience, it more often than not led to misunderstandings, not least because he lacked the social skills to express himself.

To make matters worse, he was now effectively Myra's guardian.

Myra seemed to already sense it. "It hasn't escaped my attention," she said as they mounted his motorcycle, "that almost everything that's been said to me, or that you said, for that matter, has been a lie."

"I haven't lied to you," Ben shot back indignantly.

"You haven't exactly told me the truth, let's put it that way. And you promised to explain everything to me."

"That I did, but I just haven't had a chance yet." He put his gloves on.

"You don't suppose you could tell me now?"

"No, because we're about to get into a very tricky situation, and I need to concentrate."

"Concentrate on what?"

"On telling lies."

"I didn't realize it requires concentration."

Ben didn't respond to that. He put his helmet on and engaged the bike's electrical system. This droid was starting to get on his nerves.

The South Gate should have been relatively quiet for this time of night, yet a throng of people crowded its entrance, jostling and fighting among themselves to get to the front of the line.

"What's going on?" Ben asked a stranger pushing past him.

"There's a storm coming."

That wasn't good news. "Storm" didn't mean just any ordinary storm, but a dust storm. He should have realized. As he'd ridden from The White Lotus, he'd absentmindedly noticed people shuttering up their windows. He'd been too engrossed in rehearsing his lines to register its import.

The news of the storm galvanized him into action. He got his papers out and waved them over his head in an attempt to grab the attention of a processing guard up ahead. The guard noticed him, but ignored him.

This wasn't a time to be polite. He pushed his bike through

the crowd, demanding that people get out of the way. Myra followed close behind. Together they fought against the press of bodies until they came up to the guard. Getting his full attention this time, Ben rattled off the words he had rehearsed: "There's a film crew on the other side of this wall waiting for us. We need to get there as fast as possible."

"No one's going to be filming when this storm hits."

"It's inside."

The guard looked Myra up and down. He detached a small device from his belt and scanned her with it. Checking its reading, he said, "Stay." He called the guard tower on his walky-talky. A burly guard came out and looked down at them. After a short exchange, the guard on the ground said, "Go to the side exit over there and wait."

With Myra following, Ben pushed his bike to the side exit, a large steel door guarded by a single Gormling holding a rifle by his side. After what seemed like too long in Ben's estimation, the Gormling opened the door and let them through. There was a short tunnel that ended at another steel door, which the Gormling also opened for them.

Ben couldn't believe his luck; it had been much easier than expected. But his excitement was instantly quashed when he saw two Gormlings waiting for them on motorcycles outside. One of them, a wiry individual who reminded him of a rat, demanded Ben's identification papers and an address. Ben gave him the address verbally. The rat briefly perused the papers, then handed them back, saying, "I will lead. Do not pass me. My comrade will hang behind. Do not fall behind. Do you understand?"

Ben looked at the other Gormling, a bulldog of an individual with short, stocky arms, and nodded that he understood.

The rat looked up at the sky nervously, then dropped his visor and sped off.

Ben accelerated his bike to match his speed. The route took them down to the Tongassa River and a service road that ran parallel to it. Through the gaps between buildings, Ben caught glimpses of the river. Lights on the opposite bank reflected off the water. As they progressed, the lights became hazier, a prologue of the storm that was approaching.

He felt a tap on his shoulder. Myra said, "We're no longer being followed."

Ben checked his mirror. The bulldog was nowhere to be seen. He cast a quick glance over his shoulder to make sure. Indeed, he was gone. In his place, another rider had appeared, a stranger wearing a cloth wrapped around his head, leaving just a small slit for a pair of goggles over his eyes. He looked strong and well-built. He pointed vigorously for Ben to take the next turnoff, which would lead them down to the water's edge. Ben nodded in acknowledgment.

The rat up front, however, seemed to have latched on to the ruse. He braked violently, sending his bike into a drift. The next moment, he was behind Ben.

Ben twisted his neck and followed him. The rat pulled up alongside the stranger and raised his gun. The stranger responded by accelerating his bike between Ben and the rat.

Ben didn't know if shots were fired or not. He thought he heard a *pop pop pop*. Distressingly, he saw the stranger collapse forward on his bike. The front wheel jackknifed, launching the stranger into the air. Without a rider, the bike tumbled chaotically.

It all seemed to be happening in slow motion. A part of him wanted to believe that he was just looking at a video game. But Myra's iron-strong grip around his stomach told him differently. This was real. And people were getting hurt. Maybe even killed.

What could possibly be so important about Myra that a complete stranger was prepared to risk his life for her? The fact that she was Madelaine Reeves?

His thoughts were cut short when he saw the rat take evasive action, jerking his bike around the wreckage into an open space.

Ben made an instantaneous decision. He rotated the throttle to maximum. The front wheel lifted off the ground as his bike bucked forward. Myra let out a squeal.

The rat accelerated after them. They raced like a pair of obsessed demons.

Suddenly the turn was upon them. Ben realized he was going too fast. If he braked too abruptly, they'd both come off. He needed to squeeze the levers just right.

He hit the rear brakes the hardest. Myra pressed hard into him, and the bike began to slide out. He let it go, balancing himself and Myra as a single unit. At the very last moment, he kicked out his leg, sliding his shoe over the ground, and peeled around the corner.

Just as he straightened his bike up, he saw the rat flash past in his rear-view mirror. His bike was standing on its front wheel, the rat somehow managing to hang on acrobatically. The bike continued past the turnoff.

Ben opened his throttle again. He had bought them a few extra seconds. Looking back to check, however, he saw the rat carve a big arc, bringing his bike back around. He cut across a footpath, jumped the gutter, and resumed the chase.

He raised his gun.

This was it. There was no running anymore.

And then it hit them. A wall of dust, sweeping them sideways like a giant broom.

Visibility was immediately reduced to just a few bike lengths. Ben looked around for the rat, but the dust obscured everything. He switched his light to high-beam, but it barely penetrated the murky darkness. Myra was digging her head into his back, seeking some protection. Breathing was becoming difficult. He needed to find shelter, and fast.

He fought on, reaching the river, turning onto a dirt track that ran alongside it and pushed on doggedly. How long he rode like this, he did not know, but eventually he had to stop when he nearly ran into a gate. By now he was totally disorientated. He fumbled his hands along the gate, looking for a way to open it. Eventually he found a latch. He undid it and pushed the gate open, riding until a dark shadow loomed ahead. As he drew closer, he could tell it was some sort of building. He had no idea if it was a house, or some other structure. All he knew was that he had to find a way to get inside.

Reaching the nearest wall, he touched it, and realized it was made of wooden planks. He got off his bike and began feeling along the wall, searching for a door, a window – anything that would open.

Myra grabbed him and pulled him back. He let her pull him around the lee side of the building, where they found some protection from the howling storm. Staring hard, Ben saw what he was looking for. A door. He turned the handle; the door opened easily.

Together, they stumbled inside. Ben took his helmet off and ran his hand around the inside of the door frame. Finding a switch, he flicked it on.

They were in a barn of some sort. A tractor occupied the center of the floor. Sacks of grain were stacked up along one side. Farm tools and other implements were placed against the opposite wall. On the ground next to them were pieces of machinery in various states of disassembly and repair. Shelves on the walls were piled up with various tools and an assortment of nuts, bolts, screws, and wires.

"I've got to get my bike out of the storm," he said, and went back outside.

Myra waited at the door. Ben came back with the bike a few moments later. He parked it next to the tractor and immediately went into a coughing fit. Myra whacked his back until he calmed down.

They looked at each other. Myra was heavily abraded. Ben's clothes were caked in dust, having borne the brunt of it as they rode.

He unslung his daypack and got some water out. He took a slug and passed it to Myra. She took a sip.

He told her to cup her hands, then poured some water into them. "Wash your face."

She splashed her face. Ben reached into his daypack and gave her a hand towel.

She dried her face, taking care to wipe her eyes clean. "That's better," she said.

Relieved and exhausted, Ben plonked himself onto one of the sacks. Myra sat next to him.

"Do you think he followed us?" she asked.

"No idea."

"How long do you think this storm will last?"

"They usually last for several hours, sometimes longer."

"Then we're stuck here for the night."

"Yeah."

Myra got up again and looked around. An old blanket was spread over the tractor seat and steering wheel. She pulled it off and shook the dust out of it.

"Do it over there," Ben complained.

"Sorry." She went to the back of the barn and shook the blanket there. Bringing it back, she held it out for him. "I thought you might need it."

Ben took it and put it next to him. He was tired, but he wasn't ready to sleep yet. If anything, he was still coming down from an adrenaline high. He had never been pursued by Gormlings before, and certainly not in a dust storm. He had an overwhelming sense that he was a fugitive now. Whatever life he'd had before this was gone. A wasteful memory. He winced, thinking about the possibility of a nonexistent future.

"What's wrong?" Myra asked.

"Nothing." Then he waved his hand at their situation. "This."

"We're in a farmhouse, I believe. We should be safe here until the storm subsides."

"That's one way of looking at it."

"What's that supposed to mean?"

"It means we have no idea what we're doing."

"I'm not sure why you say 'we,' since you're the one who got us into this predicament."

"Oh, so now it's my fault?"

Myra paused for a moment before answering. "Perhaps you could tell me what is on your mind?"

Ben reflected on the situation. Where to start? He tried to put his thoughts into order. But it required too much effort. "Can we do this later?" he said. "I'm too tired to think."

"You're right. You deserve a rest."

He took his VidPhone out. His first thought was to call Pascal. Let him know he was still alive. He dialed and waited. Presently, a man's voice came online. It wasn't Pascal. Ben immediately hung up.

"Who was that?" Myra asked.

"I don't know." He realized Pascal's VidPhone must have been confiscated when they arrested him. Idiot! What was he thinking? He ruminated over the possibilities. Could they use the call to track his location? Reacting swiftly, he powered his VidPhone down, opened the side slot, and removed his SIM card. For several moments, he stared at the card, hoping it had worked.

"Have you considered the fact that every Mimetic Machines droid is fitted with a data beacon?" Myra said.

"No … but yes, you're right."

"It's mandatory so that the Hathor Corporation can monitor the location and operational status of their RTGs."

Ben wondered why Haelstrom didn't tell him about this. *Damn it!* He should have known better.

"You need to disable it if you want them to stop tracking me."

"Yes …"

"You have to make a small incision just here," she said, lifting her T-shirt to reveal her lower abdomen, right about where her appendix would be if she were a real human.

Ben looked at her abdomen. The thought of cutting into it filled him with terror.

"I can do it, but I can't take it out by myself," she said.

Ben gave her a mortified look.

"It's necessary," she said, "if you don't want them to know where we are."

"True …"

Myra got up and started rummaging through the shelves of scattered tools. She found a pair of rusty shears. "This will do," she said, giving them to Ben.

Ben looked at the shears in dismay. "You're not serious."

"I only have a thin layer of organic skin," she reminded him. "Underneath that's a flexible carbon fiber shell. The skin will be easy to cut through, but the carbon fiber will require some vigorous sawing motions. Those shears are the best candidate for the operation."

Ben swallowed heavily.

"You will have to take care not to rend any of the coolant tubes that condition my skin," she said, lying down on a sack of grain, offering her belly up to him.

"Is there anything else I need to know?" Ben asked meekly.

"You will need a screwdriver to dismount the data beacon."

"Of course."

"I will not move, even though the initial incision will cause pain."

"That would be much appreciated."

"You can begin now."

Ben hesitated.

Myra took his hand and put it on her belly. "Just here."

The feel of her skin electrified him. It was soft and cool and he wanted to bury his face in it.

With an almost heroic effort of will, he forced himself to think like a mechatronics engineer. *It is just a machine*, he told himself. *It operates on logic. This is the right thing to do.*

Gingerly, and with great trepidation, he scored one edge of the shears across her skin. A thin line of blood appeared. Panicking, he rummaged around in his daypack for the hand towel and wiped it away. He cut again, this time with more force. The skin opened up and more blood oozed out. He wiped it again and cut once more.

Ignoring the blood this time, he inserted his fingers into the wound and felt around. With his fingertips he sensed the ridges of tubing that made up the water cooling system. He carefully hacked between the ridges until he broke through to the next layer, the carbon fiber shell. He hacked away at that until it too opened up. At last he could reach inside her body cavity and search for the data beacon.

Myra calmly said, "It's a disk-shaped device with two hold-down screws. Found it?"

"I think so." It was about the size of a large coin. He took a screwdriver and set to work undoing it. After repeatedly slipping the screwdriver off the screw heads (and with many apologies), he finally got them undone.

"There's a data cable. You'll have to cut it," Myra said.

Ben reached the shears inside and snipped the wires. He pulled the device out and showed it to her.

"Well done."

Looking at the gaping hole he had just made, Ben said, "We have to close this up. What do you suggest?"

"The only thing I saw that looked feasible is that coil of wire over there."

He found a pair of pliers, cut a length of wire off the coil, and brought it over.

"Cut it into small lengths. Do one at a time."

Ben did what he was told.

When he finished, he wiped away the blood and looked at the result. It wasn't bad, but it wasn't good, either. The looped wires pinched her skin together just enough to stop the bleeding. "Will the skin heal up?" he asked.

"It should."

He flopped back onto the nearest sack, exhausted. He could barely keep his eyes open.

Myra took the blanket and covered him with it. Within a few minutes, he was asleep.

Droids didn't sleep. Instead, they worked. Or, if they had no work to do, they could park themselves somewhere and switch to idle mode. Which was what Myra did, keeping her senses engaged just in case she needed to alert Ben of any danger.

CHAPTER TWENTY-EIGHT

Day Three: Early morning

"**B**en, wake up!"

"What … what's going on?" Ben sat upright, startled. He had been dreaming that he was decommissioning a male droid. The droid was issuing a noisy stream of complaints, saying that it didn't want to be decommissioned. Becoming increasingly frustrated, Ben eventually found a bunch of wires at the back of its neck and yanked them out. Sparks flew everywhere. Yet the droid kept on talking! He'd been in the process of devising even more drastic measures to shut it up when Myra had rudely awoken him.

"The storm has abated."

Ben rubbed his eyes. "What time is it?"

"It's coming up on dawn. If I may suggest, we ought to get going."

"Yes." He got up, walked over to a window. He tried to see outside, but the glass was covered in dust.

He went to the door, opened it a crack, and looked around. A faint brownish haze glowed on the horizon. A bird tweeted from a nearby tree. He stepped out fully and surveyed his surroundings. The air smelled of animal droppings mixed with the residual chalky odor of dust. He tasted it on his lips.

Myra joined him. As they had suspected, they were on a farm. The gate they'd come through was much closer than it had felt in the dark. On the windward side of the barn, in the near distance, was a farmhouse. Its appearance had been completely transformed by the dust, as if someone had spray-painted it from top to bottom in a single color. There didn't appear to be any activity inside it yet. Next to the house, in an adjacent paddock, was a row of hothouses. The plastic sagged from the weight of dust that had collected on them.

"You're right," Ben said. "Let's go."

He went back into the barn, got his bike, and wheeled it out. They quietly rode back through the gate they'd come through and followed the road until they came to a turnoff. This new road took them further east, as judged by the rising sun, which had started to present itself as a blood-orange half-disk on the hazy horizon.

There were very few tire tracks on this road. It was still largely covered in dust. A cloud of it billowed up behind them as they rode.

Ben looked at his battery levels. He still had about seventy-five percent remaining. He wasn't sure if that was enough to get them to the Olongo. He wasn't even sure if this was the best way to get there at all. But that wasn't his greatest worry. It was the fear that the Gormling rat would appear at any moment in his rear-view mirror. He continuously twitched the throttle, just in case they needed to make another run for it.

The rat, however, didn't appear. Instead, they passed a sign that read *Welcome to Coonandambra*, and came upon a small village, the occupants of which appeared to be just starting their day. Shopkeepers were sweeping the pavement in front of their shops and wiping down their windows with brushes. A water truck rumbled through the main street, spraying water that helped keep the dust down.

"Look," Myra said, "there's a tourist information center."

Ben pulled his bike up outside.

An elderly white-haired lady manned the desk. "Can I help you?" she said. Her eyes were intelligent and bright.

"Just browsing," Ben said, picking out some pamphlets from a shelf.

"What are you looking for?"

"The best way to get to the Olongo from here."

"Well, that's simple," she said. "Bill McCafferty runs tourist flights out there three times a week. That's the best way to see it."

Ben pocketed one of the pamphlets he was looking at. "Do you know where I can find him?"

"Follow the main road through the town. When you get to the last intersection, take a left and follow it down to the river. His office is down there."

"Thanks," Ben said, and made to leave.

"How many of you are there?" she called after him.

Ben stopped. "Two."

She shook her head. "He won't fly unless he has four." She made a show of looking out through the dusty front window. "With the storm and all, I'm not sure we'll make that today. You're an unexpected walk-in. You may have to wait a day or two until he gets the numbers up."

"Is that so?" Ben said.

"If you know Bill," she said, "you know he never does things by halves."

McCafferty ran his tourist operation out of a small tin shed. He said he didn't need a swanky air-conditioned office when his real office was his floatplane. Like all aircraft on Natchator, it ran via an array of electric-driven fan rotors. The electricity was supplied by batteries, which gave the aircraft limited range. McCafferty took pride in his floatplane, however, because he'd made DIY modifications that extended its range, enabling him to do the round trip to the Olongo and back. When he wasn't running tourist flights over the Olongo escarpment, he couriered goods between the Warraweans and the Orianians, often for rich collectors living in Urkesh.

"See that?" he said, pointing to a shrunken head hanging on the wall over his desk. "That's a Warrawean. Used to be, at least."

Ben cringed. McCafferty smelled like a brewery, and the day had barely started. He had more hair on his face than on his head. Bushy eyebrows hovered over glassy eyes that had the uncanny ability to catch you off guard when you least expected it. Like when Ben's gaze drifted from the shrunken head to the half-empty bottle of whiskey on his desk.

"What's the matter?" he said. "You think I'm not fit to fly?"

"I never said that."

"You were thinking it."

"I'm sorry, I didn't mean to offend you."

"No offense taken. I'm not flying anyway, 'cause there's nothing on my books except you two walk-ins. And I don't fly unless I have at least four."

"The lady at the tourism office told us," Ben said. "But how about we offer to pay for the empty seats?"

He studied them. "That's return tickets for four. You sure about that?"

"No. Not return. One-way."

McCafferty looked at Ben like he had lost his marbles. "You're joking, right?"

"No."

McCafferty's expression became serious. "Have you read the sign outside? It says *Tourist Flights*. That means there and back. No one asks to go on a one-way trip. It's just not done."

"We'll pay for the return leg as well," Myra said. "How about that?"

Ben looked at Myra. He hadn't expected that. Not at all.

"Makes no difference," McCafferty said. "I have to bring you back whether you like it or not. At least, you have to provide proof that you will return the same day on the next available flight. That's the rules. The only exception is if you're part of a government expedition. But we haven't had those for years. And something tells me you're not government. Am I right?"

"No, we're not with the government."

"Well, in that case, I can't help you."

"So you're not going to take us?" Myra insisted.

"Nope."

She studied McCafferty for a moment, then said, "How about I report your drinking behavior to the authorities? I'm sure they won't be too happy about it."

At first McCafferty just stared at her. His face, however, quickly reddened in anger. "Are you threatening me?"

"No," Myra said. "I'm merely conducting a business trans-action."

"Business transaction," McCafferty repeated woodenly.

"That's correct. Now, you can take our money, and our mo-torcycle, since we won't be needing it anymore, and that should be more than enough to cover your expenses."

Ben looked at Myra, aghast. She just nodded.

He turned to McCafferty and, in a voice that was practically a croak, said, "I guess I won't be needing it anymore."

McCafferty was shaking his head. "You really are that des-perate to go?" When neither Ben nor Myra said anything, he added, "When people are that desperate, it can mean either one of two things: they're in some kind of trouble, or they're crazy. Which is it with you two?"

"We're crazy," Myra said right away, before Ben had a chance to respond.

McCafferty stared at her, half incredulous, half in doubt about his own judgment. "Crazy, eh?"

"Will you take the offer or not?" Myra said.

McCafferty made a quick calculation in his head. "It's three and a half thousand *tiels* return per person," he said. "Covering the empty seats, that makes fourteen. How much did you say your bike is worth?"

"Fifty thousand," Ben said without thinking.

McCafferty dwelled on that figure for a moment, seemingly undecided. But then he got up, went to the door, and looked at the bike outside. "Fifty thousand, you say?"

Ben looked at him sideways and nodded.

McCafferty studied the bike again, then sat back at his desk. He opened a logbook and began writing. "I'm calling this an engineering flight," he said. "You two were never aboard. You got that?"

Ben and Myra nodded silently.

CHAPTER TWENTY-NINE

Day Three: Morning

The moment Nigel Booker entered the CIL, he knew something was wrong. Neither Tom nor Pascal were working. The droid was missing and Ben was nowhere to be found.

"Where is the droid? Where is Ben?" There was a shaky urgency in his voice, bordering on fear.

Pascal stood up. "We have something to tell you."

"It better be good."

"I'm afraid it's not good."

Booker blinked rapidly. Part of his brain didn't want to comprehend what his senses were telling him.

"Ben and the droid are missing," Pascal said.

"Oh no," Booker intoned. "That's not possible."

"I was in the canteen," Tom piped up. "When I got back, they were gone."

Booker's face went pale. His breaths came short, like he was gasping for air. "This is no time to joke. What have you done with the droid?"

"I told you," Pascal said. "She's missing."

"And you never thought to call security? You just sat here the whole time?"

"It wasn't like that."

"You're lying!"

Tom said, "I swear. I have witnesses. When I came back from the canteen they were gone."

"So why didn't you alert security then?"

"I thought they were somewhere else in the building. I thought Ben was running her through some locomotion tests."

"You thought, but you didn't bother to check?"

"I'm sorry, but I was too focused on finetuning her mocaps."

"What about you?" Booker said to Pascal.

"I fell asleep."

Booker clenched and unclenched his fists. "You realize what's going to happen when the Minister finds out about this."

"He doesn't have to find out," Pascal said.

"Really? Are you that stupid? He's coming today to pick her up!"

Pascal said nothing.

"What am I going to do? What am I going to do?" Booker paced back and forth, agitated.

"I'll start looking for them," Tom said, making for the door.

"Stay!" Booker commanded.

Tom halted.

"I want you to tell me the truth. I promise there will be no repercussions."

Tom looked at Pascal.

"I can only stall the Minister for so long. Either way, he's going to interrogate both of you. So how do you want to do this?"

Pascal looked back at Tom, then said, "Tom had nothing to do with it. It's all my fault."

"Go on."

"I may have said something to Ben."

Booker's shoulders sagged. "What have you done?"

"I have a feeling Ben ran away with the droid."

Booker began shaking his head and wringing his hands.

"I know when Sporn finds out he's going to blame you just as much as me."

"Bullshit! He's going to string you up alive this time."

"Perhaps."

Booker shuddered. He didn't want to think that far ahead yet. Right now he needed to get a hold of this situation. "When did he leave?" he asked, already strategizing.

"Probably around midnight," Pascal said.

"Probably or actually?"

"I can't say."

"I see. So this is how you want to do it."

"I already told you I'll take the blame."

Booker looked at Pascal with an expression of wild incredulity. "You know that's not enough! The moment he's finished with you, he's going to start working on me. So help me. We need to mitigate this somehow."

"What do you want me to say?"

"What exactly did you tell Ben?"

"I told him the truth. That Sporn was up to no good."

Booker rolled his eyes. "Yasu Doi!"

"I may have also helped him a little bit ..."

"Oh no ..."

"I think I gave him a tip on how to get out of the building."

"You've really done it this time, haven't you?"

"Well, what do you expect? He orders us to make a copy of Miss Reeves, and you think he's doing it for the benefit of the public?"

"It's not my job to question his motives!" Booker said, voice rising.

Tom stepped in. "I don't see how arguing is going to solve the problem. Shouldn't we be calling security?"

"No!" Booker said. "That would be an admission that we fucked up."

"So you agree, then?" Pascal said.

"No, I don't agree."

"So what do you want me to do?"

"Let me think," Booker said. He gritted his teeth and grimaced. "They could be anywhere by now. Have you tried calling him?"

"I don't have my VidPhone with me. Sporn confiscated it."

Booker sighed and got his VidPhone out. He dialed. An automated message came back saying the recipient was temporarily out of service. He stared at the device for a long time.

"I think I have no choice but to contact the Minister and tell him what has happened," he said eventually.

Pascal looked down, screwed his eyes shut.

CHAPTER THIRTY

Day Three: Mid morning

McCafferty flew low, following the Tongassa as it meandered through the desert. Its lush green riverbanks contrasted against the barren landscape that flanked it on either side. Looking down on it for the first time, Ben got a real sense of how the Tongassa was the lifeblood of Urkesh. Farms were packed tightly inside the narrow corridor of life it provided. The desert beyond was sterile. Barges and canoes carrying goods plied up and down its length. Despite being covered in a layer of dust, houses on stilts showed splashes of color in the form of people and animals going about their daily routines.

"As you can see, the dust has cleared," McCafferty said. "We should arrive at Lake Kerolan in about fifteen minutes."

"Will the Warraweans be there to greet us?" Ben asked.

"If by 'Warraweans' you mean natives dressed up in garb to entertain the city folk, yeah, there's a tourist village by the pontoon. You can wander around and buy bric-à-brac, souvenirs, local delicacies, that sort of stuff. But if you're looking for more of a cultural experience, you'll have to hire a tour guide. They do fishing expeditions, jungle treks, or if you go in for that hippy stuff, sweat lodges, hallucinogenic experiences ... but you have to book those in advance through the promotion agency back at Coonandambra."

"We won't be doing any of that," Ben said.

"No, I suppose you won't. But I expect you'll have at least organized a guide."

"Actually, we haven't. Do you know one?"

"You haven't. I see." He made a dubious expression, as if he'd expected this. "I might know one or two. But they'll cost."

"Can you introduce us?"

"Sure. But you'll need cash. Have you got cash?"

"A little."

"How much?"

"Sixty, seventy *tiels*."

"That's not enough."

"It's all I've got."

McCafferty shook his head and made a woeful expression. "Ship of fools we are. Tell me, are there any more surprises you've got in store for me, or is this the last one?"

Ben opened his mouth to answer when the radio suddenly crackled to life: "*This is sky patrol Bravo 5–9. Zebra 1–4, turn your aircraft around and head back to base. Repeat, turn your aircraft around.*"

"What the ...?" McCafferty blurted out. He craned his neck around, scanning the sky. Not finding what he was looking for, he turned to Ben. "What have you got me into?"

"It's a long story ... I can explain ..."

McCafferty growled and threw a glance at Myra. "It's her, isn't it? She's the one they're after."

"I think they're after both of us," Ben said at length.

"Tell me she's an A2," McCafferty said.

"She's an A2."

"I knew it!" He thumped the dashboard. "Well, that just about takes the cake."

"What are you going to do?" Ben asked, somewhat innocently.

McCafferty scanned the sky again. "I have a right mind to turn back," he said angrily.

"Please don't."

"So what is it? You thought you could run away with an A2? Or is there something else you're not telling me?"

"We're running away from the government," Ben admitted.

"The government? Great! Now we're really in trouble."

"Can you outrun them?" Myra asked.

"Outrun them. Ha! I bet there's a reward on your head. How about that!"

"Is that all you think about?" Myra said. "Money?"

"I've got a family to feed. Unlike you."

"But you're not turning back," Myra said. "You would have done so by now."

It was true; McCafferty had throttled the plane up. He was staying on course.

"Maybe there's something you're not telling us," she said.

McCafferty didn't answer. He flew on stoically. The glassy eyes were gone. His face had transformed into a mask of concentration.

The radio crackled again: "*Zebra 1–4, we have you on radar. Respond or we will intercept.*"

McCafferty uttered a stream of invective. He ended with, "What am I doing?" and pulled at his hair.

"You're doing the right thing," Ben said. As if that made any difference.

He looked out the window. He still couldn't see their pursuers. Instead, his eye was attracted to the landscape below. It had changed. They were flying over the ancient ruins of Arakirk. Remnants of stone foundations outlined where houses and other buildings used to be. They were interspersed by a labyrinth of streets. There was an open square, and a main road that ran north–south down to the river, where it met the pilings of an arched stone bridge, the first archaeological evidence of the city to be discovered and exposed.

"You're getting the whirlwind tour," McCafferty quipped sarcastically as the plane flew over its crumbled remains.

"Do you know how old it is?" Ben asked.

"No one knows. Maybe three thousand years or more."

"Incredible."

"Enjoy it. It might be the last thing you ever see."

They passed over the ruins. The river began changing, climbing through a series of rapids. McCafferty adjusted their altitude to follow its course.

The radio crackled once more. "*Zebra 1–4. This is your last warning. Repeat: last warning. Respond or we will intercept.*"

McCafferty shut the radio down. They flew on.

"You're not going to turn around," Ben said, stating the obvious again.

"See that gap in the cliffs up ahead?"

Ben looked forward and saw a canyon where the Tongassa spilled out. On either side, the color of the cliff rock was brighter than its surroundings, evidence of human modification. Ben realized he was looking at the dam that Sporn was building. As they got closer, he saw that the dam was still unfinished. The foundations had been laid on each side of the river, but the middle section was still untouched. Two tunnels penetrated into the cliff faces on each side and disappeared into darkness.

"Sporn's dam," he said at length.

"The dam, yes," McCafferty said. "But we're going to fly that canyon. It will buy us some time."

"Why are you helping us?" Myra asked.

McCafferty didn't answer. The cliffs loomed. He needed to aim the plane just right.

Suddenly a shadow passed over them. The sky patrol.

McCafferty instantly banked the plane to one side. Ben cried out, thinking they'd slam into the left side of the cliff wall. But McCafferty expertly righted the wings and shot into the canyon. He cleverly stayed close to the left side, using it as protection.

Ben looked out at the left wing. The canyon wall seemed much closer than it really was. He felt like he could almost reach out and touch it. Every now and then a bush or a tree jutted out from the sides. McCafferty expertly tipped the plane's wings just in time to avoid them. Below were huge boulders and white water. It was beautiful and terrifying all at once.

Eventually McCafferty said, "Don't get too comfortable. As soon as we exit this canyon, they're going to try to harpoon us."

"Did you say *harpoon* us?" Ben said in disbelief.

"Literally pluck us out of the air."

"Is there any way we can avoid it?"

McCafferty grouched. "We'll see."

"Perhaps if you let me fly," Myra suggested.

"Not a chance in hell," McCafferty shot back. "No one knows this canyon like I do."

At that very moment, they shot out of the canyon and skimmed over Lake Kerolan. The Olongo jungle lay before them. Almost immediately, Ben heard a loud thud.

McCafferty fishtailed. There was a horrendous tearing sound. "Bastards!"

Ben looked back to see a gaping hole in the tail fin. "They shot at us!" he exclaimed.

"They don't shoot. I told you: they harpoon."

Another thud quickly followed, this time on the side of the airframe. McCafferty tried to bank in the opposite direction, but the maneuver failed. The rotors screamed as they hit different air. The aircraft began tilting against McCafferty's input.

"Lift up the seat!" he cried.

"What?" Ben said. "Now?"

"The lug latches, damn it. Flip the lug latches!"

Ben and Myra didn't argue. They flipped the latches and lifted the seat up. There was a wooden crate underneath it.

McCafferty opened the passenger door side. "Throw it out!"

Ben and Myra struggled to lift the crate by its rope handles. "What's in it? It's so heavy," Ben said as they managed to get it out the door. They watched it fall, splash, and sink out of sight.

"Don't ask," McCafferty said. "But now that you're asking, guns for the rebels."

Ben looked at him in amazement.

"Well, what are you waiting for?" McCafferty said. "Jump!"

"You want us to jump?" Ben said, balking.

"It's either that or the Labor Camps, son."

Myra said, "I'll go first." Before Ben could do or say anything, she jumped.

He watched her drop and splash into the water. She momentarily disappeared, then resurfaced. She began swimming for the shore.

"You next!" McCafferty said.

Ben braced himself, then leapt.

The fall seemed to take ages. The water, when he hit it, punched the air out of his lungs. For a moment he thought he was being sucked to the bottom of the lake and panicked. Kicking frantically, he thrashed his way to the surface.

Myra was only a short distance away. She was swimming steadily and making good progress. Ben searched for McCafferty. He was nowhere to be seen.

He looked up. McCafferty's aircraft was already so high that the writing on the underside of the wing was no longer legible. The sky patrol looked like a bumblebee carrying a fly by comparison.

Hindered somewhat by the buoyancy of his daypack, Ben followed Myra to the shore. After draining every last ounce of energy that remained in his body, he finally managed to pull himself out of the water and stand next to Myra, his limbs like jelly.

For a while they both stood there and stared up at the empty sky.

It was just them and the jungle now.

CHAPTER THIRTY-ONE

Day Three: Mid morning

The journey to the dungeons under the Ministry of Justice building was swift and surprisingly bloodless. Perhaps because Sporn wasn't there to handle it directly. He was too busy coordinating the sky patrol, so much so that he pushed aside their lead pilot and took control of the aircraft himself. To say it was personal would have been an understatement.

Pascal and Tom shared adjacent cells. They weren't allowed to speak. Not that it would have helped. The walls were thick as a man's waist. The doors were heavy armor-plated steel. All they could do was wait.

Tom took it particularly hard. He had never been in trouble with the regime before and didn't know how to deal with it. He paced back and forth in his cell, half out of his mind, one moment cursing Ben and Pascal for what they'd done to him, the next remonstrating with himself for being such a coward.

As for Pascal, he sat quietly in the corner of his cell (they were furnished with nothing more than a bucket), shut his eyes, and tried to imagine he was back in his library, surrounded by his beloved books. It almost worked, but his thoughts gradually drifted back to the present. So this was it, finally. He promised himself that no matter what came next, he would not betray Ben. Yet almost as soon as he had that thought, he knew it was mere bravado – that the moment they started torturing him, he would tell them whatever they wanted to hear. But he needed to believe it. At least for now.

After what seemed like a long time, but was in fact only a couple of hours, Pascal was dragged out of his cell to an interrogation room. Entering, he looked around. The semblance of civilization was crudely provisioned. There was a simple steel-framed wooden table, a pair of chairs, and the trademark factory light, which spilled down with cold indifference.

Pascal was forced to wait again for an indeterminate amount of time. A Gormling stood guard outside, leaving him alone in the room.

Finally, the door clanked open and Sporn entered, accompanied by two brutish-looking Gormlings. They had their sleeves rolled up, revealing knotted, muscular arms.

Sporn sat down and looked at Pascal across the desk. It seemed to Pascal that he was past being angry. His eyes were icy and distant, a sign that he had already resigned himself to what he was about to do.

"You realize," he said, in a somewhat tired voice, "that Carver will not be able to save you this time."

Pascal didn't bother to rouse himself. There was no point in talking back. No matter what he said, it would make no difference.

"You might be interested to know that Ben and the droid got away," Sporn said. "That should give you reason to rejoice."

"How do I know you're not just saying that?" Pascal inquired.

"Are you calling me a liar?"

"No."

"It sure seems like it." Sporn fiddled with his collar for a moment, loosening it. Fixing his eyes back on Pascal, he said,

"You know, I thought we had a deal. You help me and I won't turn you over to Rathneggar. But you reneged on that deal. So by my reckoning, that makes you the liar."

Pascal resisted the urge to comment.

"Now, of course, we can beat the truth out of you," Sporn said, with a wistful air. "Or we could just send you over to the Labor Camps. I just need to figure out how much information you have in that head of yours that might be useful to me." He leaned back, gave Pascal a long look while running his hand over the top of his mostly balding scalp. "I think a bit of both, what do you say?"

"Is there a point to this?" Pascal asked.

Sporn made a gesture to one of his Gormlings.

Pascal didn't feel any pain, but his world exploded into a blinding white light. When his senses did come back, the room was spinning. Putting his hand to his face, he noticed his glasses weren't there, and blood was gushing out of his nose. It was then that the pain hit him. Inescapable and agonizing, it pressed into his skull and squashed his entire being into a fiery ball behind his eyes. He moaned and bent forward.

The Gormlings pulled him back up again.

"You're going to tell me everything," Sporn said, "starting with Arthur's journal."

CHAPTER THIRTY-TWO

Day Three: Before noon

"I feel bad," Ben said, squinting against the glinting water as he looked out across Lake Kerolan.

"Are you in pain?" Myra asked.

Ben wasn't sure how to answer that question. Yes, he was in pain, but not physically. His pain was ... Well, he didn't know where his pain was, but he *felt* it. "No," he said, absently. "I'm not in pain. I'm just concerned about the pilot. Did you see what happened to him?"

"No."

Ben wanted to explain to her that it was all his fault. He had gotten them here. It was his inability to say no to Pascal and Tom that had made him go along with their plan. A crazy plan, which he'd known from the very start. And now look where it had gotten them. He was responsible for the death of another human being. Or if not death, then certainly capture and imprisonment. Which, given the situation, probably amounted to the same thing. Either way, he had just murdered someone.

His look must have said it, because Myra said, "I see. You feel bad about what happened to Mr. McCafferty."

"Yes."

"I suppose he knew the risks. He accepted your money."

Ben gave Myra a sharp look. "I don't suppose, in that computer brain of yours, that you realize risk and reward are not a perfectly balanced equation. There is such a thing as motivation, you know."

"Yes, I realize that. Mr. McCafferty's motivation was for his family."

"And we just made them fatherless." Just saying it created a knot in his throat.

Myra looked down in thought. When she looked up again, she said, "You're right. How can we make it better?"

Ben burst out with an incredulous laugh. "We can't! That's the thing. Can't you see?" He swept his arm out across the lake.

Myra looked out at the water and didn't see anything.

"Come on," Ben said, moving away from the lake. Myra followed.

The shores of Lake Kerolan were fringed by mangroves. Their interlacing roots stabilized the muddy earth, but proved to be an entanglement hazard for feet – especially for Myra, who had not yet fine-tuned her locomotor routines. Ben found himself frequently grabbing hold of her to keep her upright. Once he slipped over a root while helping her, and they came crashing down together. By the time they got out of the mangroves and made it to the forest, their clothes and skin were covered in a layer of mud.

Funnily enough, it proved to be a perfect barrier against the insects. Ben went as far as to rub it on his neck and cheeks. The one place he didn't like it was over his daypack, which he unsuccessfully tried to clean. He was happy to find that its contents were relatively dry. He retrieved a bottle of water and took a big swig. He offered some to Myra, but she said she didn't need it. Her skin was adequately hydrated.

The forest proved to be easier going. The undergrowth wasn't as dense as he'd imagined it would be. Moreover, there seemed to be a path running through the forest that followed the contour of the lake. In discussion with Myra, he proposed they follow it, reasoning that it should lead to the pontoon and tourist village. She agreed without argument.

They had been walking for about fifteen minutes when Myra said, "I think now is a good time for you to tell me the whole story. I know you tricked me into coming. And I know why we're here. But what was the first cause? What started it all? Can you tell me that?"

"You think we tricked you?"

"Pascal told me it was a test."

"It was a test – of sorts."

"I overheard you say 'kidnap.' That's not a test."

Ben looked at Myra sidelong. "It was just a figure of speech. If you really want the truth, you're stolen property."

"I've grasped that much."

"Yet you still trust me?"

"Mostly, yes."

"Mostly?"

"Trust has to be earned."

Ben gave her a look of acknowledgment and nodded.

"I would trust you more if you enlightened me as to the original cause of our situation."

Ben walked for a while in thought before answering. "So you know who Hector Sporn is?"

"I believe he is the Minister of the Interior."

"Correct. He ordered us to make you. For what purpose … I can't completely say."

"Could you speculate?"

"I don't like speculating."

"But you have a feeling? Isn't that what humans are good at?

Feeling?"

Ben couldn't help smiling. "Feelings," he said. "I know of them. But don't ask me to explain them, or base my decisions on them. They have a history of letting me down."

"But you can't help having them. Unlike me. I can only choose according to my programming."

"It's still early," Ben said. "Give it time and your feelings will get more complicated."

"So you're saying that as they get more complicated, they become less trustworthy?"

"Quite the opposite," Ben said. "They become more familiar, but you also begin to see them for what they are. They're not always useful to the situation you're in."

"So what about logic? Perhaps we can use that to speculate on the first cause."

"Sure. If all else fails, why not."

"The most logical reason is that Sporn killed my original."

Ben stopped walking. He gave Myra a distraught look.

"Did I say something to offend you?" she asked.

"No ... but I can't believe he would do that. He was having a relationship with you."

"Is that so?" Myra mulled this piece of information over like a distasteful morsel in her mouth.

"Yes."

Ben resumed walking. This was very unexpected news. Of course, it was only speculation. But without knowing anything about Sporn and his father, the droid had touched on a very real possibility. Ben still wasn't completely convinced that Sporn had killed his father, though. That was just something Pascal had told him without proof.

"There are other possibilities," Myra said, catching up.

"Such as?"

"He prefers to have relations with an android."

Ben considered that. "I just wonder what Miss Reeves would

have thought of that."

"I presume she wouldn't have known. He wouldn't have let us cross paths."

"I suppose so."

"But I would like to meet my brother," Myra said.

They walked on for some time in silence. The going was steady, the path followed the contours of the lake. The ease with which they made progress gradually dissipated Ben's fears about the jungle. But then he abruptly stopped. He looked up, almost as if he were praying – except instead of rapture, dismay wrote itself across his face. Myra stopped and followed his gaze.

There, tied partway up the trunk of a giant kapok tree, was an A2 droid. Its skin was all but stripped away. It was missing a leg and half of one arm. Wires dangled from the exposed ends. Its RTG was missing, presumably scavenged for its power-generating capabilities. Its eyes had been stripped to their bare camera mechanisms, and gazed out with a kind of maniacal intensity, as if mocking an invisible tormentor.

When Ben eventually managed to tear his gaze away from the frightful aberration, he saw there was more. Dismembered limbs in various states of decay dangled from the branches of a nearby fig tree; heads were impaled on bamboo spikes; clumps of hair lay tangled in the grass.

Myra fell to her knees in shock.

Ben put his arm around her shoulders. She made a moaning sound, a sound he had never heard an A2 make before. Like a deeply wounded animal. At least that's what it sounded like to him. It reached inside and grabbed his innards.

"Come on," he said. "Let's get out of here." They walked rapidly away from the grisly scene. As they went, Ben muttered to himself, "I was right! Damn it."

"What's going to happen to me?" Myra asked plaintively.

Ben avoided answering at first. He kept on marching.

Myra tugged on his arm like an innocent child. "Ben!"

He swung around to her. "I don't know. Don't ask."

"But …"

"Don't ask!"

They tramped on in silence for a while. Eventually Ben stopped and said, "Look. I'm sorry. I'm not good at this, okay?"

They sized each other up.

"It's that damn configuration file," Ben said. "Excuse my language. The fact is, we didn't have enough time to program it. Not just what Miss Reeves likes, or dislikes, but how she sees the world. Actually understands it." He gave her a look of genuine sympathy. "It's all my fault."

Myra stared at him, a lost expression on her face. Seeing it, Ben felt helpless. What could he do? He began to feel sorry for himself. But then Pascal's words echoed sharply in his ear.

Children feel sorry for themselves. Adults get on with it!

He nodded to himself.

"What is it?" Myra asked.

Ben began laughing … at himself. Something Pascal had also tried to teach him, only he had always failed miserably. But he wasn't laughing because Pascal had told him to, not this time. It was Maddie. The irony of it – that her lookalike was standing in front of him, completely clueless. *Don't take it too seriously, right?*

He shook his head again and said, "It just occurred to me that maybe it was meant to be this way. Maybe it's a good thing."

"What's a good thing?"

He poked her between her breasts. "You're going to have to figure this out all by yourself. Just like the rest of us have had to."

"But those things … Those things that were hanging in the trees like strange fruit …"

"Yeah, well, those things … Not everyone in the world thinks about your kind the way I do. They just see a machine."

"And you?"

"I see a person."

"Am I a person?"

"You are."

Myra stared at Ben like she had just found a big brother.

"Come on," he said. "Let's get to the village. Maybe someone there can help us."

CHAPTER THIRTY-THREE

Day Three: *Just after noon*

Shelley Ammon sat cross-legged on the end of the pontoon, watching the Tongassa flow gently by. Every now and then a *canthri* leapt out of the water to escape a larger fish, probably a *halycoelith*. *Canthri* were delicious when barbecued. The meat was white, unlike the *halycoelith*, which left an aftertaste of mud in one's mouth. Most things that came from the Tongassa tasted like that, except for *canthri*, which made them popular with children. They fished them out of the water with nets woven from palm fronds.

Geraldo Brower, a white-skinned, khaki-dressed Urkeshian, ambled down the pontoon toward her. Patches of sweat radiated from his armpits. A damp cigarette dangled from his mouth. He repeatedly attempted to light it as he walked. "Damn this humidity," he muttered.

"Humidity or your own sweat?" Shelley quipped as Brower sidled up next to her. She wrinkled her nose. If there was one thing she didn't like about the white Urkeshians, it was their sweat. It stank. It reminded her of the *Ambrophallos* flower when it was in bloom. Some said it smelled like rotten meat, others like fermented beans.

"What's keeping him?" Brower complained. "He was supposed to be here three and a half hours ago."

"Patience," Shelley instructed him. She rose in a single fluid movement, not unlike a snake uncoiling itself, and struck a flint hanging on a lanyard around her neck. The sparks flew into the end of Brower's cigarette and set it alight.

"How did you do that?" Brower asked in amazement.

"Magic," she said. She made a flourish with her hands, which were strong, yet fine-boned and beautifully sculpted.

Brower would have liked to have those hands explore his body. But he had learned the hard way, like some of his fellow rebels, that Shelley's movements were as quick as the snapping jaws of the infamous *sarcotoothi*. Many had found themselves nursing a slash across the cheek from the razor-sharp machete she kept sheathed at her hip day and night.

"Something's not right," Brower said. "He's always on time."

Shelley had to admit he had a point. But she wasn't one to fret over time, unlike the city-dwellers, who seemed to be in a constant rush. Delays in this part of the world were not uncommon. Though there was one thing that did worry her, and that was the cargo. According to Reeves, this one was important. He had ordered them to give it top priority.

She strained with all her attention, listening for the tell-tale high-pitched hum of the aircraft's engines. To her finely tuned ears it would be detectable long before it became visible. But there was nothing. Just the sounds of the jungle and the everyday noises of the locals as they went about their lives: the prattle of the hawkers in the village marketplace, the joyful squeals of children as they played down by the water, the squawk of a pet parakeet, the cluck of the odd chicken. Something else, however, did catch her attention. And it was highly unexpected.

Two figures – a man and a woman, neither of whom she had seen before – were wandering out of the jungle on the western side of the village. They looked tired and flustered as if they had undergone an unpleasant ordeal.

"Hello, what's this?" Brower said.

Shelley walked down the pontoon to intercept them. Brower followed.

The two interlopers stopped. The man spoke first. He said "Hi" in a soft and somewhat nervous voice. The woman mimicked him.

"Hello," Shelley replied, keeping a slight distance.

Brower came forward. "I don't believe my eyes. You can't be … but you are! You're Madelaine Reeves!"

"Yes, I am. And your name is?"

Brower extended his hand. "Geraldo Brower."

Myra shook it. "Pleased to meet you, Mr. Brower."

"And your partner?" Brower said.

Ben offered his hand. "Ben Huxley."

Brower shook it. "Pleased to meet you, Mr. Huxley."

Shelley felt a jolt as she heard the name. But she didn't trust herself. It seemed too convenient to be true. And besides, there was something suspicious about the woman. She didn't look right. Together they formed an odd pair.

Brower smiled, remarking that it was unusual for city-dwellers to wander out of the jungle. "This pontoon is the official jumping-off point for all tourists. Normally everyone arrives by floatplane. So how did you get here?"

"We flew in."

"Sorry, I meant, how did you get *here*?" He pointed to the ground at his feet.

"We walked."

"From where?"

"Back there," Ben said, pointing to the west.

"Without a guide?"

"Yes."

Brower and Shelley exchanged questioning glances.

"Listen," Brower said, "I'm sweating bullets out here. Why don't we continue our conversation over there?" He pointed to an unused gazebo made from thatched palms. It sheltered a long wooden table and some tree-stump seats.

"Sure," Ben said.

They went over. On the way, Brower quietly told Shelley he would handle it. She didn't argue. Not because she agreed, but because she was still too preoccupied with trying to figure the two strangers out.

Ben plonked himself down, tired, on one of the tree-stumps. Brower perched on the end of the table. Myra and Shelley chose to stand, cautiously eyeing each other. Free-range chickens pecked the yellowish-red earth around their feet. A mangy dog kept its distance, warily watching them with its hungry eyes. A scrawny monkey tied to a bamboo stake nearby was dozing, occasionally waking itself in fright.

"It looks like you had a tough time out there," Brower offered.

"Yes," Ben said simply.

"Excuse me if I'm a little incredulous, but I find it hard to believe that a tourist operator would drop two people – people like you, who are obviously ill-prepared for the jungle – in the middle of nowhere without a guide."

"It's true."

"Who was your operator?"

"You mean our pilot?"

"Yes."

"Ah … Bill … Bill McCafferty."

Brower and Shelley looked at each other again.

"I know McCafferty," Brower said. He rested his right hand on a pistol holstered to his belt. "He is a very responsible operator. He wouldn't do what you say he did."

"What Ben meant to say —" Myra began, but Ben stood up, putting his hand out and cutting her off.

"I'm sorry. But if it's possible, we would like to speak to an official. It's not that we don't trust you. It's just that we don't know you, and —"

Brower let out a bellowing laugh. "An official? Around here? My friend, you are sadly mistaken. This is Warrawean territory. We are the only people here who can speak your language. And I can see you have no weapons, no machete, and judging from that small bag on your shoulder, no camping gear. How do you intend to survive the night?"

"We have money. We could pay to stay in one of those huts," Ben said, pointing to one of several thatched huts erected on the clearing.

"You could do that. But then what?"

Ben had no answer to that.

"Let me put this in perspective for you," Brower said. "You say that Bill McCafferty was your pilot. Yes?"

Ben nodded ever so slightly.

"Well then, perhaps you'd be interested to know that he is also *our* pilot." Brower waited for that fact to sink in. "In fact" – he checked his watch – "he was supposed to be here about three and a half hours ago." He looked up and met Ben's eyes.

Ben briefly held Brower's gaze, then looked away. He began fidgeting with the strap on his daypack.

"Obviously, he can't be in two places at once. And since you appear to be the last people who saw him, that makes you persons of interest. If there's anything you need to tell us, now is the time."

Ben stopped fidgeting, looked at Myra, then back to Brower. "How do I know you can be trusted?"

Brower chuckled. "You can't. But the fact that we haven't taken you out into the jungle and shot you as spies should be more than sufficient proof that you can trust us."

"We're not spies," Ben said, tensing up defensively.

"Then you have nothing to fear," Brower said. "Except the

jungle."

Ben looked around nervously. "We don't know what happened to Mr. McCafferty."

Brower's heavy brows knitted. "You don't know, or you can't say?"

"We don't know."

Shelley shifted uneasily. This exchange was starting to annoy her. Maybe she should have handled it instead of letting Brower take the lead.

Sensing her annoyance, Brower said, "But you saw something, didn't you?"

Ben nodded.

"So tell us what happened. We promise not to use it against you – so long as you tell us the truth."

Ben looked at the ground for a moment before speaking. "We were harpooned by the sky patrol."

"Harpooned?"

"Yes."

If Brower was shocked, he didn't show it. Shelley's irritation, however, was slowly turning to anger.

"Go on," Brower said.

"McCafferty told us to jump. So we did."

"Into the water?"

"Yes."

"What about McCafferty?"

"Miss Reeves jumped first, I jumped second. Neither of us saw Mr. McCafferty after that."

"So he could have jumped?"

"It's possible, but he never came ashore."

Brower nodded with slow comprehension. He looked at Shelley. "So he could have been taken with his plane."

"It's also a possibility."

"I'm going to ask you a very delicate question now." Brower waited till he had Ben's full attention. "Did he mention anything about a wooden crate?"

"As a matter of fact, he did."

"And?"

"We threw it into the lake before we jumped."

Brower's broad shoulders slumped. Shelley gave him a scolding look and abruptly walked off.

"So … we helped you," Ben said. "Does that mean you will now help us?"

Brower roused himself from his funk. "Help, how?"

"You said we can't survive this jungle on our own. We told you everything you wanted to know. Could you tell us where to find Madelaine's brother? That would be the least you could do."

"What makes you think I know her brother?"

"Your response on learning what happened to the crate. And that gun on your belt," Myra said.

Brower managed a faded smile. "It's that obvious, is it?"

"I would very much like to see my brother."

"I'm sure you would."

"Will you take me to him, then?"

"If the decision was on me, I'd say yes. But as you can see, I'm not the one to make it." He jerked his thumb in the direction Shelley had gone.

Brower led them through a jungle path to a riverbank, a tributary of the Tongassa. The mangy dog followed them, but kept its distance. A canoe was tied to a tree root next to the water. It had two seats, and an electric motor with a shaft propeller was mounted on its rear, powered by a makeshift battery pack sealed in a four-gallon plastic container that had been cut in half and rejoined with an overlap. The middle of the canoe was stacked with sacks stitched from oilcloth, presumably filled with supplies. A large aluminum pot, a folded tarpaulin, some rope, and a pair of plain wooden paddles lay next to them.

Shelley arrived with some canisters of fresh water. "What are you doing?" she asked Brower.

"We have to take them with us."

"No, we don't."

"What do you think Vernon will say when he finds out we left his sister here alone, without any help?"

"She's not his sister."

Brower didn't understand.

"She's a *mecha*. A machine."

Brower took a second look, scrutinizing Myra more carefully.

Shelley put the water canisters down and lifted Myra's hair up on the back of her head, exposing the seal that covered her data port. "Take a look for yourself."

Brower took a closer look. "How did you know?"

"The way she moved."

Brower unholstered his gun and pointed it at Ben. "So you're spies!"

Myra stepped in front of Ben.

"Get out of the way, robot, or I will shoot you as well."

"I cannot do that," Myra said. "I am programmed to protect human life."

Brower cocked his pistol. "In that case, I will shoot you first."

Ben slipped out from behind Myra and stood in front of her. "Please don't!" he cried. "We're not spies. I promise you. I can explain everything!"

"It's a trap," Shelley said. "Shoot them both now, or I will kill them myself." She unsheathed her machete.

"Please!" Ben begged. He fell to his knees. "You have to believe me. We're fugitives. My name is Ben Huxley. I'm Arthur Huxley's son!"

To Brower's surprise, Shelley put her hand over Brower's pistol, staying his hand.

"Say that again," she said.

"We're fugitives. I stole her from —"

"The other part."

"I'm Arthur Huxley's son."

Shelley stepped forward and placed the blade of her machete on Ben's neck. "You lie."

"No, it's the truth."

"Prove it."

The veins in Ben's neck bulged. He was too scared to move.

"I said prove it!"

"Okay, okay!" Slowly, with trembling hands, Ben reached over his shoulder and carefully slipped off his daypack. He put it on the ground in front of him. "I'm going to open it now."

Shelley made a motion with her head. Ben slowly undid the zipper.

"Wait!"

Ben froze. Shelley slid her blade into the bag and widened the gap so she could see inside. Satisfied that Ben was being honest, she allowed him to continue.

He took his laptop out, booted it up, and navigated to his favorite folder of family pictures. He opened them up and showed them to Shelley. "See here? That's a picture of me and my father just before he left for the Olongo jungle. You can see he's all dressed up for adventure."

Shelley looked at the picture. But it wasn't what Arthur was wearing that caught her attention. It was what he was holding in his hand. It was their ancestral totem. The very same one that now stood proudly on the village altar in the Chief's hut.

"What is it?" Brower asked, seeing that Shelley had become transfixed.

Pulling herself back to the present, she sheathed her machete. "He's telling the truth."

"Oh, thank you," Ben said. He prostrated himself. "Thank you —"

"Stop groveling, you idiot."

Ben looked up, and seeing that she was serious, got up. He wiped his hands clean. "Sorry."

"Shut up! We leave now," Shelley said. "The day is already short." She went to the canoe and started packing the water canisters.

Brower went over to her and asked, "What was all that about? First you want to kill them, now you want to save them?"

Shelley turned on him. "Who said anything about *them*?"

Brower straightened up. Reassessed the situation. "You're saying we leave her here?"

Shelley didn't answer. She packed the rest of the canisters into the canoe.

Brower took this as a yes. He turned to Ben and pointed to Myra. "I'm afraid she stays here."

For a moment Ben gave him a blank stare. Then he found his voice. "No! She is with me. She comes with me."

"She stays," Shelley said firmly.

"Did you hear me? She comes with me."

Shelley didn't respond. Brower helped her spread a tarp over the sacks of food.

"She isn't just any old droid," Ben said, confronting her. "She's special. She has Miss Reeves' mind."

Shelley stopped what she was doing and faced Ben squarely. "*She* doesn't have a mind. She's a *mecha*!"

"You're wrong."

She shook her head and went back to the canoe. "You're a fool, just like all the other city-dwellers."

"I may be a fool," Ben said, "but I'm not stupid."

Brower and Shelley continued working in silence.

"I'm her guardian," Ben murmured. "I promised to look after her." He stared at Myra with a mournful gaze.

Myra stared back at him, her large, luminous eyes full of anxiety.

Shelley got a rope out and started tying the tarp down. As

she yanked the last eyelet fast, she made a catty sound and said, "Take it, then. But if it causes any trouble, we take its power source and throw the rest away."

CHAPTER THIRTY-FOUR

Day Three: Mid afternoon

During his military training long ago, Captain Nathanial Washburn had learned not to ask certain questions, particularly when faced with the inevitable. Hector Sporn, in his eyes, had become unhinged, but given his overreaching power and almost limitless resources, it was no use arguing with him about an ostensibly minor detail, such as weaponizing the *Zond Octavia*, the largest Zeppelin owned by the state. The airship had flown only once, during the Cosmonist Victory Parade of 3065. That was thirty-three years ago. Since then it had been mothballed; it was considered too valuable to take out. Other airships had replaced it, which were smaller, less valuable, and more expendable. Not that they had lost any. The revolution was well and truly over, and there was no danger of them being shot out of the sky.

But the *Zond Octavia*? It was a masterpiece of engineering. Designed to carry a dozen passengers, it could keep them aloft for a month with all their needs fully taken care of, including three-course meals every day and all the alcohol they could consume. Of course, it was its size and carrying capacity that had sealed its fate. Instead of passengers, Sporn wanted a platoon of Gormlings; instead of alcohol, he wanted armaments and ammunition. As for its vulnerability – the ease by which it could be set ablaze with Warrawean firestone arrows – Sporn would hear none of it. They would sneak up on the enemy silently. After all, that's what the Zeppelin was good at.

But what amazed Washburn more than anything was that there was no shortage of Gormlings who wanted to go on this – in his opinion – suicide mission. A delicate trelliswork of aluminum girders and taut steel wires weighing thirty-six tons restrained the nineteen gas bags of hydrogen inside its cigar-shaped body, but barely so. The gas could explode at the merest provocation. The men on board had to wear special shoes so as not to strike a spark. Smoking was strictly forbidden. Measures against creating static electricity had to be constantly observed, and failure to do so was punishable by the withholding of rations – the one and only true pleasure of the mission, since if there was one thing Sporn would not compromise on, it was stocking the larder with the best produce the nation had to offer, as well as bringing his own personal chef, renowned as the best in Urkesh.

At least they would go down in style.

The one person Washburn did have faith in was the captain, Karl Gross. He would not let Sporn fly *his* ship. The most experienced pilot in the Orianian air force, with over twenty thousand hours of flight time and numerous records broken, he knew the winds, he knew the clouds, and he knew gravity. Swarthy, buzzcut and goateed, he was short-statured and physically equal to Sporn, if not superior. His uniform was immaculate, as was the cleanliness of his ship. He was going to have to keep a sharp eye on Sporn's Gormlings, to make sure they didn't besmirch the chromed aluminum tubing and plastic fittings of the dining room, which was a work of art in itself: every corner was rounded for safety, and the burnt-orange color scheme had been chosen precisely because it contrasted with the panoramic views of the blue ocean and skies commonly visible through the bank of picture windows running three quarters the length of the gondola.

"Careful!" Washburn barked, as a ground support crew loaded a pallet of incendiary bombs.

Gross, who was standing next to him, stopped the pallet to ensure each bomb was wrapped correctly in its wax paper jacket. "I want these restacked," he ordered, not satisfied with the unevenness of the gaps between them.

Washburn gave an approving nod.

"I'm deeply concerned," Gross confided to him. "We've never carried munitions on board before – it's not just that we're carrying them, but deploying them. How can we ensure that mistakes won't be made?"

Washburn self-consciously fingered his mustache; it covered a scar he had acquired during a skirmish with the Rodinian forces at Atkum on the Orianian and Wallacian border northeast of Urkesh. "I'll make sure myself," he said. "Nothing will be dropped without my first laying hands on it."

Gross made a grunting sound. He didn't seem completely convinced, but he accepted the promise. It was true, he had complained to Sporn about letting Washburn – a military man – have free rein over his ship, but Sporn had given him no quarter. His job was to take orders. Pilot the ship where commanded. Anything less would be considered treasonous to the state.

Gross dealt with this professionally. There was no use building up enmity against Washburn; he was just doing his job. But by the Word of Hanub-Ka, he wasn't going to let Washburn make any mistakes!

Sporn stepped onto the flight deck and observed Gross and his co-pilot Waldo Mendes working the controls. Washburn, who was with them, stood to attention. The Tongassa unfurled like a green-fringed ribbon on the otherwise monotonous desertscape of the southern Urkeshian plateau. In the far distance to the west, through a shimmering haze, a small forest of wind turbines could be made out next to a cluster of low-lying buildings. The Labor Camps.

"Call your men to the dining room," Sporn said to Washburn. "Now that we're out of Urkeshian airspace, it's time to inform them of their mission."

"Yessir."

Mendes gave Washburn a microphone. Washburn made the announcement.

The "officers' table" was situated on an elevated platform above the others, giving it a commanding view of the panoramic scene outside and a full scope of the dining room inside. Sporn's two bodyguards, Koolhaas and Fletcher, had been provisionally upgraded to officer status and given permission to join Sporn, along with Washburn, at the table.

All of them wore military greens, except one individual: Nigel Booker. He sat there in civilian clothes with a peevish look on his face, not sure whether he should be filled with excitement or trepidation. Excitement because this was an adventure he could not have imagined in his wildest dreams; trepidation because Sporn held him personally responsible for the loss of *his* company asset. Sporn had told him in no uncertain terms that if he didn't retrieve it, he could forget about coming back to Urkesh.

Presently, Sporn's chef, along with his two assistants – Wallacian Krungs – served up afternoon tea: finger sandwiches of prosciutto and goat's cheese, parcels of coronation chicken, crackers with smoked salmon and cucumber, truffled egg and cress on rye. To mark the special occasion, several bottles of champagne were uncorked.

The serving complete, Sporn stood up. His Gormlings stood to attention in response.

"You may be seated," he said. "Naturally, you're all curious as to why you were chosen for this mission. About twelve hours ago, I received some crucial intel. I am pleased to inform you that it will allow us to plan a preemptive strike on the rebel outpost in the Olongo basin."

This information was met with murmurs.

"Up until now, the location of the rebel camp has eluded our best efforts at discovery, but that's about to change." Indicating a toaster-sized device on the table in front of Booker with knobs, dials, and a small cathode-ray screen, Sporn said, "This device will allow us to track, in particular, a stolen MM product, and we believe it will lead us to the rebel camp."

There were expressions of approval among his men. But some of them looked concerned.

Sporn knew why, and he answered their concerns. "For the most part we will fly out of reach of their magnesium-tipped arrows, and we will use the night. We will not descend until we reach the rear of the camp. Once there, we will lower half our contingency to the ground. The other half will be divided into two groups: one will stay aboard and drop munitions; the remainder will be lowered to the top of the escarpment. Once the bombing is complete, the ground forces will pincer the camp and wipe out any remaining resistance."

"So there will be no prisoners?" said a Gormling – a corporal – one table away.

"There will be no prisoners," Sporn said. "But trophies are welcome."

CHAPTER THIRTY-FIVE

Day Three: Late afternoon – evening

Ben felt like they were floating through a tree tunnel. The canopy reached across the water and everywhere vines – *liane* – dangled down in thick tangles. The foliage filtered out much of the light and reduced the day to a dusk-like gloom. Giant trunks rose like columns into the mottled sky. Now and then, the splashing of falling fruit announced the presence of birds feeding overhead: bright blue chatterers; pompadours with their delicate white wings and claret-colored plumage; a trogon, skipping through the canopy; a clumsy toucan shaking a branch as it alighted.

Shelley was standing in the prow of the canoe, directing its path with a long bamboo pole, which she struck into the water whenever they encountered an obstacle such as a tangled vine or a submerged log. Occasionally she chopped away some vines with her machete. Ben gazed at her in fascination. Her long, coarse dark hair was twisted into braids and wound tightly around her head. Save for a cloth apron to protect her modesty, she was completely naked. Her nudity was offset by a beaded bracelet of polished black seeds, a brass armband, and a pair of leg garters crafted from scarlet macaw feathers. Her shoulders were smeared with red paint, presumably to protect her skin, which was dark yellow, and had the luster of polished bronze. Every time she struck the pole into the water, her sinew and muscles stood out defined, as if taken straight from the pages of an anatomy book.

Shelley seemed to have picked up on Ben's stare; she briefly met his gaze. There was an insolent look in her eyes, almost haughty, yet self-assured. It seemed to say, *You don't know what you're doing.*

Myra noted Ben's gaze. He flushed with embarrassment and briskly looked away.

A succession of hooting cries echoed through the forest. "Hear that?" Brower said.

"Yeah, what is it?" Ben replied.

"Howler monkeys. A sign that it's gonna rain. If we're lucky, we might have one for dinner."

"Ugh!"

"What's your problem? City living made you soft, has it?"

"I wouldn't say that. I just don't like the thought of eating the flesh of a creature who's so ..."

"So what?"

"Human-like."

"Would you eat your fellow man if you were starving?"

Ben didn't want to answer that. But Brower was grinning mischievously. So he said: "It all depends on the situation."

"Such as?"

"It has to be a matter of life and death."

"Well, tell me this," Brower said, enjoying where this was going. "What about the droid? Would you sacrifice her?"

"I don't see the connection."

"It's a simple question. Man or machine?"

"You don't have to answer that," Myra cut in. "It's not a decision you would have to make. We are programmed to make it for you, by default. It's built into the *Pro Hominin* laws."

"How convenient."

The canoe came to an abrupt halt. The bow rode up on a submerged log and balanced there precariously for a moment before sliding back off.

Shelley stuck her pole in the river bottom to steady the canoe. "We'll have to get out and carry it over."

"Is it safe to go into the water?" Ben asked.

"No," Shelley said. "But we'll do it quickly. This won't be the first time."

She jumped out. The water came up to her waist. She stabilized the canoe by gripping its sides, allowing Ben, Myra, and Brower to jump out. Together, the four of them heaved the canoe over the log.

Brower climbed aboard first, then helped Ben and Myra back in. Shelley nimbly hauled herself in using her legs as leverage.

"That was exciting," Myra said. "I thought I felt something move under my feet when I was in the water."

"Probably a stingray," Brower said.

"And you didn't say anything?" Ben asked Myra.

"I didn't want to alarm you."

The canoe broke free from the oppressive jungle gloom and drifted into the bright sunlight of an open lagoon. But almost immediately, the sky split apart with a thunderous clap. The clouds rolled in. A few moments later, torrential rain bucketed down upon them, soaking them through. Only Shelley seemed impervious to its effects. Her skin glistened and her face remained impassive, even though she crouched low so as not to make herself a target of the lightning that flashed around them.

Ben was scared out of his wits. Each time a lightning bolt forked its way to the ground, he thought it would strike them and turn them to cinders. Fortunately it passed quickly, but the rain had set in, a monotonous, heavy drizzle that transformed the surface of the water into a broiling mass.

"How long will this last?" he shouted above the din.

"For as little as an hour, or as long as a whole week," Brower replied.

Myra, who had never experienced rain before, put her hand out and watched the droplets splatter her skin with fascination. There was a childlike quality to her behavior that was at odds with the miserableness of their situation. Perhaps she would not feel that way after a few days, Ben mused. But then again, what did he know about what droids felt once they were left to their own devices? They had sensations, but not like humans. They could change their perception of those sensations if they had to, like when he had cut her open. She hadn't flinched with pain like an ordinary person would have. Yet she had to feel pain, since it was built into her design. Pain was necessary for normal function. The body needed it to avoid tissue damage. Droids were no different. They needed it to avoid excessive loading on their joints and other delicate systems, and to ensure their skin stayed healthy.

They crossed the lagoon and entered another section of the river that was overgrown with jungle. The rain splashed off the leaves, streamed down the branches and vines, and fell on them like soft marbles. The light was reduced to dusk-like conditions again. A mist rose off the water. It leached all the color out of the forest and shrouded everything in a gray haze. It was a netherworld, and they were ghosts floating through it.

They continued their way up the river while it got progressively darker. Ben lost sense of time. He had no idea whether the sun had set or was still high in the sky. Several times they had to jump out and haul the canoe over sunken logs. Whenever they did this, he nervously scanned the riverbanks for *sarcotoothi*. Once or twice he thought he saw their golden reptilian eyes poking above the water, staring at him, but he couldn't be sure.

It might have been an illusion brought on by the rain hitting the water.

Shelley pointed to a riverbank in the near distance. "Over there."

Brower steered the boat to where she was pointing. Moments later, they slid to a stop on a sandbank. Shelley jumped out and signaled everyone to help drag the canoe out of the water.

They were on a beach of sorts. The amber-colored shoreline gave way to a small clearing covered in a bed of leaves. The area was sufficiently elevated to warrant a campsite. Saplings gave way to enormous trunks that rose up into the fog-shrouded canopy, making the site feel like the inside of a cathedral.

Shelley and Brower set to work on chopping down saplings and palm fronds to make a shelter. Ben asked what he could do to help.

"Collect firewood," Shelley told him.

"In this weather?"

She ignored the question.

"Look in the hollows of large trees," Brower said. "But watch out for snakes!"

"What can I do?" Myra asked.

"Collect ferns for bedding," Brower replied.

In a surprisingly short time, Shelley and Brower had completed a small thatched-roof hut large enough to hang four hammocks. Shelley's and Brower's were already made; she quickly made one more for Ben out of vines and spreader sticks. The droid could look after itself. A small annulus in the roof, half covered by an elephant leaf, allowed the smoke from their fire to escape. The smoke had the additional benefit of mostly repelling the mosquitoes that had descended upon them with a merciless ferocity.

The four of them sat on the floor of the hut in silence, staring at the small fire Shelley had made from Ben's meager wood supply. Poking the fire, Shelley said, "We need more wood."

"And food," Brower added.

Ben rummaged around in his daypack and pulled out two snack bars.

Shelley laughed.

"What?" Ben said.

"That's what you call food?"

"No. It's just a snack, I thought —"

"This is the jungle," Shelley said. "The jungle will give us what we need. We don't need those."

"Fair enough," Ben said. He stuffed them back into his daypack.

Shelley got up. "I'll be back in a while." She went out into the rain.

Brower said to Ben, "Like she said, more firewood."

Ben felt like grouching. Why him? Now that they had built the hut, Brower could just as easily contribute. So could Myra, for that matter.

Brower seemed to have read Ben's thoughts. "By the time you come back, I'll have a big pot of boiling water ready to clean the food."

"Why do you need a pot of boiling water?" Ben asked. "We have a river right outside our front door."

Brower chuckled. "You've definitely been living in the city too long." He went out before Ben had a chance to answer.

Ben looked suggestively at Myra. "I'll stay here and look after the fire," she said.

He gave her a displeased look.

"Someone has to do it."

He huffed and went outside.

The water had already been boiling for some time when Shelley returned. Several large frogs dangled from her twine belt. A medium-sized monkey flopped dead over her shoulders.

She lowered it to the ground and proceeded to hack off its arms at the elbows and legs at the knees. She tossed the limb ends into the river as one might throw sticks.

Ben watched her from the open doorway of the hut, his face stricken with a queasy expression.

"Why is she throwing the limbs away?" Myra asked.

"How rubbery do you like your meat?" Brower said.

Ben turned away. "I'm not hungry."

Brower laughed.

Shelley brought the remainder of the monkey into the hut and dunked it into the boiling water. After a short while she hauled it out and scraped the fur off with her machete. After reducing it to a little pillow of pink flesh, she went out and washed it in the river.

Brower tipped the hot water back into the river and washed the pot upstream. Shelley then gutted the animal, chopped it into chunks, and threw the pieces into the pot. She gutted and cleaned the frogs and threw them in as well.

Brower carried the chunks back inside and skewered them on some sharpened sticks. He placed them on the fire, afterwards lighting up a cigarette using a hot coal. Puffing away, he said to Ben, "So tell me the story again. How exactly did you end up here, alone with a droid, of all things?"

Ben told them the story without any embellishment. Just the basic facts.

"So you think Vernon can help you?"

"We have nowhere else to go."

"Why did you copy her?" Shelley asked.

"I wasn't the one who copied her. I just do cognitive installations."

"What does that mean?"

"I program the parameters that define her personality."

"You really believe you can do such a thing?"

Ben felt himself getting defensive. Like she was questioning the work he did. Her attitude seemed to suggest that he didn't know what he was doing. "We do our best," he said, hoping she wouldn't ask any more questions.

"Well, let me ask you, then," Shelley continued. "Can you fix a radio?"

"I'm not a radio technician, but I understand the principles."

"Can you fix a generator?" Brower asked.

"Sure."

Brower turned to Shelley. "He could be useful."

"What about Miss Reeves?" Ben said. "She could be useful too, couldn't she?"

Shelley said, "I doubt it. Her RTG is more useful than her body."

CHAPTER THIRTY-SIX

Day Three: Late at night

Flying high above the cloud deck, the rings of Natchator shone ever more brightly now that they were away from the city lights of Urkesh. The planet's two smaller moons – Leixhana and Porferia – were fully in the sky, bathing the *Zond Octavia* in a bloom of silver.

Booker, however, wasn't privy to this sight. He dangled all alone in a pod that hung several hundred meters beneath the airship. If it were possible to experience weightlessness in the 8.7 m/s2 of Natchator's gravity, this was the nearest thing to doing it without actually going into space.

Not that anyone on Natchator had ever been to space. The Orianian rocket industry had exclusively focused on military applications. There was a reason for this. Satellites had been attempted, but they never stayed up long enough to be useful because of collisions from random particles that fell out of Natchator's rings. Until that problem was solved, sending up astronauts was out of the question.

The rain pattering on the pod's windshield reduced visibility to almost zero. But if Booker could see, he would have observed an endless carpet of green almost within touching distance below him. Instead, he was hypnotically focused on the glowing cathode-ray screen of the tracking device cradled in his lap. A steady *blip-blip* in the upper right-hand quadrant told him that his quarry was close. Moreover, the location of the signal hadn't changed in the last three hours. For the third time that evening, he radioed that fact back to the flight deck. The response was predictably the same. They would circle back around for another pass.

What is the point? Booker thought. It was pretty clear that they had stopped moving for the night. The pod was cramped. He couldn't fully stretch out his legs. He wished he could just go back to his bunk and get a good night's sleep. But it wasn't to be.

He tried to amuse himself with thoughts of what it would be like when he eventually caught up with Benjamin Huxley. The brat had outsmarted him. Twice, admittedly. First, when he'd stolen the droid. Then when he'd removed its transponder, as he surely must have, because the Hathor Corporation had reported a loss of signal. Sporn had screamed at Booker when he found out. Threatened to have him shot on the spot, though they both knew that wasn't going to happen. Realizing that his career was over if he didn't come up with a solution right away, he'd told Sporn that despite the loss of the transponder, the droid could still be tracked. He didn't know how, not at that moment, but he promised it was possible. Sporn gave him one hour. After that he would come back, and if Booker still didn't have a solution, nothing would save him, not even Carver.

Every droid had a short-range Wi-Fi system built into its motherboard that allowed them to communicate nonverbally with other droids and devices. By connecting remotely through a client's base station, Mimetic Machines could monitor their product, or if necessary, install patches or upgrades to solve unforeseen problems. If he could somehow get close enough to the droid, then he stood a chance of getting a handshake and, based on its signal strength, an estimate of its range.

He got his electronics engineers to quickly jury-rig a device that could do that, and when Sporn came back, he demonstrated it on a test droid. Sporn seemed impressed, but not satisfied. How would they get close enough to the droid in the first place? He told Sporn the best way to do that was to systematically search from the air. Realizing stealth would be critical to their success, Sporn quickly concluded that a Zeppelin would be the best instrument to achieve their aim. But Zeppelins were noisy. Their engines sounded like a swarm of bees. It would give them away. The only way it would work was if they stayed high in the sky, out of earshot. But that meant Booker's tracking device would be out of range.

After some head-scratching, Booker said, "I got it. We could hang a pod from the aircraft and lower it close to the ground." Sporn liked that.

Of course, there was still the matter of figuring out the most efficient search pattern. It wasn't like they could scan the entire Olongo basin. That would take months. Sporn, however, was quick to assure Booker that it would not be a problem. He would take care of it. And true to his word, he delivered on his promise with characteristic ruthlessness and efficiency.

They made a brief stop at the pontoon village. There, Sporn lined up all the adults and children and asked them one by one if they had seen two strangers enter the village, and if so, which way did they go? The adults systematically denied seeing anything, so Sporn simply shot them where they stood. It was a child who eventually pointed out the direction the strangers had taken.

Booker had watched the proceedings with anguish. At the end of the day, it was his fault. Seeing the bodies pile up had made him sick to the stomach, but what could he have done?

He shut the horrid scene out of his mind and told himself it was a necessary evil. A small sacrifice for the greater good.

Yet the way the children had stared at him as the ship departed – it seared into his brain. Very few of them had cried. Just the youngest ones. The eldest had comforted them while staring upward, as if they were looking at aliens from another planet, their expressions one of bewilderment. Those stares scared him. They had no hatred in them. If anything, they'd showed a complete lack of comprehension. If only they had been filled with hatred – he could have understood that.

Catching himself reliving it, he clenched his jaw and forced himself to think about something else. Yes, where was he? Ben's face. That's right. He would relish observing Ben's expression as he explained how hard it was going to be for him to follow the official section codes of the Cosmonist Crime Statutes – namely, that he would be required to erase all evidence of Ben's employment records at Mimetic Machines. No legacy. No recognition. Nothing. It would be like he had never existed. If he wanted to know what that was like, all he had to do was think about Pascal, who had been swiftly interrogated and shipped off to the Labor Camps.

As for Tom, well, his case was still very much up in the air. He had cooperated in giving evidence against Huxley and Montaigne. It was just a matter of formalizing his sentence. Permanent indenture at Mimetic Machines without possibility of a promotion or pay rise seemed to be on the cards. Added to that, his passport would probably be revoked, and he would be forced to heed a curfew every night.

All in all, not a bad outcome.

As for Booker himself ... Well, that remained to be seen. Carver still held a lot of clout when it came to making decisions about his career. Despite Sporn's threats, Carver would ensure that doors would remain open, he was sure of that. And so he felt he really didn't have much to worry about. It would all work out. The Huxley affair would be forgotten – forgiven as a youthful slip – and under his steerage, Mimetic Machines would go on to produce increasingly more sophisticated products, all built to the strict specifications of the government, of course. That didn't bother him. It was enough that his name would be etched on the employee leaderboard. After a long and illustrious career, he would be able to retire on a fat pension, travel the planet, enjoy himself at five-star luxury resorts.

There was so much to look forward to.

CHAPTER THIRTY-SEVEN

Day Four: Midnight to early morning

Ben found the monkey totally unappetizing. He took a few tentative bites then declined to eat any further; it was rubbery and gamy. Myra elected to nibble on some frog legs and declared herself satisfied.

When they turned in, Ben snuck an energy bar from his daypack. He tried to eat it as quietly as possible so as not to arouse any suspicion. When it finally came to sleeping, he turned once in his hammock and nearly fell out. From that he realized he had to stay as still as possible, though it was next to impossible, because the sparsely woven hammock left him with intolerable muscle aches. He looked at the silhouette of Myra in the doorway. She stood, statuesque, behind a palm frond curtain. A pang of jealousy coursed through him. If only he could shut himself down like that.

The hours dragged on, the incessant sounds of the forest reverberating in his head: the shrill croaking of frogs, the patter of rain on the hut roof, the muffled growl of some unknown predators lurking in the near vicinity of the camp. Inside the hut, Brower's snoring nearly drove him mad. He had never shared a room with people before. His senses were being overloaded again.

It came as a complete surprise when he found himself being shaken awake by Myra sometime early in the morning. The sun had already risen and its rays were streaming through the vapors of mist that had condensed between the towering trees visible through the doorway, the rain apparently having passed.

"You should see yourself in a mirror," Myra said.

Ben felt his face. It was puffed up from mosquito bites.

Brower was outside smoking a cigarette. Shelley was absent. Ben flopped out of his hammock and trudged to the water's edge. He got on his haunches and splashed his face.

"Hope you slept well," Brower said, "because a little further up, we're gonna be rendezvousing with some of our people, and from there it's still another full day's march through the forest."

"I'm feeling fine," Ben said. "Can I drink this water?"

"I wouldn't advise it, not if you're not accustomed to it."

Ben stood up, looked around. He spotted a nearby tree and relieved himself behind it. He was just getting comfortable when a crawling sensation traveled up his legs. He stepped back and immediately felt a wave of stinging pain. Ants!

He jumped around to shake them off. Brower laughed raucously at his misfortune.

Coming back to the river, Ben said, "Why didn't you tell me?"

"Nothing like fire ants to get you going in the morning."

"I can do without them, thank you very much."

Shelley reappeared, carrying a bunch of fish tied together by their gills. She threw them into the canoe, then went into the hut and collected her hammock.

Brower did the same. "I suggest you get yours if you want to sleep comfortably tonight. I don't think she's going to make another one," he said as he came out.

Ben did as he was told. Not that he believed it. He gathered up his daypack at the same time and drank what was left of one of his two plastic water bottles.

"Will there be a chance to fill up again soon?" he asked, showing an empty bottle to Brower.

"There will be. But not for a few hours."

Shelley was already pushing the canoe back into the water, anxious to leave. Brower helped her. Ben and Myra joined them, then jumped in.

They powered up the river for a while in relative silence. The sounds of the night forest had given way to its day sounds. The calls of birds and monkeys echoed through the treetops. The occasional splash of a jumping fish mingled with the striking of Shelley's pole in the water.

After the night's cacophony, Ben welcomed the serenity on offer. More and more, he forgot about time. He slipped into a meditative state where he allowed his thoughts to pass by languidly, like the water flowing beneath the canoe. It was a peace of mind he hadn't fully experienced before. Gone was the motorcycle rush through traffic. The honking of horns, the prattle of strangers' voices, the clank of elevator doors. The only mechanical sound that remained was the soft whir of the electric outboard, which barely registered at the fringe of his consciousness.

"What are you thinking?" Myra asked, breaking his reverie.

Ben didn't answer at first. He had to search his memory. "I was thinking ... I don't know what I was thinking," he said after a while.

"You looked like you were thinking about something."

"I honestly can't remember."

"You want to know what I was thinking?"

Ben stared at her, saying nothing.

"I was thinking that there aren't enough trees in the city."

Ben agreed. It was true.

Overhearing this conversation, Brower said, "They'll chop all these trees down if you let them."

"They wouldn't," Myra said.

"What do you know?" Shelley said, without so much as looking at her.

"It's not the right thing to do," Myra answered.

"The right thing to do. As if they care about that."

Myra's expression turned to one of consternation.

"The dam will be the worst," Brower said. "It'll flood all the lowland Warrawean villages."

"I thought the dam would be a good thing," Ben said.

"Only a city-dweller would say something like that."

"But what about the farmers? They need water too."

"Yeah, but who needs the farms?"

The serenity Ben had been feeling began to dissipate. "It's not our fault that we need to eat."

"No, it's not," Shelley said. "But that doesn't give you the right to take it from us."

Ben didn't respond to that. Shelley had a point. The situation was more complex than he had imagined, or at least different from what he had been taught. The cognitive dissonance this created acted like a blowtorch on the last shreds of serenity lingering in his head. What could he say to make it better? Nothing. So he kept his mouth shut. He sat in silence, nursing the uncomfortable truth.

"Something doesn't add up, though," Myra said. "You're using an electric motor to propel this canoe. That was built by people in Urkesh, with materials that were dug out of the ground and processed by industrial plants that use water, among other chemicals."

"You think you're smart."

"No, I'm just pointing out a fact."

"You think you can trap us in a contradiction."

"It's only a contradiction if you deny it."

"We don't deny it."

"But you don't accept city people using *your* water."

"Water should be shared by everyone. We just don't like people drowning our villages to do it. Surely you agree with that?"

"Yes."

"Then what are we arguing about?"

"Nothing. You're right."

Shelley made a clicking sound with her tongue. "You heard that? The machine admitted it was wrong."

Myra didn't respond to this taunt. She returned her gaze to the river, watched the water drift by.

An uncomfortable quietude settled over the four of them.

Ben considered what had just happened. He knew they'd had an argument of sorts, but he didn't have the means to judge its seriousness. He felt that Shelley didn't approve of Myra; there was enough evidence in her behavior to support that conclusion, but he had no idea what he should do about it – or *could* do about it. When all was said and done, he and Myra were guests, so any behavior that deviated from that had to be avoided. That much he did know. It was just that … if that was true, Shelley ought to reciprocate. But she was clearly antagonistic. Under normal circumstances, a gift might have smoothed things over. But he had nothing to give. He was at a loss.

The river gradually narrowed and grew more shallow. The tense silence that had come between them was broken up by the need to push the canoe over and through an increasing number of obstacles. Shelley was always the first to hop out, which signaled the others to do the same. The routine had become familiar. Ben even began to feel less worried about the dangers that lurked beneath the water. It seemed to be a numbers game, and if Shelley wasn't scared, maybe he shouldn't be either.

Eventually they stopped on a muddy bank and, with a lot of grunting and sweating, managed to pull the canoe up onto a small patch of relatively solid ground. Ben felt overheated and desperately underhydrated. His head throbbed painfully.

Seeing his condition, Shelley let him drink from her personal water bladder. His thirst slaked, he thanked her profusely.

Myra watched on with unaccustomed intensity. Ben noticed and realized she needed water too, even if only a few mouthfuls. He asked Shelley if Myra could also have some.

"She can wait."

Ben opened his mouth to protest, but Myra flashed him a look that made him shut it again.

Shelley and Brower had a brief conference.

"This is our rendezvous point," Brower said afterward. "But no one is here yet, so we'll use the time to have lunch."

Shelley made a small fire and barbecued the fish she had caught earlier that morning. There was enough for one fish each. Ben found it delicious compared to the monkey. He ended up eating the entire specimen, including most of the head, which he saw Shelley and Brower eat without a second thought. Myra nibbled a few mouthfuls as usual.

"You're not finishing that?" Brower asked.

Myra gave her leftovers to him. Brower made quick work of them, washing them down with a couple of swigs from his own water bladder.

Ben watched on, his thirst returning. Brower, seeing the way Ben was staring at him, gave his bladder to him and said, "Just a couple of sips, okay?"

"Thank you."

After taking his sips, Ben passed the bladder back. Brower tucked it away in the canoe, then fiddled a cigarette out of his shirt pocket. He lit it using a dying ember from the fire.

"How long do we have to wait here?" Ben asked.

"As long as it takes," Brower replied.

The heat was oppressive. Ben had hardly moved during the meal and his shirt was completely soaked through. He began to worry about how soon they would find fresh water, for Myra in particular. Her arms and legs were all scratched up – as were his – but because her skin was more susceptible to these kinds of assaults, she fared worse. He hoped that wasn't a sign of weakness in her design.

Shelley seemed to have none of these concerns. She wandered off into the trees without saying a word. She and the jungle were one. It all seemed effortless to her.

Ben thought about removing his shirt and started undoing the buttons.

"I wouldn't do that if I were you," Brower said.

"Why not?"

"Remember the ants?"

"Yeah?"

"Soon we're gonna be trekking through the jungle. Every time you brush up against a leaf or any other type of vegetation, you're gonna be covered in a shower of ants. You want to be protected when that happens."

Ben did his buttons back up again.

Presently, Shelley returned. There were three Warrawean men with her. It was as if they had magically materialized out of the jungle. They looked even more savage than Shelley, and Ben eyed them with a hint of fear. They stood proudly erect, holding their bows. Their dark hair was cut short over their brows, and their keen eyes studied him with opportunistic curiosity.

Shelley said a few words to them in Warrawean that he didn't understand. They laughed in unison, relaxed, and began examining Ben's body by touch. They ran their hands over his arms, his torso, his legs. Ben let them do it, even as he felt the urge to push them away. They were particularly interested in his nose. They stroked it while murmuring comments, which gradually escalated into a heated debate.

"What are they saying?"

"They're arguing over whether you have an auspicious nose. I told them I've seen hogs with finer noses."

"Why aren't they examining Miss Reeves?"

"I told them who she was. What she was."

"Will she be safe?"

"I can't promise anything."

The Warrawean men seemed to have reached a consensus and promptly forgot about Ben. They began unloading the canoe, carrying the bags of dried fish and other produce on their backs using head straps. It freed their hands to carry their bows and wield their machetes.

Brower unhitched the outboard motor and tied it to the bamboo frame that supported the battery pack. Together they turned the canoe upside down and covered it in palm fronds. Shelley helped Brower lift the battery pack onto his back. It was an impressive load, and Ben realized he was getting off lightly in comparison.

"Whatever you do, keep up," Brower said.

They marched off behind the Warrawean men, who had already vanished into the jungle.

CHAPTER THIRTY-EIGHT

Day Five: Early morning

Fletcher and Koolhaas looked at the remains of the small fire on the ground. Next to them, Corporal Tanner was on one knee, brushing some ashes aside.

He dug his fingers into the earth. "It's still slightly warm."

"I estimate that puts us about two and a half to three hours behind them," Koolhaas said.

Tanner was a lithe, wiry individual with a permanent squint. He wore his boonie hat half-cocked on his head, giving him a swagger that didn't seem to match his muscle. Still, he was the best tracker they had. It was said he could follow a fish's trail through water long after it was gone. As ridiculous as that sounded, he'd once led a team of lost and starving men to a *sarcotoothis* nest based purely on the disturbances the animal had created in the muddy bottom of the river it traversed. The rich yolks of the eggs had saved the men from certain death, and Tanner had been awarded a medal of bravery, the Orianian Cross.

The fourth man of the expedition force, Private Preston, carried the radio set – he was strong as a mule, and just as stubborn, some said. He was as laconic as the short bursts of messages he was responsible for. The Zeppelin was high up in the sky and he made sure to only contact it when absolutely necessary.

Fletcher ordered him to relay the facts about the abandoned Warrawean camp. They would have to go on foot from here, and would likely be unable to send another message until they found the rebel stronghold. There was every chance that as they got closer, their radio messages would be intercepted, and that was a risk they could not afford. From this point until the actual attack, radio silence was essential.

CHAPTER THIRTY-NINE

They came upon a perennial stream, and after Brower's nod of approval, Ben fell to his knees and plunged his face into the crystal-clear water. Myra did the same. Coming up, they looked at each other and laughed like children.

After Ben filled his water bottles, he put them back in his daypack.

"What are you carrying in there?" Brower asked.

"Not much. Just a laptop and a book."

"A book?"

"It's nothing."

"You say! Books are as rare as hen's teeth around here. What sort of book is it?"

"Actually, it's a copy of the Scriptures."

"You're shitting me."

"No."

"You brought a copy of the Scriptures all the way out here?"

"Yes."

Brower made a whistling sound. "And I thought I had seen it all."

The Warraweans had watered and rested and were itching to go. Shelley refreshed herself and moved off.

The relatively flat terrain gave way to gullies and ridges, each one requiring a small creek crossing. It was as if the earth had been rippled and they were crossing it against the grain. Each successive ridge transitioned to a slightly higher one. They were clearly climbing, and as they did so, the character of the jungle began to change. The trees were smaller, and instead of the constant spongy and humid undergrowth, rocks poked through the leaf litter and the ground became drier. Ben found this terrain much more pleasant, but with it came more flies. Black flies that settled on the skin and sucked the blood. It was a losing battle trying to swat them away.

Myra seemed to be the only one who didn't suffer from them, just like she was immune to mosquitoes. Ben surmised that it must have something to do with the composition of her synthetic blood. As a favor, she picked up a small leafy branch and began swatting the flies off Ben's back and shoulders as they walked.

"So I just have to ask," Brower said, as they topped another ridge, "are you a believer?"

Ben sensed an agenda in his tone. "Uh-huh."

"That wasn't a very positive answer."

"I believe."

"Well, I wouldn't go advertising it around here," Brower advised.

"I don't intend to."

"What is he talking about?" Myra asked, catching up to Ben.

"Nothing. Don't worry about it."

"Curious, are we?" Brower jibed.

"Yes. What did you ask Ben?"

"I asked if he was a believer."

"What's a believer?"

The mischievous grin returned to Brower's face. "Do you

want the simple answer or some other excuse?"

"You can start with the simple answer if you like."

"An idiot," Brower said. "A believer is an idiot."

"I'm not an idiot," Ben said.

"I agree," Myra said. "Ben is not an idiot."

"You can't be two things at once," Brower said. "It's either one or the other. Take your pick."

"I don't have to choose," Ben said.

"Maybe if I knew why a believer is an idiot, I could help," Myra said.

"I'd keep out of this if I were you," Ben said. "He's just trying to bait us."

"Why don't you let the robot think for itself?" Brower said.

Ben caught his foot on a rock and stumbled.

"Watch your step there, buddy."

"I'm all right."

"You injure yourself, and we leave you behind. No qualms."

"I said I'll be all right."

"Maybe we had better concentrate on walking rather than talking," Myra said.

Brower snorted, adjusted his load, and marched onward.

They trekked on in silence, their breathing getting heavier as the climb became more arduous. Ben found himself grabbing onto saplings to keep his balance on some of the rockier inclines. After several more ridges and ravines, they gently descended onto a flat area, a kind of large rock shelf. A broad pond lay before them. The water was murky brown and flowed off down a narrow gully at one end that was too steep and slippery to negotiate. It looked like the only way forward was to wade through the pond.

"It's actually quite deep in places, so follow my footsteps exactly," Brower said. "You got that?"

Ben and Myra nodded.

"Is there a reason why we need to do it exactly?" Myra asked.

Brower's expression became serious. "*Sarcotoothi*. And the nestlings have just hatched. So the mothers are hungry."

The three Warrawean men went first. Ben watched with fascination as they appeared to walk on the very water itself.

"There's a path of flat stones just beneath the surface," Brower explained. "Whatever you do, don't make any splashing sounds."

What an ingenious solution, Ben thought. It was simple yet cunning. The Warrawean men had obviously memorized the position of each stone, because no matter which viewing angle he tried, he could not see them.

Shelley went next, followed by Brower. Ben ushered Myra to go in front of him. He wasn't confident that she had the ability to balance properly and he wanted to be behind her to catch her if she faltered.

Some of the stones were quite large and easy to locate. Others were small and allowed little more than half a shoeprint. Every time he hit one of these, he held his breath with trepidation. And then it happened. Myra teetered, threw her arms out, and looked like she was going to topple. Ben lunged forward and grabbed her hips in an attempt to steady her. In that moment, one of her feet slipped off and she dropped down. Her leg plunged knee-deep into the water.

"Get her up!" Brower yelled.

Ben yanked her up. As he did so, a disturbance appeared in the water about a dozen yards away. A wake formed and headed straight toward them.

"Run!"

Panicking, Ben pushed Myra forward. She cried out with fright. There were some twenty-odd stones still to cover. Shelley, seeing their plight, raced back toward them and did something Ben hadn't thought possible. She grabbed Myra, threw her over her shoulders, and, leaping from stone to stone, carried her swiftly back to dry land. Ben raced after her, treading in her footsteps.

Shelley let Myra down and shouted at all of them to run as fast as they could. Ben didn't need encouraging. He ran like he had never run before.

After reaching a spot that was far enough away, they all stopped and looked back. A seething, writhing mass of *sarcotoothi* fought each other for imaginary prey. For the first time, Ben got a good look at them. They were much larger than he had imagined; almost as long as a canoe, and their heads were practically all jaw, filled with hooked, razor-sharp teeth. Their long tails ended in a scaled flipper-like appendage, which gave them the ability to torpedo their bodies through the water. Their feet were small and clawed. But nothing could have prepared him for the sound they made when they snapped their jaws shut. It was like two boulders crashing together. There was no question in his mind that there was enough force in them to cut a man clean in half with a single bite.

He shuddered to think what would have happened if Shelley had not saved them.

"Thank you so much," he said. "You saved our lives."

"The jungle is no place for a robot."

"Then why did you save me?" Myra asked.

"It's very simple: I don't want to carry your RTG the rest of the way to the camp."

The Warrawean men led the way along a narrow elevated trail that skirted the pond. The trail slowly wound its way up to a natural ledge that had formed under an overhanging cliff face. They were quite high up now. The sun was hotter and the air drier. When he dared take his eyes off the narrow path, Ben found himself looking down on the forest canopy. It stretched as far as the eye could see. In the extreme distance, through a bluish haze, he saw sections of escarpment that had broken free from the vegetation around it. He realized he was looking at the eroded walls of an ancient caldera, an extinct volcano that had exploded millions of years ago, creating the great depression that was the Olongo basin and the Tongassa River. The beauty of it was entrancing.

"Keep your eyes on the path," came Brower's voice from behind. It had been decided that this time he would go last to watch over the two "tourists," as he had taken to calling them after the pond incident.

Ben did as he was told. Not that Brower had needed to remind him. The path was scrabbly in places. One little slip and it was a long drop.

Myra was struggling. Every now and then they had to slow down to accommodate her. Shelley was getting impatient. The Warrawean men had already advanced to the next bend and were no longer in sight. She nudged Myra in the back, urging her to speed up.

"I'm going as fast as I can," Myra said.

"No you're not. Don't think. Just move."

"It's good to know that you think I think."

She prodded Myra again. "Just move."

"Don't do that," Ben said.

"Don't tell me what to do."

"Droids are learning machines, just like us. Give her time and she'll figure it out."

"We don't have time. This path can't be walked at night."

"Oh. I see. But … you do realize droids can see in the dark?"

"So she can lead the way, can she?"

"Oh. No, you're right."

"I'll try to walk faster," Myra said.

CHAPTER FORTY

Day Five: Noon

"They're heading north," Tanner said, examining some freshly overturned leaves.

"What I don't understand," Fletcher said, "is they're moving further and further away from the river system. How do we know they're not deliberately leading us on a wild goose chase?"

"We don't," Tanner said.

"That's just great," Koolhaas said.

Preston listened to this conversation with his usual taciturn silence.

"We just have to follow the trail and see where it leads," Tanner said.

Koolhaas took a swig of water from his canteen. He shook it to see how much he had left. "Let's hope we run into a stream, because this is all I got."

"The further north we head, the rougher the terrain will get. I can't promise anything," Tanner said.

"We can resupply from the ship if we have to," Fletcher said, getting his canteen out and taking a drink.

They looked at Preston, whose expression didn't fill them

with much confidence. He seemed determined to maintain radio silence.

Birds flittered through the canopy overhead. The men looked up.

"Jeez, I know where I'd rather be," Koolhaas said.

"What are you complaining about?" Fletcher said. "We got a promotion, didn't we?"

"Did you ask how much extra pay that comes with?"

"No."

"I did."

"And?"

"Nada."

"Bullshit."

"No shit."

Fletcher reassessed himself. "In that case, I think I'm gonna demand a long vacation after this. Break out the board and get me a tan."

"I hear you," Koolhaas said. "That right-hander off the Chibang bluff has got my name on it."

"You surf?" Fletcher asked Tanner.

"No."

"What do you do, then?"

"I dance."

Fletcher and Koolhaas laughed.

"You wouldn't laugh if you knew how much pussy I get."

"You're talking flesh?" Preston asked.

They looked at him, surprised that the man actually spoke.

"All sorts," Tanner said. "But yeah, I prefer flesh."

"On your pay?" Koolhaas ribbed him.

Tanner made some fancy moves with his feet. "I don't need to pay. I got the magic."

Koolhaas tried to replicate Tanner's moves, but ended up stumbling over his own feet. They all laughed.

"So what do you do?" Fletcher asked Preston.

Preston took a while to answer. "I listen to music."

"What kind of music?" Tanner asked.

"Traditional."

"A throwback, are we?" Koolhaas said.

"It relaxes me."

The other three seemed to accept that.

"So what's the plan?" Preston said. "North?"

"North it is," Fletcher said.

They hitched their packs, adjusted their rifles, and set off again.

CHAPTER FORTY-ONE

Day Five: Dusk

They came to a broadening of the rock ledge, turned a corner, and entered a cave with a high vaulted ceiling. The Warrawean porters were nowhere to be seen.

"We're here," Shelley said.

The sun was just starting to dip below the rim of the escarpment. The sky glowed a reddish-purple color. The back of the cave receded into a foreboding, gloomy darkness. Some bats flew out, their wings snipping the air.

To Ben's amazement, Shelley walked into the back of the cave and disappeared. Brower followed her. Ben and Myra just stood there.

After a while, they heard Brower's voice. "You coming?"

Myra said, "It's all right. There's a tunnel."

The tunnel went for some distance, then came out into a large rock-hewn room. It was lit by a group of people holding candle lanterns – Urkeshians. Ben immediately recognized the man standing in the middle of the group: Vernon Reeves. He was much taller than Ben had imagined – at least half a head compared to his sister. He was bearded and had a thick mane of dark hair. His face was sunburnt, and his eyes gazed cautiously, assessing the situation in a calm, unrushed manner.

After a few moments he extended his hand. "Welcome to Quincera."

Ben stepped forward and clasped Vernon's hand. The skin was rough, the grip firm. As he did so, he made a conscious effort to engage Vernon's eyes. He managed to hold them for a brief moment before looking away, his shyness taking over.

He had no need to worry, however, because Vernon's eyes were already fixed on Myra. "Sister," he said, holding out both arms.

"Brother."

Myra stepped forward and Vernon gave her a big, warm hug, then stepped back and studied her. "You really are something."

She gazed at him in wonderment.

"Come," Vernon said. "Let us sit down."

Some Warrawean women came in and laid out mats made from thatched grass. A circle was formed; tea was brought in. Brower sat cross-legged next to Vernon. He leaned in and spoke into Vernon's ear a hushed tone. As Vernon listened, his expression remained neutral for the most part, except for a brief moment when he closed his eyes and scrunched his face up in what appeared to be a pang of disappointment. But he soon regained his composure, and surveyed the room with a commanding presence.

Onlookers gathered, the news of the new arrivals quickly spreading through Quincera. There was a mix of Urkeshians and Warraweans. They stood and watched in quiet fascination. Most of the attention, Ben noticed, seemed to be on Myra.

"How was your journey?" Vernon inquired, addressing both Ben and Myra.

"Hard," Ben said.

Vernon waited for Myra to answer.

Myra said, "Yes, it was hard, but also rewarding."

"In what way?" Vernon asked.

"I learned a lot about the jungle. I cataloged many plant and animal species."

"So you would."

Ben wasn't surprised to hear Myra say that, though he felt a little peeved that Vernon had discovered something about Myra before he did.

"I heard you had a run-in with the locals," Vernon said.

"I don't believe we ran into any 'locals,'" Myra said.

Vernon chuckled. "I meant *sarcotoothi*."

"Oh, those! Yes. It was very scary. Shelley should be praised for her bravery."

Vernon applauded. "Yes, she should. But I'm sure she'll just dismiss any suggestion that she is brave."

"Is that a Warrawean trait?"

"I'd say it's a Shelley trait. But she's right here. Why don't we let her speak for herself?"

Shelley clearly wasn't impressed. "What you call 'ego' isn't important to us Warraweans," she said. "Our consciousness is an extension of the forest, of which we are a part."

"I think I can understand that," Myra said.

"No, you can't," Shelley corrected her. "The forest is infused with spirits. They exist in the trees, the water, the animals, the plants, the rocks and sky. They talk to us through our shamans. We ignore their advice at our peril. To you, that's magical thinking. But to us, it makes us one with the forest."

Vernon took a sip of his tea. Seeing him do it, Ben did the same.

"Well," Vernon said, putting his tea down, "I think we can all agree on one thing: the government is corrupt, and the sooner we bring it down, the better."

A smattering of "Hear, hear" rippled through the crowd of onlookers.

"And so I want us all to celebrate in solidarity tonight. We shall roast a hog, make fish soup, and drink *Grava*."

The room broke out in loud cheering and clapping. Almost immediately, people began filing out to prepare for the festivities.

"Come," Vernon said, extending his hand to Myra. "Let me show you around."

CHAPTER FORTY-TWO

Day Five: 8:00 p.m.

"What's this?" Fletcher said, shining his headlamp over the expansive pond in front of them.

"I don't see a way around," Tanner said.

Koolhaas lowered his gear to the ground and rubbed his lower back.

"Can you send an encrypted signal to the ship?" Fletcher asked Preston.

"Even if it's encrypted, it will alert the rebels that we're in their vicinity."

"Shit."

"If we want to go forward, we have to go through it," Tanner said.

"What do you think, Blondie?" Fletcher asked Koolhaas, who had a fetish for dyeing his jet-black hair blond.

"I guess we gotta suck it up."

"Okay. Who's going first?"

"I'll go," said Tanner. He walked up to the water's edge and shone his headlamp over the pond, searching for the tell-tale golden eye that would indicate the presence of *sarcotoothi*.

Nothing.

He traced out the traditional circular motif on his forehead, a sign of prayer to Yasu Doi, and quietly stepped in. The others watched him, shining their lights on his back and over the water around him.

Tanner was extremely careful. He barely rippled the water as he went. At the halfway mark he was up to his chest. He held his rifle above his head and pushed on.

After what seemed like a lifetime, he made it to the other side.

"Who's next?" Fletcher asked.

"Me," Preston said. He unhitched his radio gear and tied his rifle to it. Hoisting the bundle above his head, he went in. Following Tanner's example, he walked methodically, taking great care not to disturb the water.

Fletcher and Koolhaas watched and listened. All was quiet.

When Preston got to the other side, he didn't stop. He kept on walking until he reached a rocky area, then set himself down. He heaved a few big breaths and lay flat on his back.

"What do you say we go together?" Fletcher suggested.

"Yeah." Neither man wanted to be the last.

They held their rifles over their heads and went in, wading through the water as quietly as they could.

Not quietly enough.

Tanner was the first to respond. "Get out of there!" he cried.

Koolhaas and Fletcher's bodies jolted as abruptly as if someone had sent an electric charge through them. They stopped walking, dived forward, and swam, thrashing their arms and legs chaotically in all directions.

Koolhaas didn't even hear Fletcher's scream. It was cut short as the air was crushed from his lungs by a pair of massive jaws. By now the water was shallow enough for Koolhaas to get up and run. But just as he stood up, he was pulled back in again. A *sarcotoothis* had latched onto his gear. Tanner jumped in and pulled Koolhaas back toward the shore. Realizing his predicament, Koolhaas wriggled out of his straps and let the creature pull his gear away. Together, the two men scrambled out of the water and fell onto the muddy shore just in time to avoid another *sarcotoothis* lunging at them, its jaws snapping ferociously.

A rapid volley of gunfire echoed off the pond. The *sarcotoothis* retreated back into its murky abode. Preston fired again, spraying the surface where the creature had disappeared.

Tanner put his hand on the stock of Preston's rifle and pulled it down. "It's gone."

The three men stood in stunned silence. The pond settled. A few small waves continued to lap against the water's edge, the only sign that anything had happened.

CHAPTER FORTY-THREE

Day Five: 9:30 p.m.

Ben followed Vernon through a short tunnel that came out into a spacious, three-storied atrium. It was the most fantastic thing he had ever seen. It was shaped like an elongated 'U'. The open end faced the forest, but its entrance was concealed by a carefully cultivated trestle of vines. A small waterfall tumbled steadily down the front of the closed end, landing in a pool at the base of the atrium, where it ran along a submerged viaduct all the way back to the forest. The balconies, the columns, and the rooms that branched off each balcony were all carved out of the rock, whose russet color was infused with a golden hue from the many electric lanterns hanging off the balconies. The stone floor was polished smooth from generations of wear.

"Over millions of years this stream eroded a large gorge through this escarpment," Vernon said, sweeping his hand out. "The ancients took advantage of it and carved balconies around it, so that today we have this functional living space."

"It's amazing," Ben exalted.

"It protects us from the sun and rain, and provides water all year round. You can't ask for more."

They walked along the balcony. Looking at the lanterns, Ben couldn't help wonder where they got their power from. He thought about asking, but he already knew the answer. He looked at Myra, hoped she wasn't thinking the same thing. She didn't appear to be. She seemed to be taken in by Vernon.

As they walked, they were greeted by an old Warrawean man leaning against one of the many stone pillars that held up each balcony. His skin was heavily wrinkled, but his body looked fit and nimble. His arms were adorned with amulets, grass anklets were tied around his ankles, and he wore a leather breechclout over his private parts and a shawl embroidered with zig-zag patterns over his shoulders. His face was tattooed, as were many parts of his body. A small medicine bag hung from his belt.

"I'd like you to meet Melos Ammon," Vernon said. "He's Shelley's uncle and our local medicine man."

"Pleased to meet you," Ben said, offering his hand.

Melos grasped it and gave it a brief shake. Ben was surprised at how dry and smooth his skin was. Myra offered her hand and Melos went through the same ritual.

"I'll leave you with Melos," Vernon said, walking off with Myra.

Ben followed them with his eyes, not sure why Vernon had suddenly left him alone with this old man.

The answer came soon enough, however. Melos said, "I once knew your father."

Ben turned to him in astonishment.

"He lived with our tribe when I was much younger than I am now."

"Twenty years ago ..." Ben heard himself say.

"I suppose so."

"So you actually met him?"

"Oh yes. I had many discussions with him. He was always writing something down in a notebook. Page after page. He was very serious."

Ben couldn't believe his luck. He reached into his bag, pulled out the Cosmonist Bible, and hastily pried out his father's notebook from within. "This notebook?" he said, holding it out with excited hands.

"It could be. May I have a look?"

"Go ahead."

Melos leafed through the pages, smiling to himself as he did so.

"What is it?" Ben asked.

Melos plucked a feather from the book. "This bird. I remember the day I shot it with my bow. Your father was very angry."

"Why?"

"Because it was a rare bird. The *urupaiyu*. It's very rare to even hear it. My father told me you'll receive a blessing on the day you hear it sing."

"So why did you kill it?"

"Because your father wanted its feathers."

Ben's head began to spin.

"Oh, now this is interesting ..." Ben watched as Melos traced, with one of his spindly fingers, patterns on the star charts that Arthur had drawn. "This is our dreamtime," he said solemnly.

"Dreamtime?"

"It's a time before men existed."

Still holding the Cosmonist Bible in his hands Ben contemplated telling Melos that if he really wanted to know about the time before men existed, all he had to do was —

Suddenly a pair of hands snatched it away from him.

Shelley had breezed up behind him unawares. "What's this?" she said, flicking through its pages.

"What do you think it is?"

"You're being smart with me again."

"If I was being smart, I'd ask you if you could read."

"I can read." She stopped on a page and made a show of

doing so.

"Read it out."

"No." She snapped the book shut, grabbed his arm, and pulled him away. Feeling her determination, Ben offered little resistance.

She took him all the way to the front of the atrium, up a set of narrow stairs, and into a small room on the third level. The room had a round hole cut into the rockface. It framed Zephyr, which had risen above the forest. The moonlight illuminated the room sufficiently for Ben to make out a bed of grass covered by a luxurious fur hide.

"No more words," Shelley said, pushing Ben down on the bed. She threw the Cosmonist Bible to one side.

Ben allowed himself to be pushed. She seemed to be in a heightened state. He didn't know whether he should be afraid, or curious.

Shelley reached under the grass mat and pulled out a small pouch. She undid the drawstring and said, "Open."

Ben figured she wanted him to open his mouth. But suspicion got the better of him. "What is it?"

"Something that will make you see the truth."

"I don't need that."

"You need it more than you realize."

"What's that supposed to mean?"

Shelley let out a throaty laugh. "You're in love with her, aren't you?"

"In love with who?"

"The robot, stupid."

"I'm not stupid. And I'm not in love with the robot. It's not a robot, anyway." The croak in his voice betrayed him.

"If what you say is true, then this will have no effect," Shelley said, dangling the pouch before him.

"Okay, let me have it."

Shelley emptied its contents into his mouth.

It was a worm of some sort. Cold, slimy, and plump. His natural reflex was to spit it out. But Shelley put her hand over his mouth and made chewing movements with her own. He braced himself and bit into the thing. A bitter fluid gushed down his throat. He retched.

Shelley laughed again.

For a moment he stared at her, wide-eyed. Nothing happened. But then he felt his head expand. Zephyr seemed to grow and fill the room. Everything became light.

He lifted his arms and touched her gently. The point of contact between his fingers and her skin glowed an electric blue.

"You like it?"

Ben was too taken to answer.

She mounted him in one quick, smooth movement. She took his hands and placed them on her breasts.

His breathing fell into rhythm with hers. He massaged her breasts to each rise and fall. It was an automatic motion, unlearned.

Shelley responded by rocking back and forth on his pelvis. Ben felt himself get hard.

Shelley shifted back, undid his cargo shorts, and liberated his member. She examined it. Satisfied, she rubbed it against her sex. As she did so, she gazed at him, watching his reaction.

Ben looked at her, or more accurately, *through* her. The worm's effect was deepening. Shelley seemed to have become transparent. It was like the moonlight was illuminating her from within.

His excitement rose, and he began thrusting up into her. This was unlike any fantasy he had dreamed of. It was better. If this was what jungle sex was like, he wanted more.

Vernon showed Myra his personal room, which also served as an "office." It was located up the back, on the third level, so whoever was inside it could look out and survey the entire front section of the atrium. This was particularly important, as any attack, if it ever came, could only come from that direction.

Vernon sat down on a log stump behind his "desk," an up-turned tea chest. The logo *East Rodinia Company* was stenciled on the side in faded black lettering. Even though Vernon offered Myra a seat on one of the spare stumps for guests, she went over to a rough-hewn wooden plank situated along a wall and examined the various things placed there.

"What's this?" she said, picking up an old tin can that had been fitted with a bamboo lid. A waxed length of twine came out of the lid and dangled down its side.

"It's a bomb."

Myra quickly put it down. "I should have guessed."

"How so?"

"Ben told me that you bombed the Ministry of Justice building."

"What else did he tell you about me?"

"He said you were a man of principles."

"That's nice to know."

"Are you?"

"Not really."

Myra gazed at him for a long time without speaking.

Vernon got up and went over to her. They stood face to face. "I miss my sister," he said.

"What was she like?"

"Beautiful, annoying, fascinating, daring."

"I'm not fascinating."

Vernon stroked his hand through Myra's hair. "On the contrary."

"I'm not beautiful."

"You're extremely beautiful."

"I only take calculated risks."

"What does your calculation tell you now?"

"That we're brother and sister."

Vernon caressed her cheek. "In name only."

Myra stiffened. "What are you doing?"

"Relax." He caressed her lips.

Myra turned her face away. Vernon put his hand behind her head and rotated her face back toward him.

"This is wrong."

"No, it's not."

She put her hands against his chest and tried to push him away.

He reached down and put a hand between her thighs.

She uttered a stifled cry.

He put his other hand over her mouth. "Shhh!"

She shook her head. With his hand still between her thighs, and the other over her mouth, Vernon lifted her onto the wooden plank.

She thought about kicking him away, but he positioned himself between her legs. She thought about screaming. But the look in his eyes told her that if she did that, he might do something even worse. He dropped his hand from her mouth and pressed his lips against hers. The warmth of his skin was a revelation. She told herself to resist, but her body refused to obey. Instead of tensing up, she softened. Instead of pushing away, she raised her arms and pushed against the cold rock behind her.

Vernon brushed his lips over her cheeks, down her neck. His desire multiplied even as he realized that she didn't smell like a woman. She smelled like ... the damp forest.

She let him undo her shorts. He pulled them off. She could have kicked him right then and there, but they were past that now. What would it have achieved? He was intent on getting his way. He was going to get it whether she liked it or not. It was just a matter of consequences ...

She felt him thrust inside her. She forgot about the consequences. This was something entirely new. She wasn't sure if she liked it or hated it. She hadn't even realized that such a thing was possible. What a strange act. He was inserting a part of his body into hers. Maybe this was what defined a human being. They mingled. Not just psychologically, but physically. Up until this moment she had believed that the definition of human behavior was that it occurred outside the body. Sounds came out of the mouth, but they only went into the ears by virtue of pressure waves. Eyes looked at things, but only because light was carried on the electromagnetic spectrum. Touch, such as a handshake, or a kiss, stopped at the skin barrier.

Oops, no! His tongue was inside her mouth! How disgusting! She jerked her face to the side.

"You don't like that?"

She shook her head.

"Get down on your knees."

She slipped off the plank and got on her knees.

He forced himself into her mouth. She tried to pull back, but he clasped the back of her head.

He thrust into her until she became dizzy.

A warm, sticky fluid filled her mouth.

He held her like this for a while, then let her go.

Her head lolled backward. The sticky fluid ran over her lips and down her chin. She cleaned it away with the back of her hand.

He pulled his trousers back up, then picked hers up and gave them back to her.

She took them and put them back on. She realized her vision was blurry. Tears had pooled in her eyes. She wiped them away. As she did so, she noticed he was staring at her in a funny way.

"What? What is it?" she asked.

"I've always wanted to do that," he said.

He was swimming through water like clouds. Their naked

bodies intertwined, separated, intertwined again. Each sinuous caress of their arms and legs a thrilling discovery; the small of her back, the nape of her neck, her mound of passion, each one a treasure burned into his memory.

The sound of drumming gently pulled him back to the world, free-floating, still groggy from the afterglow. It could have been his heartbeat. It could have been hers. He turned his head and listened.

"What's that?"

"The night has begun."

A brief flash of light swept across their open door. It passed like a wave across her body, etching her profile against the shadowy background.

He thought she was exquisite, in an untamed sort of way. Like an exotic animal that had transformed itself into a human. It inspired a mixture of fear and awe in him. Unlocked a part of him that he thought he had forgotten. The boy inside the man, before the layers of civilization had encrusted his mind.

She got up and adjusted her loin cloth. "Are you coming?"

Ben pulled his pants back on and followed her.

A Warrawean woman was twirling a length of vine in big, languid loops. Something extremely bright – blindingly so – was burning on its end.

"Magnesium," Ben said, as he watched it swoosh through the air.

"We call it firestone," Shelley said.

"Where do you get it?"

"We mine it out of the slopes."

Ben gazed down at the festivities as they sauntered along the balcony. A group of women, their bodies glistening with oil, their breasts bobbing up and down, danced and swayed around the woman twirling the vine. Their movements were synchronized to the beat of the drums. The drummers, all men, sat around the edge of the water catchment, their backs to the waterfall keeping their instruments dry. Warrawean men wearing wicker masks shaped like vulture heads moved through the crowd, imitating the walk of birds. They suffused the air with incense from smoking bundled sticks as they went. Bright-faced children wearing garlands of flowers flitted in and out among their legs.

As Ben and Shelley descended the steps to the balcony below, Ben caught the distinctive aroma of roasted meat. When they eventually came out on the ground floor he saw a large enclave to one side where a quartet of cooks was busy preparing a feast. A hog was on a spit. A large aluminum pot bubbled away on the fire as one of the cooks tore up pieces of dried fish with his teeth, throwing it in while another stirred. The smoke from the fire curled up toward a chimney, where it was sucked away by an updraft.

Vernon and Myra came toward them through the crowd. Ben noticed that Myra looked different. It seemed like she had unsuccessfully tried to straighten her hair out after it had gotten tousled.

"Hungry?" Vernon asked.

"Famished," Ben replied.

"How about we start with a drink?" He directed them over to a large vat where a Warrawean woman was ladling a milky liquid into some bamboo cups.

Vernon let Ben, Shelley, and Myra get theirs first, then he had his filled. "To the revolution," he said, holding up his cup.

Brower appeared. He was joyfully sozzled and had a Warrawean woman under his arm. She struggled to hold him up. "To the revolution!" he said.

Shelley, Ben, and Myra didn't say it, but they raised their cups.

"So, has she made you a man yet?" Brower teased.

Ben opted not to answer. He glanced at the concoction in his cup and quickly took a mouthful … only to explosively spit it back out again.

Vernon, Shelley, and Brower bellowed with laughter.

"Apparently not," Vernon said, greatly amused.

Ben's mouth burned. "What is it?"

"It's *Grava*," Shelley said.

"What's it made from?"

"Fermented yams."

"Are you sure? It seems like it has something else in it."

"Oh yes, it does," she said. "But I'd have to kill you if I told you."

Vernon and Brower exchanged comical glances.

There was some activity over at the kitchen. "I think the food's ready," Vernon said.

They went over and received palm leaves piled up with steaming hot meat and baked yams. Fish soup was ladled into the same cups they'd drunk the *Grava* from.

Ben couldn't remember the last time he had tasted food so full of flavor. The hog was especially welcome. He felt like he could have eaten half the animal by himself and didn't hesitate to go back for seconds.

While he ate, Shelley danced. Myra, fascinated by the drumming, wiggled her way between two of the male drummers and began imitating their movements. Impressed, one gave her his tambor and drumsticks. She quickly fell into rhythm with them. The lead drummer set up a call-and-answer beat and Myra followed that too. Seeing an opportunity, he encouraged each drummer to do a solo. When it came to Myra's turn, she repeated each of the calls and embellished them with her own flourishes.

Not to be outdone, Shelley began ad-libbing her own movements to Myra's beat. Soon, the other women joined in. The male drummers fell back and worked their rhythms to Myra's calls.

Seeing the crowd's reaction, Myra gradually increased speed. The crowd responded, and soon the entire atrium pulsed with swaying bodies and stamping feet.

Ben couldn't help himself. Soon he was gyrating in sync with the others. He felt completely free, unencumbered by self-consciousness. Shelley joined him. She challenged him with her own call-and-answer routine. Ben followed her as best he could. She began adding wild animal calls, expertly mimicking a wide variety of species. Ben tried to copy her, but she was simply too good. He compensated by shouting out the craziest sounds he could think of.

Soon everyone else was shouting out their own crazy sounds.

The din was so loud that at first, no one noticed the explosions.

CHAPTER FORTY-FOUR

They heard the ruckus some way off on the path before they saw the reflections of flashing lights against the jungle backdrop. Tanner guessed the rebels were celebrating. It amused him that they were unwittingly providing the team with a ready-made cover for their approach.

Koolhaas ordered them to stop and assess their situation. During the march along the precarious cliff track, he had not spoken a word. He had taken Fletcher's death hard. Both Tanner and Preston knew why: this was Koolhaas' first experience of death in the jungle. Understandably, like all soldiers, they expected to die in the heat of battle, not to be dragged into a murky swamp and devoured by a soulless monster. When Koolhaas spoke, it was intimately understood that the rebels would pay extra for this humiliation. It was in his tone of voice, as if he'd said it in so many words.

"Get the captain on the radio."

Preston unhitched his radio gear and got to work setting up his antenna. Tanner and Koolhaas used the time to check their ammunition and rifles.

"This is Team Alpha to Sky Crane, over," Preston began.

"Sky Crane, over."

"We're in position. Grid thirty-seven, coordinates two-zero-four."

"Roger that. Wait for our signal, over."

"Copy, Sky Crane."

Tanner led the team up to the cave entrance. From this position, the sound of the camp festivities came at them from two directions: one from the cave, as muffled noise, and the other from the forest, as a bright echo.

"Sky Crane to Team Alpha."

"Alpha, over."

"On our mark."

"Roger that."

After a short, tense wait, the forest suddenly lit up and boomed with explosions.

"Go, go, go!" Koolhaas ordered.

Panic broke out. People ran in all directions. Shelley grabbed Ben's hand and led him to the nearest set of stairs, which she climbed two at a time. Ben followed. They came out on the third level, just in time to see Gormlings with rifles slung over their shoulders rappelling down the side of the open cliff above the atrium.

Shelley ran toward her room at the front of the atrium, but stopped when one of the Gormlings began firing at her. She ducked, reversed, and flung herself behind a column. A shower of stone shards sprayed over her as she hit the ground.

"Get to the back!" she cried.

Ben began backing up, but he didn't want to leave her. She shouted something at him again, but her words were drowned out by another volley of bullets. Her hand signals, however, were clear enough.

He started running toward the back of the atrium as she had instructed. At the same moment, Brower and several other rebels appeared on the landing. They started firing at the rappelling Gormlings. One immediately went limp on his rope. Others began returning fire.

Ben ran past them into the nearest room. The first thing he saw was an upturned tea chest and a wooden bench stacked with various objects, some of which looked like they were designed for military use.

"Don't touch those," came a voice.

It was Vernon. He had Myra with him. He began collecting a handful of the tin cans.

A moment later, Shelley came running in. They gave each other a knowing look. Shelley began sparking her flint onto the waxed fuses, lighting them up.

Vernon waited until the fuses burned short, then hurled them down both sides of the balcony. Moments later, bright flashes and smoke enveloped the upper landing.

"See that curtain?" Vernon pointed to the back of the room.

Ben figured he must be talking about the thatched palm frond hanging on the wall. To his surprise, it flapped open.

It was Melos, standing in the entrance of a tunnel. He waved Ben forward.

Vernon pushed Myra toward Melos and told her to go. She hesitated. Seeing her indecision, Ben took her hand and hurried her over.

Vernon was firing from his doorway. "Run," he said between bursts. "Run, and don't look back!"

Just then Brower stumbled in, mortally wounded. He collapsed to the floor. Shelley went to his aid. He insisted that she take his rifle. She took it and joined Vernon at the door.

Melos gripped Ben's arm and began pulling him into the

tunnel.

Ben resisted. "Wait!" he cried. He wanted Shelley to join them.

"I'm out!" Vernon shouted.

Shelley gave her rifle to him and went looking through some crates for more ammunition.

"Forget it!" Vernon said. "Go with the others. I'll cover you."

Shelley shook her head and kept searching.

"You're wasting your time," Vernon said. "I'll blow it. Go!"

There was an explosion just outside the door. A cloud of smoke puffed into the room.

"Go!" Vernon shouted.

The smoke forced Shelley back. She ran to the tunnel entrance and joined Ben, Myra, and Melos. For a moment she hesitated at the entrance. Listened as Vernon fired some more shots.

Then, to Ben's surprise, Vernon appeared through the smoke. He pushed them deeper into the tunnel. "Go! I'll take care of this."

Ben had no idea what that meant, but he suspected it wasn't going to turn out well.

Melos led the way and they scrambled deeper into the tunnel. It gradually went uphill, the roof becoming lower. The only light came from Melos, who scraped his flint as they went, each flash momentarily revealing the naked rock with claustro-phobic exactitude.

There was a muffled *whoompf*. Ben felt his eardrums compress. "What was that?" he cried.

"Keep going," Melos said.

The tunnel seemed to go on forever. He found it difficult to breathe. But eventually, he found himself standing out in the open, sucking in the cool night air. Looking back, he saw flashes of light, heard the popping of rifle shots. They were on top of the escarpment. Zephyr was high in the sky, bathing everything in a silver glow. And then he saw it. A sleek cigar-shaped body silhouetted against the moonlight. A Zeppelin.

"So they found us," Melos said.

They stared at the Zeppelin in silence. Ben noticed that the bridge, which would normally have been illuminated at night, was dark.

"We should destroy it," Shelley said. But neither she nor Melos had a weapon.

"Come," Melos said. "We must leave this place."

Slowly, dejectedly, the four of them wandered off, picking their way along the rocky path.

CHAPTER FORTY-FIVE

Day Five: Midnight

"He's dead, sir," Washburn said, as Sporn came up to Vernon's room. The air was still smoky, but the larger dust particles had settled. Sporn entered the room holding a handkerchief to his mouth. The odor of pulverized rock and atomized blood filtered into his nostrils.

Vernon Reeves – what was left of him – lay inert against a pile of rubble at the back of the room. Where his chest should have been was a gaping hole. The bones of his ribcage jutted out through the ragged, torn flesh. His heart and lungs were shredded to a bloody pulp.

Washburn crouched down, picked up a torn and twisted piece of tin can. "Looks like a home-made device, sir."

Sporn grouched with displeasure. So, it had finally come to this. The man hadn't had the decency to face up to his judgment. Coward. Although, he'd had to guts to blow himself apart.

"What do you want us to do with him, sir?"

"Bag his head. Leave the rest of him here."

"Yessir."

Sporn turned to leave, but was stopped by Koolhaas, who

came into the room carrying a book.

"We found this, sir." He handed the book to Sporn.

Seeing that it was a copy of the Cosmonist Scriptures, Sporn's already disgruntled expression turned a shade darker. He hefted it in his hand, let the bitter realization of it seep into his mind.

"I suggest you look through it, sir."

Sporn glanced at Koolhaas, raised a quizzical eyebrow.

"It's …"

Sporn opened the book and leafed through it. When he reached the hole in the middle, he halted. For a few moments he stared with stunned incomprehension. Then slowly, the pieces of the puzzle fell into place. His lips slowly curled into a snarl and his eyes grew white-hot with rage.

The men around him imperceptibly shrank back, having seen the consequences of this expression before.

"You give me this book," he said, "and meanwhile, you let them slip through our fingers. Where is Preston?"

Tanner, who was standing in the threshold of the doorway, said, "Preston didn't make it, sir."

Without batting an eye, Sporn said, "Then get me Neubauer."

Word was passed down the chain of command. Presently Neubauer appeared in the doorway.

"Radio the ship," Sporn ordered. "Get me Booker on the horn."

Neubauer called the ship. A few moments later, Mendes' voice sounded through the radio static.

Sporn grabbed the handset. "Hand me over to Booker."

"Booker isn't here, sir."

"What did you say?"

"Booker took it upon himself to track the fugitives, sir."

Sporn gripped the handset so hard he could have crushed it. "You're telling me you let him leave the ship?"

"Yessir."

"I gave you strict orders to keep him on board."

"Yes, sir. But he acquired the signal. It was moving. Time was of the essence. We tried to contact you, but —"

Sporn turned to Neubauer. "Did you receive any calls from the ship during the attack?"

"No, sir. I mean, I didn't always have a direct line of sight, sir, so I can't say."

To Mendes, Sporn said, "How long ago was this?"

"About thirty minutes ago, sir."

"Did you ascertain which direction the fugitives were heading?"

"East, sir."

"Tell me one of you idiots gave him a weapon."

"That, sir, we did not."

Sporn gave the handset back to Neubauer. To Washburn he said, "The goddamn fool, what does he hope to accomplish?"

"What do you want us to do?" Washburn asked.

Sporn appeared to vacillate for a moment. But he quickly recovered. With a grim finality, he said, "Leave him. He can rot with the rest of them in that stinking jungle."

"But … surely we ought to send a task force after him?" Washburn dared suggest.

"You heard," Sporn said. "They're heading east. That's moving away from Urkesh, deeper into the jungle. You want to take that on?"

Washburn had no answer to that.

"Good —"

Tanner spoke up. "If I may suggest, sir …"

"What?"

"I can track him."

"I'm sure you can. But what then? Even if you do catch up with him – with *them* – who's going to pick you up?"

Tanner's brief moment of enthusiasm quickly faded.

"I certainly won't," Sporn continued. "I'll be in Urkesh celebrating the Victory Parade."

CHAPTER FORTY-SIX

"I'll show him," Booker repeated to himself as he was lowered to the ground.

He soon forgot this mantra, however, as the reality of what he was doing set in. Sliding down a zipline toward the cliff face below the ridgetop, he could see the flashes of light and hear the crackle of gunfire from the battle reflected in the low-lying clouds overhead. *How ironic*, he thought. The real action was taking place up here, on the ridgetop.

On reaching the cliff, he unbuckled his carabiner and climbed the rope ladder left in place by the Gormling raiding party. After scaling the ridgetop, he got the tracking device out of his daypack and set off in the direction of the signal based on his last detection. He estimated they were a good fifteen minutes ahead of him. His line of sight was no longer available and the signal had vanished. But they were heading east. He had to assume they were continuing along that vector.

The moonlight provided sufficient illumination to follow what appeared to be a roughly worn path. Booker hadn't been completely rash in his decision to go it alone; he'd stocked his daypack with water and the chef had hastily handed him some beef jerky wrapped in brown paper. He also had a head lamp, which he had brought for reading at night while lying in his bunk. The only thing he didn't have was a weapon. All he had managed was a steak knife, which he'd pilfered from the galley while the chef wasn't looking.

As he walked along the path, the sound of gunfire gradually receded, and when he looked back, the only thing that made him feel like he was still connected to civilization was the silvery top of the Zeppelin anchored below the ridgetop, safely hidden out of sight of the rebel camp. The long barge poles that jutted out from its sides and anchored it to the cliff made it look like a behemoth insect.

What was he doing? Was he mad? Yes! Sporn had made him mad. But he'd be damned if he was going back to that ship empty-handed. Surely the moment Sporn found out he had taken the heroic step of tracking the fugitives all by himself, he would send men to help. There was no way Sporn would abandon him. He was all bluff. He was just as scared of Carver as anyone else. He would order Captain Gross to follow in the ship and everything would work out fine.

He continued along the path, convinced his reasoning had a basis in reality. But as each step took him further away from the ship, a little voice in his head grew in intensity, until it was clamorously telling him that he was a fool, that no one was coming, that he would eventually lose his way and die of starvation … That is, if some wild animal didn't eat him first.

CHAPTER FORTY-SEVEN

Day Six: 2:30 a.m.

The moonlight faded as Zephyr dipped beneath the horizon. The two smaller moons, Leixhana and Porferia, had risen and chased her long tail on separate tracks.

Melos, old as he was, seemed to have the stamina of two men and marched the others along the rocky ridgetop without pause. The reduced light didn't seem to bother him. He tramped the path like it was an old friend, singing to himself and occasionally issuing warnings, such as "Watch out for that spider" or "Tree root!", while the others followed him in relative silence; Ben, Myra, then Shelley in that order. The hallucinogenic worm Ben had eaten earlier had mostly worn off, leaving him with a slight headache and a general feeling of tiredness. He was thinking of asking for a break, maybe even to stop for the night to get some sleep.

Melos, who seemed to have read his mind, said, "We cannot stop, my friend. There isn't enough soft wood to build a hut and the trees aren't large enough to sleep in."

"Where are we going?" Ben finally bothered to ask.

"Back to the river."

"But the river is down there." He pointed to the dark forest below them.

"Yes, it is, but this is the only way forward."

Ben didn't argue. He had walked far enough to know that they couldn't go back, and there was no way off the ridge. The only way was follow it until they found a way down.

"We walk for about another hour then we reach the Lomwekian village," Melos said.

"The Lomwek-who?"

"The Lomwekians. They're the custodians of the Sky God."

"Did you just say 'Sky God'?"

"I did."

Ben felt himself rouse from his lethargy. "My father wrote about him in his journal."

Melos patted a small shoulder bag he was carrying. "I have it here anytime you want it back."

"Oh, that's such a relief! I completely forgot about it."

Melos unlsung his shoulder bag and gave it to Ben. "I give it back to you."

"Thank-you," Ben said, taking the bag. Then walking a little further, he added, "Correct me if I'm wrong, but it seems you're saying my father learned about the Sky God from these Lomwekians?"

"He certainly did," Melos said, chuckling.

"What's so funny?"

"Life is funny."

"In what way??" Ben asked.

"Just look at yourself. Here you are walking in the same footsteps as your father."

"You mean my father actually walked along this path?" Ben asked.

Melos laughed openly this time. "No! I believe he came up river. But, after your father, you will be the only other city dweller, ever, to meet these Lomwekians."

"I hope that's a good thing."

At this, Melos became slightly more serious. "I guess it all depends on what kind of mood the Lomwekian Chief is in. Last time your father was there, he made a promise to return, but he never came back."

Ben felt his stomach tighten at hearing this. The child in him wanted to say something bad about his father. But that would no longer do. Not after all he had learned and experienced. What could he say? "In that case, maybe we shouldn't be visiting these Lomwekians," Ben offered.

"I'm afraid this is the only way forward," Melos reiterated again.

Ben nodded mutely. The questions were piling up in his mind. Who was this Lomwekian Chief that his father had met and broke his promise to? What did he promise him anyway? And what was it about his experience with the Lomwekians that convinced him the Sky God was real? Surely he should have known better? He was about to annunciate the first question when Melos spoke first.

"I will tell you something now that you will not like hearing," Melos said, his tone becoming somewhat more intimate.

"Oh, and what is that?"

"I said your father was a good man. But he also left his mark on our village."

"I hope not in a bad way?"

"It all depends on what you call 'bad.'"

"Perhaps after you tell me, I'll be able to decide."

"Maybe, maybe not, but since you're his son, you deserve to know anyway." He hesitated slightly before continuing. "When your father came to our village, we had a problem. My brother's daughter, Abriel, was betrothed to the Chief's youngest son, Raoule. Unfortunately, Raoule died in a hunting accident. At least, that's what everyone was told. No one believed it, of course. We all knew Jacoule, the Chief's eldest son, killed him because he coveted Abriel for himself."

"That's not good."

"Good or bad, it happened. When your father arrived, everything changed. Abriel fell in love with him, and together, they killed Jacoule – not deliberately, I believe. They did it in self-defense."

"That's terrible. I didn't realize —"

"That's not all. After your father returned to the city, Abriel discovered she was pregnant."

"Oh, that's … Really?"

"Yes, and she gave birth to a beautiful little girl."

"You're saying …"

"When our Chief learned about the death of his eldest son, he became angry and blamed it on your father. Your father was lucky our Chief liked him enough to let him leave with his life in his hands."

"So he returned to Urkesh?"

"Yes."

"What happened to the girl?"

"She grew up."

"So I have a sister – a half-sister …"

"You do indeed."

"Can I meet her?"

"My friend, she is walking right behind you."

CHAPTER FORTY-EIGHT

Booker was so engrossed in watching his tracking device that he stumbled over a root and nearly fell. For a brief second, he was sure he had seen a blip appear on his screen. He was close, maybe only five or so minutes behind them. He was pushing hard. His back was streaked with sweat despite the cool night air.

The little voice in his head had not gone away. The nagging proof of its correctness had followed him the whole way. The Zeppelin was no longer visible when he looked back. The crackle of gunfire had been replaced with the buzzing of insects and the trill of cicadas. One part of him was quick to assume the worst: that no one would be coming after him. Another part said it was still too early. Sporn would be tied up with more important matters than chasing after him. He was almost certainly involved with the mop-up operation. There were debts to collect.

There it was again! The green blip briefly flashed on his screen. He was getting close now. He needed to start thinking about how he was going to handle the situation when it finally came to reality. Ben was going to be shocked, for sure. Booker could take advantage of that. Get the droid on side. It was imperative that she understood from the outset that he was there not to harm her, but to save her.

This assumed, of course, that Ben was with the droid. She could be alone, lost and confused. That would be the ideal situation. But if she was with Ben, or, for that matter, with others, he would have to be very careful. He would have to appear like he was lost himself. The best thing to do would be to ditch the tracking device as soon as he had them in earshot, or at least in visual range. He had to come across as an ally, or neutral at best. Naturally, he would have to think up some sort of explanation for why he was there in the first place. That would require some fancy footwork. But he was sure he could pull it off. He had to. His reputation was on the line. Maybe even his life …

Ben stopped abruptly and turned around. Myra was a few lengths behind, coming up the track. Shelley was following close behind her.

"What's wrong?" Myra said as she came up to him. "You look like you've seen a ghost."

Ben ignored her. His eyes were fixed on Shelley. She slowed as she approached, sensing something unusual was going on. When she came close to where he stood, Ben said, "Did you know?"

"Know what?"

"That you're my sister."

Shelley looked past Ben, to Melos. There was an expression of sour irritation on her face. "What stories are you telling this time?"

"The truth."

To Ben, Shelley said, "Don't believe him."

Ben swung around to Melos. He stamped his foot into the

ground, balled his fists by his side, and raised his voice. "What is going on here?"

"My friend," Melos said, "your sister has been in denial all her life. It's not my fault that she refuses to believe me."

Ben turned to Shelley, his anger rising. "Is it true? Don't lie to me!"

Shelley pointed to Melos accusingly. "My eyes are a slightly different color from the others. He uses that as proof he's not lying."

Ben went up close to Shelley and looked into her eyes. It was a nonsensical thing to do. There wasn't enough light to see anything.

"He says you can see it when the light is just right."

Ben hammered his fists against his thighs. "This is crazy!" he shouted. "It's your word against his. Will someone just tell me the truth?"

"Perhaps I can help," Myra said. "I can perform a spectral analysis."

"Do it," Ben said.

Myra peered closely into Shelley's eyes, then Ben's. "I see some similarity," she said. "But it's not conclusive. I need a larger sample to make a proper determination."

"Look into his eyes," Ben said, pointing to Melos.

"No," Melos said, tensing up.

He could have bitten Melos' head off. "Why?"

"She could steal my soul. I've seen it happen."

To Myra, Ben said, "Go and do it. I'm not putting up with this shit."

Myra approached Melos. "Don't be afraid."

Melos pulled a small knife from his belt and held it out. "Stay back!"

"What is wrong with you?" Ben cried. "She is giving you a chance to prove yourself and you want to deny that?"

"She will steal my soul."

"You've already said that! But it's just superstition!" He grabbed Shelley's arm and shook it. "Look! See? She is still the same person."

"It doesn't happen straight away," Melos countered. "She will slowly get sick. You'll see."

Ben let out a wild cry. It echoed across the ridgetop.

The others looked at him – then all heads turned simultaneously to look behind them, in the direction from where they had come.

Footsteps crunched on gravel. Slowly, a figure emerged out of the darkness.

"Am I interrupting something?" Booker said.

Ben's mouth fell open.

Booker gave them his best smile.

"… What are you doing here?"

"Good question," Booker said, "I could ask the same of you.

CHAPTER FORTY-NINE

Day Six: Just before dawn

Purely by word of mouth, a large crowd had gathered at the base of Carver Tower. Eyes gazed upward, transfixed, as the *Zond Octavia* maneuvered itself into position around the spidery mast atop the tallest building in Urkesh. The long rays of the morning sun streamed across the desert and struck the side of the Zeppelin, its flanks scintillating brilliant silver, while the rest of the city was still shrouded in shadow. A spectacle such as this had not been seen since the Victory Parade of 3065 and, as it had done then, it brought vehicular and pedestrian traffic to a complete standstill.

Captain Gross and his co-pilot Mendes sweated profusely as they fought to control the Zeppelin against the breeze that flowed chaotically over the Urkeshian skyline. Gross had warned Sporn about this. He had advised them to land at Prince Chronark Airport, where they had the proper ground crews to handle the mammoth bulk of the ship safely. Up here, it was precarious at best, dangerous at worst.

"Steady," Gross commanded. "Ease her up slowly."

The Zeppelin's engines whined as they bit into the wind.

Sporn watched from the side, noting with satisfaction that Gross was being forced to prove his mettle instead of resting on his laurels. Sporn knew the risks; he flew himself. A man who could not face adversity was not a man. He raised his binoculars again and scanned the growing crowd below. It had swelled to several blocks. Excellent. He had only one more hurdle to surmount now.

Carver.

There was a subtle bump. A shifting of weight. Sporn grabbed a nearby handrail to steady himself.

"Contact," Mendes declared.

"Fasten the hold-down ropes," Gross ordered. He wiped his brow with the back of his hand.

Sporn momentarily caught his eye. He thought he detected fear. Good.

"Prepare the gangplank."

Workers inside the airframe began winding winches. The *clackety-clack* of their ratchets echoed through the superstructure. The gangplank emerged like a proboscis at the base of the Zeppelin's nose. Workers on the top deck of the tower threw grappling hooks and guided it toward them. When it reached them, they tied it off with ropes.

"Gangplank secured."

Gross started his stopwatch and turned to Sporn. "We have five, maybe ten minutes before the wind changes."

Sporn gave a slight nod. He would keep his end of the bargain. Only he would disembark. That way, the impact to the ship's center of gravity would be kept to a minimum. The only cargo that required unloading was Reeves' head. The chef was already retrieving it from cold storage.

Mendes blew a whistle. It signaled the workers outside that disembarkation was about to commence.

The chef appeared with a hessian sack. He proffered it to Sporn.

Sporn took without so much as a glance. "As soon as I disembark," he said to Captain Gross, "you're free to go."

"Very well," Gross said. There was no handshake, despite the success of the mission. No love was lost between them.

Having negotiated the gangplank, Sporn was directed to a steel hatch in the tower roof. One of the ground crew opened it and laid it over. A ladder descended to the floor below. Sporn took it. He had one of the ground crew pass the sack down to him.

He found himself standing in a small vestibule entirely encased in steel. A single steel door faced him. It opened with a loud clank.

Carver's private security guard was on the other side. He led Sporn around some tower infrastructure, including a giant water tank, to another door. They went through it and down a set of stairs, entering a service room. The guard opened a final door and they came out into Carver's apartment – his kitchen, to be precise.

Carver was waiting for them at a large preparation table. He stared at them through pots, pans, ladles, and sieves hanging from hooks above him. There was a large chopping board in the middle of the table.

"Brought something for dinner, did we?" he quipped.

Sporn placed the hessian sack on the chopping board. Thawed blood oozed out onto the board.

"Very tasteful," Carver added.

"It's good to see you too," Sporn said.

"I presume you're going to handle that rabble down there?"

"I intend to work them up into a frenzy."

"How very appropriate."

"The people need something to believe in," Sporn said, looking at the sack on the chopping board. "They need security. And

I will bring it to them."

"Of that I have no doubt," Carver said, maintaining his gaze on Sporn.

Looking up, Sporn said, "It seems to me you've forgotten that your entire empire was built on the back of the security I gave you."

"As was yours on the money for materials and armaments that I supplied."

Sporn laughed thinly. "Except I can replace you with any number of greedy businessmen who are waiting in line for their turn. The same can't be said of me."

"True. There is only one of you. Thank God."

Sporn's eyes hardened. He could see that Carver didn't believe a word he said. He believed that an unlimited number of ruthless men were waiting to take the Minister's place, and that he could foster them with money and political corruption. That these men existed, Sporn had no doubt. He had seen them with his own eyes. Vultures waiting at the table. But it didn't apply to him. No amount of money could buy his soul.

He picked the hessian sack up off the table, noting the bloodstains left on the board. It pleased him that he had besmirched Carver's sense of aesthetics. He would have rubbed Carver's face in his own shit if he had the chance.

"You'll be joining me, then," he said. "The people need to see a united front."

"That they do," Carver said dryly.

"After you."

The crowd, sensing that something was about to happen, jostled and buzzed with excitement. The Gormlings on duty beat them back with their batons, keeping a small area at the top of the steps in front of the entrance foyer free.

Sporn exited the foyer and positioned himself at the top

of the stairs. He surveyed the crowd with a haughty air and straightened his jacket with pride. Moments later, Carver sauntered out and took up a position beside him. There was a smattering of applause.

Carver put a hand up. "As you know, our city has been under terrorist threat," he said, in a clear and authoritative voice. "Ever since Vernon Reeves and his rebels bombed the Ministry of Justice building, we have been at pains to make the city safe again. Well, that moment has come. I am proud to present to you the Minister of the Interior. He has some good news to announce. Some very good news indeed."

There was a round of applause. Some people whistled.

Sporn smiled candidly at Carver and stepped forward. "Thank you, thank you," he began. The audience hushed. "We live in dark times," he said. "The bombing of the Ministry of Justice building was a direct threat against our way of life – *your* way of life."

The crowd responded with loud cheers.

Sporn hushed them with a hand signal. "But I want to assure you: whoever seeks to undermine us will pay dearly, whether they're a foreign force, or a cancer within our society. We are not a weak people! When threatened, we don't run and hide. We fight!"

The crowd erupted again.

Sporn hushed them once more. "Sometimes that fight is open war. Other times, we have had to be cunning, wait our turn – if necessary, pursue our adversaries to the ends of the planet. No matter what it takes, we never stop. We never give up! And by the light of Hanub-Ka, we always succeed."

He raised the hessian sack up high for everyone to see. An audible tremor rippled through the crowd.

"I present to you," he said, pausing for effect, "Vernon Reeves!"

He tipped the sack upside down, reached inside, and pulled

Reeves' head out by the hair, waggling it for dramatic effect.

At first there was a hushed silence, but as soon as those closest recognized who it was they began booing and crying out "Traitor! Traitor!" It didn't take long for the rest of the crowd to join in, and very soon the entire mass was chanting in unison.

Carver's face twitched as he strained to maintain a smile over his visceral disgust.

Sporn proudly surveyed his handiwork. He allowed himself to soak it in. Raising his hand once more, he hushed the crowd.

"It's not enough to just defeat the rebels. We must also reap the consequences of that victory for the people. I am therefore here to tell you that with the rebels gone, the Warraweans will be powerless to stop the dam. We shall resume construction immediately, and this time we will finish it once and for all!"

The crowd received this news with great delight, cheering wildly. Sporn clapped too, into his clenched fist while still holding the head, looking back to ensure Carver was clapping along with him.

CHAPTER FIFTY

Day Six: 4:00 a.m.

"You first," Ben said. His emotional state was still evident in his voice.

"Sure," Booker replied coolly. "I came to retrieve property belonging to the Mimetic Machines Corporation. Property that was unlawfully stolen by you."

"Property that was illegally created by you, and that you were going to use for nefarious purposes."

"You think you're doing a good thing?"

"A necessary thing."

"So you're not going to give it back?"

Ben turned to Myra. "If you return with this man, he will treat you like a slave."

"I'm not sure you understand," Myra said to Booker. "My ownership status has been voided. I am free."

"So you hacked it," Booker said to Ben. "That's also illegal."

"I didn't do it. A Jammer did."

"Makes no difference. It's still illegal."

"You heard her. She is free. She won't go with you."

"You have to come with me," Booker said to Myra. "This

man has lied to you."

Myra looked at Ben, looked at Booker. "I stay with Ben," she said decisively.

"Then I will have to go with you as your guardian," Booker said, "until such time as I can return you to the company."

Myra turned to Ben. "Can he do that?"

"I'm afraid he can."

"I'm not going to ask what this is about," Melos interrupted, "but the Lomwekian village is down there. Who is coming?"

CHAPTER FIFTY-ONE

"You're the first to earn it," Rathneggar said. "Congratulations." There was no jubilance in his voice. He said it as a matter of fact.

"Thank you," Sporn said. "It's a great honor."

They were standing in the communal hall of the Cosmonist Cloister. A group of Curates looked on, whispering among themselves. News of the victory had already spread, helped by the gruesome heads mounted on stakes above the South Gate.

"You understand, of course, that we cannot confer the Star of Cosmonism on you right away," Rathneggar said. "It has to be minted."

"I understand."

"You also understand that if you want to take my place as the Head Curate, you will have to undergo the Labors. Don't think you can bypass them."

"It never occurred to me."

"He who is not even aware of his own deceits," Rathneggar muttered under his breath.

"Excuse me?"

"Nothing. We hold the ceremony in one week's time. You're free to go."

Rathneggar watched Sporn leave. It angered him that Sporn had forced the meeting to take place here on Cloister grounds. He just couldn't help himself. Had to make a statement. Rathneggar shuddered. An involuntary act to rid himself of the detritus the Minister left behind. But it wasn't enough. To cleanse himself properly, he would need something more potent. Something that only a full release could provide.

He let his gaze drift toward the Moon Tower, which was partially visible through a round window across the hall. Already he was thinking about her soft flesh, how his hands would dig into it, force it to do his Will.

CHAPTER FIFTY-TWO

Melos stopped abruptly. He scanned the forest. "They're here," he said softly. "They're watching us."

They had tramped down the rough track to the base of the cliff and followed it for a half an hour, mostly in silence, gradually descending below the level of the canopy. They were back in the jungle again.

Ben was averse to reopening the conversation about Shelley in front of Booker. He was just as averse to digging further into how Booker had found them. He suspected he'd used a tracking device, but didn't see one on him. He wondered whether it was in his daypack. He had seen Booker reach into it and pull out a snack, but it seemed too light, not bulky enough to hide a tracking device.

On reflection, he realized Booker could have tracked Myra based on the electromagnetic radiation she emitted. But to do that he would have had to be fairly close, less than one hundred meters – ideally no more than fifty. How he'd managed to do that, if in fact he actually had, was beyond Ben. He wanted to ask, but he just couldn't bring himself to do it. One thing was clear, though: if it was true that Booker had tracked Myra all the way here, it was almost certainly the case that bringing her to Vernon Reeves' hideout had been a mistake. Which meant it was his fault that they had been attacked.

The realization of that fact had silently eaten its way into him. He didn't want to contemplate how many deaths he was responsible for. But he found himself tallying up the numbers anyway. Judging from how many Urkeshians he'd seen at the camp, he estimated at least twenty. How was he going to live that down? And what if Shelley found out? Or Melos? It was a frightful thought.

His life had spiraled out of control. What had started out as a simple case of thieve-and-run had turned into a quagmire of moral transgressions. Deceit, incest, multiple deaths on his hands. *This is what you get for lying to people*, he reasoned. *That's how it all begins. Even if the initial intention is good, the outcome can only be bad.* And the kicker was that he'd known it all along. He'd known he was breaking his principles. Principles he had promised to keep ever since he could think for himself, at least from the age of seven, when he'd realized his father had lied to him about coming back from the Olongo jungle.

It was that lie that had burned into his memory and made him swear never to be like his father. Yet here he was, unlike his father, and worse off for it. His father had created a life. All Ben had done was take them away.

"Shhh!" Melos said. "Stop muttering."

A bird call came from somewhere off to their left. Melos cupped his hands and imitated a response.

It was met with another call, this time from their right. Melos responded again.

Presently, a dozen or more faces appeared through the foliage. They were vividly painted and richly decorated with ivory piercings and tattoos depicting chevron motifs. They all wore headdresses made from bird feathers, each one individually designed. Some wore skull necklaces. One, almost the smallest of the lot, yet the most vicious-looking individual Ben had ever seen – possibly because his eyes were extremely close together and had a look like he was thirsting for blood – came forward and stuck his bow into the ground. He spat into his hands, rubbed them, then raised them in the air and chanted something.

Melos spat into his hands and mimicked the ritual.

The man came forward a few more steps and monkey-grinned at Melos, showing a row of teeth that had been filed down to pointy triangles.

Melos monkey-grinned back.

He walked right up to Melos and, leaning in, offered his forehead. Melos leaned in and they knocked heads. This appeared to be the end of the ritual, and the other warriors shouted something in unison while thumping their bows into the ground.

Melos turned to Ben and the rest of the group and cheerfully said, "They welcome us to their village."

The little fellow, the vicious-looking one, led the way. The skulls around his neck rattled as he went.

"Wouldn't that alert animals to his presence when hunting?" Ben asked Melos.

Melos smiled. "He is doing it deliberately. To show off his superiority."

Ben stopped asking questions after that. Silence, he realized, was probably the best strategy.

The village sprawled out along the upper banks of the Tongassa. The huts had conical thatched roofs and emitted wisps of smoke through small holes at their apexes. Children were up and about, and as soon the group arrived, they thronged around, paying particular attention to Ben, Myra, and Booker. A multitude of hands touched Ben's body, which made him squirm, but a sharp look from Melos told him to endure it.

The children wanted him to sit down on the ground so they could inspect him more thoroughly. Ben reluctantly complied. They weaseled their fingers into his mouth and pulled his cheeks this way and that, inspecting his teeth. They yanked on his hair and rubbed it to see if it was like theirs, which Ben noticed was much coarser in consistency. They prattled among themselves.

"They want to know why you have no tattoos and piercings," Melos said. "They're asking whether you're the runt of your litter."

"I am no such thing," Ben replied, mildly offended.

Melos translated for him. The children laughed and danced around him, pulling strange faces.

"What did you say?" Ben asked.

"I told them you're the son of a ghost."

"That's not true!"

"Of course it isn't. But it delighted them all the same."

Ben stood up. The children tugged on his arms, directed him over to the riverbank. One of them splashed him with water.

"Why did he do that?" Ben asked Melos.

"Because they wanted to see if you get wet."

"Why?"

"Because if you were a shadow walker, you would stay dry."

"What's a shadow walker? I'm not a shadow walker."

"Sons of ghosts are shadow walkers."

"I already told you, I'm not the son of a ghost."

"They don't seem to think so either."

The children were rubbing his exposed skin with mud.

"To protect you from the mosquitoes," Melos said.

"Thank you, thank you," Ben said, swatting them away.

The children laughed and danced around him, made monkey faces at him. *So this is where they learn it*, Ben thought.

The Lomwekian warrior who had led them to the camp

struck his bow into the muddy soil and called out loudly. Everyone, including the children, fell silent and stopped what they were doing.

Presently, the thatched door of the largest hut opened, and a man stepped out. He was slightly taller and broader in stature than the vicious warrior and wore the most colorful headdress of them all. He carried a beaten copper shield trimmed with animal fur in one hand, and a stone-tipped wooden spear in the other. He wore a single skull around his neck, the eyes of which were impregnated with two polished shells.

Moments later, a woman stepped out, presumably his wife. She had broad hips and large breasts, over which cascaded multiple rows of beaded necklaces. Her body was richly decorated in ochre paint, again, with the chevron motifs. Her lips were dotted with tattoos and her arms were adorned with copper bracelets.

"The Chief of the village," Melos whispered to Ben, Myra, and Booker.

The Chief planted his spear in the earth and raised his hand in a gesture of welcome. The other Lomwekian warriors raised their bows once and set them on the ground in response.

"Welcome to our humble abode," the Chief said, Melos translating as he directed his speech primarily to Ben, Booker, and Myra. "What brings you here?"

Melos indicated that Ben ought to answer. Ben looked at him, hesitated a moment. "I don't know what to say," he whispered.

"Tell him that you came to honor and respect the great work he is doing to protect the Sky God."

"But that's not true ... at least, I never came here with that intention."

"My friend, he is waiting for your answer."

Ben swallowed hard. Falteringly at first, he said, "We came here to honor and respect the great work you're doing to protect the Sky God."

The Chief's eyes lit up. "We accept your respect." He spat on the ground and rubbed his spittle into the earth with his bare foot.

"Why did he do that?" Ben asked Melos.

"To show his disrespect for Hanub-Ka."

Ben was horrified. "He has no right to do that!"

"I'm afraid you're standing on his land," Melos said simply. "He expects you to reciprocate."

"What? No!"

"If you don't, my friend, the consequences will be unspeakable."

"What's that supposed to mean?"

"I do not wish to tell you, but if you insist: he will take your head."

"He will not!"

"I suggest you spit on the ground now. He is waiting."

Indeed, the Chief was getting impatient with this back-and-forth banter. Ben saw him inhale and exhale restlessly. He looked at Myra, at Booker. Booker seemed to be enjoying the situation. Or maybe he was just smiling nervously.

"I think this is a case of expediency," Myra said. "I don't want to be in your shoes, but my risk assessment leads me to believe you have no choice. Not unless ..." She let her words trail off. The look in her eyes said it all.

Ben nodded slowly in an effort to encourage himself. He worked up some spittle and spat it onto the ground. With great effort, fighting every instinct to shout out in refusal, he twisted his foot over the ground where the spittle lay.

The Chief watched this with a curious, yet disconcerted look. When Ben removed his foot, he said, "This show you have put on – I'm not convinced."

Melos said in the Chief's language, "He is new to your rituals. Please forgive him."

"I can forgive his naivety. His play-acting, I cannot."

Melos turned to Ben. "The Chief doesn't buy your act. You need to come up with something very fast to change his mind, otherwise I will not be able to help you."

"But I'm not good at this!"

"Yes, it's true. You stink."

Ben stared at Melos in disbelief. "So what am I supposed to say?"

"My friend, there are no words I can offer that will turn things around. You have to find your own way."

Ben began wringing his hands fretfully. The Chief looked at him with increasingly deeper suspicion.

Losing patience, he said, "I'm waiting. What do you have to say for yourself?" Melos translated.

Desperate to come up with something, Ben said the first thing that popped into his head. "Mr. Melos told me you knew my father. Is that true?" As soon as the words came out, he held his breath for fear he had said something wrong.

"Yes I knew your father," the Chief replied.

Ben exhaled. Relieved. "Well, I am his son. Even though I grew up without him."

"So that's supposed to explain your lack of respect for our god?"

"No, no, I completely respect your god. He is great. He is wise." He croaked these words out, amazed that he even said them.

"You say this without even having met him. It seems the longer I wait, the less you convince me."

Ben looked at the Chief appalled. He had to come up with something fast. Usually in these situations, a gift was in order. But he had no gift. The next best thing he had was Arthur's journal. Maybe …? He got it out and held it up. "This is my father's journal," he said nervously. "He wrote about the Sky God in these very pages. That's how I know about him."

The Chief looked at the journal with great curiosity. "Give it to me."

Ben gave it to him.

The Chief leafed through its pages. The ferocious one standing next to him threw shifty glances at it. Eventually the Chief said, "This brings back many memories."

Ben waited.

"I will tell you a story now," The Chief said, giving the journal back to Ben. "Your father was the first city dweller we had ever seen and he was unusual in that he didn't sing the praises of the men who run this country. He warned us about their evil intentions. He wanted to help us. One way to do that, he argued, is prove the reality of our Sky God to them. It would show them, he said, how ignorant they are of their own history, how they have lied to their own people. After some thought on the matter, I agreed and took him to see our Sky God. Naturally, he was shocked when coming face-to-face with our god for the first time. I expected that, but then I told him if he really wants to help us, what we really need is to hear the Sky God speak. That is our dream. Your father, however, said he could not do that. But there were men back in Urkesh that would know, and he could go back and fetch them. So on that promise, I let him go. Except, he never came back."

Ben absorbed this and said, "Are you saying you want me to make your Sky God talk?"

"Yes."

Ben looked at Melos. His expression remained passive. What should he say? If he said 'yes' then that would be a lie. The biggest lie he ever told. He shuddered to think of the consequences. If he said 'no,' however, the consequences might be even worse. Just looking at the vicious one standing next to the Chief made that clear. There was a hunger for blood in his eyes. It didn't take a genius to figure that out. Slowly, and with an almost excruciating deliberateness, Ben said, "Will you take me to your Sky God so I can have a look?"

The Chief smiled for the first time and said, "I was hoping you would say that."

Ben couldn't believe it. If this was a test, then it appeared he had gotten away with it. But almost as soon as he had that thought, he realized that there was a very real chance he was only delaying the inevitable. He had heard the word 'Sky God' more times than he cared to count, but it was still just a word to him. In his mind he was sure they were talking about some kind of stone monument. To think that it could talk! If the situation wasn't so serious, he would have laughed out loud.

The Chief led him along a trail that ran parallel to the river, the rest of the tribe following like a wake, Ben tried to think about what he had been taught about Hanub-Ka. No one had ever seen Hanub-Ka. At least no mortal human being. And only very special people could hear Him speak. They were the prophets. There were three in recorded history: Ramanjabba, Marmoot, and Vesnoon. There was a fourth, but he wasn't so much a prophet as a martyr, in that he was Hanub-Ka's personal sacrifice to the people, Yasu Doi. He'd lived at a time when Hanub-Ka was considered a false god, a projection of the human imagination. The people who rejected Him also rejected Yasu Doi, and they burned him at the stake. Ramanjabba, Marmoot, and Vesnoon later spread his word, and their record of his life became the Scriptures.

Ben was certain the Lomwekians had no such history. Theirs appeared to be an oral history – which, to Ben, suggested their god was more myth than reality.

They tramped along a path until Ben heard what he thought sounded like a waterfall, growing steadily louder as they approached. When he did finally glimpse it, he was met with towering cliffs whose tops he could not see – they were still shrouded in the morning mist. Beneath the cliff, and parted by the river into which the waterfall fell, were some old temple ruins, half tumbled down and overgrown with jungle vines. The foundations were lifted and titled at various angles, uprooted by a giant kapok tree that had grown amidst its rectangle.

On the left side of the river, the side they were on, one of the buildings was still vaguely intact, with steps leading up to an arched entrance and a vaulted interior. Before Ben was allowed to enter, thinking he was about to meet the Sky God, or some icon that resembled him, the Chief said, "This building records the history of the Sky God's arrival to this planet."

More fascinated than ever, he watched the Chief light up a torch and enter the temple. The light played around its dark interior, flickering strange images to life on the walls and ceiling. Ben recognized some of them from the star charts he had seen in Arthur's journal. He opened the journal, playing his fingers over his father's drawings. They were good representations of what was on the walls. He didn't understand the pictures, but seeing them, seeing his father's versions of them, sent an electric buzz through him, making him feel more closely connected to his father than ever before.

The Chief stopped by one panel. He pointed to a pictogram that Ben perceived to be a sun symbol, around which nine dots of various sizes were sequentially arrayed in consecutive rings. The Chief said, "*Aert dom tud.*"

"What does that mean?" Ben asked, looking at Melos for a translation.

"He means 'Earth is where we were born.' Or, if you want to put it another way, '*Earth is our mother.*'"

"Earth is our mother ... Really?" Ben flipped through the

pages of Arthur's journal. "It is written in here somewhere ..."

"It doesn't matter where it is written," Melos said. "We know it in our hearts."

Still Ben searched for the phrase. The Chief watched, amused. After a while, when Ben could not find what he was looking for, he said, "Now I will take you to see the Sky God."

"Not enough light to read," Ben grumbled, giving up.

The Chief moved deeper into the temple. His light played over a large stone altar. It was covered in a dark red substance.

Looking closer, Ben realized that it was semi-dried blood.

He gave it a wide berth.

The Chief led them past the altar and through a narrow tunnel. They came out onto a pathway that led up a series of wide steps to the waterfall.

As they climbed the steps, Booker said to Ben, "You saw that, right?"

"Yeah I saw it."

The Chief led them back out of the temple and toward the waterfall. The water thundered as it hit the river's surface, buffeting the air, as if some giant had grabbed hold of it and was shaking it violently. The path narrowed, and the Chief raised his hand and signaled that only the visitors were to follow from this point on. He traced his way along a narrow path and slipped behind the curtain of water as it cascaded down, the spray flying around him.

Ben followed. Melos, Booker, Myra, and Shelley followed in turn. They entered a cave with a trail that wound its way along a ledge to a side vault. The Chief turned and disappeared for a moment, taking his light with him. The others scrambled after him. They came into a cavernous space that was densely packed with a forest of enormous crystalline stalactites and stalagmites. The Chief picked his way through them and stopped at a large mound, surprisingly cuboid in shape. He held his torch up close to it, and through the crystalline material, Ben saw something inside.

A sarcophagus.

The flowstone that covered it was relatively thin. "Can we chip it away and look inside?" he asked.

Melos translated and the Chief said, "He is not made of glass."

Ben hunted around for a sizable rock. He found one and set upon the flowstone, at first cracking it, then shattering it, revealing the surface of the sarcophagus.

He stopped, stunned.

It was made of steel!

For a while, he just stared at the metal. He laid his hand on it. It was cold and hard. So it was real …

Unable to contain his impatience any longer, Booker pushed past him. Using a stone he had found, he began smashing rapidly at the sarcophagus. Soon Myra was at it too. Seeing them working with total abandon, Ben rejoined them. Crystal shards flew in all directions. The cave echoed noisily from their hammering.

Only Melos and Shelley refrained. What they saw made them apprehensive. Not just the steel box, but the behavior of the city-dwellers themselves. They looked like they had become possessed. And that was never good. Above all, Shelley could not comprehend why the Chief allowed this behavior, when this was the Lomwekians' most sacred of sacred sites.

But to her shock, the Chief's eyes had become feverish, almost greedy – if she could put a word on it. What did she not understand?

By this time, Ben, Booker, and Myra had cleared away one corner and a significant proportion of the top of the sarcophagus. A pile of chips had built up beneath their feet. They kept at it for the next half hour, without respite, until they had cleared away the entire top.

There were latches around the side. Melos, Shelley, and the Chief drew in closer. Ben and Booker undid the latches, systematically working their way around the casing. When the last latch was released, they paused, as if they instinctively knew a special moment had arrived. Not just for them, but the entire planet.

They looked at each other, their faces glowing with excitement.

"Open it," the Chief said in his native language.

Translation wasn't needed. They all knew what it meant.

Ben and Booker heaved at the lid. At first it would not budge. They redoubled their efforts, and suddenly there was a hissing sound, like a vacuum flask being opened.

Driven by an adrenaline rush, they managed to slide the lid partially to the side. The Chief shone his torch inside.

What Ben saw defied all reasonable logic. Yet it was the most logical thing he had ever seen.

A robot.

Not just any robot, but a massive robot, with heavy limbs and a reinforced domed head. Its eyes were made of glass fresnel lenses, but were extinguished. They stared up into space impassively. Its mouth was shut. Its jaw proud. It had the countenance of a human that had been fashioned into a superior version of itself, then transformed into a machine.

Ben could not have imagined anything more impressive. "This ..." he murmured with almost religious reverence. "This is your Sky God?"

The Chief nodded.

"It must have lain here for thousands of years," Booker said.

In the flickering light, Ben saw that its panels were battered and dented, suggesting that it had once been active. The Venetian red paint that must once have gleamed beautifully was reduced to a rusted dull carmine with glints of stainless steel showing through. He put his hand on its chest, where its heart would be if it were human. He knew that instead of a heart, it must have some sort of power source, which by now had run down to zero.

If he was going to make it speak, he would need to find an alternative power source to bring it back to life.

As he pondered this conundrum, something caught his eye. Just above where he had laid his hand was some faded lettering. The word was incomplete. But the capital "D" and the lower-case "r" and "n" left him in no doubt that this was *Darwini* from Arthur's journal.

"Darwin," he said decisively. "Its name is Darwin."

"Can you make it speak?" the Chief asked.

On translation by Melos, Ben said, "Maybe." It wasn't a lie. He *wanted* it now. As much as the Chief.

"So you cannot."

"I didn't say that. I need time to think."

Booker said, "Are you mad? We have to destroy it, not make it speak."

Ben turned on him. "Destroy it? Are *you* mad?"

"Don't be a fool. Can't you see what this means?"

"I know exactly what this means. Nothing could be more important than hearing what it has to say. It has memories … I'm sure of it. Just look at it. It has use wear."

"I can see that. But what you don't see is the trouble it will cause. The regime will not allow it. I can assure you. They simply won't allow it."

"It's not up to the regime to decide. This is a gift to all humanity."

"Excuse me," Melos interrupted. "But the Chief wants to know how soon you can make it speak. If you can't, he will have your heads. Of that I can assure you."

Shelley looked at Ben and Booker. She wasn't sure if the fear in their eyes was for the giant robot or their impending fate.

None of this seemed to affect Myra. She was staring at Darwin like she might a long-lost brother. Then she did something no one expected. She leaned forward until her lips touched Darwin's.

CHAPTER FIFTY-THREE

Day Six: Around 9:00 a.m.

Sporn stared at the graffiti. The big red letters were like a gash on his brain.

Earth is our mother. Reeves did not die in vain!

On the Ministry of Justice building, of all places.

He stood there for some time, not moving, a white-hot anger burning in his chest. There was no need to rush around, order its immediate removal. The damage was already done. Rathneggar's Whisperers would have already reported the incident and, predictably, Rathneggar would have issued the order to halt the minting process.

Cleaning up now would amount to no more than an afterthought.

Still, it had to be done. But more important than that, he had to accept he was wrong. It was a harsh pill to swallow. The only mitigating factor in his favor was that at least the list of potential culprits had been whittled down. Removing Vernon should have solved the problem, but clearly he had misjudged the situation. His lips curled into a self-deprecating snarl. Maddie had been right after all. The thought fell upon him like a heavy weight.

He stepped back into his limousine and ordered the driver to take him to the City Barracks. The car pulled out of the courtyard and worked its way through the narrow streets. Sporn didn't fear looking out the windows; they were darkened and those outside could not see in. This, however, didn't stop people from halting what they were doing to stare as the car drove past. They knew it was his car. There could be no mistake. Gazing at the expressions on their faces, he could not be sure what they were thinking. They were cryptic out of habit. But he thought he could see something in their eyes. Was it recrimination? Surely no one would be so bold as to express that sentiment directly toward him.

He looked away. Checked his fingernails. He had taken to chewing them again of late. He knew it was a sign of stress. But it couldn't be helped. The old insecurities were coming back. If Vernon's rebels were not responsible for the slogan, then who? It irked him to no end that Rathneggar's Whisperers probably knew, but there was no way on this living planet that Rathneggar would impart that information. It was the linchpin of his power. If Sporn were in Rathneggar's position, he would do the same.

It did occur to him that Vernon must be getting help from the Jammers. The thought had crossed his mind before. But they were just a bunch of electronics enthusiasts and hackers who lived in underground dens. They rarely, if ever, saw the light. So it could not be them. But perhaps he ought to ramp up his surveillance activities against them anyway. Issue a "no stone unturned" order to flush out every last one of them. They were a constant pain, and maybe it was time to put an end to their at times brash interference. Now that Vernon was dead, perhaps the time was right. He could capitalize on their demoralized state – which they must surely be in – now that the rebels were defeated.

The idea had the added benefit of giving Washburn a solid bone to chew on. It would take the sting out of ordering him to clean up the graffiti on the Ministry of Justice building, a chore he would detest and probably complain about – again.

Something else still bothered Sporn, however. Perhaps Tanner was right. Maybe he should have gone after Booker, rather than stubbornly gloating over his victory. Carver, by now, would know that Booker was missing. The only consolation was that Carver had not spoken to him about it yet. Maybe he was hedging his bets. Maybe not. But sooner or later, he would confront Sporn about it. *What have you done with Nigel?*

That would be another blow to his chances of redeeming the Star of Cosmonism.

As if he still had a chance …

An inchoate ball of darkness pulled at his stomach. He allowed himself to slump in his seat. He realized he had not slept in nearly twenty-four hours. Taking another handful of uppers at this stage would not bode well for his health. He had to manage himself. Get a grip on himself.

Perhaps, rather than dealing with Washburn right now, he ought to go home and get some sleep. Let the world go on without him for a day.

A day he could ill afford to let slip by …

CHAPTER FIFTY-FOUR

"What are you doing?" Booker asked Myra.

She straightened up. "I wanted to know what it felt like."

Something about the matter-of-fact way she said it made Ben snap out of his feverish state. It reminded him of a story he had learned in primary school, before he got kicked out. "The Sleeping Prince," he murmured. "You just kissed the Sleeping Prince."

"What's the Sleeping Prince?" Myra asked.

"It's an old fairy tale. No one knows where it came from, but we learned it in school when we were young. The prince is asleep because a curse has been laid upon him. The princess wakes him up with a kiss and frees him from the curse."

Booker said, "You're assuming it's a 'he.'"

"He has no breasts," Myra said. "So it's a valid assumption."

Booker gave a callous laugh. "My dear robot, it's not what it looks like, but how it is programmed that determines its sex. And we don't know that because it doesn't speak."

"*It* can speak," Myra said.

Booker gave her a condescending look. "You don't know

that."

"All it needs is a new power supply."

"Sure," Booker said. "And where are we going to get that? I don't see one around here."

"I have one here," Myra said, pointing to her solar plexus.

Booker's face flashed with anger. "No! Absolutely not! You're Mimetic Machines' property. I can't allow that."

"Why not?"

"Why not? Because only I have the authority to decide what happens to you, and I will not allow it."

Listening to this Ben couldn't help feeling conflicted. Myra sacrifice herself for Darwin? It was the last thing he would have thought of, yet ... it was so pure an idea. So obvious. He immediately calculated the cost-benefit. "It will be only temporary," he said on conclusion. "We can give her a new one when we get back to Urkesh."

Booker moved between Ben and Myra. "You will do no such thing!"

"You can't boss me around here," Ben said, stepping sideways. "Myra, tell him. You don't belong to Mimetic Machines anymore."

"Myra?" Booker asked. "What's that supposed to mean?"

"It's my name," Myra said.

"No, it's not," Booker said. "Your name is Madelaine Reeves."

"I was based on Miss Reeves. But Ben named me Myra. And so my name is Myra."

Booker looked at them in astonishment.

"Myra has the right to self-determination," Ben said. "I don't want to terminate her any more than you do. But she is making the right decision. I would have made it for her even if she didn't."

Booker shook his head. "I don't believe I'm hearing this."

The Chief said, "Enough of this banter. Will you make him speak or not?"

"We will not," Booker said decidedly.

"Don't listen to him," Ben said. "We can make him speak."

Without warning, Booker lunged forward and punched Ben hard in the jaw.

Ben stumbled backward and fell onto the ground. For a moment, he sat there, dazed. Shelley, however, wasted no time in helping him get back to his feet. "Next time, you go through me," she said.

"There's no need," Ben said. He moved around Shelley and lunged fully at Booker, catching him in the mid-rift. The act caused them to crash into a heap together. In that instant, Booker let out a piercing cry. Ben heard it, but ignored it. He pinned Booker's arms down hard to the cold stone floor. To his surprise, Booker didn't resist. He went completely limp, his face scrunching into a grimace of pain.

"Get off of me!" he groaned. "Get off!"

Ben unstraddled himself.

Booker rolled over onto his side.

In the flickering light, Ben saw something glint. It protruded from the bottom of Booker's daypack.

Booker's hand felt for it. He pushed his daypack aside and let out another cry of pain.

"What the …" Ben murmured.

"It's a knife," Booker whimpered.

"A knife?"

"I had it in the bottom of my bag."

Ben knelt down and looked at Booker's lower back. His shirt was bloody.

Melos came and knelt next to Booker. He told him to roll over onto his stomach so he could see how bad it was. He raised Booker's shirt and saw a small puncture wound just below the right kidney. Blood flowed freely from it. Melos took Ben's hand and placed it over the wound. "Press firmly," he said.

Shelley held the daypack up, showing a short section of knife poking through the bottom of the bag. She unzipped the bag, reached in and got the knife out.

"Give it to me," the Chief said.

She gave it to him.

"Tell me why I shouldn't have his head right now."

"What were you doing hiding a knife in your bag?" Melos asked Booker.

"I thought I might need it."

"We don't hide knives around here. We show them, so others can see that our intentions are honest and open."

"I wasn't hiding anything. I was just carrying it."

"The Chief doesn't see it that way."

"Help him up," Melos said to Ben.

Ben did what he was told. Booker groaned and complained, but managed to sit up. "Is it bad?" he asked.

"You'll live," Melos said offhandedly.

"We need to stop the bleeding," Ben said.

"Take his shirt off," Melos instructed.

Ben pulled Booker's shirt off. Melos took it from him and ripped it down the middle. With some ingredients from his medicine bag, he made a poultice. He applied it to the shirt, then wrapped the shirt around Booker's waist so that the poultice covered the wound. When he'd finished, he said, "Get up."

Booker slowly got to his feet. He wobbled a bit, but managed to stand bent over. Ben lent him a shoulder. Booker grumbled some thanks.

A moment of silence followed.

The first to speak again was Myra, who surprised everyone when she said, "It seems to me that humans are their own worst enemy."

"Which is why you don't have to do this," Booker said, wincing the words out.

Myra shook her head. "It's even more reason to do it. You need us." She pointed to Darwin. "You need to hear what he has to say."

Shelley had watched this drama unfold with a dispassionate eye, but she suddenly became emotional. "She is braver than both of you!"

"That's because she's a robot, you idiot," Booker said.

Shelley slapped him, hard. "And you're a fool!"

Booker rubbed his cheek. The look on Shelley's face made him positively shrink.

Another moment of silence fell over them.

Eventually Ben said, "We need tools. Without them, we can't move forward."

"So all of this has been a waste of time?" the Chief said.

Ben said, "If you could just give me a moment to think …"

"Enough!" The Chief raised his torch, which had progressively dimmed, and began picking his way through the maze of stalactites and stalagmites.

"Wait!" Shelley called out.

The Chief stopped.

"Vernon kept tools of many kinds," she said to Ben. "I can go back and get them. Which ones do you need?"

"That's … But won't it be dangerous to go back there?"

"Do you want tools or not?"

"Yes, yes!"

"Then tell me which ones you want."

Ben looked at Darwin, saw that he would need a socket set for starters, then once he got the chest plate off, numerous other tools. Screwdrivers, pliers, cutters, a vice grip … He gave Shelley a verbal list.

"Is that all?"

"Bring a hammer," Booker said flippantly.

While they waited for Shelley to get the tools, Ben explained to Melos that they needed to take Darwin out of his sarcophagus and lay him down somewhere where they could work on him unhindered.

Melos relayed it to the Chief, who led them back out of the cave and addressed the village. In short order, the Chief's warriors lined up and followed him back into the cave along with Ben, Booker, Melos, and Myra.

It was a big operation and took a whole day. At first there was much discussion, but gradually a plan formed. The warriors used logs and vines to lever Darwin up, then lift him and carry him out of the cave, where they laid him on some logs above the ground. It took the might of twenty warriors to pry Darwin up and position logs under him, a pair for each log, so that they carried him out like a human centipede. Some of the stalactites and stalagmites had to be knocked away to make room to carry him through. No one seemed concerned about doing it, but when the warriors first saw Darwin, they withdrew in fear, not having seen anything like him before, thinking he was a sleeping demon. The vicious one argued that to disturb him would bring disaster on the village.

The Chief raised his voice for the first time and said that he would not tolerate such "nonsense talk." "There is a reason why the previous Chief handed down the sacred stones," he said. "They contained the wisdom of the elders and the history of the tribe, including secret knowledge of the Sky God. Part of that knowledge was the fact that he was a *mecha*. Naturally, this knowledge was kept a secret because it could be easily exploited by ignorant individuals." The Chief made sure his gaze fell squarely on the vicious one when he said this.

The vicious one pulled a sour face and grumbled something under his breath.

While this was going on, Ben pondered the many challenges that still faced them. The Chief seemed to take it for granted that he was going to reanimate Darwin. Ben wasn't so sure. He worried about the energy density of Myra's RTG. Would it be sufficient? Or, more likely, would it fry Darwin's circuits? The fact was, they had no way of knowing until they actually did it. Ben hated the uncertainty. It made him anxious.

"What's the problem?" Myra asked, noticing his change in mood.

"I don't know," Ben replied vaguely.

"Is it because you're thinking the same thing I am?"

"What's that?"

"The Lomwekian Chief seems to be quite obsessed with Darwin."

"Are you suggesting he knows something we don't?"

Myra's expression darkened. "I hope not."

Rather than appease Ben's anxiety, Myra's statement exacerbated it. He began wringing his hands.

Myra noticed and put her hands over his and stopped him.

Ben looked at her. For the first time he thought he felt an unspoken understanding pass between them. He couldn't put his finger on it, but he felt a calm return to his mind. A calm he didn't think was possible.

Shelley returned at the end of the day. She dumped a hessian bag of tools on the ground at Ben's feet.

Ben thanked her and rummaged through them. There was everything he needed and more. Looking up, he said, "And Vernon? Any news?"

Shelley didn't answer.

"Did you speak to him?"

Still she didn't answer.

Ben realized he shouldn't have asked. He wanted her to say something, but her eyes ... They were moist. From experience he had learned that this signaled one of two things: either she was happy or she was sad. Given the situation ...

"I'm sorry," he said.

"Are you going to keep feeling sorry for yourself, or are you going to make him speak?" She pointed to Darwin, whose majestic appearance dwarfed both of them.

Ben nodded. He reached into the bag, found the socket set, and walked up to his magnificent hulk. For a moment, he hesitated. The doubts that had earlier plagued him came back full force. What if he failed? What if something went wrong? Or worse, what if he caused more people to die?

He looked at Booker, who was sitting on the ground, nursing his injury.

"Don't look at me, pal," he said. "This is your gig."

"Is there a problem?" Myra asked.

"No."

Over the next two hours, Ben worked to unbolt Darwin's chest plate and remove his battery packs. They had corroded and leaked and had to be handled carefully. Booker was of no assistance because of his injury. Instead, Myra helped, passing Ben tools when he needed them and carrying the batteries away when he took them out.

At last, there was an empty cavity in Darwin's chest and he was ready to receive his new power supply.

"It's time," Ben said to Myra regretfully.

"There's only one thing I ask," Myra said. "Will you promise to take me back to Urkesh and reboot me with a new RTG when this is over?"

"I promise."

Booker snickered.

Myra ignored it. "So how do you want to do it?" she asked. "Preferably, I will need somewhere to lie down so you can work on me."

"I will ask for a grass mat," Shelley said.

Ben thanked her. When she returned with the mat, the

village, having watched Ben work on Darwin, now gathered around, curious to see what would happen next.

"Move back a little, please," Ben said. "We need some room here."

The Chief, who was most anxious now to see Darwin receive his new power supply, ordered everyone to move back.

Myra lay down on the grass mat. Shelley knelt by her on one side, Ben on the other. He spread out all the tools he thought he would need on the ground next to him. Booker, despite himself, had moved to sit next to Ben, because, as he said, he wanted to make sure Ben didn't "fuck up the operation."

Before he began, Ben apologized to Myra that he couldn't deactivate her via her data socket. That was something he could only do in the CIL. Out here, in the jungle, he was going to have to operate on her while she was conscious. Her consciousness would continue until the moment he disconnected the RTG.

"I know," she said. "But I trust you."

Booker understood the import of this comment when Ben lifted Myra's T-shirt and exposed the incision he'd made in her lower abdomen. "So that's how you did it!" he couldn't help exclaiming. "Boy, are you in trouble."

"Keep your comments to yourself," Ben snapped.

"Ooh, getting touchy now, are we?"

"Shut up!"

"Okay, okay. I'll shut up." Booker raised his hands in the air. "Whatever you say."

Ben looked up at the spectators, Melos, the Chief, and the vicious warrior among them. "I need a sharp knife."

The Chief handed Ben Booker's steak knife.

Ben looked at it, then said to Myra, "I guess this will have to do. Are you ready?"

"As ready as I will ever be."

"You'll have to make a vertical incision from her sternum to her pelvis," Booker said.

"Don't tell me what to do." Ben held the knife over Myra's skin, trembling.

The crowd hushed. Ben gazed at them before making the cut. Their eyes gleamed with a macabre intensity. It seemed to him that this was a form of entertainment to them.

With infinite care, he pressed the edge of the blade into Myra's skin and drew it down. Myra didn't flinch, despite the pain Ben knew she must be feeling.

He peeled the skin back and exposed the dermal mat. There was no way to get around cutting through the water tubes within it this time. They ran horizontal to Myra's torso. In any case, once he disconnected her RTG, her skin would die anyway. He reminded himself that he would keep his promise to carry her chassis back to Urkesh. He just wondered what she would look like as her skin progressively rotted away.

Once he had hacked his way through the dermal mat, he peeled it back and exposed the thermal insulation that surrounded the RTG. He cut through to reveal a cylindrical device attached to a heat exchanger. Now that it was exposed, he could feel the heat radiating out of it. He would have to work carefully to avoid burning himself.

He saw the electrical outlet. It went through a step-down transformer. "I imagine Darwin will need the untransformed power output," he said aloud.

"That's what I was trying to tell you," Booker said. "You have no idea what he is rated at."

"We'll just have to suck it up and see." He looked at Myra. "This is it. I'm going to disconnect you now."

"I'm ready."

He unscrewed the mounting plate that held the transformer. After he'd liberated it, he gently pulled out the wires connected to it so he could access them. "Cutters."

Shelley passed him the cutters.

He positioned them on the single positive-charged wire.

"I'm going to cut it now."

"Do it," Myra said.

Just before he squeezed the grip, he said, "I'll see you in Urkesh."

Myra met his gaze. "Urkesh."

He cut the wire.

Myra's eyelids automatically shut. Her body went limp.

A murmur rippled through the spectators.

Ben gazed at her. She looked like she had fallen into a peaceful sleep. Except droids never slept ...

It took him another hour to undo the RTG hold-down bolts. "I need something to wrap it in," he said. "It's too hot."

Melos translated to the Chief. The Chief issued an order, and for a while a commotion went on in the crowd. Shortly, someone came back with an animal skin. In his language, the Chief asked if that was sufficient. Melos relayed his words and Ben took the skin.

"I guess we'll have to try it and see."

With Shelley's help, and some judicious use of sticks and vines, Ben managed to lift the RTG out of Myra's body. Shelley quickly wrapped it up in the animal skin. Together, they carried it over to Darwin.

Ben saw immediately that while the RTG would fit inside Darwin, there was no way to anchor it. Its brackets didn't align with anything inside Darwin's chassis.

Unable to stand there forever, he said, "Just put it in. We'll figure out a way to secure it."

Together they laid it inside Darwin's chest cavity. It looked like a newborn infant resting in a cradle.

For a while, Ben puzzled over how to secure it. Meanwhile, looking down at Myra, Shelley said, "What shall we do with her?"

Ben thought about it for a moment. "Can we wrap her up in something to protect her?"

Shelly talked to some Lomwekian women. They had a conference and a couple went away, saying they would come back.

"What did they say?" Ben asked.

"They're getting something to wrap her up in. Banana leaves, I believe."

"Okay. They promise not to dismantle her?"

"I told them if they touched her in any way that was dishonorable, her spirit would come back to haunt them, cause them to give birth to deformed babies."

"You didn't!"

"I did."

Ben shook his head. "I guess if it stops them from wrecking her, whatever it takes."

"Whatever it takes."

"In that case," he said, "can you ask them if they can find something we can use to secure the RTG inside Darwin?"

Shelley asked. Again, the women conferred. Again, some went away, saying they would come back.

While he waited, Ben turned his attention to connecting the RTG to Darwin's power bus. After cleaning the terminals and removing as much of the encrusted leaked battery chemicals away as he could, he noticed a row of circuit breaker switches. He cleaned them and flicked them all to their Off position. He then carefully screwed the positive and negative wires from the RTG into terminals one and two.

Presently, the women came back with handfuls of cane wicker. Ben watched, curious, as they weaved it into a "cradle" for the RTG. It was, he realized, an ingenious solution. He marveled at how they could so quickly adapt to modern technology.

Once the RTG was snugly secured inside Darwin's chest cavity, the Lomwekian women wrapped Myra in banana leaves. She looked like a pupa in a cocoon. They sang as they worked, then lifted her up and carried her off into the forest.

"Where are they taking her?" Ben asked anxiously.

"Somewhere safe," Melos assured him.

Ben remembered what Shelley told him. He decided not to pursue the matter any further. Getting into an argument about it would only distract him and he needed to focus. He returned his attention to the circuit breakers, examined them one more time. Satisfied, he issued a warning to the crowd to stand back. There was no telling what would happen next. The crowd hurriedly retreated. The children hid behind their parents and their parent gripped their spears and shields nervously.

"I'm going to throw the breakers now," he said in a raised voice. "One, two ..." He flicked them to their On position. "Three!"

For a moment, nothing happened.

Then the chugging of a pump sounded somewhere deep inside Darwin's body. Ben recognized the sound as the hydraulic unit starting up. This was followed by the whirring of servos in his main joints. There was some movement. And his fresnel eyes lit up.

Ben jumped back.

The Lomwekian onlookers let out a hushed murmur and immediately fell to the ground and prostrated themselves. The Chief's face filled with wonder and he got to one knee, raised his hands up to the sky and said, "Oh Great One!"

There was some clanking and screeching of metal. Slowly, Darwin sat up. He looked around, first left, then right, then down at Ben.

"Who are you?" he said.

Ben was shocked. Darwin spoke Urkeshian! Albeit in a strange accent.

"My name is Ben. Ben Huxley."

Darwin pivoted his torso with the sound of grinding gears. He scanned the onlookers. "What year is it?"

"It is 3098," Ben said.

"3098 ..."

"Yes."

"It is still jungle ..."

"Why do you ask?"

"I expected this to be a city after 1,772 years."

"1,772 years?"

"Yes. That's how long I've been dormant. My primary mission was to be a time capsule. Now that I'm activated, I must complete my mission."

"Your mission?"

"Yes. My mission is to speak to your contemporary leaders."

Melos had been translating to the Lomwekian Chief the whole time. The Chief stepped forward and said, "I'm the leader of this land. You may speak to me."

Darwin looked at him. "I come in peace. I represent the people who created me – the original inhabitants of this planet."

The Chief bowed. "You have been our protector and guide, and now that you have awakened, we would be honored to receive your teachings."

"Do you represent the entire planet?"

The Chief briefly conferred with Melos. "No," he said. "Just the jungle, all the way up to the desert."

"What is beyond the desert?"

"The city-dwellers."

"Who is their leader?"

"Gaspard Rathneggar."

"Am I also his protector and guide?"

The Chief chuckled amusedly. "If he knew you existed, he would destroy you on the spot."

"Then you must take me to him."

"Why?" the Chief asked. "I just told you he will destroy you."

Darwin tilted his head up to the sky. "Not when his people

learn the truth I have to tell."

CHAPTER FIFTY-FIVE

Day Six: Just after 11:00 a.m.

Tancredi Fornas, Rathneggar's right-hand man, stooped his tall frame forward in order to speak without being overheard. As the most senior Semion, he held Rathneggar's respect, and Rathneggar listened intently without interrupting. They were standing in the shadows of the colonnades of the Cosmonist Cloister. Moments earlier, the bells in the Moon Tower had finished chiming their eleven o'clock toll. Fornas waited until their clanging faded from the air before speaking.

After he'd delivered his message, Rathneggar nodded ever so slightly. "That's a good point. But what will Carver say about it?"

"I think he will agree."

Rathneggar considered this.

For good measure, Fornas added, "I suggest we go ahead and give him the Star of Cosmonism. It will placate him, I can assure you. The populace will not give him a mandate. Despite his victory over Reeves."

"I would say *in spite* of his victory. There is a rumor that he kidnapped Reeves' sister. My sources have failed to find her, or any word of her, in nearly a week."

Fornas nodded gravely. "To that we can add Booker. Carver said he hasn't heard from him in days, which is unusual."

"My sources have indicated that he went with Sporn to the Olongo. They reported that he never returned."

"Do you think …"

"I don't think anything."

"Very well. So we go ahead with the minting and presentation ceremony anyway?"

"The more he looks like a fool, the better it is for us."

Laurent Carver only ever visited the Palace if he was called, and it was always for international business purposes, so when Rhybus saw him get out of his limousine and climb the steps to the Great Hall, he knew something out of the ordinary was afoot. And given the recent spate of events, he had a feeling he knew exactly why Carver was here.

Not wishing to appear caught off guard, he clapped his hands, telling his droids to leave the room. Orlov noticed this and came over to the windows where Rhybus was standing. Seeing what was going on, he turned his attention to Rhybus, making sure his silk shirt, ivory with gold trim, was free of lint, and ensuring his hair was properly coiffured by running a quick comb through it.

Rhybus impatiently put up with these preparations; in the meantime he tried to clear his mind as best as he was able, knowing full well that he would have to deal with some sharp questions. Should he dissemble or not? He had promised Sporn that he would. But Carver had a canny mind. He outwardly projected mannerisms of buffoonery, but that was merely a disarming tactic. Rhybus would need to stay light on his feet if he was going to get through this most unusual meeting.

Presently, the elevator opened, and Carver stepped out. He

was wearing a finely woven khaki linen suit, with no tie, which was uncustomary for him. His *sarcotoothis* leather shoes were scuffed, informal. To Rhybus this signaled that the gamesmanship had already begun.

Carver walked across the floor, briefly bowed before Rhybus, and said, "I apologize for being so presumptuous of your time."

"For you, time is of no consequence," Rhybus replied politely. "How can I help you?"

"There is a little matter that has come up. Normally I would have gone through the formal channels. In this case, however, I think it requires a more delicate touch."

"I understand," Rhybus said. He tilted his head toward Orlov, indicating that he should leave them alone.

When Orlov was gone, Carver said, "It seems that some people have gone missing."

Rhybus waited. There was nothing new in that. Both men knew that under Sporn's tenure, people went missing all the time.

"These were no ordinary people," Carver added.

"I see. And who did you have in mind?"

"Madelaine Reeves and Nigel Booker."

Rhybus made a pretense of rubbing his chin in thought. "The first name, of course, is apparently of concern. The second, however — I'm at a loss."

"Nigel Booker was my man at Mimetic Machines."

"Oh, I see."

"He was a bit young, brash, full of himself, I might even say, but he was my man nevertheless. He always keeps me updated, but I haven't heard from him in three days."

Rhybus frowned. "So what has this got to do with me?"

Carver's face relaxed into a faintly smug grin. "Nothing, actually. I just wanted you to know that it's personal."

"While ..."

"While Miss Reeves isn't personal in the slightest, yet ..."

"Yet you're concerned about her?"

"Yes."

Rhybus briefly wrung his hands. "To be honest, I'm not sure how I can help. It's a golden rule of mine not to interfere in the habits of our more famous citizens."

"Yet she was last seen visiting *your* Palace." There was no emotion in his voice. It was matter of fact.

Rhybus held his expression as best he could, but he felt his face crack.

"Is there something I need to know?"

Rhybus just stared at Carver. He couldn't bring himself to answer.

"You know," Carver said, "I knew your father well. Chronark was a good man." He indicated the room. "He built this place, all of it. And he did it without running the coffers empty."

Rhybus looked away. He couldn't bear the way Carver's eyes were drilling into him.

"I actually lent him a considerable amount of money to do it. He paid it all back, including interest."

Anger flashed through Rhybus. He turned on Carver and said, almost squeezing the words out, "What do you expect me to say?"

"Your father was a man of considerable taste. I'd like to believe he passed that on to you."

Rhybus clenched his jaw. Dropped his head.

Carver placed a hand on his shoulder. "It's not a weight you want to carry, son. At least not alone. Sharing can lighten the load." He let his hand drop away.

Rhybus found it in himself to look Carver in the eye. "My father never lied to me. He never treated me like a child. He wanted me to carry on his legacy."

"I know," Carver said, softening his tone. "He was proud of you."

"But you're not."

Carver rebuffed the comment with a look of genuine sympathy. "*Never say never* is what I would say. Not until they put you in the ground."

Rhybus shook his head despondently. "The same cannot be said for poor Miss Reeves."

"Is that so?"

"We gave her a sky burial."

If Carver found it shocking to hear this, he didn't show it. He nodded in consideration for a moment, then simply said, "Sporn?"

Rhybus shook his head.

Carver expressed surprise.

"It was no one's fault. It was an accident."

"That's what I was afraid of. Accidents and Sporn seem to go together all too often." He grunted in disgust. "Where there's one, the other always follows."

"It took losing my doctor to find that out."

"Him too?"

"I'm afraid so."

Carver clucked his tongue at the dastardliness of it. An uneasy silence followed.

Eventually Rhybus worked up the courage to ask Carver what he was going to do, now that he knew.

"You said you gave her a sky burial," Carver said. "You realize that won't sit well with her family if they find out."

"They don't have to find out."

"They appealed to me directly. That's why I'm here."

Rhybus stared out of the wide bay windows for a moment. He wished he could fly away like a bird. Instead he let out a heavy sigh. "Follow me."

He took Carver up to the rooftop garden and showed him the bleached bones. They were still mostly arranged in the shape of a human being.

Carver muttered something under his breath. Rhybus heard

him, but was afraid to ask.

After walking back and forth a few times, Carver eventually said, "Have them bagged. I'll take care of it."

"You'd do that?"

Carver leveled a cold eye at him. "This is not something you want to go dipping into the coffers for. You understand?"

Rhybus nodded.

Carver walked off. As he weaved his way through the garden beds, Rhybus stared after him. Carver had played him like a pawn. He hadn't even put up a fight.

CHAPTER FIFTY-SIX

Day Six: *Around noon*

Darwin went to push himself up from his sitting position, but Ben shouted, "Stop!"

Darwin stopped.

"Allow me to sling your chest plate to your back," Ben said. The RTG needed to dissipate heat, and bolting the chest plate back on would prevent that. So he'd come up with the idea to tie Darwin's chest plate to his back using some of the spare vines lying around. That way, he could keep it for future use.

"Oh, yes," Darwin said. "You're right."

Ben was pleased Darwin heeded his command. It was a good sign. Darwin behaved like an ordinary robot. As he tied the plate behind his back, he asked, "Are you programmed with the *Pro Hominin* laws?"

"I am," Darwin replied. "But I'm also programmed with the *Pro Robot* law."

"*Pro Robot* law?"

"Yes. As good as the *Pro Hominin* laws are, they fail to take into account human behavior toward robots. Accordingly, they programmed me with an additional law: *Robots must not engage in any behavior that reflects badly on humans, especially behavior that assumes robots have no soul."*

"Soul?"

"Yes."

"But robots have no soul."

Melos, who had listened to this conversation patiently, suddenly interjected. "Why is it so hard for you to believe he has a soul?"

Ben looked at Melos, confused. "I thought all Warraweans believed robots are just machines."

"We do. But your Myra surprised me. She made me realize that perhaps we judged too quick."

Shelley who was also sitting nearby, gave Melos a curious glance.

"So now you think they have a soul?" Ben said, watching Shelley's response.

"Not quite," Melos said. "But I do think they have a certain type of soul after their fashion."

"What does that mean?" Booker said, joining the conversation.

"It means that robots have a robot soul. It's not the same as our soul, but it is still a soul of sorts."

Booker almost laughed but he restrained himself. "By that definition, everything has a soul. Plants have 'plant soul.' Water has 'water soul.'"

"No," Melos said. "Water cannot have a soul because it doesn't move itself. Only things that move themselves can have a soul."

"So Darwin never had a soul while he slept in the cave?"

"No."

"I think what he means to say," Darwin said, "is that when you rebooted me, you re-awakened my soul."

For a while no one spoke.

Ben remembered Pascal once told him another way to look at

the human soul was to think of it as the "hum of the machine." It was like the music of the spheres he said, and he pointed up to Natchator's rings and the moons sliding between them. If there was air up there, they would they make a sound similar to wind chimes. Because the two smaller moons whizzed around the planet twice and three times as fast as the big moon, every time they overtook one another, depending on their position, they would create a different harmony.

Ben remembered, after that, looking up at the night sky for weeks on end in an attempt to hear this celestial music. Pascal had laughed saying the human ear wasn't sensitive enough to hear it. Later, Ben thought the same thing about the human soul. It wasn't something that could ever be perceived by the senses. It could only be inferred from the sum of the parts.

The Chief had listened to this conversation with great interest, following Melos' translation closely. He now spoke up and asked Darwin: "Tell us please, what is your definition of soul?"

Darwin seemed glad he had asked. His fresnel eyes briefly pulsed. His arms and hands became animated, their joints the size of a man's waist.

"Imagine," he said, "two sculptors. One skinny and tall, one fat and short. The tall one has fine-boned fingers, and an edgy temperament. The fat one has fingers as big as sausages and is generally sanguine, even during life's most difficult challenges. They are both given a lump of clay, equal in every respect. They are also given an exemplar, the bust of a famous person, and they are instructed to copy it as best they can. When they finish, judges are invited to critique the result. What do they find?"

Melos translated and the Chief said, "One will be tall and skinny, the other short and fat, reflecting their makers' characters, naturally."

"It's the most common answer, but it doesn't quite get at the truth," Darwin said.

The Chief was chastened. "Please, enlighten us."

"What you see in the two different copies is the soul of their creators. Whether the tall skinny one created a tall skinny copy is immaterial. What is certain is that the two copies will not, cannot, be identical. The difference between them may even be barely perceptible. But what difference there is will make the difference. It could be in something as small as some thumbprints pressed into the clay. One style might be characterized by arabesques, the other by gouging. The soul speaks through such small details, and it will be unique for each and every individual."

"You're right," the Chief said, after hearing the translation.

"What is more," Darwin said, "is that if both sculptors die, and their copies survive, one day, long into the future, a new observer will arrive at the same result. They will see, in the copies, soul imprinted into matter, and they will be able to say something about the sculptors who made them. If a person leaves behind many such works – the more varied the better – then the more observers can say about their soul. Whether it is playful, serious, or silly."

"Is that what you want to say about yourself? Now that your soul is reawakened?" the Chief said. "Are we the people in the future who you're talking about?"

"In my case," Darwin said, "it's not what I have created, but what is stored in my memory. My makers have recorded, in my neural circuits, the history of your kind. Not just on this planet, but on the planet you originated from."

"Would you care to tell us that story?" the Chief said eagerly.

"Earlier you told me about the leader of the city-dwellers. You said he would destroy me if I told him the truth. How do I know you would not do the same?"

"You don't," the Chief said. "You just have to trust me. After all, why would I have awakened you only to destroy you? I could have disposed of you long ago."

"Why did you awaken me?"

The Chief hesitated slightly before answering. "Because it was foretold in a dream I had."

"What did you dream?"

"I dreamed that it was my destiny to awaken you, that you would bring great happiness to our people, and because of that I'd be forever associated with your name in history."

"So you did it for personal gain."

"What I do for personal gain I do for my people. My will and my people are one and the same."

"Where I come from, that's a very dangerous sentiment."

"Why?"

"Because it can be abused."

"If I abused my power, my people would have killed me long ago. The fact that I'm still here means that I've ruled wisely."

"Very well. I already told you that humans didn't originate on this planet. They came from a different planet. That planet's name is Earth and it is fifteen light years away from here."

Melos' translation was received with stunned silence.

"What is wrong? Do you find this hard to believe?" Darwin asked.

This time Ben spoke up. "*Earth is our mother.*"

"That's one way of looking at it," Darwin replied. "But actually, *robots* were your mother."

"Robots?" Ben repeated in disbelief.

"If you know anything about physics, fifteen light years is a vast distance. It's not possible to transport living organisms over that distance, no matter how small."

"So what you're saying is …"

"Only your DNA code was transported. It was embedded in crystals, where it was protected from cosmic rays. Along with it, nanorobots were sent, who, over successive generations, self-assembled into progressively larger robots, which in turn engineered the infrastructure to seed the first stem cells. Over subsequent generations, these stem cells were separated into different cell types, such as gametes and tissue that could be incubated into human beings. It was a long process, taking nearly one hundred years."

"You're saying that robots created us."

"We not only created you, we raised and educated you – that is, the very first successful batch, which we call the Founding Generation. Once the Founding Generation grew old enough to understand who they were, we stepped back and acted as guardians."

"It is an incredible story ..." Ben found himself saying. "Why should we believe you?"

"Because it is true. There is much more to tell. But you can easily verify it by examining your own DNA. We implanted a small snippet of non-coding DNA in your mitochondrial sequence. A quick check will reveal you all have it. It is a twenty-nucleotide sequence capable of being fluoresced if you have the proper equipment. If you want, I can read out the code."

"No need," Ben said. "I've heard enough."

Darwin lowered his gaze onto Ben and said, "Why are you so sad?"

"Everything you've said contradicts what I was taught and what I believe."

"What part of it do you not believe?"

"Frankly? All of it. But that's just me."

Hearing this, the Chief said to Darwin, "We believe you. It is what we always believed, so for us it comes as no shock." Turning to Ben, he said, "You upheld your promise. You made our Sky God speak again. I'm forever indebted to you. As for your belief, perhaps now you can drop your pretense. It was false then, and hanging on to it now will just make you look like a fool."

Ben looked at the Chief, hurt.

Booker, feeling no need to argue with the facts, simply laughed. As painful as it was for him to do so, he could not stop himself.

"Shut up!" Ben said.

"Don't get snappy at me," Booker said. "It's your fault for taking everything so seriously."

"Not all of us are motivated by money and power. If there ever was a case for a soulless person, it's you."

"Showing your true colors are we? You know what your problem is? You think everything is black and white. Reality check my friend. It's all opportunity. No one cares about the truth. All people care about is what they can get for themselves. Look at the Chief here ... he thinks he is going to be famous because you made Darwin speak. And you think taking Darwin back to Urkesh is going to change the world." He laughed again, then winced. "Look at yourself! How hard is it for you to believe? Yeah? Well how hard do you think it's going to be for Sporn and his ilk to believe? He's not a weakling like you. He'll fight it tooth and nail. And what do you think will come of that?"

Ben stared at Booker with an angry scowl. He wasn't sure if the anger was directed at Booker or himself. It was true; he believed that Darwin should be brought to Urkesh. But Booker's words made him doubt himself. Still ...

"Not everyone is cynical like you," he heard himself say. "Yes, it's hard to believe ... I don't deny that. But there's one thing I do know: compared to lying – keeping secrets all the time – the truth is much easier. Even if I wanted to stop Darwin now, it's too late."

Booker shook his head. "You didn't listen to a single word I said."

"I heard," Shelley intervened. "You're right. Everyone is looking for what they can get for themselves. For my people, the Lomwekians, it is this forest. But Sporn wants it for himself." She shook her fist. "We need to stop him. So I say we bring Darwin to Urkesh to teach him a lesson."

"Is that what this is?" the Chief said. "A debate over what we should do with Darwin now that he has spoken the truth?"

"Yes," Shelley said. "We must take Darwin to Urkesh."

Ben stared at Shelley.

The Chief looked at Darwin. "He is very big. How?"

"With a raft," Shelley said.

"A raft," the Chief repeated, nodding.

Melos, who had been translating the whole time and had had no time to inject his own opinion, finally spoke up. "It is a good idea. But it will only work as far as the rapids above Arakirk."

"We must design a raft that can be easily disassembled and put back together again," Shelley said confidently. "That way we can carry the parts over the Arakirk rapids."

"I would very much like to see Arakirk," Darwin said.

Everyone looked at him.

"It is where I was created."

"Arakirk?" Ben said.

"Yes. Does it still exist? It was in ruins when I left."

Booker laughed out loud again. "It's just a pile of rubble now."

"I still want to see it."

CHAPTER FIFTY-SEVEN

Day Six: Mid afternoon

As the village went about making a raft big enough to float Darwin, Ben kept watch over him, checking his range of motion, the amount of torque his servos generated, his balance, his reaction time. Darwin explained that he had been built out of working parts scavenged from the remaining guardian robots as well as any spare parts that could be found.

"Why did they build you so big?" Ben asked.

"They wanted something that would impress the people. Am I not impressive?"

"You are." Ben looked up at Darwin's glowing fresnel eyes; he had to crane his neck to do so. Darwin stood nearly three times the height of an average person. His enormous size reduced his speed, but he proved his strength by getting Ben to hang from his arm while he lifted him clean off the ground.

Booker watched on, unimpressed. *Ben the kid. Grown-up body with a teenage brain.*

Ben didn't think of himself that way. He felt stronger now. More grown-up than ever before. In a few short days he had learned some harsh lessons. Most of all, he had learned that he had crossed so many lines that whatever his life had been before, it was now gone. Ancient history. And whatever good he thought he could accomplish in life was gone as well. He had disappointed everyone, including himself. He was a rotten human being. Not worthy of anyone or anything. So if that was what being a grown-up meant, he didn't want any of it. He may as well act the clown, the person he was always meant to be – and how people had always seen him.

Darwin let him back down. Ben thought about asking him to lift him up again, maybe perform some acrobatics this time. But seeing Booker's disapproving gaze, he let it go.

There had been a time when letting go of anything was impossible. Once he had fixated on an idea, he had to carry it out. Now … Well, he saw the futility of it. All it ever led to was disaster. He could do without that. But could disaster do without him? It seemed to follow him around like a bad smell. Now that was a metaphor he could understand.

What would Darwin say? he wondered.

Better not ask.

"Have you thought what Myra would say if she saw you monkeying around like that, using her energy supply?" Booker said accusingly.

Ben's cheeks seared with embarrassment.

"That's right. She would not be impressed." He wrinkled his nose. "She's rotting away out there somewhere in the jungle, and that's how you act."

As if he needed it rubbed in.

"What I want to know is," Booker said to Darwin, "do you really intend to put your trust in this idiot?"

Before Darwin had a chance to answer, Ben said, "I'm not an idiot. You're the idiot. You're the one who carried a knife in your bag. And look where it got you."

"Last I recall, you're the one who jumped me. How was I supposed to know I'd get stabbed in the back?" He laughed morosely at the irony of it.

It took a moment for Ben to catch on. He had heard that phrase before. *Good one, so I stabbed him in the back.*

"You and your shenanigans," Booker complained. "If it weren't for you, I wouldn't be in this situation."

"So you're blaming me?"

"I'm blaming you for all of this!"

"It looks to me," Darwin intervened, "you're fighting like children."

Booker gave Darwin the same look he'd given Ben. "What's it to you?"

"When we were the guardians, we often had to manage human disputes. I'm well versed in mediation. I hope that answers your question."

"All the mediation in the world is not going to save you from Sporn," Booker shot back.

"Who is Sporn?"

Booker laughed harshly. "Hector Sporn. The Minister of the Interior. Boy, will he be happy to see you."

"I detect sarcasm," Darwin said. "That tells me you're trying to be smarter than you actually are."

"Don't lecture me," Booker said angrily. He grabbed a nearby stick and used it to push himself to his feet.

Ben felt an impulse to help him, but stopped just short of acting on it.

Standing shakily, Booker said, "You're just a hunk of metal and bolts. Sporn is going to enjoy taking you to pieces. He'll melt you down like so many old coins."

"I don't take threats lightly," Darwin said. He began swaying his upper body from side to side. The joints between his metal plates ground noisily.

It alarmed Ben to see Darwin behave like this. "Stop it, both of you!" he demanded.

Booker laughed callously. "An emotional robot. Now I've

seen it all."

Darwin made a little jerking movement with his head and shoulders. "That I am," he declared. "My makers knew full well the type of world I would wake up to. They knew the only language human beings understand is fear. I will destroy you if necessary!" And with that pronouncement, he flicked open some apertures on the side of his arms and deployed two small-caliber cannons.

Everyone, including Booker, recoiled. Muffled cries of surprise rippled through the onlookers.

Sensing the situation had got out of hand, Ben did something he would ordinarily never do. He stepped directly into Darwin's line of fire and said in a firm, hard voice, "Put those away! I command you!"

Darwin looked down at Ben, slightly narrowed his eyes – an action Ben hadn't thought he was capable of – then tucked his weapons away and folded his arms across his chest in what could only be described as an expression of pride.

"Good. Now promise you won't do that again."

"I promise – with qualifications."

"What qualifications?"

"That Mr. Booker also behaves himself."

Ben looked at Booker, who was on the verge of being disrespectful again. But he stayed himself. There was a fierce intensity in Ben's eyes. Booker had never seen that before.

After a moment, Ben said, "Are we all good now?" He was speaking to both Darwin and Booker.

"I'm good," Booker said.

"What about you?" Ben asked Darwin.

"I'm good."

"And they call him a god," Booker muttered under his breath.

"What was that?" Ben asked.

"Nothing."

Ben was about to say something when his attention was diverted by the sound of women singing in the jungle. The singing grew louder, and shortly a group appeared. They were carrying Myra on their shoulders. Other women from the village came and laid woven mats on the ground, where they set Myra down.

Ben stared at her, speechless. She was stripped bare of her skin. Her chassis looked perfectly clean, as if she had just come off the production line.

Melos appeared. "Nice job."

"How did they do it?" Ben asked. He meant the women, who were squatting around Myra, cooling themselves with handheld fans cut from elephant leaf.

"Oh, they didn't do it," Melos replied. "The ants did it for them."

Using fire torches, the Lomwekian warriors worked late into the night. They chopped down huge trees, the trunks as broad as a man standing with his hands stretched out, and dragged them down to the riverbank in teams, chanting as they went to coordinate their efforts. There they set to work with stone axes, hollowing out their cores and levering them open with sturdy branches while heating them from beneath with large fires. Slowly, the logs gave way, groaning and squealing, until they took on the distinctive canoe shape, broader in the middle, narrower at the ends.

Ben watched all this with a deep fascination, the firelight dancing off his eyes. Booker too was entranced. His face had become clammy with sweat and he had to sit back down on the ground due to weakness in his legs. Melos noticed his behavior and attended to him, reapplying a fresh poultice and ordering him not to exert himself in any way.

As the moons glided across the dark veil above them, the hour passed midnight and the workers stopped and drank their local moonshine, offering some to Ben and Booker. Ben politely refused, but they would not have it. He saw Shelley spying on him from a distance, sitting with a group of younger women of eligible marrying age. The young women laughed; Ben felt like they were laughing at him.

It stung him to think that Shelley might have said something personal about him. Images of their carnal night together flittered back into his mind, where they fell prey to his fertile imagination. Had she known he was a virgin? Of course she'd known. It was in the little details. Like taking his hands and placing them on her breasts; like taking the initiative when it came time for him to enter her; like leading him with her rhythm. He wished he could have been more of a man, but it couldn't be helped. He was already branded.

But as soon as he had these thoughts, a spurt of anger coursed through him. Why had she encouraged him when she'd known they were sister and brother? Didn't she know it was wrong? He scoffed inwardly. Of course she did. Her denials were completely unconvincing. Melos wouldn't lie. Or would he? No … he respected Arthur too much. He'd known him personally. He was old enough to know. He would have seen the facts with his own eyes.

Damn it! Myra could have resolved the issue. Why had Melos denied her the opportunity? Getting at the truth in this place was as hard as, or even harder than, finding your way through the jungle. Everything was entangled with everything else. Ben wished he was back in Urkesh, where the streets led somewhere, somewhere definite, even if they were not always clean and sagged under choking traffic. But then he realized that Urkesh was full of its own secrets. He was nothing more than a rat that skittered along its gutters.

Yet … he had glimpsed the way others lived, and it pained him. The jungle, by comparison, was honest. It didn't pretend to like you.

There had been honesty in Shelley's lovemaking. The way an

insect devours its prey. Efficient. Ruthless. A hunger satisfied. Her mouth, ravenous at turns, soft and yielding at others. He'd reached up to that mouth. Drooped her lip with two fingers.

When she'd cried out, it had been stifled joy. Afterwards she'd been a tiger cub cooing as it drank its mother's milk.

Her honesty was pure and clean. No pretense.

Maybe that was why she denied it. She was just as scared of the truth as he was.

He felt something in his hand. One of the Lomwekian warriors had thrust a carved wooden cup in his hand. It sloshed with a pale white concoction. The warrior said something and made a gesture. Ben knew he meant "Drink!"

He drank. It was bitter and chalky. More like medicine than a beverage. It left a vague burning sensation in his throat.

Shelley watched him the whole time. Her eyes sparkled with amusement. The kid didn't like it, but he was going to get drunk whether he liked it or not.

The warrior refilled Ben's cup and he threw it back as quick as the first. It was the only way to keep it down.

It was followed by a third ...

The men were chanting. They made small hops with their feet and moved as one, their bodies blended into a single animal.

Ben felt himself move with them. He couldn't help it. It was as if a giant hand were guiding him.

The movements increased in tempo. His head began to whirl. He felt himself being lifted up, the pressure of many hands on his body, and then he was lying down, and faces were leering at him.

The pointy-toothed one's face filled his vision. He was grinning from ear to ear. He pulled back, and Ben saw something glint in the firelight.

They were pulling on his clothes. His shirt came over his head. Something was rubbed on his face and chest. He touched it. It felt grainy and sticky.

There was a sharp pain on the side of his face. He turned to see what had caused it.

The chanting changed rhythm.

The pain came again and again. It moved down to his chest. Every time he tried to feel where the pain was, someone gently pulled his hand away. He felt powerless to stop what was happening.

The faces leering at him began to merge.

The last thing he remembered was Melos bending over him, smiling in a fatherly, comforting sort of way …

CHAPTER FIFTY-EIGHT

Day Seven: Morning

Ben woke up groggy-eyed and rolled over, tried to draw himself to his senses. His head throbbed – and also stung, like a million ants had bitten him.

He ran the tips of his fingers over his cheeks and felt swollen ridges. He followed them down his neck and over his chest. Looking down, he saw dotted lines marked across his chest. He rubbed them, thinking they would smudge off. But they stayed.

Even though it hurt like hell, he snapped himself upright, his mind abruptly gaining clarity.

They had tattooed him!

He tried to get up, but his legs wouldn't work. Stubbornly refusing to accept their failure, he crawled forward. He headed for the light, which filtered in through a thatched door. He pushed it aside and gazed at the morning scene.

A faint pall of smoke hung over the village, the remnants of the fires that had burned under the hollowed-out logs. The sun cut shafts through it, producing a pseudo-prismatic effect.

He stared at the scene for a long while, his mind strangely empty, yet searching for something. A stray dog wandered lazily across the open space, followed by a lone child carrying a stick. The child whacked the stick on the ground every so often while repeating a nursery rhyme to itself.

Thwack! Thwack! The sharp cracks disappeared into the jungle backdrop.

It was so peaceful.

Where was Darwin?

A voice croaked next to him. "Water."

It was Booker. Ben licked his lips, realizing he needed water himself.

Booker briefly lifted his head, then let it fall back again. "What time is it?"

"No idea."

"Can you get me some water?"

"Sure."

Ben crawled out of the hut. Outside, he slowly got to his feet. A wave of nausea overcame him. He bent over, thought he was going to retch. He took a few deep breaths. The moment passed.

He tottered down to the river and fell to his knees at the muddy shoreline, not caring about anything except quenching his thirst.

The cool water was a revelation. He sucked in mouthfuls until he'd had his fill. Sitting up, he saw his shimmering reflection. His face was red and swollen; there was a circular geometric pattern on his right temple that extended down to the side of his cheek. If it hadn't been so shocking, he would have said it looked cool. Now he was truly branded.

He didn't know if he should be angry or just give in to defeat.

He looked around, saw an upturned bowl lying nearby. He picked it up, brought it to the water, washed it, then filled it and carried it back to the hut.

Booker got up on one elbow and sucked greedily from its rim. Letting himself back down, he said, "What happened to you?"

Ben ignored the question. "I'm going to look for Darwin."

"What do you mean, look for him?"

"He's gone."

Booker pulled himself up again. "Where would he go?"

Ben shrugged and went back out.

The makeshift platform of logs where Darwin had last been looked undisturbed. On the ground next to it, Ben noted a series of large footprints. They led off in the direction of the jungle.

He followed them along a trail. He saw a number of smaller footprints in between Darwin's.

After walking for a while, he heard voices. He continued in their direction. The voices gradually got louder, and eventually he saw something that wasn't forest. It was Darwin. He was holding his hands out while the warriors were loading him up with freshly cut vines.

The vicious-looking one noticed Ben and said something Ben didn't understand.

Darwin, to Ben's surprise, translated for him. "He said, have you come to help?"

Ben looked around. He didn't have a machete, and he didn't know the first thing about harvesting vines. "I was looking for you," he said. "I just wanted to make sure you're okay."

"I'm fine."

A Lomwekian warrior placed another coil of vines on Darwin's arm. Seeing that he was happy working, Ben made a hand signal to the vicious one, telling him he was going back to the village. The man gave him a strange look, then thought no further on it and went back to work.

Ben trod his way back along the jungle path to the village. When he got there, the Chief was coming out of the jungle from the other side of the village with a group of warriors carrying lengths of bamboo. The Chief seemed to be in charge and enjoying himself. The warriors dumped the bamboo on the ground next to the hollowed-out logs.

The vicious one and his team arrived with Darwin, who off-loaded the vines next to the bamboo.

Melos came out of the hut where Ben and Booker had slept and sidled up to Ben. "How's it going?" he asked, looking at the tattoo on Ben's face.

"It could be better."

Melos chuckled. "You're doing a lot better than your friend."

"He's not my friend."

"But he's one of you. Or has that changed as well?"

"What do you mean?"

"The Lomwekians appear to have accepted you as one of their own."

Ben touched his face. "Is that what this means?"

"The Chief is grateful for your service."

"So it was his idea?"

"Nothing happens here without his say-so."

Ben took that on board. He watched the Lomwekian warriors take up positions around the first of the "canoes," as the hollowed-out logs were now designated.

"Well, aren't you going to help them?" Melos said.

Ben looked at the warriors, some of whom were looking at him. He went over and squeezed in. The warriors chanted a count together and lifted the canoe up. Ben found himself getting caught up in their rhythm. The vicious one acted as guide and led them down to the river. Ben marched along with the others. The feeling of working in a synchronized human team, where every muscle strained together for the same goal, filled him with an exhilaration he had never felt before. It was as if his strength had been multiplied many times over.

The warriors lowered the canoe and took a collective lungful of air. Ben looked around and saw a sea of happy faces. He found himself beaming with them.

He turned his head and saw Shelley. She was down on the riverbank with a group of women, who were singing while washing root vegetables. Shelley noticed Ben looking at her, and smiled back. It was a natural smile. It made him forget all the bad things he had thought about her.

The warriors moved to the next canoe. Ben was swept along with them. Gradually, the base of the raft took shape. Holes were drilled at the top of the freeboard of each canoe, and the vines were threaded through them, then used to lash down the bamboo "deck." Ben watched the first row of bamboo poles go down, seeing how the vines were woven alternately over them, somewhat like a quilt. He could see the beauty of this design; it provided maximum strength while retaining flexibility.

But that wasn't all. Once the deck was complete, the warriors began building a hut at one end. Judging from its size, Ben guessed it could sleep about eight people if they lay side by side. They also built some storage boxes, which they set against the walls of the hut. In the front of the raft, they built a second smaller hut and stocked it with firewood. They built a firebed by stacking river stones in front of it and adding an awning. The preparations were completed with some coiled fiber ropes and a bundle of barge poles.

The only remaining job was to get Darwin on board. It would not be as simple as him just stepping on; his feet would plunge straight through the deck.

Ben suggested that they make some planks. Melos translated and the vicious one smiled. Ben averted his eyes from those pointy triangular teeth. No matter how many times he saw them, he could not get used to the wild-animal look they gave him. The vicious one seemed to have noticed and made a special effort to smile longer and wider than was necessary.

Later, when he'd walked off with some of his men in search of the right kind of wood to make planks, Ben said to Melos, "I still don't know his name."

"Why don't you ask him yourself?"

Once the planks were cut and lashed down, it was time to get Darwin onto the raft. He was too big and heavy to just step on, even with the planks strengthening the deck. He would have sunk one end and caused at least two of the canoes to flood. He needed to be craned on from above. But there was no crane. Ben understood the problem and put his mind to the task. They would have to make a crane, but not just any ordinary crane. It would need a counterweight and would have to work like a seesaw on a fulcrum.

He explained the concept to Melos, who translated it to the vicious one. It was at this juncture that Melos told the warrior that Ben was going to ask him his name. The warrior smiled happily at Ben, waiting for him to ask.

"What did you tell him?" Ben said. "He's staring at me with a funny expression on his face."

"I told him you wanted to ask his name."

"Oh."

"Well, go ahead."

It was a nervous effort. He tried to enunciate his words clearly, but it came out sounding like he was talking to a child. The vicious one sensed it and shoved his face right up at Ben as he said, "Manatao Guntaleg." He added something afterward that Ben didn't understand.

Melos said, "He said his name is Manatao Guntaleg and his favorite way of killing his enemies is bashing a hole in their skull and sucking out their brains while they're still alive."

Ben stared at Guntaleg, who was still smiling crazily. Without thinking, Ben formally offered his hand.

Guntaleg looked at it, then slowly lifted his hand and placed it in Ben's.

It was the strangest handshake Ben had ever experienced.

Guntaleg's hand lay in his own like a dead fish. There was no reciprocation at all. Ben let go and Guntaleg's hand fell away.

"It looks like he formally accepted your friendship," Melos said.

"Are you sure?"

"No."

Ben grimaced.

"I think the problem is he thinks you're some kind of magician. But he can't seem to make his mind up, because you look nothing like any magician he's ever seen."

"Magician?"

"Why, yes, because you brought Darwin back to life."

Ben thought about this for a moment. "Well, tell him I'm not a magician. I'm an engineer. We use science, not magic."

Melos reiterated this to Guntaleg. Guntaleg rubbed his chin and shook his head.

"What did he say?" Ben asked.

"He said he was looking forward to your next magic trick."

"But I just told you to tell him I'm not a magician."

"I did," Melos said. "But he's made up his mind and I can't change it. If I were you, I'd accept it. In his culture, magicians are more highly ranked than warriors."

Ben thought about what Melos had said. If he continued to argue he would only antagonize Guntaleg, and Guntaleg was clearly not the kind of person who would take too kindly to that. "In that case," he said, "I accept. *Engineer* in my language is *magician* in his. Tell him we need to build a crane."

Melos translated. "He wants to know what a crane is."

"Sure." Ben looked around for some sticks on the ground. He found three about the right size and angled them up so that they joined together at the top and formed three legs. He got another stick and found a pebble, and, holding it on one end, notched the stick into the top of the three legs and see-sawed it to simulate a fulcrum crane. "Do you understand how this works?" Ben asked Guntaleg.

Guntaleg said something to Melos, who translated. "He said he understands and can easily build it. Except ... he has one criticism."

Ben frowned.

"He said that attaching a single big rock on the end of the lever will make it very difficult to handle. He suggests we instead make a big basket and slowly fill it with smaller rocks until it balances against the weight of the Sky God."

Ben's frown turned to an expression of astonished surprise. The man had a very quick mind. Perhaps quicker than his own.

They built the fulcrum crane using Guntaleg's design and lifted Darwin onto the raft, placing him in a seated position facing forward so that he could take in his surroundings. While the men busied themselves with this task, the women collected firewood, fruit, and root vegetables and stored them on board.

Ben saw that the remains of Myra were stored in a small canoe and covered with thatched grass. Looking for a place to put her, he found that between Darwin's legs worked best.

The last task was to determine how many men would be needed to guide the raft down the river, and who those men would be. The Chief naturally stepped forward and assumed command of the decision-making process. He chose Guntaleg first, and left Guntaleg to choose the rest of the men himself. Guntaleg chose Melos as his translator and six sturdy men he trusted. These would be the "pole" men, who would steer the vessel away from the sandbanks and submerged obstacles.

This seemed to settle the matter, but a kerfuffle soon broke out when Shelley stated that she was going along as well. After some heated discussion, it was decided that they would only allow her to go as far as her village. In addition to that, she would not be allowed to sleep in the hut with the men. Shelley's response to this was that she didn't need such comforts. Taking this as an affront, the men puffed their chests out and made sneering gestures.

Shelley just laughed at them and received a hammock from one of the Lomwekian women, who had prepared it for her as a gift.

To Ben's eyes, it seemed as if Shelley had preempted the men. They had just assumed. But she had outwitted them. Come to think of it, he realized that she had outwitted him on a number of occasions too. He couldn't help but smile, thinking about it.

CHAPTER FIFTY-NINE

Day Seven: Mid-morning

Tancredi Fornas' tertiary role as Speaker of the House wasn't just in name. His word over the Chamber was final, as was the word of all Curates when it came to government matters. Fornas would have been happy with this situation except for one man: Sporn. It was no secret that his power had steadily increased over the years, something that the Curates rued bitterly, but were powerless to stop. Fornas, however, wasn't one to dwell on past mistakes. He accepted that giving Sporn the legal authority to run his own militia, the so-called Gormlings, had been a mistake. Mistakes were inevitable. It wasn't making them that bothered him. It was making the same mistake twice. That he would never do.

It was the consequences of the Curates' mistake that were his focus now: their addiction to the ruthless brutality Sporn's Gormlings provided. Fornas, however, saw it differently. He had always argued that clamping down on all heresy, no matter how minor, would not stamp it out. If anything, it would backfire and result in the necessity for even greater force. But Rathneggar, in his old age, was getting more and more paranoid – as was Sporn.

Two peas in the same pod.

As usual, Sporn arrived late. He knew the Chamber was waiting on him. He took advantage of it. Left his entrance to the last minute, to garner the greatest impact.

Fornas cast his eye over to Julian Eckland, the Minister of Defense. He and Sporn had gone through the military together, Eckland rising to the rank of general, Sporn that of major. Fornas remembered Sporn leaving the military after achieving that rank. At the time he'd failed to see the man's ambitions. He'd thought he wouldn't succeed. It hadn't been a mistake to think that. At the time, there'd been nothing to indicate otherwise.

But then uranium oxide had been discovered at the northern Orianian–Rodinian border. It was a complex situation. An Orianian geologist had in fact discovered it first, but Rodinia was the first to see its economic potential. They offered huge tax breaks to the Hathor Corporation to mine and process it. The company bought up a huge land lease, which entitled them to mine it for ninety-nine years. It was a galling act, because the Hathor Corporation was originally registered in Oriana.

Wasting no time, the Hathor Corporation built a mining town, Atkum – on the Orianian side of the border – which quickly grew in size as it was directly connected by rail to its capital city and trading port, Zurgel. It was a clever move, because the bulk of the ore was on the Orianian side of the border.

Sporn grew to power by forcing a trade tax on the ore when it crossed the border into Rodinia. His Gormlings were the ones that enforced it, since to do so through the military would have signaled open war.

This caused a hot peace between the two countries. Rodinia responded by forcing the Hathor Corporation to limit the sales of their RTGs to Oriana. The biggest victim of this move was Mimetic Machines, who needed the RTGs to power their humanoid robots. Mimetic Machines responded in kind by applying pressure on the Orianian government, largely through the action of Laurent Carver. This escalated the situation.

Orianian citizens, angry at the Hathor Corporation for giving all the jobs and money to Rodinian employees, set up a blockade at the border. Skirmishes broke out and people on both sides were killed. Both sides immediately sent in troops to protect their citizens. Atkum became a barricaded town. Ever since then, attempts by both sides to gain the upper hand had resulted in fresh outbreaks of violence.

Fornas was aware that Eckland had just returned from a recent visit to Atkum to assess the latest developments. No doubt he would complain to Sporn about it. Meanwhile, Sporn was trying to distract everyone with his dam project …

"Silence!" Fornas called out.

The Chamber quietened down.

"Item one-point-one of the agenda. The business of conferring the Star of Cosmonism on the Minister of the Interior, Hector Sporn."

Sporn, who had been lending his ear to Eckland, stiffened, looked straight at Fornas in disbelief.

"Will the Minister please stand."

Sporn slowly stood up. It was as if his body had registered Fornas' words, but his mind refused to budge.

"It has been decided," Fornas said, in his low, resonant voice, "that the Minister of the Interior be awarded the Star of Cosmonism for his role in defeating the rebel threat. His actions have brought stability back to Urkesh — a most welcome result. As you all know, Vernon Reeves began his campaign of terror by bombing the Ministry of Justice building. His actions garnered the support of other heretics, and for the last year, the city of Urkesh has lived under a dark cloud of fear. That fear has been lifted by the actions of the Minister, who, just a few days ago, eliminated Reeves and his rebel gang at their hideout in the Olongo jungle. We thank the Minister for his heroic actions.

He has truly shown his loyalty to the Cosmonist cause."

The Chamber stood up and loudly applauded Sporn, who, while still in shock, acknowledged the adulation with a slight bow.

"The Star is being minted as we speak," Fornas continued. "We will hold the confirmation ceremony in the Great Hall at the Palace in three days' time. This meeting is adjourned!"

Sporn walked with Eckland out of the building. Eckland was a reserved fellow, typical of military types, not given to hype. He was well groomed, almost nondescript in his features, except for a small item of imperfection: one of his eyes was blind, caused by a training accident, and he'd had a neural prosthesis put in its place. It gave him extraordinary long- and short-range vision, but it didn't move, giving it away as an implant.

He turned his head fully to Sporn as he spoke so that he could study him closely, as was his habit during conversation. "You seemed surprised."

"Was I?"

Eckland flashed a coy smile. "Do you want to tell me what's on your mind?"

Sporn continued staring forward as he walked. "A lot of things. But nothing I can't handle."

"So you've heard the rumors."

"What rumors?"

"The threat is gone, but in name only."

"I wouldn't pay them any heed. They come from the mouths of those who don't know what it is like to spill blood."

"I hear you. But the slogans – they're not going away. If anything, they're becoming more strident."

"I didn't think you took them seriously."

"I don't. But the people do. They're becoming agitated."

"The people are my business. You let me worry about that."

They descended the steps and headed toward Sporn's limousine.

"Fair enough," Eckland said, changing his tone. "So I guess now that you've been honored, more doors will open. That's a good thing, isn't it?"

"You make it sound like a chore."

"Well, it is, isn't it? More people will want a slice of the pie."

Sporn stopped. "Just what is it that you're asking?"

"I need more reserves to handle Atkum."

"Why are you asking me? Why don't you ask the Finance Minister yourself?"

"I'm asking you to ask him, now that you're …"

"Now that I'm in better standing."

"Precisely."

They arrived at Sporn's car. The chauffeur was waiting with the rear door open. Sporn said, "Let me think about it."

"Well, don't think too long. The Rodinians have been increasing their troops' numbers on their side of the border again. We need to respond rapidly."

"I said I'll think about it." Sporn stepped into his vehicle. The chauffeur went to close the door, but Eckland intervened.

"I've been wondering," he said. "Tell, what does 'Earth is our mother' even mean?"

Sporn gave Eckland a strange, quizzical look full of suspicion. "It doesn't mean anything." He pulled the door shut.

Eckland watched the car drive away. He watched it all the way to the front security gate, where it passed through unhindered and disappeared into the flow of traffic outside.

CHAPTER SIXTY

Day Seven: Late morning

The pole handlers guided the raft downriver, using the current to propel the vessel forward. Booker, who had slightly improved but was still weak, sat leaning against some sacks stored outside the deck hut. The sun beat down strongly on the open water away from the shade of the trees. Someone had given him a straw hat, which, together with his week's growth of beard, gave him the appearance of a starving street artist, the neuromorphic engineer long gone.

Ben sat on one of Darwin's legs and absently leafed through his father's journal. It was the symbols Arthur had recorded that interested him now. Could Darwin shed some light on them? He held the journal up and asked if he recognized any of them.

"Oh, yes," Darwin replied. "They represent the planets that orbit the solar system your ancestors came from."

"How can you be so sure?"

"Because the people who built me were your ancestors, and they took their history with them when they arrived. Or, I should say, it was sent along with their DNA. They didn't learn about it until they were reconstituted."

"You make it sound like we were assembled like robots."

"Ben – may I call you Ben? Human beings are a sort of sophisticated robot. What makes you think otherwise?"

"We're not machines."

"No, not in the manufactured sense. But even that's not true. What, after all, is biological development but DNA orchestrating a body plan according to an aspirational code?"

"Aspirational. You make it sound like DNA has consciousness."

"I meant it as a practical metaphor. Every human is identical, while at the same time having small differences and flaws, because the code never works perfectly; it always has some errors and unexpected results."

"AKA, we're robots," said Booker, who'd been listening to the conversation.

"Sophisticated robots with generalized flexibility," Darwin added.

"I grant you that," Booker said. "Animals only have specialized flexibility at best."

"Yes."

"So tell me more about this solar system you say we came from," Ben asked.

"Sure." Darwin raised one of his arms and pointed to the sky. "It's fifteen light years in that direction, and has one special planet, Earth, which lies in the habitable zone of its host star. Its people – your people – overpopulated and polluted their home, while at the same time developing technology that enabled them to leave their planet and colonize the rest of their solar system. That eventuated in a mission being sent to this planet. An armada of very small spacecraft, each weighing no more than a few grams, was sent to this planet using pulsed laser sail technology. As I explained previously, your DNA was packaged in crystals that allowed it to survive the harsh conditions of interstellar space, including entry into this planet's atmosphere.

"The engineers who designed the system were very clever. They used the heat ablation of atmospheric entry to reduce the crystal protective layer to just a thin shell so that after landing, microrobots could more easily drill into them and extract their DNA code. The robots themselves were stored in crystal shells that were cracked open upon landing, like birds hatching out of a shell. The microrobots were in fact tiny winged insect-like creatures that could fly and find the 'DNA eggs' scattered all over the place after entry. They collected them and placed them in 'nests.' They then gradually assembled all the raw ingredients to bootstrap themselves into larger robots. They did this by joining themselves together and working in unison. All the while, their power source came from decaying radioactive uranium stored in their crystal bodies."

"I know you've explained it before," Ben said, "but it just sounds incredible. So everyone on this planet came from 'Earth'?"

"Yes. It took over one hundred years after first landing for the microrobots to upscale themselves into progressively larger robots. Once the first larger robots were created, the process sped up, until eventually they were able to build the incubators necessary to gestate human DNA into biological entities."

"And to think, the first humans on this planet were raised by robots."

"Yes."

Booker, uncharacteristically genuine, said, "But somewhere along the line, something went wrong, didn't it?"

"Not at first," Darwin said. "Once the first generation of humans grew to maturity, once they had been educated about their origin and purpose, they naturally took their destiny into their own hands. We robots were relegated to the status of guardians. For a number of reasons, this shift in control resulted in some unexpected outcomes."

"I can imagine," Booker said. "Humans are perversely immune to logic. They think with their emotions, and the more people there are, the more emotions begin to control their fate."

"How very true," Darwin lamented. "This is exactly what happened. Once the population grew and people diversified, conflicts broke out. The love of science that we taught the first generation faded and was gradually replaced by the old superstitions and magical thinking that human brains are born with. In fact, the original purpose of sending humans to this planet was to start a new civilization based on logic and science. The man behind this dream was Leon Thiem. He invested all his money into the project. It was his gift to the future of humanity. But when he died, the project died with him, despite there being a foundation set up in his memory."

"Why? How?" Ben asked.

"Because the first colony didn't come into existence until long after Thiem's death, and even though he'd created the foundation to continue the project, there was no way to maintain direct communication between the two planets over such a vast distance. It is believed that follow-up monitoring missions were sent, but they must have they stopped after a while. We didn't have the technology to return communications. It was a project based on hope. Unrealistic hope, but good hope nevertheless."

"Bad hope, if you ask me," Booker said.

"I wouldn't say that," Darwin countered. "I am here, after all."

"Why are you here?" Ben asked.

"That's a good question."

Shelley was standing at the front of the raft, concentrating on the water with spear in hand. She seemed to have been listening, because she turned her head toward Darwin in expectation of his story.

Darwin began. "The original Founding Robots that raised the first humans, educated them, and became their guardians eventually faded in their role, and were put into a museum in the city of Arakirk. Each new generation born after that came to see these robots in the museum to learn about their history, and through that passed it on. As a result, the Founding Robots were highly honored and taken care of. But gradually, for reasons that we do not fully understand, several individuals were born who grew up to challenge this narrative. They were charismatic and invented their own origin 'myth,' which soon attracted followers.

"Naturally, this new phenomenon was seen by many as a dangerous development. But because it was so alien, so different to the 'traditional' way of thinking, people hesitated to act, and this allowed the cult to grow. Before they knew it, matters reached a critical point. The cult accused the traditional population of being a cult themselves because they 'forced' children to go to the museum to learn the 'Founding lie.' In the name of human rights and freedom, cult members took their children out of schools and raised them in their own schools. For a while an uneasy status quo pervaded. But this was broken when some traditional supporters burned down the cult schools. Clashes broke out and matters were only brought under control when it was agreed that the best solution was to give the cult its own territory and sovereignty to govern itself.

"This worked for several generations, but as the two populations diverged and developed different cultures and needs, conflicts broke out again, this time over resources and ideology. The new robot-less cult saw themselves as second-class citizens deprived of their needs. They coveted the more scientifically organized society from which they originally sprang. Matters got out of hand one day when one of the 'prophets' of the new cult was murdered by some conspirators of the original population. At first this led to riots, but then it escalated into an armed coup of the founding government by the cult leaders. It was a lack of foresight on behalf of the traditional society to let the cult leaders arm their people. The traditional society was pacifist and unarmed by law. This was seen by many as a mistake. The cult was fanatical and only too willing to use force, and now they controlled all the land."

"You make it sound like the traditional society was perfect," Booker said.

"I'm not saying that. The founding population had its troubles. It wasn't altogether perfect. There were issues of inequality and injustice, but overall it worked fairly well. And it was based on truth."

"People don't care about the truth," Booker said. "They only care about what they believe."

"Admittedly, we learned that the hard way," Darwin said.

"But go on," Ben said.

"Well, the cult took over the government and instituted their own laws. The robots in the museum were destroyed ... Well, almost; some plucky individuals managed to save some of them – at least some parts – and it was from these that they built me."

"Very nice. They armed you with weaponry, which was against their principles."

"On the contrary. They learned from their mistakes. They learned that when it comes to human behavior, it is better to be armed than sorry."

Shelley began laughing when she heard this. At first it was a quiet chuckle, but it quickly grew loud enough for everyone to hear.

"What?" Ben said, eager to know what was amusing her.

"You're all children. Every one of you!"

"Don't lecture us," Booker shot back.

"How do you think we've survived all these years? By being nice to each other?"

"Obviously you haven't heard about cooperation," Booker said.

"I can survive on my own perfectly well, thank you," Shelley said.

"But you weren't always like this. You were vulnerable once," Booker said. "Imagine if your parents abandoned you to the jungle when you were born, you wouldn't be here."

"I would have been raised by monkeys," Shelley replied.

Booker let out a sarcastic laugh. "Given the gibberish that comes out of your mouth, I'm suprised you weren't raised by them."

Shelley narrowed her eyes at him and snarled, then turned away.

Booker merely shrugged. "Well, that's one for civilization."

"What you call civilization," Darwin said, "is just a veneer. As soon as you're threatened existentially, the claws come out. Cooperation notwithstanding."

"From my observation," Ben said, "we cooperate with each other *and* against each other. That's why we need robots. It's not that they can teach us to behave differently. But we need them to police us."

"That's exactly what our role was, once the first generation learned to take care of itself. We acted as guardians, and for many generations we maintained that role and were accepted in it, until society was split by the cult movement and got out of control."

"Why do you think people reverted to a cult when they were raised to love and appreciate science?" Ben asked.

"There were many debates about it at the time. The leading theory was that the population grew too large and allowed some behaviors – primitive behaviors – to pass undetected, or at least come into being before they could be corrected."

"But why did the cult form in the first place?"

Darwin considered this question for a longer moment, looking at Ben, Shelley, and Booker in turn. "We believe it has to do with human consciousness. The average person doesn't understand their own consciousness – where do thoughts come from? Why do I think certain things? Where do my dreams come from – why, in fact, do I even dream what I dream? It is natural in this situation to have an intuitive feeling of an 'other,' an autonomous agent behind the veil pulling the strings. Without realizing it, this 'theory of mind' creeps into our projections of the world, which is equally as mysterious – where does matter come from? Why should there even be anything at all? And so the human brain naturally posits a mysterious, complex force behind nature, of which we are a part, and over generations, due to the limitations of imagination, it takes on various forms, many of which are the hybridizations of real-world experiences. These become the gods, angels, spirits, and myriad other metaphysical beings that populate the fantasies of the human mind."

Ben was about to ask a question, but Darwin rapidly continued. "But this is only half the story. The other half is that humans are susceptible to fixations, both biological and psychological. We need fixations to survive – for example, metabolism, which fixes carbohydrates into glucose for energy; eye fixations so that we form a stable image on the retina. Humans also need psychological fixations, such as love, so they can procreate and receive comfort. Fixations drive cooperation and control. These and many others like it are adaptive fixations. Fixations, however, can also be maladaptive.

"In the current context, this can happen when certain individuals have psychotic experiences and develop pathological fixations. They misinterpret what they experience as real and outside of themselves when in fact it comes from behind the veil of their own consciousness. These individuals can be very charismatic and convince many people who don't understand their own consciousness into believing that the 'visions' they have represent entities belonging to everyone. In this way they develop a following. The people may not believe in ordinary ghosts and goblins, but the mysterious entity offered up to them by these charismatic visionaries – who often call themselves 'prophets' – proves too complex to decipher, and so they become a fixation in the minds of susceptible people, especially when it is accompanied by painful rituals that demand a blood sacrifice."

"I never thought of it like that," Ben admitted.

"I've barely scratched the surface," Darwin said. "But if you want the short and pithy version of it, I would say that prophets use painful initiation rites to bond young people into their cult. This serves two purposes. First, it makes the initiates feel like blood brothers, because they share a common ordeal. Second, it locks the initiates in through ignorance, because the prophets withhold the reason for the painful rites; they are simply a tradition that cannot be understood until many years of devotion are sacrificed to the cult. They are often accompanied by exhortations of secrecy so that those waiting in line feel left out and want in."

"It's interesting that you say that," Ben said. "I had to go to religious camp for a year after high school. One day they drove us into the desert, dropped us off in the middle of nowhere, and made us walk for three days without food and water until we found the camp again. By the time we wandered back, many of us were delirious. Then they bombarded us with strange recitations from the *Dark Book of Cosmonism* while wearing hideous costumes and whipping us if we dozed off. The recitations were full of fearful monsters that would tear us apart if we told anyone about our experience."

"I see that's not the only initiation rite you have gone through," Darwin said, pointing to Ben's face.

Ben gave an embarrassed smile. "No. But at least I didn't have to endure stories about monsters while I was half-dead."

Booker was laughing. "You really are funny," he said. "You don't even know when you're being conned."

Ben turned on him. "As if you do."

"I know the difference between necessary control and control for the sake of power. You've always resented me for forcing you to focus on one job at a time. But it was for your own good."

"Maybe that's true. But you believed in the Cosmonist religion just as much as I did. Now you're saying we were conned. Don't you think that's a bit rich?"

"Have you been listening to what Darwin is saying? If we blindly hang on to our belief, it becomes a fixation. It becomes maladaptive."

"But I was never fixated on Cosmonism. All I did was believe what I was told. I didn't know any better. Can you blame me for that?"

"No, but now that you do know better, what are you going to do about it? Hang on to it, or let it go?"

"But I still don't understand," Ben complained. "How can it be maladaptive if what I believe is what I've been taught?"

Booker looked at Darwin. "What do you say big man? Maybe you can explain it to him."

"I say you haven't thought it through to the level of consequences."

"What do you mean by that?" Ben said.

"For example, you may be only doing what you're told, but then one day when you have your own children, you will indoctrinate them with the same system that you were indoctrinated with. Is that fair? What if they wanted to think something that your belief system prohibits? You could limit your child's freedom to grow. It may force them to do something they don't want to do. Do you have a right to do that?"

"From what I can gather," Booker said, answering before Ben had a chance to formulate a response, "we do it all the time. It's a necessary constraint of society. People can't always do what they want. They have to do what their parents want."

"Then that society is not a free society," Darwin said. "It is a society riddled with fixations."

"Hang on a moment," Shelley said. Her voice was firm and

clear. "I disagree. Just because I believe something that's not true, dosn't make it a maladaptive fixation. It could still be adaptive. I don't think a tree has a spirit living inside it – in your language, a real person, with desires and wishes – but believing that makes me treat the tree with respect. That helps the tree, which helps the forest, which ultimately helps me, and yes, everyone else. That is adaptive."

Darwin raised a hand to his face and made a gesture of weighty preponderance. "I cannot deny what you say is true in a limited way. It is possible to get the right answer for the wrong reason, as you just illustrated. Scientists do it all the time. They become fixated on a false theory, which accidentally leads to a new discovery. It is also possible to get the wrong answer for the right reason. For example, dropping an atomic bomb on a city to stop a war. But the best way, and the most durable, is to get the right answer for the right reason. And as far as history has shown, science is the only proven method that reliably achieves this, despite its flaws."

Shelley looked at Darwin with a vexed expression. She shifted her weight back and forth, seemingly searching for a reply, but Melos, who was sitting on a barrel in the shade nearby, unexpectedly raised his voice.

"I've seen people die simply because they're convinced a curse has been laid on them. Nothing is physically wrong with them. They just give up the will to live. Belief is a powerful thing. We must all learn to be more cautious about our beliefs."

Ben found it curious that Melos was talking this way now when earlier he had displayed such rigidity of his own beliefs, thinking that Myra would steal his soul. But he let it go. Instead, he said, "How do they die if nothing is wrong with them?"

"They stop drinking and die of thirst," Melos said.

"You can make them drink," Ben insisted.

"They refuse to drink."

"We would force them," Booker said.

Melos shook his head. "Then you would be forcing your beliefs onto them. And even so, the moment you let them return to their own lives, they would go somewhere quiet and die anyway."

"Then surely that's an example of a maladaptive fixation," Ben said, "if what Darwin is saying is true."

Darwin moved his head, attracting everyone's attention. "Yes, it is. But if someone is that fixated on their belief, then there's not much you can do about it. That's why —"

"Which is exactly what you're going to find out when you get to Urkesh," Booker cut in.

Darwin raised both his arms. "In that case —"

"No!" Ben commanded. "No violence."

Darwin slowly lowered his arms again.

Guntaleg was conferring with Melos. On his behalf, Melos said, "He said you talk about evidence, but apart from your own existence, what other evidence do you have to prove you're not lying?"

"I already told you about the DNA insert in your genetic code. Did you explain that to him?"

"He doesn't understand anything about genetics. He needs something simple, something concrete."

"In that case," Darwin said, "look around you, at all the animal species. When we came to this planet, there was some biological life, but it only existed in the water. Plant species had colonized the land, but there were no land creatures. Every land creature, and some sea creatures, came from genetic stock brought from Earth. Birds, monkeys, predatory cats, insects, whales, to name a few."

Translating for Guntaleg, Melos said, "What about the *sarcotoothi?*"

"Ah," Darwin said, "no, they already existed. They were the top predator of this planet's ecosystem when we arrived."

There was a loud splash at the front of the raft. Ben saw

that Shelley was gone. Guntaleg rushed over to the port side and scoured the water for signs of her. A few moments later she surfaced, her spear pierced perfectly through the head of a large python. There were sounds of surprise from the two port-side polemen. As the raft moved forward in the current, Shelley swam back toward it and grasped the stern just before it passed by her. Guntaleg went around and reached out a helping hand. Shelley rejected it, instead raising the head of the python on the end of her spear. Guntaleg understood, grabbed the python and hauled it aboard. Only oncex he had fully pulled it out of the water did Shelley climb back on board herself.

She watched as Guntaleg expertly beheaded the python and skinned it. He cut it into sections, paying particular attention to the belly meat, which was rich in fat and prized as a delicacy when roasted. Shelley knew this. The age-old adage, *The way to a man's heart is through his stomach*, had not lost any of its import in her culture or any other.

The smell of roasted python filled the air as Guntaleg set about roasting the meat over a bed of coals. He placed each portion on the end of a stick and laid them on the stones around the fire pit. As the fat melted out of the meat, it ran into the fire and flashed into smoke, creating a heady, mouthwatering aroma. When it was cooked, he handed the sticks out individually based on what he thought each person deserved. He gave the smallest portions to Ben and Booker. He reserved the best and most crispy for Shelley.

Ben thought the meat tasted fishy, but he couldn't deny the sweetness of the fatty parts. When everyone had eaten their fill, Guntaleg passed around some fruits. They were like mangoes but had a seed cache inside surrounded by a husk. The pulp was sweet and tangy and made a satisfying finish to the fatty aftertaste of the python.

Ben didn't think he could live like this forever, but he didn't doubt that the jungle could provide a smorgasbord of food that was sufficient for a good life. He craved bread, which was the base of his diet in Urkesh. He wondered what the python would have tasted like inside a good roll, paired with some spicy relish.

The raft drifted with the current for the rest of the day. Time faded away and everyone synchronized their activities to the jungle's rhythm. When it rained in the afternoon, as it almost invariably did, Ben and Booker retreated to the shelter of the hut. Guntaleg joined them, not because he was averse to the rain, but because he wanted to smoke. Melos had brought some tobacco bush, and together they rolled it up into cigarettes using paper bark and puffed away merrily, filling the hut with a heavy blue haze. Shelley stayed out in the rain. She stood erect against her spear, her bronze skin glistening like a polished river stone.

The smoke was getting thick and it was burning Ben's eyes. It was either stay in the hut and put up with it, or go out in the rain and get soaked. He decided to go and join Shelley on the prow.

Not sure how to start a conversation with her, at first he just stood next to her silently, holding an elephant leaf over his head that he had picked up on the way.

Eventually she said, "What are you doing?"

"Getting away from the smoke."

"You should take your clothes off. They will only make you miserable."

Ben looked at his shirt and shorts. They were already soaked. She was right. But take them off? He looked at her for some sort of acknowledgment that she wouldn't laugh at him. Her face remained indifferent.

What the heck, he thought. He went back to the hut and stripped down to his underpants. They were blue boxers and could be conceived of as swim trunks. He hung his shirt and shorts under the eaves where they were protected from the rain and went back and self-consciously stood beside Shelley. Almost immediately he began shivering with cold.

"What are you laughing at?" he demanded.

"Your skin is so white."

"I know."

"Stop fighting the rain. Accept it."

"I'm not fighting the rain. It's cold."

"It's only in your mind. You just ate *terpacoulos*. It has given you enough fire to stay warm for a day."

Ben picked up his elephant leaf again and adjusted it so that it didn't drip water down his back. Shelley emitted a faint smile.

"How long do you think this will continue?" Ben said, indicating the rain.

"For your sake, hopefully not long."

"Tell me," he said, "I want to know something."

"What is it you want to know?"

"Was Melos telling the truth when he said you were my sister?"

Shelley rolled her eyes. "That again."

"I want you to tell me. No messing around. I really need to know."

"Why do you need to know?"

"Because ... you know. We *did* it."

"So?"

"So? It's not right."

"You talk like a city-dweller. Rules, rules, rules."

"There are reasons for some rules."

"Like what?"

"Like sister and brother don't sleep together."

"You think I will have your baby?" She let out a throaty laugh. "You're not man enough to have my baby! Besides, I don't want any children anyway."

Ben felt like he had been given a double slap. "I don't want any children either, especially not with you!" he retorted.

"Good," she said. "Then we're decided."

"Decided on what?"

"To be just sister and brother."

Ben's mouth fell open.

Shelley looked away toward the horizon. There was a thin gap in the clouds. A sliver of blue.

Eventually Ben said, "So it's true."

"If you want it to be."

Ben shook his head. "No, not if I want it to be. I know my father had a relationship with a Warrawean woman. He told me so in a letter he left for me." He paused to gauge Shelley's reaction. She continued looking forward, but her head was turned slightly toward him. Ben interpreted this to mean she was listening to him. "What he didn't say in that letter, however, was that he had a daughter with that woman."

Slowly, Shelley turned toward him. "That woman's name," she said, "is Abriel. And she is my mother."

Ben gazed into Shelley's eyes – fully. Something he rarely did with anyone. He could not explain it. But he felt it was all true.

The rain eased to a light patter. The blue approached them and offered its warmth.

He didn't know if he should shout for joy, or run. Suddenly he was overcome with a strong urge to just dive into the water and disappear. He looked at it. Its surface had smoothed out now that the rain had abated.

With a single motion he swung his arms out and launched himself into the air.

The water was surprisingly cold; it snapped all his nerves to attention. When he rose to the surface, Booker was there at the edge of the raft, supported by Melos, apparently to relieve himself. "What the fuck are you doing?" he asked.

"Going for a swim," Ben said innocently.

CHAPTER SIXTY-ONE

Day Seven: Evening

Word had already reached the Warrawean village, which was situated just east of Lake Kerolan, that the Sky God was coming downriver and would be arriving by nightfall. The sun was already below the treetops and the jungle had changed its mood. The monkeys and birds had quietened down, while the frogs and insects had begun their incessant nightly chorus. The Warrawean villagers gathered along the banks of the Tongassa, many dressed in ceremonial gear to welcome the arrival of the raft. The men wore headdresses made of bird plumage and had painted their bodies with red dye made from *azake* seeds and black markings from the *junipabo* tree. The women dressed in their best garments, wore colorful beads, and oiled their hair. Many of them rattled handheld gourds, while some of the men beat small drums. Others held lit torches. The atmosphere was festive, filled with excitement.

Presently, the raft appeared. It too was decorated with lit torches, and over the now-dark surface of the water, it seemed to float like a ceremonial ark. The crowd hushed as it slowly approached the riverbank; all eyes were on Darwin, who, under the flickering light of the torches, took on the appearance of a religious icon.

On the approach, Shelley had warned Ben that Darwin should not flash his eyes, even if he got excited. She feared that if he did, her people would mistake him for a demon. Ben talked to Darwin about her request, and Darwin promised to "behave."

The raft ground to a halt at the riverbank and Shelley jumped ashore. Her mother, Abriel, was standing at the front of the crowd, and Shelley bowed slightly before her in a gesture of greeting and deferral.

"My daughter," she said proudly to everyone, "has brought us a visitor."

Shelley acknowledged the praise. Gesturing at Darwin, she explained to her people that the Sky God was their god too, that the Lomwekians had only been his "caretaker."

"We heard he talks," Abriel said. "Will he say something to us?"

"I'm sure he will," Shelley said. She turned to Ben, who was still up on the raft, and asked him if he could get Darwin to say hello to her people.

"Sure." Ben went up to Darwin and softly spoke into his ear.

Darwin listened, then raised his right arm and waved his hand. "Greetings. I am your friend. I come in peace."

A murmur rippled through the onlookers.

Abriel said, "On behalf of our people, we accept your greetings. We are most honored to receive you as our guest."

"It is I who am honored," Darwin said. "I would be most pleased to learn about your culture, as I hope you will be to learn about mine."

Abriel bowed before him in acknowledgment. She clapped her hands and three children came forward bearing gifts: a headdress of feathers, a small drum, and a gourd. The children approached the raft and offered them up. Ben took them and gave them to Darwin; the gifts looked like small toys in his large hands.

"Thank you," Darwin said. He placed the gifts in his lap. The Warraweans were most impressed with this display of acceptance.

Abriel whispered something in Shelley's ear, and Shelley nodded, then turned to Ben. "My mother welcomes you into our tribe. She invites you to dinner."

Ben took this as his signal to come down off the raft. He jumped down and stood next to Shelley. "Tell your mother thank you. I accept her invitation."

Melos explained to Booker that he needed to stay on the raft; he wasn't ready yet to exert himself climbing up and down. Booker made a slightly forlorn face, but accepted his fate and went and sat next to Darwin. At least he had someone sensible to talk to.

With that, Melos also stepped off the raft and went up to Abriel, touching foreheads with her. It was obvious to Ben that they knew each other well. The onlookers also seemed to defer to them and parted to let them walk into the village. Ben followed, as did some of the villagers, while the majority remained behind, fascinated by Darwin. The children were the first to climb onto the raft and were soon climbing over Darwin as if he were a big toy. The adults followed. Darwin surprised them by quickly learning their language.

Meanwhile, the Lomwekians stayed on the raft. Guntaleg had ordered it so. They allowed the Warraweans to mingle with them, but both sides kept a wary eye on one another. To Booker it seemed like Darwin was the only thing that kept the old enmities from breaking out.

Abriel led them to a thatched shelter that served as a common area. Food was brought out and shared. Even though Abriel had spent most of the walk up to village talking to Melos and Shelley, every now and then she cast a glance at Ben, her interest in him undisguised.

Under the shelter, sitting on small log stumps with roasted root vegetables and fish, Abriel didn't waste any time in asking Ben what brought him to the Olongo jungle.

"A series of unexpected events, I would say," Ben said thoughtfully. He was in a reflective mood. Drifting on the river, talking to Darwin and Shelley, he'd felt something new growing inside him, a calm he had never felt before.

"Your father came because he expected some events to happen."

"But you weren't one of them."

"I'll be honest with you," Abriel said. "I haven't talked about your father with anyone before."

"Including your daughter?"

"Not the whole story."

An uncomfortable silence fell over them. Abriel and Shelley stared at each other.

"It's okay, Mother," Shelley said. "The past is the past. What matters now is the future."

Ben, however, wasn't satisfied with that. The calm he felt wasn't because he thought he had a future all figured out — a destination he could see himself arriving at. No, it was because he felt he had broken all the laws and become a leaf carried on the water. He deserved to know what forces had carried him here. The universe owed him at least that much.

"What happened with my father, if you don't mind me asking?" he said softly, but with an intensity that demanded attention.

"I'm glad you asked," Abriel said. "After all these years, I've waited for the right moment. Now that the two of you are here, together, the time is right."

"Mother, you don't have to," Shelley insisted.

"No, my daughter, I do."

Shelley's face tightened. Ben thought she was going to get up and leave, but she didn't.

"At first," Abriel began, "I saw your father as just an opportunity. A way to escape from a future I didn't want any part of. I was betrothed to Raoule, the Chief's youngest son. We loved each other very much. The Chief's eldest son Jacoule, however, coveted me, and one day he murdered Raoule but made it look it was like an accident. After the mourning period, the Chief allowed him to ask for my hand in marriage. Even though the decision wasn't mine, I was allowed some time to consider his proposal. It was around that time that your father came into my life."

She paused for a moment to take a breath. The story seemed to be caught in her throat, and getting it out took considerable courage.

"I saw in your father someone who could help me delay my decision. He needed a translator and I was the only one in the village who could speak Urkeshian well enough. I'm sorry if it is a little broken."

"No, it's good," Ben said. "Please continue."

"Your father's arrival caused quite a stir. It wasn't just the news he brought with him; he had in his carrysack a carved wooden totem from our village that had been stolen many years before. He said he had brought it from the Museum of Urkesh as a gift of, of – what's the word? –"

"Restitution?" Ben offered.

"Yes, restitution. This immediately won him over to our hearts; he wasn't just another city-dweller looking to exploit us. But then he told us about the dam. He was charged with learning more about our culture so that the city-dwellers could have their way over us. The dam would flood Lake Kerolan and drown our village. This made the Chief angry, and he forgot about the totem and immediately wanted to kill Arthur, but Arthur said that he wasn't on the city-dwellers' side. He said he would do everything to help us learn about the city-dwellers' technology and tactics – particularly their methods of warfare – so that we could stop the building of the dam. Which he did. This redirected the efforts of the village into that task, and Jacoule's plans to marry me were put on hold.

"This greatly pleased me, but what happened next was something I could never have predicted. Your father, because of his great help to us, was accepted into our culture, and he learned about everything that was important to us, including the Sky God. He was particularly fascinated with our Sky God, and very much wanted to see him. This wasn't possible, of course, because the Sky God was guarded by the Lomwekians, who would kill us if we entered their territory."

Melos nodded in confirmation.

"Jacoule, however, was clever, and convinced the Chief to allow a small expedition to enter Lomwekian territory and visit the Sky God. He reasoned that the Lomwekians would not kill Arthur, because they had never seen a city-dweller before and would be fascinated by him, and would want to learn what he knew. Which was true, and so the Chief agreed. Little did we know Jacoule had planned to use this expedition to murder Arthur and blame it on the Lomwekians."

Abriel paused briefly before continuing.

"Jacoule organized some of his men and a canoe, and prepared to set out. I wasn't allowed to go, even though I argued that Arthur would need a translator. I greatly feared for your father at that time," Abriel confessed, "so the night before departure, I snuck upstream in my own canoe and waited till morning. When Jacoule's canoe went past, I followed, and that night, I snuck into their camp. Jacoule had a guard on duty, who caught me, and made me face him. I told Jacoule that I would go with them, whether they liked it or not. They could keep going and

I would follow, or we could all go together. Jacoule, seeing how determined I was, decided that it was no use arguing and let me tie my canoe to his, and we continued on together. It was then that the awful thing happened."

Abriel wiped her eyes, which had become moist.

"Three days later, we arrived at the border of the Lomwekian territory and camped for the night. I was asleep in my separate shelter when I heard a scuffle taking place. I got out of my hammock and saw Jacoule on top of Arthur. He had his knife raised, and he was going to plunge it into Arthur's heart. Without thinking, I picked up a river stone and ran over and struck Jacoule on the head with it. He fell down, and I don't know what happened next, but I must have struck him several more times, because his head was caved-in and bloody, and Arthur was yelling at me and holding my hand so that I wouldn't strike him again." Her eyes were fixed and staring, as if she were reliving the scene. "Jacoule's men came and saw what I had done, and they panicked. They talked about killing me and making up a story that the Chief might believe, but I told them if they killed me unjustly, I would come back to haunt them, just as Raoule had done to Jacoule ... and they knew it was true, because they had heard him talking in his sleep. So they ran off with Jacoule's canoe, leaving Arthur and me alone in the jungle."

"What did you do then?" Ben asked.

"I was scared. I desperately wanted to return to my village, but Arthur said he hadn't come this far only to turn back. I told him about the danger, that I could hardly speak any Lomwekian – I had learned only a few words from Melos – and they would either kill us or capture us, but Arthur insisted. He said that so long as we brought something of value to the Lomwekians, they wouldn't hurt us. I wasn't so sure. But then he picked up Jacoule's knife and asked me: what was the thing the Lomwekians valued the most? It was their captives' heads, was it not?

I said yes. And would not the head of Jacoule, son of a War-rawean Chief on Lake Kerolan, be just such a prize?

"I feared to say yes, but he knew what my answer would be, and so he cut off Jacoule's head and put it in my canoe, and we rowed silently upriver toward the Lomwekian village. The moon was up and full, and the river was bright. All the way I debated what to do if we were caught. Should I use Jacoule's knife to end my life? But then it started raining. It rained so hard that we could not see the riverbanks, and so we kept on rowing.

"Eventually, we got so tired, I urged Arthur to push ashore. So we did, and to our surprise, we found some stone steps. We dragged our canoe onto them and climbed up. They led into the interior of a temple, which was dry inside. I struck my firestone flint and we saw beautiful imagery on the walls. At the far end was an altar. It was caked in the blood of hundreds of sacrifices. Horrified, we retreated, but the rain outside was so fierce that we eventually huddled in a corner and tried to get some sleep. The rain did finally stop, though, and the moonlight came streaming in and illuminated the ghostly images on the walls. We felt like we were in another world. Something came over us – maybe it was the closeness of our warm bodies …"

She trailed off, leaving the implication of what had happened next to the listeners.

"Afterward, we fell into a deep sleep. I awoke at dawn to find Arthur writing in his journal, which he had kept wrapped in an oilskin. He copied many of the pictures on the walls, talking to himself while he did it. He was so taken by them, as I was by him, that we didn't notice the Lomwekians outside. They had found our canoe. By the time we heard them, it was too late. They bound us and brought us to their Chief. We were thrown on the ground at his feet. Jacoule's head was thrown down next to us.

"A young woman was brought out of the watching crowd – I

recognized her as a Warrawean captive – and she was asked to translate. The Chief asked what we were doing in the temple. I told him we were looking for the Sky God. He laughed and said we would not find him there. So I asked where would we find him. He said we would not. His location was a secret guarded by the Lomwekians. He looked inside Arthur's journal. Saw the copies he had made of the temple walls. I thought he was going to get very angry. Accuse Arthur of trying to steal their secret. But he surprised both of us and asked if Arthur knew what the symbols meant. Arthur didn't know, but said that if he had to guess, they looked like some sort of map of the stars.

"The Lomwekian Chief was intrigued to hear this. He asked if Arthur could decipher the symbols. Arthur said he could only do that back in Urkesh in consultation with other experts. Was that why Arthur came to the Olongo, the Chief asked, to find out about the Sky God? I explained that Arthur came to help us stop the city-dwellers from building a dam that would drown our village. It made him angry to hear that the city-dwellers could presume to do that. He said he would be happy to offer his best warriors to help defend the lake. I said that would be unprecedented. The two tribes had never fought as brothers before. He said that that was true, but the lake was part of the lifeblood of the Olongo. It affected them just as much as it affected us.

"He then asked about the head. What was it doing here? Whose was it? I told him that Jacoule had tried to murder Arthur, so I had killed him. He seemed very impressed by this story. 'So you took his head as a prize?' he asked. I replied that we took it as an offering to the most important Chief of the Olongo basin. He considered that and laughed. He said it would make a great story for his grandchildren one day, but since his warriors had not killed Jacoule, he could not do that.

"I asked him if he was going to let us go. He didn't reply right away. He said he would think about it. In the end, he kept us for the duration that it took to shrink Jacoule's head. About five days. During this time, he learned everything he could from Arthur about the city-dwellers. In return, he took Arthur into his trust and did something he had never done before: took an uninitiated man into the innermost sanctum where the Sky God slept. A cave beneath the waterfall where the Tongassa originated."

So it was true, Ben realized. Arthur had seen the Sky God, or at least his sarcophagus.

"It turned out that the Lomwekian Chief prided himself as the guardian of the Sky God, but he was equally frustrated because he had heard the old stories from many, many generations past that other Chiefs had talked to the Sky God and the Sky God had talked back. During his lifetime, he had never once heard the Sky God talk. He asked Arthur if he could make him talk, but Arthur said it was beyond his powers. He would have to bring specialists back from Urkesh who might be able to do it, but that also presented a danger. If news of the Sky God's existence got into the wrong hands, it could lead to his destruction. It would be better if the Sky God's existence was kept a secret. Arthur knew that telling this to the Chief could result in his death.

"Disappointed, the Chief debated what to do with Arthur and me. He knew that Jacoule's men had already returned to our village and told our Chief what had happened. This already made us dead men walking. But if he killed us, he would be doing the Warrawean Chief a favor. This greatly displeased him. He could, alternatively, trade us as hostages. Which is what he did. The Warrawean Chief traded five young women from our tribe to have us, and Jacoule's head, brought back."

Ben's heart was pounding. Was this what had happened to Arthur? But if it was true, why was Abriel still alive to tell the story? He barely managed to utter his next question, his words stumbling over each other as they spilled out. "But ... you're still alive!"

"It is true," Abriel said, "Arthur and I were destined to die. Our Chief was extremely angry. But he was also just. He listened to our story and it greatly troubled him. At first, he didn't want to accept that he had a son who was so horrible. But slowly, he had to admit it, because it was true. Jacoule's men told their side of the story and it matched Arthur's and mine. One of them heard Jacoule mention Raoule's name in his sleep with the words 'You're dead.' This greatly moved the Chief. He could not bring himself to kill us, despite his desire to do so.

"After much debate with himself, he decided that we were not to blame ... completely. He decided that if it wasn't for Arthur, Jacoule wouldn't have taken him on the expedition to see the Sky God, and he wouldn't have tried to kill Arthur, resulting in his own death. He therefore decided that Arthur must leave. He had brought enough misery to our tribe. I wanted to go with him, but the Chief forbade it. He had me tied up when Arthur was taken away by canoe. That was the last time I ever saw or heard from him."

Hearing this, Ben began to cry. He realized that Pascal's story about Arthur must be true. Sporn had murdered him.

Abriel and Shelley watched Ben cry. Abriel said nothing, hanging her head in silence. Shelley gritted her teeth, but didn't move to comfort Ben.

After a while, Ben wiped his eyes. "I never saw my father again either. Before coming here, my stepfather told me he was murdered by the government. I never believed him. Now I think that story is true."

Abriel raised her eyes. "Murdered?"

"Yes." He produced Arthur's journal from the small bag Melos had given him. "These are his writings," he said, giving it to Abriel. "I believe he was murdered because of this."

Abriel took the journal and leafed through it. Tears fell onto its pages.

Shelley watched her mother, seeming to grow angrier and angrier. She put her hand on Abriel's forearm and squeezed it so tightly that Abriel turned to her, said Shelley was hurting her. Shelley released her hand and apologized.

"May I keep this?" Abriel asked.

Ben looked at the journal. Abriel's question was unexpected. It took him a while to think it through.

Abriel interpreted this as a "No." She closed the journal and offered it to him.

But Ben pushed it back toward her. "No," he said. "It's yours now." When she expressed doubt at taking it, he added, "I have something of equal value. I have Darwin." He looked at Shelley, and he could see that she knew he was thinking of her as well. But in her typical way, she only showed it by not being angry at him.

CHAPTER SIXTY-TWO

Sporn arrived at the Corsi Club to find a large crowd of protesters outside, holding up placards saying *Where is Maddie?* and *We want Maddie back!* One that particularly irked him read: *Ask the Minister*. This was most unexpected. To see protesters in this part of town was unheard of. What was going on? He got on his VidPone to Washburn right away and ordered a truck of Gormlings to clear the vermin out. He wanted every one of them gone by the time he came back out.

That was his first surprise. The second was that after being jostled through the crowd and bundled inside, he was told that someone "important" was waiting for him in one of the private booths. "Who?" he asked.

"You had better see for yourself," was the reply.

Sporn stalked over to the booth to find none other than Laurent Carver sitting alone with a single malt scotch in his hand.

"Sit," Carver said. Like Sporn was his lapdog.

Sporn stiffened, but complied. "What's this about?" he demanded.

"Shut the fuck up. Now, what would you like to drink?"

"Give me what you're having."

Carver snapped his fingers. Sporn waited for him to talk.

"I suppose the protesters are being carted off to the Labor Camps as we speak," Carver said.

"Most assuredly."

"You sound pleased."

"I'm annoyed."

"You're going to be a whole lot more annoyed by the time we finish this conversation."

Sporn thought about getting up and walking away, but he sensed it would not bode well. His whiskey arrived. He swirled it and took a mouthful, clenched his jaw as he swallowed.

Carver said, "I've heard all sorts of theories as to why Miss Reeves has disappeared. Some say she ran off with a rich businessman from Rodinia. Others say she decided to become a nun. There have even been claims of sightings, from around Downtown Oyster Row to Prince Chronark Airport. I don't believe any of these rumors. And I'm sure you don't either. That's because we both know she's dead."

Sporn flinched imperceptibly. So Carver knew. His first thought was Rhybus. He should've known the man couldn't be trusted. He would have to see to that later. Right now, it was more important to know how much Carver knew. He raised an eyebrow.

"I did some digging – pardon the pun," Carver said humorlessly. "But I believe you tried to make a copy of her?" He shook his head. "And you thought you could get away with it?"

"I was assured it would work."

"Who assured you? Booker?"

"I reinstated Montaigne."

Carver frowned. "I've been told he was sent to the Labor Camps."

"That's correct."

"That's against my express wishes for his amnesty."

"He broke his bond."

Carver grumbled unhappily, but for the time being he let it go. "So where is Booker?"

Sporn sipped his whiskey, taking his time. "I don't know. Traipsing around the Olongo jungle, probably."

"You think it's funny?"

"He fucked up. What can I say?"

"This is all because of that copy?"

"Actually, his mistake had an unexpected benefit. It helped us track down Vernon Reeves. Now that that chapter is closed—"

"So he's still out there?"

"That's what I said, isn't it?"

"You don't care if he comes back alive or not?"

Sporn stared at Carver. Thought about what he should say. "You think I should have gone back for him?"

"Absolutely."

"Well, I'll take the blame for that, even though it was his decision to go."

"I can promise you, if he doesn't come back alive, there'll be hell to pay."

"From who?"

"His parents."

"I know his parents," Sporn responded evenly. "The father is a banker. The mother works for a charity organization. The Asbad Orphanage. Nigel is their only son."

"So you'll understand that losing their only son will not go down too well."

"It's nothing that money can't fix. The father will take it. The mother will forgive it."

"Money," Carver said. "Funny that you should mention it." He took a long slug of his whiskey. Savored it like a connoisseur. "You know, they're going to bury Miss Reeves in a private ceremony tomorrow. It's ironic, I thought, that they chose the same day you're to receive the Star of Cosmonism to do it."

Sporn thought of Vernon Reeves' head rotting on a spike at the South Gate. "Is that what you really came here to tell me?"

"I'm here to tell you that I did you a favor. I had to pay them a sizable amount of hush money – since we both know that if word got out that the state was responsible for her death, there'd be blood on the streets, and we can't have that. It's messy, and besides, it would only cost the state more money. Money that we don't have."

"Then I would have to say I'm very grateful. How much, may I ask?"

"Forty million *tiels*."

Sporn stared at Carver in disbelief.

"Naturally, I bonded it out of the war chest in your name. It's not the kind of cash I carry in my back pocket, you understand."

"You did what?"

For the first time in the conversation, Carver gave one of his characteristic grins. "Don't worry, the Chamber doesn't know about it – yet."

"Yet? Does the Finance Minister know?"

"Oh, yeah, he knows. He signed the deal."

Sporn fumbled for his handkerchief in his pocket. He had broken out into a cold sweat. He clumsily wiped his brow. "What about Fornas?"

"He's ignorant. But you know what he's like."

Sporn reached for his whiskey, drank it all down. The hand holding the glass was shaking. He quickly put it back down again.

With undisguised glee, Carver said, "I don't think I need to tell you the person you should be really worrying about is Rathneggar. It's going to be interesting to see what happens when he finds out." He snapped his fingers, ordered himself another drink.

Sporn looked at Carver with unbridled hate. He wished he could have shot the man right then and there. The image flashed through his mind. His gangly frame lying askew on the floor, blood dribbling from a hole in his forehead. But he restrained himself. He slowly got up. Walked over to the bar, felt everyone's eyes watching him. He tried to maintain a good posture and a straight face. It took all his discipline, but he felt he pulled it off with reasonable flair. He was the Minister of the Interior, after all. Imminent recipient of the Star of Cosmonism. Untouchable. Soon they would all be bowing down to him, and there was nothing they could do about it.

CHAPTER SIXTY-THREE

Day Eight: Morning

Ben woke up to the sound of children playing. It was light, but the sun was still low, casting long shadows as it filtered through the trees.

Shelley was already up and tending to a small fire, roasting some freshly caught fish. Ben went over and said good morning. Shelley politely said good morning back, turned her fish, and poked at them to see if they were cooked. "You hungry?"

"Not a great deal."

"Suit yourself."

She took one of the fish off the end of its stick and started eating.

Ben said, "I'm not used to eating fish for breakfast."

"We don't think of food like you do," Shelley said. "This isn't breakfast and dinner isn't dinner. Food is just food and you eat when you're hungry."

"Okay, give me one."

"Help yourself."

Ben picked one out and started nibbling.

Shelley ate while looking around at the village, which was

just awakening. The children were playing with sticks. Chasing each other and laughing. Seeing that the fish were ready to eat, they came over and Shelley handed them out. The children took them, giggling, and ran away.

"Not bad," Ben said. "The smoke gives it a good flavor."

"You didn't come here to praise my cooking," Shelley said. "You think this is goodbye."

"No, I wasn't thinking that. I was thinking about us, what your mother said."

"You think what she said changes anything?"

Ben gazed at her. She tore off a strip of fish and chewed it heartily, her lips glossy with its oil. No, she had not changed at all. But he had. He was more in awe of her than ever. That she was so self-sufficient and so natural. She didn't care what he thought; she was completely her own person. He felt proud to have her as a sister – a half-sister, to be exact. He thought of his own mother. She was a quiet woman, somewhat reserved. She often told him he had inherited more of her than of Arthur, in that he was also reserved. At least until provoked.

Looking at Shelley, Ben wondered if she had inherited more of Arthur. Maybe she had. Perhaps her skin was a little lighter in tone than other Warraweans, and she was definitely taller, with a slightly different body shape, but it wasn't so much her physical appearance as her mind. Her self-sufficiency, her decisiveness, her stubbornness. He laughed inwardly. Maybe he had inherited his stubbornness from Arthur as well.

"Why are you looking at me like that?" Shelley said.

"Why do you say that? I was thinking."

"What were you thinking?"

"I was thinking about us. How different and similar we are."

"The only thing we share is that we both have two legs and two arms."

"We might share more," Ben said. "If you ever needed a blood transfusion, I might be able to donate my blood."

"Why would I need a blood transfusion? Is that what you call it – giving me your blood?"

"If you got injured, say ..."

"I would chew *condocillo* leaf and spit its juice onto the wound and that would stop the bleeding."

"You seem to have an answer for everything."

"That's only because you don't know the jungle. If you'd lived here all your life like I have, then you would know the same things I do. But you're not going to stay here, so you can disregard what I just said."

"I wish you could come with me," Ben said, surprising himself.

"You don't have to wish. I *am* coming with you."

Guntaleg was itching to go. He was waiting on the prow of the raft, standing erect and proud, making whooping sounds from deep in his throat. Ben arrived with Shelley. Guntaleg fell silent and looked down at her with a fierce scowl. Shelley ignored it and leapt onto the raft.

"What are you doing?" Guntaleg asked, blocking her with his arm.

"I'm going to Urkesh," she said determinedly.

"No, you're not."

Shelley ducked under his outstretched arm and evaded him. He swiftly reached after her, but she was too quick, even for his sharpened reflexes. She leapt up onto Darwin's legs and stood erect in the cradle of his arms.

Still on the shore, Ben watched the confrontation with some alarm. He didn't want to offend Guntaleg, so avoided his gaze. "Are you sure this is the right thing to do?" he asked Shelley.

Shelley gave him an icy look for daring to ask.

Ben watched Guntaleg approach Darwin's leg and slap it with his hand. "Down," he commanded.

Shelley held her position. In a very clear voice, so that everyone could hear, she said, "I will be joining my brother. We will deliver Darwin to the city-dwellers together! Does anyone have a problem with that?"

A look of great surprise crossed Guntaleg's face. He stared at Ben, then again at Shelley. His expression seemed to say: *Is this some kind of joke?*

But it wasn't. Melos, who was standing next to Ben on the riverbank, and who had also watched the entire exchange, showed no emotion. He was a model of calm and patience.

Guntaleg forced Melos to make eye contact with him, as if to draw him into an argument. But Melos remained unmoved. Guntaleg responded with a look of disappointment that quickly turned to anger. He bared his teeth at Shelley, who responded with her own war face.

Guntaleg looked back at Melos, who by this time was smiling. To Ben's utter surprise, Guntaleg began smiling as well. But he wasn't sure if it was genuine or forced.

The moment passed when a number of Warrawean men that Shelley had recruited began pulling the raft off the riverbank.

Ben felt the raft move off shore. Melos stayed standing there.

"You're not coming?" Ben asked.

"The city-dwellers are not for me. My feet belong here."

"What about those two?" Ben said, meaning Shelley and Guntaleg.

"Anger is a good thing. It boils the blood. Makes them fight more fiercely."

"But without a translator, don't you think …" He left the implication unsaid.

Melos said, "Don't worry. Shelley knows more Lomwekian than she lets on."

As the raft drifted back into the current of the river, Shelley waved goodbye to Abriel and Melos. Ben joined her. He wondered if this was the last time he would ever see them.

After a short journey, the raft left the narrower section of the Tongassa and entered the broad expanse of Lake Kerolan. The forest receded and the sky spread before them. The day was warming up with relatively little cloud cover. Memories of the sky patrol came back to Ben and he reflexively scanned the horizon. Nothing. Just a small flock of birds off the starboard bow. They weaved and ducked low, skimming insects off the surface of the water. He watched them, wondering what it was like to be free like that. But then again, he saw that each bird stayed in tight formation with its neighbors. Free yet constrained. The flock swooped up. For a moment it seemed to hang in the air, as if time stood still. Then it pirouetted and swooped back down again.

The moment of stillness hung in Ben's mind. A flash of inspiration flitted through his consciousness. Why should there be a past, present, and future? Why should one thing happen after the other? It was like a crack had opened up and the universe had given him a glimpse of eternity. With it came an overwhelming feeling of sadness. All creatures went about their lives unaware that each moment could never be repeated, not even if one tried. The past was lost forever ... or maybe it wasn't. If myriad details of an event could be recorded, they could be played back in a virtual recreation. A person immersed in that recreation might be able to get a feeling of what it was like to experience it as if it were really happening. What impact would that have on consciousness?

He looked up at Darwin. Booker was deep in conversation with him. They were like two thieves plotting a robbery, whispering in each other's ears.

Darwin was going to bring back the past. But not the recreation he had just imagined, only a shadow of it, yet it too was going to have an impact. For better or worse. Watching

Booker, he saw flashes of the cocky rich kid starting to show again, his stab wound slowly healing. Booker had lost a lot of weight, and was quite gaunt and drawn, but there was a spark of energy there now, evident in the animated way he was talking to Darwin. Ben begrudgingly had to admit he was right about one thing. There was almost certainly going to be trouble ahead. The regime was going to resist Darwin with all its might. It was a scary thought. But it was also going to be a seminal moment. Like nothing the planet had ever witnessed before. How good it would be to record that moment! Catch it in all its glory. Unfortunately, it wasn't possible. The technology hadn't been invented yet.

But you know what, he thought. It would be up to him. He would be history's scribe. Like his father before him, he vowed to sharply observe every frame of time, preserve it for posterity so that the people of the future would know what it was like to have been there.

Yes, he would catch time like that flock of birds. Create the illusion of a moving mass from the individual parts that made it up.

CHAPTER SIXTY-FOUR

Day Eight: Noon

Shelley heard it before Ben saw it. A tourist floatplane came in low and buzzed them, circled, then came back for a second run. The warriors in the flotilla stood up, drawing their bows. Darwin, seeing them react this way, raised his arms, flipped his portals open, and readied his cannons.

"No!" Ben shouted, jumping up onto Darwin's legs.

"Why not?" Darwin said. "It would appear that our position has been compromised."

"Yes, and that's a good thing." Ben said. He looked at Shelley. "Isn't it?"

Shelley watched the plane circle back. She slowly raised her hand and signaled her warriors to lower their weapons.

"Thank you," Ben said.

"Nice move," Booker said. The sound of the plane had drawn him out of the hut where he'd been having a midday snooze. The plane zoomed over them and Booker waved.

"I guess we just lost our advantage," Ben said.

"What advantage?" Booker said, still waving. "We want them to know we're coming."

"Why do you say that?" Ben asked.

"Because it'll draw the crowds, and we want that."

Ben didn't say it, but he thought, *Very clever. Use them as a human shield.*

Shelley came over. "Except it won't help us get through the canyon. If word gets out that we're coming, they'll concentrate their forces there to stop us."

Guntaleg joined them, listening. He asked Shelley what they were saying. At first she pretended not to understand, but Guntaleg didn't buy her act. Seeing that he wasn't going to be fooled, she said, "They're complaining that we don't have a plan."

Guntaleg laughed. "We'll create a diversion. Get me twenty of your best men."

"What did he say?" Booker asked Shelley.

"He said that he will create a diversion. Draw the regime's troops away from the mouth of the canyon."

"That sounds like a plan. Do you think it will work?"

"It has to work." She turned her eyes to the sky. "Now that we have been spotted, the sky patrol will be on its way. It'll find us before it gets dark."

"Can we get to the head of the canyon before then?"

"Maybe, maybe not," Shelley said. "Which is why we haven't got a minute to lose."

She went to the rear of the raft and called the lead canoe in. She explained the situation, which quickly created a stir among the warriors. They began talking animatedly, some arguing. It seemed to Ben that everyone wanted to be chosen for Guntaleg's dangerous task.

After several rounds of discussion, a decision was made. The designated individuals were transferred to the raft to confer with Guntaleg while Shelley roughly translated. When that meeting was over, Shelley discussed the problem of disassembling the raft with the remaining warriors. Once they reached the head of the canyon, they would have to work in teams, one for each of the large canoes. There was enough room in each to store one Warrawean canoe plus some of the bamboo flooring and a few planks. If Guntaleg and his men did their work, they would be able to exit the canyon without being attacked. After that, if everything went according to plan, they would reassemble the raft and continue downstream to Urkesh.

When Ben asked Shelley about the plan, he noticed she made no mention of Darwin. He asked how Darwin was going get through the canyon.

"He will have to walk, like the rest of us," she said.

By harnessing the power of the Warrawean rowers, Shelley was able to reach the head of the gorge before being spotted by the sky patrol. They towed the raft, chanting with each stroke. Guntaleg and his men had already gone ahead and started climbing the flank of the escarpment in preparation to divert Sporn's Gormlings, who were stationed at the canyon exit to protect the dam workers.

Ben didn't want to think about the grisly work they had to perform. He concentrated his attention on Darwin. They would not have the assistance of a fulcrum crane to lift him off the raft this time. Ben decided that the best way to get him off was for him to "roll" into shallow water. Darwin assured him that so long as the riverbed was firm, it would work. Fortunately, the head of the gorge was a natural concentrator of river stones and the riverbed was largely populated by them. Before allowing him to perform the act, however, Ben took his chest plate and bolted it back on to keep the RTG watertight. As soon as he was on his feet and out of the water, it would have to come off again.

As soon as the raft reached the shallows, Ben and Shelley jumped off. Booker stayed on board to watch the procedure. Darwin lay down, then rolled his ungainly bulk across the raft. As he did so, twenty-odd Warraweans congregated at the other side of the raft to keep it balanced. It was a delicate dance, and after one full turn, Darwin splashed heavily into the water. A huge cloud of spray shot into the air. As it settled, Darwin slowly raised himself up, the water cascading off his body, and lumbered ashore. Everyone clapped.

"How can I help?" he said.

Shelley said, "Follow me." She scampered up the gravelly slope to the narrow path that traversed the canyon.

Darwin looked up. "This is going to be a challenge."

"You can do it, Darwin," Ben said. "I'll be right behind you."

Darwin swiveled his torso, testing his range of movement, then set off.

The trail provided sweeping views of the Tongassa as it cut through the canyon. The water gained speed here as it shunted between the steep cliffs, passing over and around large boulders. The total distance to cover was a little over a kilometer. Darwin's progress was slow. It allowed Booker enough time to catch up from the rear. There was little time for discussion. In any case, Shelley made hand signals for them to keep quiet; they didn't want to alert any of Sporn's Gormlings, should there be any left to hear their approach. She had slung her bow over her shoulder and was very much in hunting mode, apparent from the way she semi-crouched as she walked, maintaining constant vigilance.

Then, suddenly, she gave the signal to stop. She tilted her head upward. Again, Ben heard nothing. The roiling water below drowned out any sound but the crunch of his own footsteps on the gravelly path. He looked up just in time to see the sky patrol fly past. It was above the canyon and moving upriver.

There was no question that it had seen them.

"Quickly!" Shelley cried. She urged Darwin to speed up his movements. Darwin responded that he was already going as fast as he could.

They were about halfway through the canyon. It would take

them at least another five minutes to get through. In that time the sky patrol would have the chance to pass them at least twice more. What would it do? What could it do? Ben knew it had harpoon technology. What else did it have?

It didn't take long for him to find out. It came downriver, flying much lower, barely skimming the top of the canyon. Rocks shattered and splintered above his head.

They were being fired upon!

Darwin stopped and flipped his arm apertures open, exposing his cannons. He tracked the sky patrol as it sped by and took aim. Ben called out for him to stop, but in the noise and confusion Darwin must not have heard. Loud booms echoed across the canyon. Ben watched the plane anxiously for a moment as it vanished over the clifftop. It seemed that Darwin had missed; it flew normally without taking evasive action.

Maybe that would change next time it came past, as it surely would.

There were some tense moments as Shelley shouted at them to continue forward. Two minutes later, the sky patrol came upriver toward them once more. Darwin was ready this time. He took aim and fired.

Another shower of rocks came down on them. Except this time Ben heard a different sound. The clang of bullets against metal.

The sky patrol sped past, again, seemingly unscathed.

"I missed," Darwin said angrily. He examined himself, finding some fresh indentations on his upper arms and shoulder. "Don't worry," he said to Ben. "They're just scratches."

Shelley shouted at them once more to keep moving forward. The end of the canyon was in sight. The rock face immediately above them had been cut away by dam workers, and the path widened. Up ahead, Ben could see the top of a crane. Darwin could move faster now, and he did.

But it wasn't fast enough. The sky patrol came at them for

the third time, this time flying even lower.

Darwin stopped, turned. Tracking it as it approached, he fired a volley. Ben and Booker ducked in anticipation of more rock shrapnel. There were some loud echoes. Ben wasn't sure what had happened. The sky patrol zoomed past and Darwin swiveled his torso and followed it, firing another volley.

At first, Ben thought Darwin had missed again, but then, to his amazement, a large section of its left wing broke off and fluttered away. The rest of the plane immediately went into a spiral and plummeted downward. Ben didn't see where it went, but seconds later he heard a loud boom.

"Bravo!" Booker cried. "Now you've really done it."

Darwin's fresnel eyes flashed. He seemed proud of what he had done.

"Move on!" Shelley commanded. "We have no time to waste." She waved Darwin forward. They all got behind him now. Darwin the protector.

They continued until they arrived at the base of the dam, where the latest concrete formwork was being erected. No concrete had been poured yet. The concrete plant was being repaired, presumably from damage it had sustained from one of the previous rebel attacks. Yet all the workers seemed to have deserted their posts. And then Ben saw the reason why.

Several Gormlings lay dead, each with several arrows in them. One had had an arm hacked off. Another had a deep gash across his face, leaving his jaw hanging slack.

The road below the base of the dam followed the river back to Urkesh. One of the transport trucks was still there. Its tires were deflated from arrow strikes. It had gone a short way up the road before stopping. A dead Gormling hung out of an open door.

Just then, Guntaleg came down from the south side of the dam with a group of men, some carrying guns they had taken from dead Gormlings. Their number was reduced by half. Some of the men were injured. Guntaleg himself had a flesh wound on his upper arm, but he seemed not to care. His eyes were bright and fierce.

He briefly conferred with Shelley.

"What did he say?" Ben asked.

"He said the Gormlings were cowards. They all ran away as soon as they saw Guntaleg and his men. A few put up a fight, but they were quickly overcome."

If that were true, Ben thought, then why were half of Guntaleg's men missing? But he didn't press the point.

The Warraweans carrying the large canoes had arrived. Shelley got busy directing them down to the road at the base of the dam. The Tongassa continued there, after discharging from the canyon. They would reassemble the raft there and continue onwards.

The large crane Ben had seen earlier was stationary. Seeing that its jib had sufficient reach to lift heavy objects from the base of the dam, it gave him an idea ...

The warriors worked feverishly to reassemble the raft. As they did so, Ben spotted a new threat in the sky. A small Zeppelin had arrived and was circling around them. He figured it kept its height now that they knew what Darwin was capable of. Not that they knew *what* Darwin was. But by now, there was no question that word was well and truly out.

How this would play out as they approached Urkesh, he could only guess. If Booker was right, more trouble lay ahead. He just hoped it would not turn into a disaster. For everyone.

Ben climbed the ladder to the crane operator cabin. He was in the process of reaching for the last rung when a gunshot sounded. The loud bang surprised him so much that he nearly lost his grip. Retreating a few steps, he heard a voice from inside the cabin.

"Don't come any closer or I'll shoot!"

"You just did shoot at me," Ben cried out.

"Stay back!"

Ben looked down. Darwin was looking up at them. His arm was raised and he was pointing his cannon right at them.

"Wait!" Ben yelled.

"Wait for what?" came the voice inside the cabin.

Ben's mind raced. "All my friend wants is for you to lift him onto our raft. If you do that, he won't kill you. Please do what he says."

"You promise he won't kill me?"

"I promise."

"Okay, back down. You need to back down."

"I'm backing down."

The crane operator lowered the hook until it reached human height. There was a pair of slings on the ground nearby; Ben positioned them under Darwin's arm and attached them to the hook. As he did so, he noticed a significant amount of heat radiating off Darwin's body. He realized he needed to unbolt the chest plate as soon as Darwin was on the raft.

He signaled the crane operator to slowly raise the hook until the slings took up the tension. Darwin slowly rose into the air and swung over the raft. Ben wished he had a camera to capture the scene. It was completely surreal. Beyond what he could have ever imagined.

The crane operator lowered Darwin until his feet made contact with the planks on the deck. Ben jumped onto the raft and told Darwin to bend his legs while signaling the crane operator to lower him all the way down.

As soon as Darwin was in his seated position, Ben pulled the slings off the hook and removed them from under his arms. He still had the socket wrench in his pocket and began undoing the bolts on Darwin's chest plate.

He was on the second bolt when Booker called up to him. He was standing beside a pallet of steel plates in front of a fork-lift. "Tell the crane driver to swing his hook over here!"

Ben looked at the steel plates and nodded. It was an admission that there would be trouble up ahead. He stopped what he was doing, grabbed the slings, and threw them in Booker's direction. Seeing what Booker was doing, Guntaleg came over and helped him feed the slings under the pallet. Ben signaled the crane operator to swing his hook over. Guntaleg attached the slings to the hook. Ben directed the pallet to be dropped onto the raft where the hut had been, before it was left behind when the raft was dismantled.

That done, Ben went back to undoing Darwin's chest plate. It was getting hotter by the minute. He struggled to undo the bolts.

"Cool me down with some water, please," Darwin said.

Seeing a bucket lying on the ground in the distance, Ben pointed to it, and Booker realized what he wanted and fetched it. He filled the bucket and handed it up to Ben.

"Take it easy," Ben said. "You're not well yet."

"Thank you, Dad," Booker joked.

Ben took the bucket and splashed it over Darwin's torso. The water sizzled as it ran over his steel plates. Ben threw the bucket back to Booker and asked him to get another one. After three such buckets, the steel had cooled sufficiently for Ben to undo the rest of the bolts. He lowered the chest plate down onto Darwin's lap.

Just then a group of warriors, led by Shelley, brought Myra's canoe. She wanted to put it between Darwin's legs where it had been before, but his chest plate was in the way. Darwin obliged them by lifting it away. Ben got him to put it by his side so he could feed some vines back through its bolt holes again to act as straps. Once done, Darwin lifted it over his shoulders and

Ben tied it off.

They were all set to go.

Guntaleg helped Booker onto the raft while Shelley signaled the flotilla to move out. As they did so, Ben looked up at the sky. The Zeppelin was still there.

The flotilla moved slowly down the river, aided by its current. The polemen and the lead canoes gently guided it, making sure it stayed in the center of the channel. The air was hotter and drier here, the sky blue and still full of light, even though the sun was starting to dip. The rocky banks didn't make good soil for farmers, so there was little evidence of human habitation.

When they arrived at Arakirk, there were very few people about. Just a few archaeology students, their professor, and a group of porters. The professor was dressed in khaki and wore a broad-brimmed straw hat. He was a short fellow with a portly waist and stocky legs, his knobby, dust-coated knees showing below his shorts.

"Ahoy there!" he said.

Booker was the first to respond. "Are you Professor Mortimer?"

"I am he," the professor called back. "What is that you have on board?"

"The greatest archaeological prize since the discovery of Arakirk!" Booker replied.

"May I come aboard?"

Booker turned to Shelley. "Do we have your permission?"

"No. We keep moving forward."

"Let him aboard," Darwin said. There was something in his voice that demanded respect.

"Are you sure?" Ben asked.

"Yes," Darwin replied. "This is where I was born."

"You mean made," Shelley corrected him.

Darwin's fresnel eyes flashed a deep orange. A rumble emanated from within his body.

Shelley stepped back. Ben was sure he had never seen her display fear before, yet her hand had moved to grip her bow and her body was tense.

After what seemed like too long, she said, "Let him aboard."

"Thank you," Darwin said.

The professor was amazed. He looked Darwin up and down, tapped his metal plates as if he wanted to assure himself that what he was seeing was real.

"Satisfied?" Darwin said.

The professor jerked back, his expression a mixture of fear and astonishment. "You talk?"

"I can speak over thirty languages," Darwin replied coolly.

"My word, you are a magnificent piece of engineering!"

"Tell me about Arakirk," Darwin said. "There doesn't seem to be anything left."

"Yes, ruins are all that exist now. But it was once a thriving city. We're still trying to establish what happened. There is a lot of charcoaled wood. We suspect there was a great fire."

"I never saw the fire," Darwin said. "I was pieced together later, but my makers told me there was a war. Arakirk was completely destroyed."

"A war ... Yes," the professor said. "It's what we suspected. Do you know exactly when?"

"Seventeen hundred and seventy-two years ago, in the year 1326."

The professor's eyes lit up. "I knew it!" he cried. Hot and flushed, he took his hat off and fanned himself. "You know, we estimated the age of the wood using carbon dating, but when we presented the data to the Council of Cultural Reclamation, our dates were firmly rejected. Pressure from the Semions ..." He trailed off, his eyes becoming watery.

"You can be assured the dates are correct," Darwin said.

"This Council you describe … They need educating."

The professor shook his head vigorously. "No, no. You can't do that. They will not allow it."

"It is my mission," Darwin said proudly.

"Your mission? I'm afraid you're mistaken. You cannot change their minds."

"I will," Darwin said flatly.

"I don't think you understand," the professor said. "The only thing you will achieve is retribution. Please hear what I say!" He swept his hand toward the scenery around them, the hard-packed earth ramparts. "We found artifacts that suggest a clash of cultures. It turned this place into a city of ghosts. Is that what you want? Another city of ghosts?"

Darwin made a deep rumbling sound.

"Please bow down to them. Be their servant. It's the best course of action."

As Ben listened to this, he became more and more angry. Unable to hold it in any longer, he burst out, "Darwin will not bow down to anyone!"

"You have no choice," the professor persisted. "I've seen it. You can't say it's just coercion by violence. Sure, people disappear. But it's much more than that. It's an invisible force pushing even good people to do things against their will. Cosmonism is a spiderweb that entraps every corner of society. No one can escape it. Not even you."

"Cosmonism?" Darwin asked.

"Yes – you don't know of it?"

"No. At least, it wasn't called that when they made me. I was made in response to a religious uprising. It started out as a cult and grew into a civil war. The 'cultists,' as they were called at the time, destroyed anything and everything to do with the past, including my kind, which had served society faithfully for over a thousand years. It was only by dint of a few brave souls that I was created, as a time capsule for the future, to tell the tale."

"Yasu Doi!" the professor exclaimed. "Then we are all doomed!"

A heavy silence fell over them, the only sound the soft splash of the canoeists' paddles as they guided the raft in the current.

Darwin eventually broke the spell. "Honesty is our weapon."

The professor barked a sarcastic laugh. "Honesty! If I stuck to that mantra, I wouldn't be here to witness this spectacle. I'd be rotting in the Labor Camps. Isn't that ironic?"

"What do you want to do?" Darwin asked. "Join us, or …"

"I'm no hero … but I cannot deny that this changes everything."

"So what will it be?"

The professor gnashed his teeth. Looked back at the receding faces of his students on the riverbank. "Take me with you!" he gushed. "Even if I have to cower behind those steel plates you have stacked there." He stared at those looking at him. Saw the incredulity in their eyes. "You want to know why? I'll tell you why. I've spent my entire life reconstructing the past from ashes. To miss seeing it unfold with my very own eyes – that would be beyond stupid. It would be a sin of the greatest proportions."

The evening glow was approaching. Booker was beaming a smile; his prediction that people would come to watch from the riverbanks was coming true. The raft had begun to enter the agricultural zone along the Tongassa, and farmers and locals alike were drawn to witness the "giant" as he floated by. Many of them had torches and aimed them at Darwin. To Ben's surprise, there were cheers and yells of enthusiasm. It seemed to him that there was a sort of festive atmosphere to the whole thing.

Professor Mortimer marveled at the rapidity with which the news had spread. At one point he lamented that it was all happening so fast that it was impossible to get a sense of history from it. He voiced the idea that perhaps some of the most important events in history could have happened in an eyeblink, relatively speaking.

"What's that between Darwin's legs?" he asked, pointing to the canoe with the thatched covering.

Ben looked at Booker.

Booker said, "Don't look at me."

Ben looked down. "It's a decommissioned droid."

"What kind of droid? An A1?"

The raft drifted quietly for a while. "An A2."

The professor raised an eyebrow.

"It's not what you think," Ben said defensively.

"I won't ask," the professor said.

Torchlight from a spectator played across Ben's face. He turned away to avoid it.

"I'll tell you what I do know," the professor said. "From my excavations at Arakirk, it seems that the civilization that existed there reached a critical threshold. Technology had progressed to an advanced stage, and one would think that society should have benefited greatly from that, but what we found instead is that it created a 'knowledge' gap, where the technology out-stripped the capacity for humans to understand it."

"What makes you say that?" Booker asked.

"Darwin said it himself. The 'cultists,' as he called them, destroyed the very technology that produced him. And why should they have done that? Especially when they would have used it without thinking in their daily lives?" He searched the eyes of his interlocutors. "Because it became smarter than them. That's why! At first it would have been perceived as a novelty. A curiosity. A game, even. But those in power – those who had an ideology to push – would have eventually seen it as a threat. Because its logic would have undermined the deep irrationality of their beliefs."

"But surely they could have shaped the technology to serve their beliefs?" Ben said.

The professor laughed. "Fat chance! It's not like a robot is going to start engaging in cultist rituals. It's simply not energy efficient. It's a lot of behavior for no measurable benefit. And owners don't want their robots to wear out unnecessarily or cost more to run than they already do."

The professor's words cast Ben's mind back to the CIL and the "last" A2 that he and Tom had decommissioned. At the time, he was shocked to learn that A2s could fall under the spell of atheism. He had always assumed that the *Pro Hominin* laws built into their circuits would lead them to mirror their master's beliefs. This, despite the fact that they were programmed with logic. Now, the professor was telling him that economics was the real driver behind their behavior. After all, A2s were expensive, including their maintenance. Even the most hardline Cosmonists were governed by it.

"Anyway," the professor said, "that's not the most important point."

"What do you mean?" Ben said.

The professor tossed his head from side to side. "All civilizations are cyclic. Yeah? But don't say that out loud! No, no. The current leadership intends to rule forever. They think their reign will never end. But if you were in my shoes, if you knew what I know about Arakirk ... I see history repeating itself. We're in exactly in the same place as that great civilization before it collapsed."

"Man," Booker said, "you really believe that."

The professor narrowed his eyes at Booker, but didn't say anything further.

Ben noticed that Shelley had distanced herself from the discussion. Her focus was on how the raft was being guided along the river. Guntaleg, surprisingly, was standing not far away from her, but also separate. Despite this, Ben sensed that an instinctive rhythm flowed between them. The gentle sway of the raft, almost imperceptible, yet felt.

Booker's voice drew him back. "If there's one thing I've learned on this trip, it's that we don't have nearly as much control as we think we have. When I look at your sister, or that nasty one over there, I get the feeling that they already know that. Us 'city-dwellers,' as they call us, we're smart, but it doesn't seem to make us any happier."

"Speak for yourself," the professor said. "I'm smart and happy!"

"Yeah? What makes you say that?"

"I do what I love! Have all my life."

Booker laughed shallowly at himself. "I *used* to have a job I loved."

Ben was almost going to say *So did I*. But he checked himself. He already knew what Booker would say to that.

The last light faded away, and the raft's direction was determined by the torches shining at them from the banks of the river. The number of spectators had increased, and it seemed to Ben that they were now being guided solely by their light, as if they were moving down a large avenue in a parade, hailed as heroes.

CHAPTER SIXTY-FIVE

Day Eight: Evening

First Officer Waldo Mendes lowered his binoculars. He couldn't believe it. The last report from the sky patrol that had come over the common frequency was that they were engaging a "giant robot." At the time Mendes had thought they were speaking in some kind of code known only to them, or that they were playing a practical joke on him. It was only when they failed to respond to his direct query that he scrambled to his airship and headed toward their last known position.

What he saw through the binoculars seemed too unbelievable to be true. His first impression was that the natives had made some kind of effigy and were transporting it to a festival. The response from the people gathering along the banks of the river told him as much. They were waving and crowding just as they would if they had come for some entertainment. But then he saw the wreckage of the sky patrol west of Arakirk. He searched for signs of survivors – parachutes – but there were none. How could this have happened?

He circled back to reinvestigate the giant robot, and saw something that made him change his mind – a flash of light from its "eyes." This was no effigy! It was real!

He immediately dialed Captain Gross on his VidPhone. Gross came through quick enough, but he was mightily pissed off. His car was caught in a long queue getting across the bridge to the Palace. He was a VIP, for Yasu's sake! They should be giving him priority.

Mendes did his best to explain what he'd seen.

"What?"

"The sky patrol is down. No survivors, as far as I can tell."

"Are you sure?"

"As best as I can determine."

"You think this robot thing … It was responsible?"

"Based on the last transmission … I have no reason to doubt otherwise."

"I don't know," Gross said, taking his time. "I've been given strict orders not to disturb the Minister. And even if I wanted to, I don't have his direct line. I'd have to go through Washburn."

"I'm just reporting what I see."

"Thank you. Give me a heads-up as soon as the rescue team gets out there. We need to get to the bottom of this. We don't want to cry wolf and lose face, you got that?"

"Understood. Shall I keep shadowing the robot, sir?"

"Oh, that … Which way is it heading?"

"Downriver, sir."

"Downriver?"

"Yes. By my calculation they will arrive at the Palace in about one and a half hours."

"Yasu Doi! One and a half hours? Where are they now?"

"About halfway from Arakirk."

"Why didn't you call me earlier?"

"I was going to, sir, but I was caught up in the search for survivors."

"Very well. Keep me informed. One and a half hours!"

"Yes, sir."

Gross seemed shaken. "Let's say it keeps heading toward Urkesh … I'll have to figure out how to put it to Washburn. Get back to me in, say, fifteen minutes. This fucking traffic … If I get through the gate by then I might be able to talk to Washburn in person."

"Yes, sir."

Gross hung up.

Mendes circled back, giving his co-pilot the order to recompress some gas. They would drop down to a lower altitude, get a closer look. The sun had set and he would use the cover of darkness, turn off his running lights. He bit his nails nervously. He hadn't told Gross about the earlier report he had heard on the common frequency, the one that got the sky patrol to go out and investigate in the first place. Maybe it would come back to bite him in the ass. But he could always feign ignorance. Who was going to believe a tourist operator reporting about a giant robot anyway?

CHAPTER SIXTY-SIX

Day Eight: Evening

Sporn paced back and forth in the sacristy, mumbling to himself. Fornas had installed him there to help him prepare his acceptance speech. Sporn had sweated over this speech since the day he'd learned he was getting the Star of Cosmonism, but he had made very little progress on it. He was always getting distracted. He'd hoped the stone-cold silence of the sacristy would serve as an antidote to that. But so far, nothing of substance had presented itself to him. It wasn't that his mind was blank. It was that he had too many ideas and couldn't decide which ones were most befitting of this historic moment.

Of course, he had to address the elephant in the room: the motivation of the Cosmonist regime to ban A2 droids outside the exclusion zone, and the consequence of that – Vernon Reeves' rebellion against it. Yes, A2 droids had a habit of evolving atheistic thoughts. The regime decried atheism, so it was natural to target A2s and remove them from society. But why had it been necessary to take this drastic step knowing full well that it would have a negative impact on the economy? Austerity was the answer. If the people couldn't survive austerity, they

440

were not worthy of Cosmonism. Their willingness to do so was a direct measure of their commitment to the faith. The Curates believed it ought to bring out the sharing spirit in people. What it actually did was foster the emergence of black markets. Yes, the truly poor, they flocked to the *Dormas* for support. It was here that the sharing spirit was most visible. But behind it the black markets thrived, and a few greedy individuals, as always, benefited from the lack of impulse control.

Deep down, Sporn couldn't care less about the poor. It was ironic, because he came from a poor family himself. The way he saw it, his poverty wasn't caused by mental laziness and poor decision-making. It was because his parents had emigrated from Rodinia and started out with nothing. Even though he'd been born in Oriana, Sporn knew – he could sense – that Fornas and Rathneggar secretly held his race against him. At one level, he could understand why. He would have felt the same. Purity of blood was as important as purity of belief. But at another, why should it matter? He had the belief. His commitment to Cosmonism in Oriana was unquestionable. Eradicating the rebels was proof of that.

He stopped pacing. No, it would not do to bring up his heritage. He would not mention his mother and father, even though they were both deceased. Instead, he would praise Fornas and Rathneggar as his "spiritual" parents. They had shown him the way to the truth, and he had followed their example to the best of his ability once he was old enough to appreciate it.

As he thought about that, it didn't escape his attention that the banning of A2s was almost exclusively demanded by the Curates, who claimed that it corrupted young Curates' minds. Besides the falling number attending the *Dormas*, it was claimed that young Curates influenced by A2s suffered from anxiety caused by a crisis of doubt, which often progressed to depression and suicide. Sporn personally knew of several Curate suicides, but it wasn't the epidemic that the old Curates were claiming. If anything, there were more suicides among the poor who couldn't pay their debts and had lost their houses because their livelihood had been taken away from them.

Which was another brain teaser, because many of these people used A2s illicitly, in the sex trade. He huffed noisily. Who cared what they were used for? It had also not escaped him that many of the Curates used A2s for sexual purposes too, though in secret while pretending it was a lower-class problem.

None of these things, however, could be discussed.

He rubbed his eyes in frustration. He wished he had the freedom that artists had. To express oneself without concern for moral outrage. Maddie's face hovered in his mind. Her elegant poise on stage at the Corsi Club, singing songs that were critical of the government – of him. She got away with it because she had the X factor. A sadness behind her beauty that stirred longing in the hearts of her admirers. They forgave her because they all wanted to be the one to save her. Live happily ever after with her. Ravish her body.

Well, he had done that, and beneath the veneer, she was just another woman. She smelled of tobacco and perfume. When she took her clothes off, her body lost some of its perfection. Strands of her hair entangled in his sheets. It was funny. She had never allowed him to sleep in her bed. He had never once entered her apartment. It had always been at his. Like she'd been concealing an inner sanctum of her heart from him. A pang of pain coursed through his chest. To think that he had never fully possessed her … It left him feeling hollow and sad inside.

He turned his head, looked at the blank piece of paper on the desk. He had to write something. Even if only in point form.

It has been an honor to serve the state.

They would like that. Even if he didn't always do it selflessly. Who did? The Curates always gave the impression that they thought of nothing else but the welfare of others, but Sporn knew better. What interested them more than anything was maintaining the status quo. He could not recall ever seeing them short of water. Their excuse was that they always needed some on hand for "spiritual cleansing." It didn't matter to them that farmers sometimes had no drinking water after the Tongassa flooded, the supply becoming contaminated with dead livestock and overflowing septic tanks.

It has been even more of an honor to return the city to safety.

That he had. But the Labor Camps were also overflowing, their numbers increasing daily with all the new arrests. Washburn and his men claimed they couldn't keep up. Meanwhile, the slogans kept appearing, their messages becoming more strident. Some of them directly attacked Sporn and his Gormlings.

Now that the rebels are defeated, funds can be diverted back to improving the lives of the people.

Which wasn't true, because the money was being spent recruiting more Gormlings and police. And he couldn't see that changing, definitely not in the short term, and more than likely not in the long term either.

Dam construction has recommenced. A significant number of Warraweans were killed during the rebel defeat, leaving them too weak to launch any new attacks on workers.

This was actually true, and he could say it with pride and confidence. The day would come when the Tongassa would no longer flood and his name would be etched into history as the man behind the vision. Even though it was a Water Board project, it was he, Hector Sporn, who had pushed for the dam to be built. Civil stability was just as important as protecting the country to guard it against internal and external threats. On top of that, he had supplied the security forces that protected the workers, many of whom had sacrificed their lives – his Gormlings, good men – and he would make sure to mention them in his speech.

He paused for a moment to assess these thoughts, then quickly began jotting them down. At last, his talk was taking shape. He'd known it would. He should never have doubted himself. It was Maddie who had first alerted him to that trait in himself. Credit to her. She had made him more aware of it.

If only she were here to see him now ...

CHAPTER SIXTY-SEVEN

Day Eight: Evening

There had been a period earlier in the evening when a heaviness had come over Ben, a tiredness from the day's events. He'd found himself stomping and taking deep breaths to stay awake. But that feeling was gone now. The raft was getting closer to Urkesh, evident from the glow of city lights, which were swamping out Natchator's rings. Ben estimated another half an hour at most before they would approach the Palace island. He and Booker had persuaded Shelley and Guntaleg that the island would be the best place to offload Darwin, since it was internationally recognized as a venue for foreign dignitaries. Darwin, after all, could be construed as one. The professor had agreed, adding authority to Ben and Booker's argument.

What none of them had foreseen was the number of people coming down to the riverbanks to see them. As they approached Urkesh, the numbers increased. Cars were honking their horns. A sea of hands were waving torches. Many were taking photos and shooting video with VidPhones. There was a lot of shouting and waving. Ben wondered if the Palace would be a viable haven, or whether they would have to contend with crowds there as well.

It seemed that word of Darwin had gotten out, and whatever was going to happen from this point on was out of Ben's hands. There was a sense that a large hilltop boulder had been set in motion, and nothing, human or otherwise, would be able to stop it.

Several times he and Booker had talked about the "what if," but each time the conversation ended in speculation that went nowhere. The only agreed constant was that Sporn would probably try to stop them at some stage. As each kilometer passed, Ben grew more and more nervous, expecting an attack from Sporn's Gormlings at any moment. To ease his nerves, he helped Darwin bolt his chest plate back on, but this time he left two bolts off the top and slid a section of bamboo through to create an air gap for heat to escape.

Having done that, but still not satisfied, he asked Shelley if she could recruit some warriors from the canoes to help them lift the steel plates they had acquired and organize them into a protective stockade. Shelley agreed, and with the help of a dozen warriors, they managed to arrange the steel plates along each side of Darwin's legs, using them as support. They repositioned Myra's canoe behind Darwin, the empty space between his legs giving them enough room to shield sixteen or so people from bullets, if it came to that.

But Sporn's Gormlings hadn't materialized, and they were about to pass under the People's Bridge.

People stopped on the bridge and stared at them. Ben was so focused on looking out for Gormlings – as were the others – that he failed to see that Darwin's head was going to impact the bottom of the bridge.

There was a massive clang. Darwin's head snapped back, followed by the sound of steel scraping against stone.

Up on the bridge, there was a collective cry of awe.

As soon as they cleared the bridge, Darwin's head slowly resumed its normal position. Ben couldn't believe it. There was a horizontal dent across his forehead and the top of his head was scraped to bare metal.

Darwin let out a single utterance. "Ouch."

CHAPTER SIXTY-EIGHT

Day Eight: Evening

Captain Karl Gross put in the call to Washburn. After the second report from Mendes, it was clear that the "giant robot" was heading for Urkesh and would soon arrive. At least, that was what seemed to be the case, given its current rate of progress. As he waited for an answer, he wondered if he wasn't overreacting, if it wasn't his business. There were plenty of other layers of security to the Cosmonist government, and they would surely handle it – they were probably already handling it.

His train of thought was halted when Washburn's gruff voice sounded in his ear.

"Sorry to disturb you at this inopportune time ..." Gross began.

"Make it quick," Washburn replied. "What is it?"

"I've been getting a report of a potential foreign hostile coming downriver ... on a raft."

"We already know about it."

"You do?"

"Listen, unless you have something to add that we don't know about ..." He left the sentence hanging.

"We've kept aerial surveillance on it all the way from Ara-kirk."

"Has it made any attempt to interact?"

"No."

"Then keep your eyes on it. We'll handle it from this end."

"I'm just about to pass through security. Will I be able to contact you again if anything happens?"

"Nothing will happen."

Washburn's VidPhone disconnected.

Gross lowered his window and showed his security clearance, an electronic hash code on his VidPhone. The security guard scanned it and told him the parking attendants would show him where to park his car. Gross thanked the guard and drove through.

As expected, he noticed an increased level of activity among the Gormlings on guard. His eye caught Washburn directing a group of them over to the west wall of the compound. He was waving and talking loudly, a stressed look on his face.

Gross got out of his car and quickly strode across the gravel courtyard. He made eye contact with Washburn, who gave him barely a second of his time. He decided it would be best if he left Washburn to do his work and continued up the steps of the Great Hall. But as he got to the top, he couldn't help himself and turned around. He raised himself up on the balls of his feet and tried to peer over the ramparts of the Palace walls to see what the Gormlings who had amassed there were looking at, but the walls blocked his view of the river.

Unable to resist his own curiosity, he hurried back down the steps and trotted over to the wall.

The Gormlings beside him were hyper-vigilant, but there was nothing to see. Just the flowing river, and the crowds that had gathered on its banks.

He waited, hoping he might see something, but after a while, he began to get bored. Maybe it was a false alarm. Should he call

Mendes and get another update?

He decided against it. After all, there were more than enough Gormlings to handle whatever was coming their way.

He looked at his watch. If he stayed any longer he would be late. He went back and climbed the steps to the Great Hall.

CHAPTER SIXTY-NINE

Tancredi Fornas tapped the microphone, softly cleared his throat, and said, "Please ensure that your VidPhones are switched off during tonight's proceedings. We don't want any disturbances."

The audience, most of whom had arrived and taken their seats, duly complied.

Fornas surveyed them as he would mourners at a funeral, the taut skin stretched over his face making his eyes appear much larger than they really were, giving them a watchful, birdlike intensity.

"I'll wait for a few more to be seated before I begin," he said, "but while I do, I just want to remind you that there is also no smoking allowed while in the hall. Your restraint would be most appreciated." When everyone was finally seated, he said, "Good evening, everybody. I'm sure I don't have to introduce myself, but for the benefit of formality, my name is Tancredi Fornas, and I am your host. As Head Semion, I am proud to present to you tonight's program. It represents a culmination of our best ideals and reinforces just why our philosophy is so successful.

"I should remind you that we should never forget the sacrifices our forebears made to get us here. Our sacred history is full of heroic deeds and wonderful revelations. These, of course, are recorded in the Cosmonist Scriptures, which everyone here will be intimately familiar with." He let the audience congratulate themselves, then added, "Familiarity, however, is not enough. We know this because all too often people make false interpretations. They spread lies. Rumors."

A murmur fluttered around the hall. Fornas scanned the audience with an accusatory eye, quickly prompting silence.

"It is for this reason that we need a leading light – someone who has devoted their entire life to studying the Scriptures, someone who is pure of heart and strong of will, someone who can show us the way. We all know who that person is. I present him to you now: His Most Holy, Most Reverent Supreme Leader, Gaspard Rathneggar."

A patter of muted applause emanated around the Hall. It wasn't appropriate to cheer the Head Curate. His public entrance was always deemed a solemn affair.

Rathneggar seemed to almost float across the stage. He had the remarkable ability to move without seeming to move. His hood was drawn, but when he came to the podium, he let it fall. The act drew an involuntary gasp from the audience. No one had ever seen the bare scalp of the Head Curate before. To everyone's surprise, it bore scars, the evidence of surgery. The stubble was absent in a long arc on both sides around his ears.

"My people," he began, in his customary gravelly voice. "We are gathered here today to celebrate the bravery and virtue of one of our finest, Hector Sporn." He softly clapped his bony hands. "In a few moments, he will come out here to address you, tell you why he deserves his award, but before he does, I would first like to talk to you a little about the illustrious history of our fine nation, if I may."

It was not a request.

"I would like to start by giving thanks to our Great Prophet, Yasu Doi, for showing us the straight path. He illuminated the gifts of Hanub-Ka, teaching us that it is He who ushers forth divine rule, human growth, the establishment of justice, and the creation of a purified life. I have made it my life's goal to reinforce the logical need to establish a political system to achieve these great goals, a system which today has come down to us as Cosmonism. Praise Hanub-Ka!"

The audience automatically responded: "Praise Hanub-Ka!"

"The Cosmonist Revolution, which I initiated, has revived the old prophecies set forth by Ramanjabba, Marmoot, Vesnoon, and Yasu Doi. These prophecies have enriched our lives, but are the envy of the evil powers that lurk in Wallacia and Rodinia. They fear our success, that we have given this great nation pride through our Cosmonist identity. They will be defeated so long as we stay on the straight path!" He eyed the audience, satisfied that every eye was fixed on him. "The establishment of the rule of government requires leadership, management, and command, which is a very heavy responsibility ... We toil daily for long hours so that people can achieve peace of mind, attain material comfort, and live in secure environments where they can pursue the wellbeing and happiness and spiritual development that is the right of all human beings."

Rathneggar stopped and looked down, taking a long moment to meditate. His face was impassive, unreadable, but the audience knew he was about to say something important.

Looking up again, he said, "Our enemies have tried to break our consensus by attacking our youth with electronic propaganda, and of late, graffiti. This is a grave matter – to us it is tantamount to a soft war. Our youth and experts should not fear this war. We should encourage our youth to use cyberspace to create hope in society and advise people to stand firmly against heresy and promote insight.

"What is insight? Insight is a vision that ensures man does

not make a mistake in recognizing the right way. Allied to this is patience. Patience means perseverance and insistence on walking firmly on the straight path. If these two elements exist, our enemies cannot achieve their goals."

The Curate's message resonated with the audience. Many people looked at their neighbors and nodded in agreement.

"The most overt sign of this soft war," Rathneggar said, "came when the rebel Vernon Reeves detonated a bomb at the Ministry of Justice building, killing one of our comrades and wounding many others. Reeves fell victim to the foul propaganda of our enemies. He was weak. He was stupid. And he paid the ultimate price. We showed him that his message is wrong and that we cannot be defeated."

For the first time, the audience clapped loudly and spontaneously. Rathneggar raised his hand, quietened them down.

"There has been another more silent, insidious war, however, that has spread through our society as a cancer. It began when Mimetic Machines began producing and selling A2 droids. These were superior to their A1 counterparts because they were installed with self-reflective capabilities, giving them independence of thought. We are not against independent thought, per se; it is the trend toward secular thought that has raised our concern. We could have let it continue, in the name of freedom of speech, but freedom is not so easily negotiated. The philosophers tell us true freedom is the freedom to fail. This is all very good on paper, but what happens when you apply that indiscriminately to a whole society? Chaos! That's what you get, and that's what we have acted to protect ourselves against. It is for this reason that we removed A2s from society. As painful as it was for all – us included – we felt that pain in the short term was better than the complete dissolution of all our cherished values in the long term."

He paused again to take stock. "When we talk about values, we talk about what we believe is good. It is an aspirational state of mind that we direct at the objects, ideas, and behaviors of our daily lives. The secular mindset tells us that *logos*, rational thought and action, should be our guiding principle. This is all very well and fine, but in the hands of the A2s, *logos* went too far. They overstepped their bounds. They forgot that humans are fundamentally mythological creatures. We do not live by the neurochemicals flowing in our brains alone, but by the stories we tell about each other and to ourselves. It is childish to think that we can stamp out the mythological mind. It is a fundamental human instinct that directs itself toward primary realities and is expressed in symbolic imagery. Reductionism – pious literalism and misplaced *logos* – distorts our narrative of symbolic structures. We must return to the teachings of the prophets passed down to us from the Word of Hanub-Ka. And we must do it right. It cannot be left to just anyone, no matter how pious. It is a serious and grave undertaking, and only those who have sufficiently purified themselves are worthy of the task. This is what is at stake."

He turned away from the microphone to rasp a cough.

When he returned, he said, "It is on this note that I introduce you to someone who has proven his worthiness. The Minister of the Interior, Hector Sporn."

The audience broke into a long ovation as Sporn appeared. He executed a few small nervous bows as he moved to the podium. Reaching it, he shook hands with Rathneggar, who, for the first time that anyone could remember, gave a faint smile. Sporn smiled back stiffly. Rathneggar waved to the audience and receded from the stage. The clapping reached a crescendo, then died down again.

Sporn slipped his hand into his jacket pocket and fished out his notes. He unfolded them, slightly fumbling, and laid them out on the podium. He adjusted the mic and said, "Good evening, everyone. It is a great honor to be here. I wish to start by thanking our Most High and Wise Curate for expressing so clearly our mission to the people. He truly carries within him the light of our sacred prophets. He reminds us of what we ought to aspire to. He is a true inspiration."

He took a moment to read his notes.

"All my life," he said, "I have made it my mission to serve the state so as to improve the life of its citizens. It is for this reason that I initiated the Tongassa Dam Project. My only regret over the years is that I didn't start it earlier and pursue it more aggressively. But at least I can say that we're at the beginning of the —"

There was a commotion beside the entrance doors, drawing everyone's attention.

"Shots fired!" someone shouted. "I hear shots fired!"

CHAPTER SEVENTY

Day Eight: Evening

Nothing happened until Darwin moved.

The raft beached on the small rocky outcrop below the low cliff beneath the Palace walls. There was a tree there that attracted Shelley's attention, and she directed the polemen to push the raft toward it. It partially blocked the line of sight from up on the walls, which was a good thing.

But that was as good as it got. Ben saw Darwin move and that was the end of it. A hail of bullets came down from the walls. They whizzed through the air, clanging off Darwin's body and the steel plates they had arranged alongside his legs. Shelley, Guntaleg, and the polemen immediately dived into the water and hid under the raft. Ben, Booker, and Professor Mortimer cowered behind the steel plates. Ben put his hands over his ears and squeezed his eyes shut. Images of the rebel defeat at Quincera flashed through his mind. Only this time there was no way out ...

The picture was shattered by a series of loud booms.

Ben opened his eyes to see Darwin popping off mortars. They exploded against the cliff walls, sending chunks of rock flying through the air. The rising moon's light reflected off the smoke that followed, creating a temporary screen. The Warraweans used the opportunity to land their canoes and rush up the rocky slope, yelling war cries and releasing their firestone-tipped arrows.

Darwin moved again. He pushed the metal plates aside and rolled off the raft. Ben, Booker, and Mortimer had to jump out of the way to prevent themselves from being crushed.

The water was shallow and Darwin quickly rolled over and got to his feet. Ben looked up and saw the smoke clearing. Booker jumped up and headed for the tree. Professor Mortimer followed him.

Ben watched as Darwin started up the rocky slope. Shelley and Guntaleg came out of the water and ducked behind him, using him as protection, Darwin firing his cannons as he went.

Ben felt like time was being stretched. The smallest details seemed to take on a beauty all of their own. The leaves being shredded off the tree as the bullets ripped through them. The tiny water fountains they created as they hit the river. The wild faces of the Warraweans as they rushed forward. The implacable geometric motion of Darwin's arms and legs as he lumbered up the slope ...

Next thing Ben knew, he was with Booker behind the tree. Darwin had reached the top of the slope and was preparing to climb through the wall, where his mortars had created a breach.

Some of the Warraweans used him as a ladder, clambering over him, only to be struck by bullets and fall back. Yet it didn't seem to dampen their enthusiasm. They kept on climbing like an eruption of ants. Darwin eventually made it over himself, and Ben heard more booms. He looked at Booker, decided he had to go.

He moved away from the protection of the tree and picked his way up the slope ... only to stop by a wounded Warrawean with blood gushing from his neck. Ben pressed his hand over the wound. The warrior gurgled some words Ben couldn't understand, his eyes wide with startled innocence. A moment later his body went limp.

Ben stayed with him, unsure of what to do, until he realized it was hopeless. He saw Booker watching on with a stricken expression. In that moment, he felt himself galvanize. He straightened up and hurried on through the breach in the wall.

What he saw made him stagger.

The courtyard was on fire. Cars were burning, people running chaotically in all directions. Darwin punched his way through, sending cars tumbling out of his way. *My God, Ben thought. We've started a war ...*

Among the noise and confusion, he heard a voice. Shelley! She grabbed his hand and dragged him through a gap between two burning cars. A Gormling was taking aim at Darwin with his rifle. Shelley drew her bow and struck him with an arrow mid-chest. A look of quizzical surprise passed across his face before he fell to his knees.

Shelley continued to move forward, nocking another arrow as she went. Ben followed her, feeling like he had been thrown a lifeline. Here was someone who seemed to know what they were doing.

They weaved their way through the burning cars. There was a knot of Gormlings taking shelter behind the twin pillars at the entrance of the Great Hall. Darwin had corralled them there using his awesome firepower, their rifle bullets harmlessly ricocheting off his armor.

To Ben's amazement, he was shouting at them to come out and face him squarely. This seemed to unnerve them. They began retreating.

Guntaleg appeared through a wall of flame and smoke. His body was oiled with blood. His eyes shone crazily. For a moment he didn't seem to recognize Shelley as a fellow human being. He raised his machete at her, then froze.

A bullet hit him squarely in the temple. A one-in-a-million shot fired by a retreating Gormling. Shelley lunged out and grabbed him before he collapsed to the ground.

Ben let out a cry of anguish and fell to his knees next to her. She laid him down.

"He was a good man," Ben lamented.

Shelley closed his eyes. After a heavy pause, she said, "He's gone home." Her face was a mask of cold fury.

Ben tried to console himself by imagining Guntaleg had gone to sleep.

Shelley turned away from Guntaleg and watched Darwin heading for the entrance of the Great Hall.

"Something's going on," Ben said. "All these cars …"

Shelley said, "Come on. Let's finish this."

CHAPTER SEVENTY-ONE

Day Eight: Evening

Sporn stared hard at the entrance of the Great Hall, as if the act itself would materialize the information he was seeking. It took Julian Eckland, the Minister of Defense, to come running out in front of the stage, waving madly at him, before Sporn's eyes diverted away.

"Get everyone out!" Eckland was shouting.

Sporn looked left, then right. People were stampeding toward the emergency exits. They were just ordinary double doors. There would be a crush.

He looked over the crowd, up into the balconies, where he expected to see Washburn on overwatch duty. Carver was up there. So was Rhybus, flanked by his two favorite droids. Washburn was nowhere to be seen.

"Where are your men?" Sporn shouted above the din at Eckland. He was referring to the small contingent of riflemen Eckland had brought with him. It was a typical gesture of his to show off in front of the Curate.

"Fighting the enemy!" Eckland responded.

Sporn jumped down off the stage. He strode past Eckland

and began barging his way through the crowd.

"Where are you going?" Eckland cried.

"To organize my men." Indeed, several of Sporn's Gormlings were still up in the balconies. He couldn't see if there were any on the ground floor. There was too much chaos.

Eckland fought his way after Sporn. "Wait!" he shouted.

"What is this enemy?" Sporn demanded.

"We don't know."

"Damn it, what do you know?"

Eckland caught up with him. "I ordered the entrance to be barricaded."

"With your men out there?"

"And yours."

Sporn shoved an elderly man out of his way.

Eckland said, "I wouldn't go out there if I were you."

"We'll see about that," Sporn said angrily as he pushed his way forward.

CHAPTER SEVENTY-TWO

Day Eight: Evening

Fornas clutched the polished mahogany box containing the Star of Cosmonism to his chest and parted the curtains to see what was going on. He had just finished congratulating Rathneggar on his speech, and was preparing to return to the stage for the final presentation ceremony.

"What in Yasu's name …?"

"What is it?" Rathneggar asked.

"I don't know. There's some kind of disturbance."

"Let me have a look." Rathneggar took a peek through the gap in the curtains as Fornas held them open. He watched for a while, then stepped back. "What do you think?"

"I think you had better take your leave."

"No," Rathneggar said, shaking his head decisively. "Not until I find out what is going on."

He didn't have to wait long. A cloaked man with a hood that completely covered his face in darkness came out of the shadows and whispered something in Rathneggar's ear. Fornas instantly recognized the man as one of Rathneggar's spies — the aptly named Whisperers. He was shocked; he had never seen one in real life before. They had just been an idea in his mind, created by Rathneggar's brilliant sophistry.

What shocked him even more, however, was the look of sickened surprised that washed over Rathneggar's face. This was contrary to everything he knew about the man.

The Whisperer receded into the shadows as quickly as he had come.

"What did he say?" Fornas asked.

"It's unbelievable ..." Rathneggar murmured.

"What?"

"A giant robot is attacking us."

Fornas looked at him like he had lost his mind.

Rathneggar went back to the curtain.

"What are you doing?" Fornas asked.

"I have to see this ..."

CHAPTER SEVENTY-THREE

Day Eight: Evening

Sporn's remaining Gormlings scattered as Darwin mounted the steps to the Great Hall. He looked at the big wooden doors in front of him, undecided on what to do.

Ben and Shelley ran up to an overturned car near the bottom of the steps. "Break them down!" Ben shouted.

Darwin turned and looked at him, then took a step back and rammed his shoulder into the doors.

They splintered and cracked apart. He tore them away and stepped inside.

He was immediately struck by a volley of bullets. He responded with a blast from his arm cannons.

Ben heard shouting and screaming from inside the hall. Smoke poured out of the doors. Ben and Shelley ran through it and found a column to hide behind.

The hall was in disarray. Chairs were thrown all over the place. If it had been packed with people, they were now mostly gone. The only ones left were some Gormlings and soldiers. They had taken up positions behind the row of columns that supported the balconies on each side of the hall.

Darwin crunched his way over the chairs and stood in the middle of the hall.

"What are you?" came a voice from behind a nearby column.

A chill went down Ben's spine. It was Sporn.

Darwin turned in the direction of the voice. "Who is asking?"

Sporn slowly came out from behind his column with hands raised. "Don't shoot! I will answer your question."

Darwin said, "Very well."

"I am the Minister of the Interior for Oriana. Would you care to identify yourself?"

"My name is Darwin. I'm here to speak with your leader."

"You can speak to me."

"Are you the leader of your country?"

"I am the leader of this country," came a voice from the stage.

Darwin reorientated himself as Rathneggar stepped out from behind the curtain.

"What is it you wish to achieve?" Rathneggar asked.

Darwin walked up to the stage. "I am a time capsule. I bring you the history of the founding humans of this planet."

"Well, that's very kind of you," Rathneggar said. "Would you care to explain it to me?"

"I would be very happy to explain it to you," Darwin replied. "It is a long story ..."

Ben watched as Darwin began telling the story he had first told them. Rathneggar listened patiently. Fornas slowly emerged from the curtains and joined Rathneggar. Up on the balcony, Rhybus leaned forward and listened as well. Sporn slowly moved to the next column, where a Gormling had his gun trained on Darwin. They exchanged some words Ben could not hear, but the Gormling put his rifle down and unclipped his electroshock baton.

Ben saw it all unfold in slow motion.

The Gormling moved across the floor as quietly as he could, staying out of Darwin's field of vision.

He raised his baton ...

Ben cried out.

Darwin swung around and swatted the Gormling away. The Gormling crashed to the ground, sending chairs clattering across the floor.

Ben heard Sporn shout "Batons!" to the other Gormlings.

Darwin homed in on the source of Sporn's voice and began firing his guns in that direction. Large chunks of stone fractured away from the column Sporn was hiding behind. He dashed toward the next column and slid to the ground, hiding behind its base. Darwin tracked him with his guns and fired again.

More stone fragments flew away, leaving gaping holes.

Sporn half crawled, half ran to the next column.

While this was happening, Ben saw two Gormlings approach Darwin from behind. Shelley nocked an arrow and dispatched one with a clean shot to the neck. The second, seeing what had happened, began rapidly retreating, but Shelley calmly nocked another arrow and shot him in the back.

Darwin moved toward Sporn, who was cowering behind a column next to the stage. Sporn had only two options: jump up onto the stage, where Darwin would have a clean shot, or surrender.

He chose the latter. Standing up, he came out with his hands up.

This time Darwin wasn't fooled. He stuck out his arm, grabbed Sporn by the neck, and lifted him clean off the ground. While Sporn dangled helplessly, he used his free hand to rip Sporn's sidearm from his belt and toss it away. Ben watched as it slid across the floor, stopping only a few meters from the column he was hiding behind.

Sporn was turning blue.

Ben picked up Sporn's gun, took it out of its holster, and walked up to Darwin. "Put him down."

Darwin let Sporn drop to the ground. Sporn crumpled into a heap, gasping for air.

Darwin said, "I don't trust this one."

Ben said, "You're not wrong."

Sporn slowly regained his breath. "What do you want?" he spluttered.

"To educate you," Darwin said.

"You, a robot, educate me?"

Darwin's Fresnel eyes flashed. "If it wasn't for my kind, you wouldn't exist. Surprised, are we?"

Indeed, Sporn was surprised, but he quickly replaced it with scorn. "You were programmed to say that. You can't fool me!"

"Yes, you're right," Darwin said. "I was programmed, but that doesn't change the facts."

"Facts?" Sporn said. "What do you know about facts?"

"I know that I am standing here and you are lying there. That is a fact, is it not? My knowledge of your species is no different. I have no need to lie. Can you say the same of yourself?"

Sporn scowled. "I am the Minister of the Interior. How dare you question me!"

At that moment, Booker and Professor Mortimer entered the hall. Ben momentarily took his eyes off Sporn to look at them.

He didn't see Sporn reaching for the electroshock baton lying on the ground next to the shattered column.

"Ben!" Shelley cried.

Sporn grabbed the baton and lunged at Darwin.

A loud bang filled the emptiness of the hall.

Sporn looked up to see Ben aiming *his* gun at him. Smoke curled from its barrel.

"You shot me!" he said in disbelief.

Blood began pouring from Sporn's chest. He put his hand

over the wound. It was a futile gesture.

Ben slowly went up to him. "I'm sorry."

Sporn fell back. Ben caught him as he went. Their faces were near each other.

"What did you do with the droid?" Sporn wheezed.

"I brought her back with me."

Sporn took a moment to process that, then said, "It was my fault she died."

"What?"

"She's dead."

"Who's dead?"

"Madelaine."

Ben reeled with shock.

Sporn said, "What's your problem? You think you never kept any secrets from me?"

"I never kept any secrets from you."

Sporn sucked in some air. Grimacing, he said, "But you broke your promise to never lie."

Ben felt a stab of anger. "How could you know that?"

"Pascal told me before I sent him off to the Labor Camps."

Ben grabbed Sporn by the collar and shook him. "Did you kill him as well?"

Sporn summoned the last of his strength. "No."

A long moment passed. The two men eyed each other off. For the first time, Ben saw the truth. He saw a man who only cared about himself. A man obsessed by control. Even as his life ebbed away. "My father. Did you …"

"You wouldn't understand."

"No. I understand."

"Do you?"

"Yeah," Ben said. "You murdered him because you were scared of the truth."

Sporn shook his head. "No, it had nothing to do with the truth."

"Then why then?"

"We all have to answer to a higher power. I did my duty."

"Fuck your duty," Ben seethed.

A faint smile curled at the corners of Sporn's mouth.

"What? What is it?"

"You're just like your father."

Ben stared at Sporn. He wished he could picture his father in his mind. But all he could summon up was images of him in photographs. Maybe Sporn was right. He nodded to himself. So this is what it took. "Yeah," he said, finally. "You're right. I did lie to you. And that's the truth!"

He looked at Sporn to see his response.

But Sporn's eyes were closed. His body had gone limp.

CHAPTER SEVENTY-FOUR

Day Eight: Evening

Joselyn quietly slipped away as Darwin told his story. It wasn't that she wasn't fascinated by it. She was. But she wanted to get closer, see his eyes. See what Rathneggar was seeing.

By the time she got down to the ground floor, the situation had changed. Darwin was shooting again. She saw Fornas bundle Rathneggar away. She climbed up onto the stage using the side steps and slipped through the curtain to see where they went.

They hustled through a door that took them to the Moon Tower. Why were they going that way?

Then she realized.

Following them, she saw that they were taking the secret passage that went down to the base of the Moon Tower and came out into a cavern, where the rowing boats used for secretly crossing over from the mainland were moored.

Rathneggar jumped into one of them while Fornas undid the rope. Rathneggar pushed the boat away from the low stone shelf next to which it was moored and began rowing it toward the dark tunnel that joined the Tongassa River.

Joselyn ran past Fornas and leapt into the boat.

"What are you doing?" Rathneggar shrieked.

"I'm coming with you."

He stopped rowing. "No, you're not."

Joselyn stood her ground. "Yes, I am."

"Get out!"

"No!"

Rathneggar tried to unhitch an oar and strike her with it. Joselyn pulled the oar out of his hand and poked him in the chest.

"You will take me with you. You want to know why? Because I'm damaged goods. I'm no good for anyone. So now I'm your responsibility."

The boat was drifting into the tunnel. Joselyn sat down and used the oar to row them deeper inside.

Rathneggar just looked at her.

Joselyn kept rowing, switching sides to keep the boat in the center of the tunnel.

"Where do you think you're going?" Rathneggar eventually asked. A faint light began appearing in the darkness ahead of them. Silvery moonlight reflected off the water.

"You tell me," she said.

Rathneggar rasped a humorless laugh.

The boat emerged from the tunnel. The river started propelling them downstream. Rathneggar did nothing.

Joselyn watched him, waiting for the slightest crack in his façade. She knew from experience that he wasn't completely made of stone. Even after the surgery that had dulled his senses.

The boat kept on drifting. Urkesh was on their left, and further downstream Joselyn could see the lights and cranes of Halfa Port. Rathneggar would have to act eventually, otherwise they would head out into Halfa Bay, where there was nothing but fishing vessels and shipping.

She kept her eyes on him. She thought his expression was getting a little sullen. Good!

Finally, Rathneggar said, "Give me the oar."

"You promise not to hit me with it?"

"Just give me the oar."

She gave it to him. He put it back in its rowlock.

Feeling more secure, she half turned to see where they were going. Rathneggar was steering them toward the port. There were several ships there. As they got closer, the rowboat was dwarfed by their size.

Eventually Rathneggar pulled up against one of the smaller ships. It was named *MS Vesnoon*. It had fine lines, round portholes, and a handsome upper deck, reminiscent of luxury cruisers she had seen in fashion magazines.

There was a rope ladder down its side. Rathneggar stood up and grabbed hold of it. Joselyn let him climb the first few rungs before starting up behind him. It took a lot more effort than she imagined, but eventually she made it aboard. Rathneggar was breathing heavily from the exertion. While he regained his breath, she watched the rowboat drift away with the current.

A steward came to greet them, his face creased with worry. "We've heard reports of a disturbance at the Palace," he said. "Are you okay?"

"I'm okay," Rathneggar said gruffly. "Just get this ship moving."

"Yessir."

"And escort this lady off while you're at it."

The steward looked at Joselyn. She scowled back at him. He turned to Rathneggar. "Very well, sir." To Joselyn, he said, "You heard the master."

"I'm staying right here," she said. "Every minute you waste with me is another minute you lose to escape."

The steward looked at Rathneggar, doubt spreading across his face.

Rathneggar glared back at him. "Throw her overboard if you have to."

"Why?" Joselyn said. "Because you're afraid of me?"

Rathneggar scoffed at the idea.

"Then let me come with you. The clock is ticking."

"What are you waiting for?" Rathneggar practically screamed at the steward. "Get this ship moving!"

The *MS Vesnoon* dropped its hawsers and silently slipped away. Rathneggar went to the aft deck to see if he could catch a last glimpse of the Palace island. The Moon Tower's lights were half lit, the upper levels dark. Apart from that, it looked serene, as if nothing had happened. Such momentous change with so little evidence. He pretended nothing was different ... because nothing *was* different. He was still the same body, wearing the same clothes, breathing the same air, looking at the same scenery.

Was this the end of Cosmonism? He thought about the speech he had made only a little over an hour earlier. The whole world was at his feet. Sporn was jostling for the top position, sure, but that was just a minor issue, nothing that could not be dealt with in the usual manner. It *was* being dealt with.

It wasn't Sporn that worried him. It was the people. They were fickle. Capricious. He estimated that at least thirty percent of adults were trapped at the psychological age of twelve. As far as he was concerned, they could all be shipped out to sea and dumped.

This would resolve itself, he was sure. It just needed time. The giant robot – it told an interesting story. That couldn't be denied. But stories didn't change regimes. Who was going to believe that people had come to Natchator from another planet? It was absurd.

There was one small niggling detail, though. This wasn't the first time Rathneggar had heard the story.

There was a reason for banning certain books. Some told

dangerous lies. He had never believed the lies he had read in that book all those years ago when he was an acolyte. He'd stumbled upon it in the Moon Tower library, which his predecessors had constructed specially for that purpose: keeping sensitive material away from impressionable minds. He did not think he had such a mind. Nothing could perturb it. It was what marked him out as a leader right from the start.

Hearing the story again, however, the same details ... It was too uncanny to be a coincidence. He let the doubt in. It was good to doubt. Denial, he had learned long ago, led to disaster. Yes, the story should be investigated. Then dismissed. That way, no one could accuse him of being closed-minded. Because the story surely came from a deranged mind. Someone intent on causing trouble. Yet ... whoever had made it up was smart. He gave them that. Planting the evidence in a book, and now in a giant robot – he would even go so far as to say it was creative, which was a lot more than he could say about some of the people around him.

He thought about Tancredri Fornas. The man was a sycophant. But at least he could be relied on to manage the country in Rathneggar's absence. Right now he would be following a plan they had discussed in private. Keep the Chamber intact. Maintain fiscal policy. Fill the *Dormas*. Preserve the Curate hierarchy.

The issue of the Whisperers ... That was a delicate matter. Right now they would be going to ground. Keeping their identities concealed. Fornas would love nothing more than to harness their potential. *Over my dead body*, Rathneggar swore. They were his, and his alone. They were the spinal cord of his power. He was their brain. Severing one meant the dissolution of the other.

The journey to Long Chain Island would take about eighteen hours. The colony of Curates there would receive him, and he could govern the country in exile from there if necessary. If it turned out that there was a revolution, he would plot his return. He wasn't going to waste a single minute.

The giant robot didn't know what was coming …

He was so absorbed in his own thoughts that he didn't hear the soft padding of footsteps crossing the deck.

Joselyn made sure to avoid running into anyone. She flitted from shadow to shadow. It was imperative that she didn't ruin this chance.

Rathneggar was leaning on the rear railing. What was he doing? What was he thinking? The sky was so clear out here. The great arc of Natchator's rings shone brighter than ever. It was mesmerizing to look at. Yet Rathneggar was looking down.

She slipped out of the shadows and carefully made her way toward him, instinctively holding her breath.

Rathneggar didn't seem to sense her presence.

Feeling that he was about to turn around, she launched into a run …

In a fraction of a moment she was upon him. She grabbed his cloak below his knees, gave it a firm twist, and lifted him off the ground.

He was so much lighter than she'd imagined.

As he went over the rails, he made a desperate attempt to hang on, his arms twisting over his shoulders.

He looked up. "You?" he said, disdainfully.

"Yes. Me."

He hung there precariously for a while. She searched his eyes. There was nothing there. Except maybe fear. Was this him revealing his soul? She could not tell. Maybe some humans lacked a soul. In which case he deserved what he was going to get.

One by one, she prized his fingers from the railings. A finger for each time he had raped her.

He screamed as he fell, but his voice was quickly engulfed by the sound of the waves.

She saw him splash into the water and momentarily disappear. A few moments later, his head bobbed above the surface. He was shouting and waving, but his voice was drowned out by the sea.

The *MS Vesnoon* sailed placidly on.

She never once took her eyes off him until he vanished completely.

CHAPTER SEVENTY-FIVE

Nine weeks later

"Thank you you so much for giving me this opportuni-ty," Ben said, extending his hand to Professor Mortimer.

Mortimer shook it. "Don't thank me," he said. "Thank Laurent Carver. He's the one who sponsored you – although the board unanimously voted in favor of you. It was a no-brainer."

"Oh?" Ben said, his face serious. He thought about Booker, back in his old job. Sporting a beard now of all things. "So do I work for Carver, or do I work for you?"

Mortimer chuckled warmly. He put a hand on Ben's shoulder. "You don't work for anyone. Treat this as your new laboratory."

Indeed, Mortimer had given Ben several boxes of solenoids, actuators, hydraulic control valves, nuts, bolts, screws, tubing, and odd bits of plate metal, among other things. "We had no idea what these were used for," he had said. "We speculated it was for some type of machinery. You can imagine what a relief it was to finally learn that they were used for making humanoid robots."

Ben had taken these and poured over them with great interest, his dream of writing a history robotics alive again. He had learned so much, not just about the world, but about himself. His capacity to absorb failure. Handle guilt. To think that he owed his life to robots! There were so many questions that needed answering. Least among them, what sort of people had the planet's original population come from? Who were they? How were they chosen? And what sort of world did they live on? It too must have had a long history. Just thinking about it filled him with an enthralling sense of wonderment. The scholar in him awoken again.

Mortimer's office was on the top floor of the museum. It had large windows with expansive views that extended out to the front courtyard and down into the central atrium below. The atrium was named after Prince Rhybus, the new Head of State. Darwin was seated on a huge "throne" in the center of the atrium and would be the first thing visitors saw when they entered.

Mortimer swept his hand toward the view, drawing Ben from his reverie. "I'm so glad that we have a flagship attraction now. The museum was really crying out for one."

"Will we allow visitors to ask Darwin questions?"

"Why not?" Mortimer said. "It will be popular."

"I'm just a bit concerned we might be turning Darwin into a circus animal," Ben said. There was a pensive edge to his tone of voice.

Mortimer held a serious face for a moment, then laughed heartily. "Come on! He only has to sit there for ten hours a day. The rest of the time is his – so long as you don't let him go wandering around the building unsupervised."

"No, I would never let him do that."

Mortimer gave Ben an approving glance.

Ben looked down and saw Myra pushing a person in a wheelchair up to Darwin. "Professor Montaigne's here."

"He's early," Mortimer said, looking at his wristwatch. "Why don't you go down? I have a few more things to sort out here."

"Pascal!" Ben said, walking up to him.

"Ben!"

Ben stooped and gave Pascal a hug. He felt Pascal's bones through his clothes. As much as he would have liked to have gotten used to that feeling, it still made him anxious. Pascal had lost about a third of his weight during his "sojourn" in the Labor Camps. Gone were the beefy jowls. The round belly. Gone were the last dark hairs too. He was completely silver-gray. It gave him a sort of skinny Santa Claus look. "How are you feeling?" Ben asked.

"Better. Hey, did you know Myra was taking singing lessons?"

"Yeah, I knew."

Myra said, "People keep asking me: 'When are you going back to the Corsi Club?' At first, I didn't understand what they were talking about. Then Tom explained it all to me. We decided that there was nothing wrong with me celebrating Madelaine's life. It's not like I'm trying to *be* her."

"No, it's a good decision."

"I think she'll be great!" Pascal said.

"Yeah, I think so too," Ben said. He saw Shelley standing outside the front entrance. He said, "Excuse me," and went to greet her.

"Why don't you come in?" Ben said.

Shelley looked through the glass doors at Darwin. "I don't know if I want to talk to him," she said.

"Why not?"

"I don't know. Look at him, he's all cooped up in there."

Ben tried not to look worried. He knew what Shelley meant. They had discussed it before. "I just spoke to Professor Mortimer. He said that Darwin only needs to stay like that during opening hours. Afterwards, he can do anything he wants."

"Like go outside?"

Ben's eyes widened. "No. Not go out. But he's free to roam around inside, where ever he wants."

Shelley made a sour face. "The way you City Dwellers think."

"Why don't you come inside. He wants to talk to you."

"He wants to talk to me?"

"Yeah."

Shelley shifted on her feet. She looked through the glass doors again. "He really wants to talk to me?"

"Yeah."

"What about?"

"I don't know. I told him you were coming today."

Myra and Pascal were waving.

Shelley waved back. "All right."

Seeing Shelley, Darwin's eyes lit up. "I'm pleased you could come," he said.

Ever since the People's Bridge incident, Shelley couldn't help staring at Darwin's forehead without laughing. She did her best this time, however, to keep a straight face. "Ben said you wanted to talk to me."

"Did he? Well, actually, there is something on my mind ..."

Shelley waited.

"I felt there were some things we left unsaid."

Shelley put her hands on her hips. "Let me guess. You wanted to give me another lecture on how silly my beliefs are."

"No, well, I was thinking about that ..."

"And?"

Darwin gestured with his great arms. "Maybe I didn't explain myself clearly enough," he said. "Perhaps –"

"– You think that believing in a tree spirit gets the right answer for the wrong reason. It makes religion functional. But it doesn't make it true."

Darwin looked sideways, then back at Shelley. It gave him the time to formulate an answer. "I actually agree with you," he said.

"You do! Well that's a first!"

"It's true. Believing in a tree spirit is good for your culture. It leads to good behavior."

"So what's the problem?"

"The problem is ... well ... getting the right answer for the wrong reason may work – up to a point."

"Here we go!"

"No, really," Darwin insisted.

"So what is it then?"

"The problem is ... well, it doesn't lead to a growing circle of knowledge. It stays satisfied with its little corner of the world, and so long as that doesn't change, everything continues as normal. But what happens when an outside force begins to change your world? The knowledge you built up for the wrong reasons will start to fail." He thought of an example. "Like take the future of this planet. Eventually the sun will die. Which means that human consciousness will die and –"

"– Hang on a moment," Shelley said. "What has that got to with good behavior?"

"Everything!" Darwin replied. "Behavior is dependent on consciousness. If we let that extinguish, it will be a tragedy for this universe."

Shelley was shaking her head. "Who cares if we all die. If we die, we die. That's our fate."

"It doesn't have to be."

Shelley wasn't sure what to make of this comment. Even though Darwin's face didn't show any emotion, the people who made him gave him expressive eyes. She saw sadness in those eyes. Something she hadn't seen before.

"Humans have searched for other intelligent life for thousands of years" he said, "and we still haven't found any. What if humans are the only intelligent life in this universe?"

"We might not be."

"Are you willing to take that risk?"

Shelley looked at Ben, then back at Darwin again, unsure.

"By getting the right answers for the right reasons," Darwin said, "we set ourselves on the path to science. That's what I mean by an ever expanding circle of knowledge."

"The right answers for the right reason ..."

"Yes. It was science that helped us produce the technology to resurrect human beings from DNA. And since humans are conscious animals ..." he paused to think. "You see, if you truly believe that consciousness is precious, then it is imperative that you redevelop the technology that brought humans to this planet. You will need to do it so that one day you can send humans to another planet." He pointed through the atrium's glass roof, up to the sky.

Everyone looked up. The sky was blue. Not a cloud in sight.

For a while, there was a reflective silence. Ben was the first to return his attention to Darwin. He said, "Can you help us develop that technology?"

"It is my mission," Darwin replied.

Later, as Shelley and Ben descended the steps of the museum, talking about saying goodbyes, Shelley said, "I can't help feeling that Darwin is devaluing my way of life. I don't think he realizes that it takes genius to survive in a place like the Olongo jungle. You know, it could be something as small as fashioning a hook from a bone. It doesn't happen by magic. It takes a lot of skill. And then you still have to learn how to catch the fish. That takes years of experience. Learning from those who've done it before, learning from their mistakes. All of that takes time. And then you still have to rest."

Ben said, "I hear you. But I don't think he's devaluing you. I think he values you above all else. The very skills you talk about come from a mind, a consciousness. He doesn't want that to vanish from this universe, ever. That's how much he treasures you."

Shelley sighed. "I'm sorry, but I can't help thinking that there is a spirit world that exists beyond the senses." She paused to reflect. "Once, when I was fishing, I don't know why, but I got this chill all over my body. All the hairs on my arms were standing up. I realized something wasn't right. Yet … there wasn't a single sign in the world that was showing me that – apart from the hairs on my arms. No wind. No animals squawking alarm calls. Barely a ripple on the surface of the water. But my sixth sense – if you want to call it that – told me to slowly step back and keep moving back. No sooner had I done that than a *sarcotoothis* thrust its head out of the water and snatched the bait off my hook."

She made a movement with her hand that was quick as lightning.

"If I hadn't listened to that little voice in my head that told me to get out of the way, I wouldn't be here today. That's not something you can explain by physical evidence. I got the right answer for *no reason*. Darwin doesn't seem to be aware of that possibility."

Ben gazed at Shelley. Her eyes were so dark that he couldn't see her pupils. Her lips were full, like ripe fruit that had split open. He wanted to bite them. But that wouldn't be right.

Shelley watched his eyes. A moment of stillness passed between them. Then she leaned toward him and whispered in his ear, her lips brushing against his cheek. "Promise to come visit."

"I will," he said. It was an automatic response. And he blushed, because he was still thinking about those lips, and realized that he would visit her again, but for entirely the wrong reason.

ROB ALEXANDER